Shallow

Stock

D R Shores

1

W ynter McGlynn stood at her office window, looking out across the bay and drawing comfort, as ever, from the immensity of the view.

An hour past sunrise on a cloudless day. The mountains in the distance to her left lacked their usual shroud of mist whilst the deep water ahead mirrored the blue of the sky. A westerly breeze gathered the surface of the sea and bellied the sails of the few yachts already venturing beyond the marina away to her right.

Summer, she thought, allowing herself a rare moment of nostalgia.

Resting the coffee mug on a rolled sleeve, she smoothly shifted her balance from one bare foot to the other. McGlynn was tall, long limbs toned by the exercise she found had become a necessity as well as a pleasure now she was in her forties. Dressed in customary weekday attire - white open-necked shirt over lightweight trousers with no jewellery or makeup - her angular features were kept from androgyny by the unconscious, unaffected grace of such movement.

Faint sounds from the anteroom intruded upon her memories, a discreet knock on the jamb restoring her fully to the present and announcing the start of her week.

'You're late,' she said, showing none of her surprise.

'Good morning, Director,' said Matthieu, his accent pleasing as always. 'My apologies. Mr Wiesenberg rang and I felt I should finish our conversation first.'

'Ah, in that case no problem.' Controlling her impatience to know what led to the call, she swivelled lightly into the tan

1

leather desk chair, a leg folded beneath her. 'We'll get to Jacob shortly. I've already been through the overnight messages but any other news?'

'Nothing worth disturbing you,' he replied, taking his usual seat opposite. 'Did you see the documents for the board?'

'Uh-huh. Read them yesterday. There are some points to pick up with the team later but no further action for now.'

'OK. And Thom called to make arrangements for dinner with Fredrik Nilsson. He wanted to know if you'd be travelling from here.'

'That's the plan. Did he mention whether Fredrik's bringing anyone?'

'No?'

'Can you ask him to check. I'm fine to meet one-to-one but if he's bringing a guest then Thom should come too, Malmotec's as much his deal as mine. And can you also get him to chase a response from the Monopolies Commission. We could really do with knowing whether they're likely to object before we push for completion.'

'Certainly. Did you look at your schedule yet?'

'I did. But I heard over the weekend that Danny Zhao's accepted an offer to join Boland Technologies, so what would you recommend I change and why?' she asked, testing him.

'I'd move the monthly supplier review to next week,' he replied at length. 'And ask Christopher Boland for a call instead.'

'Good. Because?'

'Because Christopher's a non-exec and hiring Zhao means he's likely diversifying into a field where there's a

2

conflict of interest,' he reasoned. 'It could also mean he objects to the Malmotec acquisition at tomorrow's board meeting. Although he'd need the other investors for an outright veto, it might cause a delay you can't afford, so you'll need to talk with him today before you'll know how to play the conversation later with Fredrik. And the least urgent item in your diary is the supplier review.'

'Excellent, Matthieu, your thinking's spot on. As it happens, I've already messaged Christopher and he's available until lunchtime so go ahead and rearrange. And if you want to go to the top of the class, see if you can figure out how I heard the news before you and how you'd find out first next time.'

Matthieu merely raised an eyebrow while making notes. Through the open doorway beyond his shoulder, McGlynn could hear muted conversation and the subtle sounds of modern-day labour as more of her staff began to arrive.

'Now, tell me why Jacob called.'

'He was confirming this afternoon's meeting and said Rohan's ready to take the stand tomorrow or Wednesday as needed.'

McGlynn's instincts responded and she leant forward, forearms on the desk. More astute than most, Jacob Wiesenberg was not prone to anxiety. That he had made an unnecessary call to her assistant nagged at her.

'How did he sound?'

'A little bit tense, although that wouldn't be unusual would it? Near the end of a big trial?'

'Mmm. But he's an old pro and we've fought several cases over the years, some of which were just as difficult as this one, so he shouldn't be any more concerned than usual.'

She pulled her lower lip into her mouth and massaged it with the tip of her tongue. 'Leave our meeting as planned but can you get Rohan to come up once he arrives. I want to look him in the eye and see if he's as ready as Jacob says.'

'No problem.' Matthieu swiped and tapped at the tablet on his lap. 'It looks as though he's due in around now. Anything else?'

'I don't think so, at least not work-wise. But tell me, how's your mother doing?'

'No better, no worse,' he replied, trying to keep his voice matter of fact. 'She has her next appointment on Thursday.'

'I remember. I've made arrangements for you to have the afternoon off so you can attend as well.'

'Thank you but it's only a check-up with the oncologist. My father will be there and I'll call them in the evening. It's six hours of travel and there's too much going on here for me to be away.'

'I understand. But some things are much more important than work and this is one of them. The chopper's free so you can be there and back in an afternoon if you must.'

'Honestly, I ought to–'

'I'm not asking, Matthieu,' she said gently, the steady grey eyes kind but resolute. McGlynn knew he was an only child, born long after Eloise and Olivier Gautier had given up hope of conceiving at all. 'I've already cleared the crew to fly you out and they're under your instruction about the return hop provided you're back before the start of business on Friday.'

'In that case I… I cannot thank you enough.'

'You're very welcome. Do you still feel up to joining one of the tables on Wednesday night?'

'For sure.'

'Great. Just let me know if you need more time with your family but, if you're here, then I want you as alert and fully focused as normal, understand? It's going to be a hell of a week so reach me day or night if something needs my attention.'

'You have my word, Director. If that's all, I'll go and find Rohan.'

'Hang on, can you also find out what Andrew's got planned during lunch. Tell him I could do with being back at the office five minutes earlier than usual.'

'Do you have a preference?'

'Always,' she said with a smile. 'But I'm not sure he'll let me get away with a run every day until the weekend.'

'Will do and, again for Thursday, *merci hein?*' Rising, he swept the tablet to sleep and took a light grip on the door handle. 'Open or closed?'

'Open's fine thanks.'

Beyond the boundaries of their professional relationship, she was genuinely fond of the young Breton with the shock of dark hair and habitual high spirits. The son of old family friends, he had joined the company's fast-track programme via a Masters from HEC in Paris. She had since kept an eye on his progress and liked what she saw. Bright, committed, quick to learn, his potential was obvious and eighteen months ago she recruited him to her personal staff. During that time he had developed a strong friendship with Thom Dalkeith, McGlynn's nephew who ran the mergers and acquisitions team and was only a couple of years Matthieu's senior. He needs another six months here, she reflected, then a transfer to one of the overseas divisions with a view to broadening his horizons and re-levelling his career. The burden of responsibility will help mature that youthful exuberance into the gravitas required when dealing with demanding customers and unreliable suppliers, let alone the big personalities he would come up against in colleagues and competitors.

McGlynn felt her blood stir at the thought of competition. The primal joy of rivalry and the improvement it engendered. Be better than your opponent, adapt or die, Darwinism made real within the dominion of mankind.

Smoothly turning her head, her eyes flattened as she looked over the rooftops of a dozen smaller blocks to a metal and glass building similar to her own.

Many decades previously, the site where the tower now stood had been the address of a private hospital in which elderly residents, sitting in high-backed chairs on austere verandas, compared ailments as they kept watch over the ocean. Nobody seemed sure whether it was the fresh air or the attempts to claim the worse affliction which had the more beneficial effect, but such therapies gradually fell out of fashion, those requiring convalescence began to demand hotel-grade comfort and the facility was duly purchased and mothballed by a healthcare conglomerate with more modern premises to offer. Over the following years, the fabric of the neglected building became dangerous and the City administration, at the command of a mayor exasperated by the group's stonewalling of repairs, eventually ordered a demolition and compulsory sale of the land out of little more than ill will.

At the time, McGlynn was searching for new quarters to accommodate her burgeoning staff and had exchanged contracts for a similar plot to the east. However, the old hospital site was in a slightly better location for commercial development with the edge of Valiance Park to the rear and closer proximity to the Blake Street subway. After making several visits to inspect the grounds, walk the surrounding streets and talk with local property owners, she decided to develop both but move the construction of her own building westwards. Architectural plans and approvals for a state-of-the-art office block were already complete and she saw no reason why they could not be transposed the short distance along Foreshore Road.

Such was the level of interest that sealed bids were invited. Determined to win, McGlynn ruthlessly exploited her network to uncover rival proposals and negotiate outside the prescribed process. However, and much to her chagrin, neither strategy worked and she was forced into an eleventh-hour submission informed solely by experience and gut feel. Notice of the contract being awarded elsewhere came swiftly, the rumour mill suggesting she had been outbid by a sum too close for coincidence, and she refocused on establishing a dialogue with the new owners, intent on persuading them to withdraw. For months her lawyers worked their way through opaque holding companies only to dead-end in the Cayman Islands. Unable to wait any longer, McGlynn reluctantly retrenched to the original site and ordered the construction of ML One.

Nearly three quarters of the way through the build, an anonymous message had revealed the next link beyond the Caymans and, from there, it had been relatively easy to determine the ultimate owner of the land she had failed to acquire. McGlynn was furious beyond reason. Polite interest from friends, family and colleagues in how her new headquarters were progressing quickly became taboo. Even the grand opening, at which six hundred guests enjoyed unmatched hospitality for an evening of society gladhanding and congratulatory speeches, failed to appease her.

Within weeks of ML One becoming fully operational, ground was broken next to Valiance Park. The designs lodged with the City's planning department were a clever manipulation of her own - triangular motifs in place of squares and a subtly different patina to the exterior alloy - but the resemblance was obvious in terms of design principles and scale. Sure enough, the building topped out nine months later to provide the waterside business district with a fraternal twin, a second dominant structure giving added inspiration to the office workers arriving each morning in pursuit of fame, fortune or simply their daily bread.

What few of these workers knew, and almost none with the same level of exactitude she did, was that the roofline of the second tower had risen precisely three feet above its elder sibling. The difference in height was imperceptible at this distance but enormous in symbolic terms. She knew the building's actual owner knew the same and how it mattered to them equally. His office was directly opposite hers, the corner suite facing the sea and the mountains, and McGlynn recalled her anger as the unspoken taunt slowly manifested in her line of sight, storey by insulting storey. Anger fuelled further by the expense of having to upgrade the top floor windows across the whole of her western aspect to ensure ongoing privacy. She remained grimly amused by the enhanced ballistic specifications of the new glass, qualities which she had no reason to believe were likely to be tested, but the finish being an imperfect match with the rest of her building still grated.

Six days, she brooded. Six days and three battles I expect to win. It may not be the end of the war but it might be the beginning of the final onslaught. Yet again she gloried in her good fortune to be born into this life, her life, to perhaps initiate and witness the dying days of a conflict spanning her generations.

With detachment she noticed the physical response to this train of thought, the slight rise in heartbeat and breathing, the tightening of her musculature and a primal arousal stemming from the adrenal glands. Controlling her next ten inhalations, she set aside the problems lying along the shoreline. There they could wait until recalled for further contemplation.

A low purring signalled an incoming call.

'Yes, Natalie?' she asked.

'Sorry to disturb you, Director, but there's a Detective Campbell here to see you.'

Christ, thought McGlynn, what does City PD want urgently enough to turn up first thing on a Monday morning?

'Ask the front desk to hold her there,' she said, playing for time. 'Offer tea or coffee and let her know I'll be down shortly.'

'I tried that but she used an ID to force her way through the barriers and is on the way up. She'll be here any moment.'

2

D espite his title, Julian Dayton – or more correctly The Honourable Julian Alexander Ulysses D'Ayton - was an ignoble man. In particular, he knew of his own inclination to laziness and hence made a great show of working harder than everyone else to disguise the fact.

Bright sunshine slanted through pockets of cool shadow as he strode across Vermont Avenue from the gates of Valiance Park, jogged up the marble steps and passed through the revolving doors of the Dayton Global Industries building. As usual, he intended to be the first to arrive in the offices upstairs.

'Morning gentlemen. Any problems?' he asked, crossing the polished floor.

'None at all, sir,' replied the senior overnight guard. 'Have a good day.'

Dayton had been having much the same two-line conversation for seven years, albeit only the last four at this location, and enjoyed the respectful attitude of his staff. They perpetuated his sense of purpose and pride despite it never having crossed his mind whether he earned this courtesy or if it simply came with his position.

Beyond the reception area, six elevators were arranged in banks of three next to the huge picture window framing a view of the sea beyond. Stepping inside the last on the right, he turned to face the chromed doors as they slid closed, partly from universal convention but mostly so he could recheck his appearance following the short commute. Today he wore the dark blue merino three-piece, closely tailored to his slim frame and matched with a white herringbone shirt and green and gold silk tie. Satisfied there were no blemishes on the toes of his shoes, that the cuffs of his shirt extended equally beyond his jacket sleeves and that his tie was correctly knotted in the centre of his collar, his eyes travelled upwards to the reflection of his face.

Half a head taller and a decade older than McGlynn, Dayton had been considered a reasonably good-looking man in his youth. When taken in the context of his personal net worth, the dark hair framing symmetrical features had made him one of the most eligible men about town. In profile however, generations of semi-aristocratic breeding were visible in an underdeveloped jaw and an overdeveloped skull hanging forwards between rounded shoulders. The thick hair had faded to leaden grey and years of responsibility and long hours had lidded and bagged the flecked green eyes, one of which was indisputably developing a squint. Not given to smiling at the best of times, he would normally feel disappointment at these ongoing losses in the fight with time and stress and gravity, but not today. He could not remember feeling so energised by the prospects of a week and was amused to find himself humming snatches of Turandot, the corners of his mouth turned unmistakably upwards.

The car slowed as it reached the end of its run, the doors parting to reveal an unoccupied hallway with plush carpet and panelling of light wood. Turning to the left, he walked past empty glass-walled rooms towards the southeast corner, a spring in his loping step. With a final glance across the open plan floor he swung towards his office only to stop dead at the threshold.

Poking out from the desk chair, which had been turned to face the floor to ceiling window, were pairs of pinstriped trousers, brightly patterned socks and patent leather shoes. The ankles were raised and crossed, the left heel resting comfortably upon one of the waist-high Easter Island sculptures flanking the glass. Presumably alerted by the sudden absence of Puccini, a foot dropped to push off the nose of the bust and the chair rotated to reveal a handsome man with fashionably styled black locks and an arrogant grin.

'Hello brother,' he said, the patrician intonation as well matched to the cut of his suit as the resonance of his voice to the muscular physique.

'What the hell are you doing here?' replied Dayton, his own voice nasal, the accent much more neutral. 'You're not supposed to be back for weeks.'

'Well, everything's taken care of and I didn't want to miss out on all the fun. Hopped a late flight and here I am. Aren't you pleased to see me?'

'Frankly no, I'm not. We agreed for you to stay on hand and make sure Fender does as he's told.'

'For fuck's sake, Jules, don't take me for an idiot. We both know that's just a poor excuse to keep me out of the way.'

The accented diminutive was sensed rather than heard. No one but Eddie presumed to address him with such familiarity, or in the derisory tone that instantly recalled his days as a skinny, acne-prone teenager. Making a great show of walking across the office to reposition the sculpture a fraction, he searched for a suitably brusque reply.

'Bullshit. We've talked about this endlessly. If we don't get first mover advantage in Asia-Pac, then the healthcare division is finished and we're back ten years in terms of our competitive positioning. We've got another year, eighteen months max at the losses you–… we're incurring there and it's bloody obvious Fender Tang's out for himself first and us second. And we might be a distant second at that if rumours are true. I need you close enough to be in control of the situation, not here.'

'Fender's my friend,' said Eddie. 'And the only guy in the region with the connections to get the first machines installed and prove the technology.'

'How do you know? Did you actually bother to try anyone else or was his the only number you called?'

'Oh bugger off. You know that's not how it works over there, it's all about the network and long-term relationships. We'd have lost access to him and his friends forever if I'd gone elsewhere. If you ever bothered to take the time for some cultural research outside your westernised comfort zone, you wouldn't be so quick to criticise.'

'And once you can remain objective and make good business decisions instead of trading favours with your old drinking buddies, you might be nearly ready to run the company,' snapped Dayton. 'We need other options at our disposal if it turns out Fender isn't as interested in a proper distribution deal as he says. Therefore I want you in Asia and therefore that's where I expect you to be.'

'Uh-huh, whatever. You keep telling yourself you're in charge and I'll keep pretending I believe it.'

The two men eyed each other, well-matched in their different ways and knowing it. Where Dayton depended on determination, self-reliance and sheer force of intellect to get what he wanted, his younger brother employed guile, charisma and, when the situation suited, occasional physical intimidation. Deciding a change of tack was required, Dayton crossed to the vast Persian rug where two sofas lay either side of an intricately carved and lacquered coffee table. Taking a seat facing slightly away from the desk, he began again in a friendlier tone.

'Listen Ed, I really need your help on this. I've got too much to do in the City and won't be able to get over until at least the end of the year. If you can hold the fort until we have the second batch of prototypes up and running, I'll tell Carl to come out for a longer secondment and oversee the transition to full production. Does that work? Why do you want to come back early anyway?'

Eddie pushed himself out of the leather and steel chair to pad across the room and drop down opposite, responding as intended to this new and more equitable seating arrangement.

'Because the action's here, Jules,' he answered, stabbing downwards with a thick forefinger. 'The apartment's great but I am so sodding bored it's untrue. Fender's still in the process of calling in favours and greasing palms and quite rightly doesn't want me or any other *gweilo* involved. There are only so many times I can call him for an update and I'm convinced I'm starting to get on his nerves which isn't good for either the business or our friendship. If I end up pissing him off, then we won't just need a new distributor, he'll actively move against us if he has other options.'

'Does he?'

'God knows but he's too clever to not have thought through all the angles. We're almost blind in that part of the world. We should have invested in local production years ago and then we'd have a much better understanding of the politics and influence. Like *she* does,' he added.

'Mmm. Well if you don't have enough to keep you busy, why don't you spend some time finding out? Start with Fender's personal grapevine. Tactfully though, Ed. Play on the whole stranger abroad thing and take advantage of their hospitality. No doubt you can persuade at least one or two of his better-looking friends to take you into their confidence, eh?' said Dayton, the conspiratorial emphasis indulging his brother's self-image. 'Once you're sure Fender's in for the long term, I've no problem with Carl or one of the others taking over. But we need this expansion to start well and you said you'd stick around to make sure he keeps his word, and not just about the distribution forecasts, agreed?'

Eddie mulled the thought as Dayton waited patiently, proficient in the use of silence during a negotiation.

'All right. I'll go back for now. But there are a few things I want to sort out first, so it'll be next week, OK?'

'Fine, thanks.' Now that he had seemingly secured agreement, Dayton's good humour began to return. 'Besides, if you're sticking around, you can come along and enjoy some of the impending highlights.'

'When's the verdict due?'

'Probably Wednesday, maybe Thursday. The technical arguments should conclude this afternoon and then there's only personal testimony left before summing up.'

'What are our chances?'

'Depends on those testimonies. I'm sure she thinks they're going to be her trump card. But we're going to win, and when we do it'll expose her for what she really is.'

'Mmm. She's been able to wriggle her way out of this kind of thing in the past. And we can't afford to be liable for damages with cash flow so tight.'

'Don't worry about it. No one's going to want to be associated with McGlynn-Lansing anytime soon which means other opportunities will open up for us.'

'Like what?'

'I'll tell you once we've won.'

Well versed in his brother's Machiavellian streak, Eddie saved his breath by not probing further. 'What does Richard think?' he asked instead.

'About the case? We haven't discussed it in detail. He's obviously aware but I suspect the old man doesn't want to be seen as closely involved. Corporate lawsuits are a bit tawdry for a peer of the realm don't you think?'

'Might be useful to get another opinion though. Dad's been through a few of these in his time and knows his way around.'

'So have I and there's no need to put him in an awkward position when we're in front. He's got enough on his mind with this trade deal nonsense - it's virtually all we've spoken about since you left.'

'Can't believe it's taking so long. But he's only an advisor isn't he? The grunt work must be with the Civil Service?'

'Totally. But they're driving him round the bend. And you and I need him to stay involved so we get as much warning as possible if it's going to affect exports costs. Our margins on the new machines are already paper thin. We'll have to rethink our whole production strategy if these extra tariffs get added.'

Much to Dayton's irritation, Eddie made no effort to stifle a yawn and stretched like a big cat, possibly a result of his overnight travel but more likely that his thirst for information did not extend into what he considered trivial financial details.

'God but I'm tired. Didn't want to wait for the jet so made the mistake of taking the redeye. First class was packed and I ended up behind a couple of old bags who bickered from wheels up to wheels down. Are you still planning to race at the weekend?' he asked, switching to a topic with significantly more interest.

'Absolutely, I've flogged myself to death in training so there's no chance I'm missing it.'

'What sort of time are you hoping for?'

'Depends on the weather but something around two-fifty or better should do it.'

'You know this heatwave's forecast to break by then. Thunderstorms. You must all be mad.'

'There's nothing like a little electricity in the air to keep one feeling alive. Come down and watch, it'll be fun.'

'Maybe. Sophia's in town so I'll almost certainly have a better offer.'

'Moretti? Didn't you two break up?'

'I did. But then neither of us seems particularly attached to anyone else at the moment so, you know…' Eddie trailed off for a second or two at the thought. 'Anyway, she's been talking to some mutual friends and apparently my name came up. Turns out she's still quite into me so I gave her a call, told her I was coming over and suggested she do the same. We're booked into the Castello on Friday.'

So this was not a spur of the moment trip after all, thought Dayton, not if the sod has already planned his social calendar.

'Aren't you getting a bit old for serial dating, Ed? Don't you find it all a bit of a distraction?'

'Ha! Not on your life. Plenty of time to find the right girl, get married and start knocking out the inheritance line once I'm back for good. And lots of emotionally stunted, desperate to please, thirty-something wives-in-waiting to be had in the meantime. You should try it, you know, might help you relax a bit.'

'I'll take it under consideration.'

'That's the spirit. Right, I'm off to find a decent cup of coffee somewhere,' said Eddie, adding insult to injury. 'Probably back after lunch.'

Dayton managed a curt nod and exhaled slowly. The morning's events had already left him disagreeably tense. What was the real reason for his insolent little brother's return, was it really as simple as the boredom he suggested? If so then fine, he could be tolerated for a few days before being sent back overseas with an even firmer set of instructions. But if not… well, then maybe he had come back early to cement his power base, or even launch the long-anticipated coup.

Eddie had been a distant figure a decade ago, literally and figuratively. In the luxurious position of having few accountabilities despite being a nominal director of the company, he had been in no hurry to submit to the rigours of a truly executive position. He much preferred bedrooms to boardrooms, fast cars to fast returns and especially playing rugby to playing the market. Nevertheless, as the next year or two rolled by, he had been forced to admit he could no longer practise the beloved sport to his accustomed level. Although still an athletic and imposing figure, the cuts and bruises began to outlast the days between matches. His pace suffered and his club, which had no connections with Dayton Global Industries to be used as leverage, were uncompromising in his deselection. However, rather than humble himself with one of several offers to play in a lower-league side, he instead quit the game and concentrated on expanding his social circle during a grand tour of Europe and North America. Towards the end of the second summer, he was dismayed to discover that all lines of credit had been withdrawn without warning. Once the available favours were called in and he ran out of spare rooms and sofas, the prodigal son had little choice but to return home and face a one-sided argument with his father during which the topics of maturity, family and duty could frequently be overheard.

As a result of Richard Dayton moving to London to take up his seat in the Lords, Julian himself had risen to the position of chief executive only weeks previously. One of his first major decisions therefore was in offering Eddie an ultimatum - renounce the profligate lifestyle, recommit himself to the business and acknowledge his elder brother as leader, or tender his resignation by the end of the month.

To his credit, Eddie gave the matter serious thought before returning with provisional acceptance and a single condition - that subject to satisfactory performance, he was to be considered as next in line when the time came. Partially persuaded by their father, Dayton had agreed. They needed a new chief of staff to help refresh the management structure and Eddie's no-nonsense camaraderie, his ability to quell any dissension by having a quiet word in private and ultimately his blood loyalty to father and brother made him the obvious choice.

True, Eddie had since worked like a man possessed, throwing his competitive spirit and sporting discipline into increasingly bigger roles and cultivating an insatiable appetite for information, absorbing the lakes of valuable data which ran like oil through the machinery of their worldwide operations. He made and learned from many mistakes but never shirked the chance to take on more responsibility or improve a different area of the Group's interests. Both within and without their immediate circle, his reputation had burgeoned as an energetic and instinctive businessman with a flair for dealmaking.

Unfortunately for Dayton, Eddie's rise to what was evidently second in command had left a problem when it came to planning for his succession. On the one hand, the wider management team respected his brother's newfound commitment and preferred his engaging leadership style to Dayton's aloofness and unforgiving judgement. On the other, Eddie had fewer than ten years of relevant experience and Dayton believed he remained oblivious to the longer-term implications of his decision making, occasionally charging down blind alleys which jeopardised their returns or wider interests. Dayton was also self-aware enough to realise he had other, less rational but considerably more powerful reasons for not yet wanting to relinquish control - jealousy, insecurity, status and influence. In private, he enjoyed having Eddie as a ranking junior. For the first time in adulthood, he no longer felt the need to justify himself in comparison with his physically stronger, more handsome and more popular sibling.

What had seemed a distant promise seven years ago had inexorably become the elephant in the room. When was he going to transfer his remaining authority and install Eddie as the senior party? Not yet, certainly, and maybe not for a long time. There had been no expectation of seeing him in person for another few months and Dayton had planned to compose arguments for further delay before raising the subject at a time of his choosing. Nevertheless, here he was, back in the City again and to be found sprawling in his own chair as a provocative statement of future intent.

Rising from the sofa, Dayton thrust his hands into his pockets and returned to the easterly window, replaying their conversation in his head. As ever, he found himself drawn to those moments where he had missed opportunities to better assert his authority, advance his own agenda or more cleverly rebut an objectionable point. Eddie had the unnerving ability to make him feel not just incompetent but inadequate as well. They had always squabbled, despite the age gap, their lack of a close emotional bond an ongoing sadness to their mother and a frustration to their father who clearly did not appreciate having to play peacemaker between the two adult children running his family business.

Leaning forwards, he pressed his forehead against the cool glass and looked down into the surrounding streets, safe in the knowledge he could not be seen with the sun at this angle should anyone, particularly anyone in the tower to his east, be minded to try. Why exactly had Eddie decided to return without warning, even temporarily? Ought he to find some pretext to contact Fender Tang directly and double check their various agreements still held? How could he stay abreast of Eddie's movements, whether they involved Sophia

Moretti or not? Was now the right moment to reset expectations about any plan of succession?

He mentally replanned the week's schedule, his earlier anticipation tainted by unexpected complexity. The good humour had disappeared again, replaced by resentfulness at having to find solutions to new problems, to unwantedly change what had been a well-constructed course of action, to work harder than he would wish.

The pavements below teemed with tiny figures heading for their many places of work, hurrying in and out of the shadows as they crossed roads largely hidden beneath slow-moving cars and darting cyclists.

'You fucking idiot,' he whispered to the glass, eyes closing as if in pain. 'Stupid, stupid, stupid.'

3

By a quarter past ten, it was becoming clear to McGlynn that her schedule would also need significant revision. After Natalie's call, Detective Campbell had arrived almost immediately, giving her only enough time to slip on her shoes and dispose of the empty mug while wracking her brain as to the reason for the visit.

Although a big woman, Campbell's weight looked mostly like muscle and her handshake was full of the self-confidence to be expected of anyone dealing daily with the worst that society offered.

'Good morning, Ms McGlynn,' she said, the beautifully modulated voice containing a trace of her Jamaican roots. 'I'm sorry to come unexpectedly and I thank you for seeing me.'

'Not at all. Natalie, could you organise some tea please. And would you let Alison know I might be a couple of minutes after nine,' replied McGlynn, deftly setting expectations. 'Please, Detective, come through and make yourself comfortable. How's your family? It's been a while since you were last here.'

'It's kind of you to remember. They're all well. How are the twins? They must be what, eleven by now?'

'Wonderful, but chaos of course. And they turned twelve in March.'

Natalie came in bearing a silver flask and china cups and they busied themselves with tea making until the door had closed again.

'Now, to what do I owe this pleasure, Detective? I don't think we've had any reason to contact the Fraud Office, have we?'

'It's not often that my visits are for pleasure, but I do appreciate the sentiment.' Campbell retrieved a small notebook from her jacket and flicked through the pages. 'And I'm no longer at Fraud, I took a supervisory role at Major Crimes last year.'

'In that case, congratulations,' said McGlynn, inwardly wincing.

'Uh-hmm. Now then, perhaps you could tell me how much you know about illegal immigration?'

'Well, I can't say it's a regular topic of discussion, so not much more than I read in the press or our security protocols, I'm afraid. I know it continues to be a problem around the world and the practice is generally seasonal where open water crossings are involved. Didn't the coastguard step up patrols after that overcrowded boat incident last year?'

'They did. And it continues to be a significant problem, not just around the world but here specifically. Last month alone we detained sixty people attempting to gain entry near Alber Cove. Cost us over two thousand man-hours. The traffickers are getting bolder and more organised, immigrants are landing with higher quality forgeries and those without documents are better briefed for claiming refugee status. They get stuck in the system much longer before being processed and deported.'

'Don't we have a moral obligation to accept human beings on that basis and offer shelter? Some of their living conditions at home, the regimes they're escaping are horrific.'

'Uh-hmm, but trying to tell the difference between economic migrants, women trafficked for prostitution, those with a criminal record and genuine refugees is getting harder every day. You might remember Mayor Santoro taking a hard line on the issue in his manifesto. Unfortunately, City PD doesn't have the manpower or the budget to keep up with the increase in numbers.'

'Ah, and next year is election year.'

'Correct, Ms McGlynn. Which means the problem needs to be fixed beforehand, or at least reduced to the level where it's no longer making the front pages. The mayor has instructed the coastguard to return more inbound boats to their countries of origin. He's also tasked the Port Authority and Major Crimes with dismantling the supply chains and given us a freer hand to take down anyone who's found to be involved, knowingly or otherwise.'

'And what does all this have to do with me?'

Campbell paused to sip her tea. 'We've been tipped off that vessels offering illegal passage are using McGlynn-Lansing's facilities.'

'Nonsense. We operate the best marine security practices there are. Every captain in our fleet has at least fifteen years of service and neither they nor our other freight partners would risk themselves or their crew by allowing it. I'm sorry, but you've been misinformed.'

'This comes from a credible source so we'll be following it up,' replied the detective, having paid close attention to McGlynn's response. 'I'm here as a courtesy and to ask for your full cooperation.'

'And you'll have it, of course. But it's a waste of resource which, as already mentioned, is better directed elsewhere.'

'Even so, I'm planning to visit your warehousing shortly. And, um, I've been asked to tell you that Mayor Santoro would also appreciate a discussion on this topic in person,' she added, appearing uncomfortable.

'What? Why?'

'I really have no idea, Ms McGlynn, I'm sure that's above my pay grade. But I've been instructed to make it clear he's expecting you.'

'Well that's… noted. I'm likely to bump into him on Wednesday anyway. Now, unless there's anything else, please speak with Matthieu on your way out and he'll give you contact details for our dockside staff.'

'Uh-hmm. That won't be necessary. But could you perhaps let…' Campbell turned back a couple of pages. '… a Mr Hugo Valente know we're coming?'

'In that case, it seems you have all the information you need,' said McGlynn, rising. 'Although I must say I'm disappointed to have my company under scrutiny in this matter. I trust there'll be no connection made in public?'

'Please don't be concerned Ms McGlynn, this is a routine enquiry. At this point,' she added, with marginal emphasis. 'Here's my new card in case you think of something relevant. Call me anytime.'

And with that she had left, leaving McGlynn to contemplate the unwelcome development. Throughout the meeting with her head of human resources, in which she displayed her usual full attention, the notion of whether McGlynn-Lansing was complicit in such an abhorrent crime as human trafficking remained close by. Now standing again at the window, she looked out across the bay, lost in thought. Her teams at the docks and across the extended fleet carried her full confidence but she had no illusions about how difficult it was to protect cargo and ships from unauthorised stowaways. The variable state of global maritime security and the huge number of places to hide aboard a container vessel made preventing the problem almost impossible.

Nathan Santoro's invitation had in some ways proved even more unsettling. Why would he want a meeting on the subject given there was no obvious connection to McGlynn, perhaps other than City PD's speculative visit? She was no expert in the field and it was odd for such a canny political operator to associate himself with anyone involved in an investigation, no matter how informally at the time. The likely answer involved personal gain. In her opinion, the mayor's ambition significantly outstripped his ability, thus making him an inconvenience if not actually dangerous, and she had no wish to be drawn into helping either him or his potential re-election. Yet she could find no plausible subtext and, despite herself, was intrigued by the real reason for his interest.

'Matthieu,' she called, waiting a moment until he appeared around the edge of her doorway. 'Three things. First, call Mayor Santoro's office and ask about his availability in the next couple of days, I'll go to him. Second, tell Andrew we'll be out on the bike at lunchtime. Third, have you found Rohan yet?'

'No, Director. But I've left messages asking him to call as soon as possible.'

'OK thanks, keep me posted. Door closed please.'

McGlynn possessed an almost preternatural ability to compartmentalise the array of problems and opportunities competing for her attention. Satisfied she was now committed to the best course of action on all fronts, she immediately dismissed the morning's events and turned her mind towards the call which Matthieu had scheduled at half-past the hour.

Christopher Boland was the most recent non-executive investor on her board, purchasing his block of shares after her father's old friend Aaron Castellane announced the intention to sell. Now semi-retired, the bulk of Boland's private wealth had been made by allowing others to buy into the company still bearing his name. At the time of his appointment, McGlynn had been unusually indecisive, balancing his substantial experience in one of McGlynn-Lansing's main fields of interest with an underlying feeling he might be difficult to get along with. Whilst she had no concerns about working with colleagues offering well-intentioned challenge, indeed she often sought them out knowing it would help maintain the highest standards, he had exhibited a vaguely antagonistic manner during their negotiations, as though he valued the debate more than the quality of the outcome. Ultimately though, she decided his credentials and network should carry the day and there had since been no cause for regret. Their working relationship became cordial, if not exactly friendly, and he had contributed heavily to accelerating her technology division's expansion, lending both good advice and access to his black book of industry contacts.

And now this. Why was he hiring Danny Zhao and why had he decided not to let her know in advance? Zhao's reputation in the elite world of quantum computing bordered on the genius. If McGlynn had known he was available she might have approached him directly, even though it would have been difficult to accommodate him alongside Rohan Mehta given the rivalry between the two men.

Glancing at the wall clock, she retrieved her earphones and returned to the window. A pair of seagulls playing on the breeze wheeled toward the glass, the faint plaintive calls an unmistakable lure to anyone who had known the ocean. She followed their looping, rolling course and then, as they turned and headed back out over the blue, let her eyes defocus.

'Call Christopher Boland.'

The first familiar purr. Two more and she knew Boland's own device would be ringing. Two more and her concern increased. Well aware he was likely to be ready and waiting for the conversation, the slight delay in picking up tacitly suggested his attitude towards the call, maybe even a power play. *Bâtard.*

Moments before she was diverted to the answering service, there was a muted click.

'Boland.'

'Morning, Christopher.'

'Ah, Wynter, a very good morning. How are you?' he brayed, the clipped pronunciation almost identical to that of Eddie Dayton. Little surprise given the two men had attended the same school in south-west England, albeit a generation apart.

'Fine thanks. How was your weekend?'

'Marvellous. We had the grandchildren over. George is filling out nicely and hoping to specialise in cardio if he gets the grades. Even Lucy seems to be blossoming, thank heavens.'

'I'm sure he'll get what he needs,' said McGlynn, knowing how much Boland favoured his grandson. Poor Lucy. 'You and Elaine must be very proud.'

'Bloody good genes, that's what we put it down to.'

'Mmm. Listen, are you coming over tonight? I thought we might meet for breakfast if so.'

'Alas not. I'm on the early flight, should be there around ten.'

'That's a shame, I was hoping to catch you before the board session, see if there's anything you'd like to add to the agenda.'

A chuckle made its way across the line.

'Ah, you've heard, have you. Good news travels fast. Who told you?'

'It's difficult to keep secrets from people who spend their lives solving puzzles,' said McGlynn smoothly. 'Congratulations on persuading Danny to join you. Quite the scoop.'

'Thank you. I know it might seem an unorthodox move but I can walk you through our strategy and settle any nerves. In fact, the opportunity for collaboration between our companies couldn't be more exciting.'

'I would have hoped for the courtesy of a heads-up beforehand. The potential conflict of interest is obvious, no?'

'Well it all happened rather quickly I'm afraid. And better that I was able to secure his services than he disappeared off to anyone, um, less friendly.'

'Indeed. Shall we add it under other business then?'

'How about coffee,' replied Boland, not taking the bait. 'I can maybe get there slightly earlier, say around nine thirty?'

'Yes OK, I'll see if I can rearrange a few things and confirm.'

'Jolly good. I read through the briefing materials with interest, by the way. They'll make for a good debate. In particular, I'm surprised you're still investing so heavily in the software team. Our previous advice was to wait until the trial is settled one way or the other.'

'You know Julian Dayton's in the wrong here, Christopher.'

'It doesn't really matter what you believe, it's what you can prove. What does that lawyer chap of yours think?'

'I'm speaking with him later but he spent the weekend briefing Rohan to make sure his testimony stacks up. Provided that goes as expected, it'll be obvious that Dayton's have had the benefit of our code for at least a year.'

'Don't be so sure. So-called expert judges can be anything but and this is a particularly technical case of he said, she said. Hmm, I'd like to see how well-prepared Rohan is. Can he join the meeting for an hour?'

'I'll find out if it's an option.'

'And given costs are going to be much higher if you lose, I suggest we also review our damage limitation strategy.'

'That won't be necessary.'

'Nevertheless, I've taken the liberty of talking it over with the others and it will be tabled tomorrow.'

McGlynn's concern increased. If Boland had secured agreement from the other three investors, there was nothing she could do to prevent a formal item on the agenda. Talking through the topic itself was of no concern, she was used to difficult decisions and responsibility for their outcome. However, the fact they had all spoken without making her aware was at best disrespectful and at worst indicative of something much more serious - a collective lack of trust in her judgement.

'That's disappointing. But OK, I'll update the board and then we can discuss whether contingency planning is worth our time.'

'Now now, Wynter, don't be upset. Hope for the best but plan for the worst, eh? We're here to help and do what's right for you and the company.'

'And I appreciate it.'

'Until tomorrow then. Let me know about coffee.'

Without waiting for a reply, the call clicked off leaving McGlynn to simmer at both the man's arrogance and the knowledge she could not afford to lose his support. Yet again, her father's legacy had left her in a position of weakness, of resorting to diplomacy rather than exerting authority.

David McGlynn had assumed control of the business from her grandfather Kenneth during an era of stable, if unimaginative, profitability. Determined to make his mark, jealous of the expansion which his great rival Richard Dayton was busily masterminding, he had immediately given orders to increase borrowing in the pursuit of accelerated growth. For a long time it seemed the new Director could do no wrong. Innovative ventures funded with cheap credit made substantial returns, a broadened range of manufactured products captured the zeitgeist of their various markets and the company outgrew an already confident global economy. A decade of success brought fresh affluence and influence to McGlynn-Lansing and its ebullient, Midas-like leader.

But then, as is generally the case when one speculates for long enough, fortune turned against him. With the unflinching clarity of hindsight, it became clear that David's optimism had been misplaced, his decisions deeply flawed. He had acquired extensive interests in Australian food commodities in the months prior to the most prolonged drought in sixty years, forged egotistic and expensive political connections with a government then toppled by scandal and brokered offshore manufacturing agreements across the Far East only to see tit for tat trade wars and an economic recession wipe out the anticipated profits. McGlynn's rapidly descended into serious financial trouble.

By this point, the replacement of several cargo planes had been put off for years longer than prudent. However, with global aluminium prices at record highs and the availability of commercial credit suddenly at record lows, there was neither the liquidity nor the collateral needed to commission new aircraft. Aware of the trouble, Richard Dayton set about exploiting the situation by offering competing services at a loss, all the while poaching key members of staff with exorbitant salaries and unsettling stories of their employer's imminent demise. Eventually it became clear that without an injection of capital the company would fail altogether.

Held at arm's length, her opinion neither wanted nor valued by a man bent on protecting his legacy, McGlynn remembered well the prevailing atmosphere of that period. Creditors started to circle ominously, a hush settled over the once vibrant family home and her embattled father spent every waking hour at the office as avenues of escape slammed shut. Early apprehension gave way to serious concern as she realised the institution dominating her consciousness since childhood could conceivably fail before she ever had the chance to lead it.

Overriding her protests, David attempted to broker a management investment deal with the four minority shareholders at that time - Aaron Castellane, Nick Turnbull, Elliott Hounslow and Brendan Stratton. In return for considerable personal outlay, each was offered a stockholding of twelve percent and the corresponding incremental dividends. As part of the agreement, none could sell their shares to the other and the Director's personal approval would be required should they wish to sell elsewhere.

The four men, vastly different characters who rarely saw eye to eye, had met in secret to discuss the offer. Recognising one of those rare moments where significant weakness creates significant opportunity, they conspired to call David's bluff by each demanding the crucial thirteen percent which collectively gave them a voting majority and hence control. After weeks of heated negotiation during which the company sank further into trouble, David conceded on the specific proviso that a McGlynn blood relative retained the position of Director in perpetuity. In his desperation, he gambled the investors or their hand-picked replacements were unlikely to ever agree a unanimous vote against him or his line.

Hence, after a century of trading as an autocracy, McGlynn-Lansing's destiny suddenly became vulnerable to differences of opinion, where consensus mattered more than being right.

With the injection of cash, the company duly restored its finances and began a protracted recovery. David never did likewise. He had been emasculated by the shift in power, unable to simply exert his will and inwardly shamed by the memory of what he knew was his own incompetence.

Routine decisions became the subject of pointless debate as the increasingly embittered Director sought and failed to re-establish his authority. Whilst McGlynn had not yet forgiven him for mismanaging the situation, she observed this slow decline with a mixture of sadness and trepidation, realising she would likely be asked to succeed him sooner than expected. Sure enough, within a year of the boardroom coup and a few months of Julian Dayton assuming the equivalent role, she had been approached by an apologetic Castellane who told her Turnbull, Hounslow, Stratton and, so sorry, he himself had come to the conclusion that the company needed a new Director. Would she consider the position?

McGlynn had known she would be their preferred choice. Of her older siblings, Michael had chosen academia over commerce long ago and Sylvie, whilst passionate in leading the company's marketing efforts, demonstrated little ambition in taking on a broader remit. The perception of the non-executives, based on the periphery to which she had been consigned during David's downfall, was that McGlynn was naive and would rely heavily on their experience. She would become a puppet dictator, obedient to the grace and favour of the four older generals.

Well, no matter. Although apprehensive of the workload in the context of her young children, she had more than enough self-belief along with a burning desire to make amends, and accepted on the proviso she could speak with David beforehand. Their meeting had been without question the worst of her life. He was livid to learn the investors wanted him replaced without consultation. Worse, that his daughter appeared to support the conclusion he was no longer fit to lead the company. David's sense of betrayal had been total and words were exchanged which could not be unsaid.

They rarely spent time together these days but, when unavoidable occasions arose, their sense of kinship was gone and McGlynn grieved for the loss of her father's love.

Being the first Director of the firm to not inherit a voting majority had hence left her sensitive to any rift with a united board. Were Boland's motives well-intended or was he using the case against Dayton's as a smokescreen to cover his own manoeuvre in hiring Zhao? When and why had he been in contact with the others outside the normal meeting schedule? She needed to find out, and preferably before they sat across a table in open forum tomorrow.

Two more pairs of gulls flew out over the edge of the tower above her head. Following them, she briefly coveted the effortless and unconcerned freedom with which they rode the thermals forced upwards by the face of the building. After a moment's play, they swooped below the horizon and her eyes came to rest on the container ships coasting lazily more than a mile offshore.

She wondered which were hers and, despite the earlier conviction, whether any held more human cargo than was declared on their manifest.

4

T he remainder of McGlynn's morning unfolded much as originally planned. As was usual before the board convened, she used the weekly management meeting to run through the reports that would be pored over, inviting comments from the room and then pursuing lines of questioning until sure everyone understood the main issues and appropriate action was being taken.

Similar to Boland, her principal concern was the level of funding for their computing division. As Damian Bailey, her head of finance, had highlighted in his briefing document at the weekend, sales revenues were increasing more slowly than anticipated despite the growing demand for quantum-based server processing. Yet costs continued to climb and McGlynn wanted to better understand the delay in new product features which her head of sales claimed was causing slippage in customer contracts.

To her frustration however, the man responsible for developing those features, Rohan Mehta, had failed to attend. Nor had he responded to the messages she and Matthieu had left and McGlynn was now undeniably concerned. To be late to the office on a Monday would have been unusual enough but to miss a whole morning, including a meeting at which he would have known his presence was expected, was entirely out of character. It seemed Jacob Wiesenberg was the last person to see Rohan, with no one from McGlynn-Lansing having spoken with him since the end of the previous week. She resolved to give him the benefit of the doubt until the end of the day at which point she would send someone to his home address.

Individual conversations broke out as the meeting ended - earlier debates yet to be settled, arrangements for follow-up activities or simply plans for lunch. With nods of encouragement for those under particular pressure, McGlynn beckoned to Matthieu as she left for her office.

'Did you confirm the bike ride with Andrew?' she asked.

'Yes, he'll be in the garage at ten past. Can I ask how long you expect to be out for? I know you said a couple of hours but–'

'Don't worry, I'll be back in plenty of time to meet Jacob at three. But if he's early, just show him in and offer him a drink.'

'Of course. Would you like me to say that we haven't seen Rohan this morning?'

'No, it's probably best I tackle it with him directly. He's liable to need calming down. See you later.'

Placing the laptop on her desk, she crossed to where the wall of built-in cupboards met the windows. What looked like a blanking panel gave way beneath her hand to reveal a short corridor ending at a polished mahogany door. Keying a nine-digit code into the pad, her fingers fast and accurate on the small silver buttons, she leant against the dark wood and stepped into her apartment.

In common with many of her peers, McGlynn had more than one place to stay in and around the City. When she signed off the drawings for ML One there was a space of more than a thousand square feet along the southern edge marked simply as "Equipment Room". This had subsequently been partitioned into a small, interconnected suite, simple and functional in its specification but finished to the highest quality by handpicked craftsmen. Over an hour's drive from the family home in Laurel Valley, the space represented convenience, security and above all privacy in her otherwise very public existence. Few people knew the apartment existed and only two, McGlynn and the housekeeper, had regular access.

After shrugging on her cycling gear, she made for the kitchenette and, with a drinks bottle filled, rode the private elevator directly to the underground garages beneath ML One, stepping out into a dim space smelling the same the world over - of metal and rubber and concrete. This section contained two cars and was separated from the main floor by a vertical rolling grid. A lean figure waited beyond with a road bike in each hand.

'Hey Andrew, how are you?' she called on the way over.

'Just fine thanks, Director. Want to tell me where we're going on this beautiful day?'

Reaching the barrier, she keyed a different combination into the adjacent pad and the mechanism rattled into life.

'The port. I'll need an hour or so there and then back before two-thirty. Does that work?'

'Sure. This week's all about technique, no conditioning. So long as you promise you'll take it easy there and back, then we're all good.'

Brookes' intonation was warm but he was firmly in charge when it came to McGlynn's training plan, a role he assumed with ease given his military background. He handed her the nearer of the cycles along with a small earpiece. The bike was built around an electric blue, aerodynamically sculpted carbon frame, set off by bright white wheel rims, saddle and handlebars. With practised ease, she swung a leg over the seat post, snapped a shoe onto the clip and screwed the tiny speaker into her ear.

'Audio check,' said Brookes. 'Then let's go.'

They pushed off and rode between the lines of cars, tyres squeaking on the polished concrete. Near the base of the exit ramp, the shimmer of hot air could be seen where the noonday sun beat down on the pavement outside and the scent and tranquility of the garage began to fade, replaced by hot asphalt and distant horns. McGlynn leant the bike over neatly, stood on the pedals and led the way up the incline.

Catching her breath as they emerged into direct sunlight, her nostrils refusing to comply without a conscious effort to inhale, she balanced to a stop, glanced in both directions, then banked right and freewheeled down Cornelian Lane, the ocean ahead glittering between vertiginous glass and metal walls. The lights at the end were already green and they crossed Foreshore Road to turn right again, onto the Esplanade directly in front of ML One. She looked up at the face of the building, still loving the aesthetics of the construction and the activities it housed, before returning her attention to the joggers and other cyclists making the most of their own lunch hours.

'Let's start out nice and slow until we've warmed up, Director,' came the voice in her ear. 'Think about those semicircles with your feet and no more than fifty percent power in whatever gear you feel comfortable.'

She changed up to the midrange, the precision of the slider snicking across the cogs appealing to her desire for quality, and concentrated on her cadence. The metronomic push downwards on one side while drawing backwards on the other, trying to keep the power delivery even throughout the rotation and equally distributed between each leg. The texture of the rubberised strip below became a blur as they reached a cruise, McGlynn out in front and Brookes a length behind where he could watch her style and offer advice as needed.

Stretching out along the shoreline, the cycle track lay sandwiched between the wide Foreshore Road to her right and the pavement of the Esplanade to her left. Pedestrians came mostly from the business district opposite, strolling casually in twos and threes, leaning on the railings or sitting on one of the many benches to eat their lunch and top up their tan, gossiping about weekends and upcoming promotions and office affairs. She inhaled deeply now, more used to the midday heat, and indulged in the smell of the salt air and the sun on her bare arms.

In the near distance, the Dayton Global Industries building dominated the skyline. Feeling its pull like a yoke around her neck, McGlynn resolved to ignore the southeast corner as they approached. The City had witnessed significant chapters of shared history between the McGlynns and the Daytons during its long evolution, most of it spiteful and destructive, and Julian Dayton was only the latest in a line of men who had sought their own pre-eminence through the demise of her company. He appeared to take such humiliating pleasure however, such a vindictive interest in the task since taking over from his father, that she had learned to despise the man and his methods as much as his aims. And to think there had once been a time when she believed the two of them might bring an end to their feuding. Well leopards can't change their spots, *tant pis*, so be on your notice Julian because I'm more than a match for you and your brother.

A voice broke through her thoughts.

'Back off the gas and relax your shoulders again please. Focus on posture and cadence. Save your energy for the weekend.'

The corners of her eyes crinkled behind the sunglasses. Brookes knew what Saturday meant.

They pushed on, the high-rise office blocks cascading into hotels and restaurants near the start of the pale, sandy beach to their left. Holidaymakers in swimwear and towels crossed without warning, children carrying balls and buckets, their parents concealed behind voluminous string bags full of paraphernalia for a day by the sea. Further along, skateboarders and rollerbladers weaved in and out of shadows cast by the stone pines planted at regular intervals more than a century ago. The marina was now clearly visible between their naked trunks, the yacht masts a skeletal forest of aluminium above the long black seaboard wall. Although impossible to tell which belonged to the 35-foot *Libertas III*, she mentally pictured the elegant lines and the teak deck and resolved to spend more time on the water this summer.

The sun was relentless. Riding one handed, she retrieved the water bottle and took a long pull, wanting to go even faster, to explore the limits of her endurance, relishing the challenge of exercising in such temperatures. They reminded her of Alpine trips to watch the Tour as a child, the stamina of the riders sprinting up near impossible inclines seemingly superhuman. To her, they remained an indelible illustration of man's ability to manage temporary pain in pursuit of glorious achievement. Knowing she was now in the latter half of her physical prime vexed her despite recognising the inevitability of age. Opportunities which had seemed limitless were being closed off one by one, by physiology rather than lack of ambition, yet she much preferred resistance to acceptance, short-lived discomfort to long-term decline.

Beyond the marina, where the Esplanade ended and the track decanted onto the last stretch of Foreshore Road, the gantry cranes of the docks came into view. Verges manicured by the City's army of manual workers gave way to functional concrete blockwork protecting Port Road from the sea on one side and the cliffs on the other. Most of the traffic forked inland but the two riders bore left and hugged the barriers as heavy goods vehicles thundered past. Reaching the tall security fence of the Port Authority, McGlynn checked over her shoulder and turned onto the service road, the slope's old cobbles serving as a rumble-strip for the thousands of shipping container tractor units which travelled there each week.

'Careful,' said Brookes uneasily.

Assured in her ability, she stood off the saddle, loosened her grip and allowed the bars to buck and jitter as the thin wheels bounced off the stones. No doubt much to his relief, she made the far side in safety and veered along the perimeter towards the port's southwestern tip.

Her facility was located in prime position. Exclusive access to nearly two thirds of a mile of quayside and seventy feet of draught to comfortably accommodate the ultra large container vessels arriving from around the world. Fully autonomous cranes could unload these gentle giants in a little over a day, straight into the compound then through the huge warehouse doors or directly onto waiting flatcars in the adjacent railway terminal. At this time of year, the containers were brim full of fruit, wine and meat from the big southern hemisphere exporters and the proximity of the onward transport options saved McGlynn thousands of hours and tonnes of lost produce. More than half of their shipments travelled inland by rail, the colossal trains navigating the switches before disappearing into the black maw of the tunnels beneath the coast road. They would re-emerge into daylight more than an hour later, well on their way towards the Capital and its waiting profits.

Reaching the compound, they freewheeled beneath raised barriers alongside an empty security cabin.

'How did that feel?' asked Brookes.

'To be honest, Andrew, it felt like nothing more than a warm-up. We can go up a couple of notches on the way back.'

'Not a chance, sorry. You know it's light duties only this week.'

'Huh. I'm fairly sure I pay your wages.'

'Sure, but I'll be out of a job unless you're in perfect condition in five days' time. So you'll do as I ask on the way back, Director. Please,' he added with a flash of white teeth in the tanned face.

'Ha! I'll think about it.' They pulled up next to a glass personnel door and she checked her watch. 'I'm going for a quick look around before I find Hugo. Meet you back here in an hour.'

Handing the bike to Brookes, she headed for the gaping aperture of the first loading bay, her cleats clicking on the hardstanding, her eyes drawn to the enormous container stacks standing like monoliths erected to an industrial deity. Up the steps to load height and through the heavy plastic strips, the coolness of the conditioned air came as a relief. While peeling off her gloves, a tall and flabby man in dark green overalls shouldered carelessly through double doors in the whitewashed block wall. He slowed a step and made a leisurely appraisal of this welcome, lycra-clad break to his routine.

'Alright darlin,' he drawled, tongue flicking out to moisten rubbery lips and appearing to grind through basic but obvious possibilities. 'You know this is a restricted area? But tell you what, you come with me and I'll give you the tour. It's nice and quiet over there by the packing stations. We could–'

However, the rest of his intentions were left unsaid as he moved almost within touching distance and McGlynn removed her sunglasses to look him squarely in the eye.

'We could what, Jonah?' she asked, voice like granite.

Jonah Turner seemed at a sudden and total loss for words.

'Um, er…I meant…that...we could...I mean, we… we should go and make sure you're signed in. Director.' A pause, the man wilting before her gaze. 'But you don't need to do that. So, er…'

'No, I don't. And nor do I expect anyone visiting one of my sites to be spoken to as you've just done, particularly by someone at your level of seniority. Do I make myself clear?'

'Yes ma'am. I'm, um, ah, sorry.'

'Sorry isn't good enough. I'll speak to Mr Valente and ask him to pick this up with you later.'

Turner opened his mouth as if to protest but then shut it again. Satisfied he had accepted her decision, she started towards the racking opposite.

'I know it's lunchtime but why is it so quiet in here? Where is everybody?'

'The next shipment's not due till tomorrow.'

'So?'

'So, er, I gave the guys the afternoon off.'

'You did what?' She stopped in her tracks, astonished their normally frenetic port operation could spare any downtime. 'On whose authority?'

'Mr Valente said it'd be OK,' he replied, face falling further as he realised there would be a second reason to expect his manager's displeasure.

McGlynn digested this new information then set off again down one of the aisles, eyes roving critically in every direction, her terse questions bringing laboured replies from Turner who panted heavily in his efforts to keep up. The cavernous space was eerie in disuse and she was unable to quell a feeling the two of them were not entirely alone. Arriving back at the loading bay, she stopped beside the doors from which he had emerged.

'OK, I'm done. Go and call round the shift. Tell as many of them as you can reach to get back here immediately.'

'Today?' Turner looked horrified.

'Yes, today. Mr Valente will be issuing new instructions at two o'clock and there'll be unpaid overtime until they're complete. The more hands you can muster, the faster you'll be finished.'

Giving him no time to demur, she depressed the release plunger, pushed against the galvanised plate and entered a brightly lit corridor. A set of metal stairs rose immediately to her left with an equivalent visible in the distance, single doorways spaced at regular intervals in between. Valente's corner office was almost directly above and she took the stairs quickly despite her cleats, wanting to reach him before he had the chance to be forewarned.

Although he no longer worked for her directly, McGlynn had known Hugo Valente for years. Through a dogged application of effort, he had risen from apprentice dockworker to run their home port operations with efficiency and rigour and she had grown used to the general absence of problems from his direction. Yet standards seemed to have fallen and she was keen to understand why. Reaching the landing, she heard a voice through his open doorway, deep in conversation.

'…of course I wouldn't,' said Valente listlessly. 'No, that's not what we agreed. You wanted…'

McGlynn found him hunched over the desk, forehead resting heavily on one hand and a phone clamped to his ear with the other, so preoccupied that her presence went unnoticed leaving her free to survey the room. A dying yucca plant stood beneath a window overlooking the railway terminal, sheafs of paperwork were deposited in piles on the green leather sofa and the oversized photographs of ships and buildings adorning the walls had begun to fade in the sunlight. The place had the same air of neglect as Valente himself. McGlynn remembered him clean-shaven in crisply pressed clothes but he now wore a grubby short-sleeved shirt and a two-day stubble on his chin. So tangible was his disaffection that the hair lost since their last meeting might have been pulled out deliberately.

She stepped forward and his head jerked up, expressions of surprise and then resignation crossing his face.

'Sorry, gotta go, I'll call you back later,' he said into the mouthpiece. 'Hello Director, good to see you. If I'd known you were coming I'd have met you on the way in.'

'Good to see you too, Hugo. How're you doing?'

'Fine, fine,' he replied, McGlynn noticing a slight shake of the head. 'There's hardly a day we're not flat out. Might have to expand again soon.'

'Nice problems to have. How are *you* doing though?'

'Oh, sorry. I'm fine too, thanks.'

'Then why is my warehouse in such a mess?'

'Excuse me?' said Valente, blinking rapidly. 'With due respect, I think we're in good shape. Wastage is down, we're coping with nearly fifteen percent more stock movements with the same number of staff. There's–'

'I'm very familiar with the operating stats. I meant literally. The racking's badly stacked and leaning dangerously in several places, the towers are missing chunks of paint which means they'll end up collapsing anyway from rust, the forklifts aren't at their charging stations, there are trip hazards in almost every aisle, plus empty pallets and loose packaging and trash all over the place. And the place smells, Hugo. It smells of rotten meat and a lack of management.'

'It's true that we've had to focus on our priorities. Getting shipments in and out on–'

'Prioritisation is what's required when we're out of capacity. But Jonah tells me he sent today's shift home which suggests we've not yet reached that point?'

'But they've been working so hard recently. I thought we should give them time off before the *Santa Rosa* docks tomorrow. It'll take a week to get her cargo unloaded and moved onwards.'

'Has there been any overtime recently?'

'No. We're managing costs at the agreed–'

'In that case nobody's being overworked and the team should be spending afternoons like these maintaining the facility. We operate one of the largest and supposedly best port operations on the continent which is the reason we win the level of business we do. If standards drop, we'll be dead in the water and then we'll be sending people home for much longer than the occasional afternoon, don't you think?'

'I guess so.'

'When was the last time Jane came over?' she asked, her disquiet increasing.

'Must've been, um, late last year. We speak most weeks though.'

'OK.' McGlynn made a mental note to call Jane Hallam, to whom Valente reported, once the difference in time zones allowed. 'Hugo, I'd like to see the physical security reports for the last three months.'

'May I ask why?' he asked, blinking again.

'Given what I've seen today, I'm concerned things may have slipped elsewhere. Nobody was manning the entrance barriers when I arrived, two of the warehouse doors were open without supervision and some of the containers in the compound weren't padlocked. It looks to me like we're completely open to theft and smuggling of all kinds.'

'But the cameras, they're continually monitored.'

'That's not the point. They're only part of the infrastructure we need for our Port Authority license. So I want to take a look at those logs.'

'No problem, I'll send them across to your office later today.'

'Now please Hugo.'

'Of course,' he said, not quite daring to sigh but shoulders sagging an inch further. 'Be right back.'

He disappeared through the doorway. Already anticipating her ride back around the bay, McGlynn moved to the window to stretch her legs and watch a train being unloaded by more than a dozen huge gantry cranes. Overseen by only a couple of bored-looking stevedores, the process reminded her of ants methodically deconstructing an obstacle, the regularity of the movement and the slow but inexorable removal of the source material. Containers without the McGlynn-Lansing logo were hoisted high into the air and carried along the wharfside before the cranes returned empty, cables dangling to collect their next load.

What on earth was going on, she wondered, cursing herself for not having picked up on these problems before now. Jane Hallam, or Auntie Jane as she was affectionately known amongst her peers, although never to her face, was a capable and resolute veteran of the McGlynn-Lansing executive team. McGlynn had known her since childhood and had complete trust in her competence which is why she found the state of the warehouse and Valente's disposition so perplexing. Why had Hallam not realised quality was declining or, if she had, why was she not doing something about it having let McGlynn know?

She heard raised voices through the partition wall and her foreboding increased. Something was broken here. After Campbell's visit that morning, she no longer felt her previous confidence in dismissing the detective's allegation. Did Julian Dayton know about their substandard port management and was he behind the tip-off to City PD? If so, was it simply a distraction, designed to inconvenience, or did he have any actual evidence that McGlynn-Lansing was complicit in people trafficking, knowingly or otherwise? She shivered in the air conditioning.

Nearly five more minutes elapsed before Valente returned.

'I'm sorry, Director, but it appears we don't have complete records for the last three months,' he said, not meeting her eye.

'Are you absolutely sure you're alright, Hugo?'

'Yes. I'm OK.'

'Right. In that case I want a full review of our security status on my desk by close of business tomorrow,' said McGlynn, the warmth gone from her tone. 'Including copies of whatever documentation is available, plus root cause analysis of why current protocols aren't being followed and a set of appropriate recommendations to fix the problems either immediately or as soon as possible.'

'But… but the *Santa Rosa*, I need to make sure she's berthed and unload–'

'That's what delegation is for. Make sure your first line understands what's expected and that they take responsibility. Specifically, I want her manifest double checked before any of the crew step ashore. Every container is to be opened or scanned for unexpected items before it's trans-shipped and the empty holds searched. I'm leaving Andrew Brookes here to oversee your work. You'll keep him up to date with progress and his instructions are to be followed to the letter. If you're not able to commit to completing the report by tomorrow afternoon, then I'll expect your resignation in its place, preferably beforehand. Do you understand?'

Valente clearly understood all too well.

'Yes. And again, I'm sorry.'

'This situation and your handling of it is totally unacceptable so sorry can wait until we're operating safely again. You should also prepare for a visit from the police, either a Detective Campbell or one of her team from Major Crimes. They're as interested as I am in how secure our cargo operations are and particularly whether we're involved in people smuggling.'

Watching closely, McGlynn could have sworn he turned another shade paler.

'Exactly,' she continued, picking up her helmet. 'I want to know how exposed we are before they do. So find a reason, any reason, to stall them until you've completed the review but then give them your full cooperation. Jonah's recalling the afternoon shift so make sure they clean up properly before tomorrow's shipment comes into the compound. Oh, and please address his behaviour towards visitors in general and female visitors in particular. I was subjected to some pretty unwelcome attention on the way in.'

Valente nodded dejectedly and McGlynn saw he would likely fail to complete his growing tasklist without some level of encouragement.

'You're a good and loyal man, Hugo. I'm trusting you and I'm here to help if you can't reach Jane. But do not let me down on this.'

'I won't, Director,' he said, straightening a little.

She left, clattering down the steps and finding Brookes sprawled in the sunshine. Outside her fitness training, his consulting firm provided ML One's physical security infrastructure and she knew he had the attention to detail currently missing from Valente's work.

'Hey, sorry Andrew but a change of plan. Are you able to clear your diary for the afternoon? Probably tomorrow as well?'

'Think so. What's up?'

McGlynn brought him up to speed and told him what she needed.

'And keep a particular eye on Hugo,' she finished, donning her gear. 'He's not himself and I don't know why. If you get any sense he's not capable of sorting this out, then I want to know immediately.'

'Roger that. Where will I find you tomorrow for a debrief?'

'Not sure yet. Give Matthieu or Natalie a call and they'll find some time for us, or we can catch up at lunch anyway. But call me in the meantime if you need to.'

Brookes nodded his acknowledgement and disappeared inside carrying his bike. McGlynn stood astride hers, surveyed the compound once more, then clipped in and rode under the barriers as the first cars arrived carrying angry looking men. She held no sympathy. The state of the warehouse reflected badly on all who worked there and, whilst Valente was responsible, there was no excuse for anyone condoning such carelessness.

Despite Brookes' earlier instructions, she pushed much harder on the return journey to ML One, conscious of the growing number of things to be done and feeling the need to be in action, to be productive, to be removing items from the list faster than they were being added.

So engrossed was she in her deliberation that Julian Dayton's office went completely unnoticed as she swept past.

5

As it happened, Dayton's office was empty. He was instead in the boardroom and doing his level best to appear confident and at ease despite enduring that most discomforting of activities - having his picture taken.

'That's great, thanks,' said the City Post photographer, snapping away with an expensive-looking camera. 'Two more. Tilt your chin up and a nice wide smile, looking directly into the lens. Smile please Mr Dayton. Please? That's it, hold it there. Good, thanks. Three or four more...'

Dayton surrendered as asked, trusting to the man's experience and hoping by the law of averages they might get at least one tolerable shot if there were simply enough from which to choose. He had agreed to the interview with the Post weeks ago, ostensibly regarding an important announcement but in reality merely an advertorial to keep their own brand presence high and their competitors out of the headlines. He understood the marketing logic but this was an aspect of the business he particularly disliked. Making the occasion even worse than anticipated, the Post had seen fit to send Sunita Malik to write the piece.

Dayton was all too aware of her reputation - ambitious, independent, meticulous in her research and a fearless investigator. She had made her name skewering upstanding but clearly flawed members of City society in the columns appearing online and in print at the Post's downtown newsstands. The meeting would have been delegated to Eddie had he known - it was far more amusing to read about another's lack of integrity than to offer up one's own for scrutiny.

Malik had selected the chair at the head of the table, immediately in front of the ancillary flash units and their white panel reflectors. Like a grand inquisitor, she watched patiently while the accused was softened up by a blunter instrument, not even having the good manners to give him any privacy in his torment. Large, leonine eyes followed his self-conscious movements as if assessing their prey, trying to gain a more profound understanding of his weaknesses prior to the impending verbal combat. Dayton knew vanity and desire would make him prone to revealing more than intended to such a beautiful woman. He needed to keep his wits about him.

At length the photographer was satisfied. Helping himself to a large glass of sparkling water, Dayton took a seat along from Malik, reclining and crossing an ankle on the opposite knee in what he hoped was a confidently relaxed pose. As she concentrated on her phone, he took the opportunity to drop his eyes to her chest, admiring how the fullness of her breasts offset the slim neck and waist in the close-fitted satin shirt. He looked up again well before she did but the pleasing mental image remained, carefully memorised for future consideration.

'Happy to record this conversation, Mr Dayton?'

'Sure. And please, call me Julian.'

'Mmm. Shall we start with these new jobs?'

'Of course.' he said then paused, both for effect and to make sure the soundbite was recorded exactly as intended. 'I'm pleased to announce that Dayton Global Industries will be creating three hundred roles over the next six months at our various locations across the City. Two hundred will support an expansion in our manufacturing facilities and the remainder are a direct investment in technology research.'

'Sounds like good news. Will all of these roles be for high-skilled, high-paid workers?'

'Well, there'll be a mix as you might expect. But in the main, this is about our commitment to the local economy.'

'And how many local jobs have you offshored to cheaper labour locations over the last year?'

The first lunge, even earlier than expected.

'Ah, we've certainly rebalanced our supply chain to ensure we have more people closer to our customers.'

'Yes, but as I understand it, most of those jobs went to low-skilled workers in countries where Dayton's currently have little or no sales revenue. I believe you've let nearly five hundred local staff go over the last year so we're really talking about a net reduction of two hundred, aren't we?'

'You could phrase it that way, although I think you're rather missing the point. These difficult decisions mean we're able to continue our investment in the City over the long term.'

'OK. So you agree that you're actually reducing local employment at this time, thank you.' She moved on before he could object. 'And what's your position on the human rights record for the countries to which you've moved those redundancies?'

'Pardon me?'

'I believe you've offshored roles to countries known to be involved in...' Malik traced a page in her notebook with a finely manicured fingernail. '...detention without trial, systemic female inequality, modern slavery and suppression of the free media. How do you feel about supporting those regimes?'

'We don't have operations in any sanctioned countries,' said Dayton, crossing his arms.

'Of course. I wasn't questioning the legality of your international business, rather I was asking about the morality of your employment policy. Should you have workers in those locations?'

'Well I certainly don't see why we shouldn't. Perhaps it's better they work for us than some of their other options, wouldn't you say?'

'Well it's not up to me, is it Mr Dayton.'

'No, it's not. But what's your view?'

'My readers will be far more interested in your opinions.'

'That's a given,' he snapped before he could stop himself. 'But I believe this is an interview, not an interrogation, and I'm interested in hearing what you think.'

'I think... that I'll say you avoided the question. But couldn't you be doing more to restrict your activity in such countries?'

'That's a lazy question, Sunita. It's not a question of arbitrarily doing more, or less, it's about balancing the interests of our workforce with those of the company.'

Arrogant bitch, he thought. She had no idea about the difficult choices required to operate a business of this size. Well-defined notions of international friends and enemies were for children and compromise was essential to maintaining their position.

'Any further comment, Mr Dayton?'

He smiled again but without it reaching his eyes.

'OK,' she continued. 'Let's go back to those hundred new jobs in technology research. What projects will they be working on?'

'That's not something I can divulge, as I'm sure even you would be able to understand.'

'Mmm. So will you still hire these roles if you're successful in acquiring Malmotec's silicon manufacturing division?'

'Eh? And where have you heard that?' he said, trying hard to keep a straight face.

'That's not something I can divulge. As I'm sure even you would be able to understand. But is it true?'

'I can't comment on speculation.'

'I believe it's more than speculation. Do you think you'll be able to make them a more attractive offer than McGlynn-Lansing?'

Dayton's pique intensified. Whilst there were plenty of disgruntled ex-employees who would no doubt delight in telling the press about job losses to foreign workers, only a very select few were aware of his interest in Fredrik Nilsson's company. If Malik knew, then it was possible the same source had also mentioned McGlynn's which, if accurate, confirmed something he already suspected - that old Swedish bastard was not playing the exclusive game he claimed. He had leaned hard on his network to try and find out whether Nilsson was talking to anyone else but it looked like this second-rate hack had somehow managed to get there first.

'If we were interested in Malmotec which, for the record, I'm neither denying nor confirming, then of course, joining forces with Dayton's always represents a more attractive option than any of our smaller competitors.'

'Do you think Malmotec would accept an offer from a business accused of industrial espionage?'

'Careful Sunita,' he fumed.

'But would they?'

'You know I can't talk about the ongoing case with McGlynn-Lansing. But as always there are two sides to the story.'

'Did your company steal their intellectual property?'

'Of course not. Our views on the matter are already well documented in court. We're entirely innocent of these vexatious charges.'

'Are you able to prove that?'

'For fu–... for goodness' sake. I don't need to. The prosecution needs to be able to prove that we did. Which they clearly aren't able to.'

'What will their tech chief, um, Rohan Mehta, testify to when he takes the stand?'

'I've no idea. Ask him.'

'It's obvious isn't it? He'll say you illegally copied their software and are using it to develop your own technology.'

'You're overstepping your brief here, Sunita,' he said, intending to place his hand on the table for emphasis but instead bringing it down hard enough to make a slap. 'I strongly suggest you return to the agreed topic before you get yourself into trouble.'

'The problem is the agreed topic just isn't very interesting, Mr Dayton.'

'Then find a way of making it so. That's your bloody job. And if you ever want to make the move to the networks you so clearly desire, then I'd recommend you improve your interview skills. You can keep that on the record if you want.'

Dayton rose from his chair, needing an end to these questions before saying something he might truly regret.

'This is even worse than facing that sodding cameraman of yours,' he groused.

Malik, knowing the most revealing part of an interview often came when the interviewee believed it to be over, stayed precisely where she was.

'Didn't you enjoy having your picture taken?'

'Does anybody?'

'In my experience, many of your peers invest large amounts of energy seeking out the opportunity. I'm just surprised you're not comfortable with the idea.'

'It certainly comes with the territory. But even after all this time, I can't say it's my favourite part of the job.'

'I see. And what is?'

'Well,' he stalled, furious with himself for ceding such an obvious opening. 'Helping the company to expand around the world and creating value for our employees and customers.'

'If you'll forgive the observation, Mr Dayton, that sounds a little trite, like something from the first page of your annual report. What is it that you actually enjoy about running Dayton Global?'

The unfortunate reality, and one he was absolutely not prepared to share with Sunita Malik, was that he enjoyed relatively little about his work.

Dayton had coveted the role from as far back as he could remember, envying the respect his father commanded without yet being aware of the prerequisites. Later, he began to appreciate the enticing opportunities available to those who wielded great wealth or power. Despite his parents' wishes for him to follow family tradition and go up to university, he had petitioned Richard to let him join the business as soon as he was old enough for a full-time contract. Patronage should ensure he was given the reins in the future even if his ability was found wanting.

Initially enthused, he soon discovered this glamorous world required an extensive and sustained application of effort and his interest duly waned. The next position, the next promotion, which always seemed to offer more prestige but require lower productivity, tended to occupy the bulk of his attention through the following decades. Nevertheless, he was careful to work hard enough without driving real change or risking real accountability such that Richard continued to sponsor his progress.

Then, with his father being unexpectedly called to London, came his chance at last. Eddie was still away gallivanting like a teenager, absent from the business for so long that Dayton was confident he would not be considered, yet the delay in being formally asked to take over the sprawling, complex conglomerate substantially tarnished his sense of arrival. Worse then followed as Richard maintained a close scrutiny of his son's work, demanding he seek approval on all major decisions. With no further advancement possible, Dayton found himself at the zenith of his career, arguably his existence, but confined by the isolation of leadership and with only an illusion of real power.

The running of the company had been an imposition on both his time and peace of mind ever since. A relentless grind, an inconvenience to be tolerated rather than a privilege to be appreciated, the stream of obstacles to be overcome, the constant worry he would make a big enough mistake to be found out for the incompetent he suspected he was, the potential shame of being forced out against his will. All these concerns served to degrade any achievement he might have otherwise felt. His staff were incapable of making their own decisions, or at least making the correct decisions, leaving him jaundiced and weary as he dragged the business through year after year of attritional trading.

And for what? Why did he choose to spend the bulk of his time in such an onerous endeavour? There was no need to increase his net worth, having inherited and accumulated more than enough to fund an agreeable lifestyle for the rest of his days. Nor was status the reason. With the exception of Richard who retained ultimate authority and Eddie who likely knew as much, no one else dared question Dayton's position. The feeling of primacy brought some pleasure but in no way compensated for the drawbacks.

Largely, he carried on for no other reason than he was capable of doing so. On the rare occasions when he looked candidly in the mirror, he found whatever motivation he had lay in the fear of failure rather than a desire to win - vanquishing Wynter McGlynn perhaps being the only exception. Most fundamentally, he suffered from a profound lack of imagination. If he was not the man who ran Dayton Global Industries, who would he be instead? Where would he spend the remaining years of his life and with what would they be filled? What was his better option, his higher purpose?

In trying to find an acceptable answer to Malik's question therefore, he was compelled to work with half-truths in a ragged attempt at authenticity.

'It's an honour… to lead this company and work on solutions benefitting today's society in ways my grandfather and his grandfather could have only dreamed about. That's what I enjoy the most, having a hand in solving these big problems of our time.'

Malik considered this briefly before trying her luck again.

'So it's about legacy, Mr Dayton? About leaving your mark on the world?'

'I'm sorry, Sunita, but I really do have a busy afternoon. If you could send across a selection of pictures and the proposed copy, I'll take a look before it goes to print.'

'Thank you but we have editorial control on this.'

'Very true. However, given the long commercial relationship between my company and the Post, which it would be a shame to compromise, I'd like to send any comments to you and Bill beforehand.'

'OK, I'll talk to him and let you know,' she said sweetly, intending to use all of her persuasiveness with the Post's editor, Bill Rutter, to have the piece published exactly as she wanted.

'Good. Let Becca know once you're done and she'll see you out.'

Leaving the boardroom, Dayton stalked back to his office, irked by the tactics Malik had used and knowing he would likely need to confront Rutter in the coming days. Bad enough if she wrote up the factual contents of the interview but worse if she attempted to combine it with the Malmotec acquisition, the McGlynn's trial or, heaven forbid, anything more personal. Although knowing it was unavoidable in his position, Dayton detested criticism.

'Becca,' he grumbled in the general direction of a desk near his doorway. 'Those people from the Post are packing up. Make sure they're gone in the next fifteen minutes.'

'Sure Julian, will do.'

Rebecca Giordani had been his PA for nearly two years. From a blue-collar background, twenty-one and smart, she had realised within the first few seconds of their interview that he was at least as interested in her appearance as in the fact she had put herself through night school while working two jobs. His occasional but awkward attempts at charm, combined with the incomprehensible patterns of his mood, meant she would have left months ago had the salary not been significantly higher than expected. Regardless, she had made herself a promise to put up with him only until the end of the summer before starting to look for something a little more challenging and a lot less demeaning elsewhere.

Making her way to the boardroom, she found the photographer halfway through stowing his equipment and the journalist leaning over the table making handwritten notes.

'Oh, hello again,' said Malik.

'Hi. Julian asked me to come and see if I could help you clear up,' she said, hiding her embarrassment that *clear up* had very nearly been *clear out*.

'No, we're fine, thanks. Steve won't be long and he gets grumpy if anyone touches his gear.'

'How'd it go?'

'If you have time, sit down and I'll tell you,' Malik replied with a laugh, the sound bright and artless even though her intentions were not quite as genuine. Dayton's assistant could be a fertile source of information.

'Oh God, was it bad?'

'For someone at his level, he's not exactly comfortable with himself, is he?'

'Ha! Not really, no. But did you at least get what you wanted?'

'We talked about the jobs you're hiring and then some related bits and pieces. Enough for me to write the article. What's he like to work for?'

'He's alright. I mean, he's very committed and works all hours. I know it must be stressful but he can be a bit hard on people sometimes. As long as he gets what he wants though, then he's OK. Uh, I hope you don't mind me asking, Sunita, but are we off the record? I don't want to get into trouble.'

'If you say we are,' she replied, closing her notebook as if in affirmation. 'What happens if he doesn't get what he wants?'

'He just gets grumpy is all. Grumpier than usual.'

'Mmm, doesn't sound like fun at all. Poor you.'

'I'm fine. It's been my first proper job since college and I've learned loads.'

Malik noted the past tense and sensed an opportunity.

'What would you like to do next?'

'Not sure to be honest. But I don't want another PA job.'

'How about the media? There might be a few openings at the Post. I could keep an eye out for you?'

'Oh, that'd be awesome,' replied Giordani immediately, her mind filling with scenes of ringing telephones, privileged conversations and dramatic deadlines. 'Thanks so much!'

'No problem. I'm actually arranging drinks after work with a few of the more senior guys. Why don't you come along and meet some people?'

'Wow, sure. What time?'

'Here's my number,' said Malik, fishing out a card with her warmest smile. 'Give me a call and I'll let you know how we're fixed.'

The equipment had now disappeared into several large cases and the photographer looked impatient to be underway.

'Guess I'll leave you to it then,' said Giordani. 'Thanks again and see you later.'

Enthusiastically retracing her steps, she had barely taken her seat before Dayton's door opened and he emerged looking only slightly less strained than before.

'Are they gone?'

'Just leaving now.'

'I'm going out for a meeting,' he said, the practised lie coming easily. 'Cancel or rearrange my appointments, it's all internal stuff anyway, and reach me on the phone if urgent. If you see my brother, tell him to call me.'

Dayton returned to his office for another ten minutes then left without a word or glance in Giordani's direction. His restlessness at Eddie's arrival had been compounded by the interview and he had decided to exercise the tension away - there was a gym and pool in the basement of his block which he would likely have to himself at this time of day. Descending in the elevator, he made a conscious effort to relax. Everything was still largely as planned, there was no need to work himself up unnecessarily.

The doors opened into a reception area much busier than when he arrived. Overnight security had been replaced by four receptionists in smart grey uniforms patiently registering a queue of visitors. A dozen or so already wearing badges waited on long leather sofas to either side of the front doors, some alone, some talking in small groups. Making his way across, he saw a few heads turn but studiously ignored them, having no interest in conversation.

Vermont Avenue remained in the building's shade but the warm air still felt suffocating. Bright sunshine lit up the park opposite, the vivid green almost too much of a contrast against the muted greys and browns of its surroundings. Many office workers lingered after their lunchtime breaks and Dayton had to resist the urge to check whether any were supposed to be working for him. Slipping on a pair of sunglasses, he turned right then immediately left up Old Fleet Road, heading away from the sea towards the city centre, intending to make a slight detour on his way home. The City lacked its usual rush hour tumult but there was no escaping the sun as he strolled northwards and within a couple of blocks he was forced to remove his jacket and tie. The few pedestrians took no notice of him, nor the occupants of the sleek cars which slid like basking sharks between the cyclists, the hissing of tyres on concrete their only sound.

Following fifteen minutes of steady progress, modern offices began to give way to irregular buildings housing a patchwork of tenants. Dry cleaners and newsagents shared old party walls with restaurants and temping agencies. Pavements became cluttered with bulging refuse sacks and signboards and shiftless people meandering between shops or lingering outside. Dayton had lost his battle with the heat and was perspiring freely.

Approaching the junction with Smithy Street, named after the many blacksmiths who had lived and laboured in the area during City's founding, he saw a large group standing on the corner. They blocked the pavement and looked out of place this far downtown; morbidly obese and dressed in cheap leisurewear, jewellery and tattoos. He noticed they bore a bovine resemblance to each other. The similarly slack jaws, lank hair and vacant eyes behind thick, heavily rimmed glasses suggested a family of sorts, although it was difficult to distinguish one generation from another. From the way they gazed up at the street corners they were probably sightseeing, and lost.

Dayton shuddered. He could have been born that way, he thought, towards the shallow end of the gene pool. Condemned to perpetual surprise through a lack of capacity to think beyond the here and now, subsisting on insecure, minimum wage jobs, state benefits, prescribed medication and a takeaway diet high in fat and low in nutrition. He stared at them with rising revulsion, trusting to the tint of his glasses to protect him from causing offence. The herd were still immobile, careless of anyone else's need to use the path, and he had to check for traffic before stepping out to make his way past.

'Excuse me,' he said under his breath, the elongated vowels suggesting the annoyance he dared not express more fully.

One of the larger males, at least he assumed this one was male given it had marginally more facial hair, heard him and looked down.

'You what?' it grunted.

'Nothing, nothing,' replied Dayton, quickening his pace so he was clear of the group, around the corner and heading westward before the situation could escalate.

Long experience had taught him he possessed the kind of face, with its high cheekbones and generally contemptuous expression, which more physically aggressive men seemed eager to punch. Even so, he had always managed to avoid an actual fistfight and had no inclination to change that record today, well aware he would be hopelessly ineffective against such an opponent. A slug of adrenaline washed into his bloodstream and his heart thumped dully in his chest.

'Ugly wanker,' he rasped through barely moving lips. 'What an ugly, fucking bastard.'

Safely away from the danger now, the fear started to subside and he snickered at his habit of cursing in private, developed unconsciously over the years. He often pondered whether it was possible to acquire Tourette's through practice or simply by not dominating the urge when it arose but the foible would be rather awkward if it became uncontrollable. The thought kept him amused all the way to Offenden Place - a shadowed alleyway where, halfway down between the refuse trolleys, he found the anonymous black door he wanted.

'Hello?' crackled a voice through the ancient intercom.

'I'm here to see Dr Voros.'

'Do you have appointment?'

'Not until tomorrow. Tell him it's Julian Dayton.'

A pause before he heard a buzz and the door cracked open to reveal a domestic hallway converted long ago to a place of work. Old posters were tacked to poorly decorated walls and the place smelled faintly of disinfectant and decay. A woman's head appeared round the corner of a doorway, impossible to tell her age given the amount of make-up she wore.

'Two minutes, OK?' she asked, adenoidal and disinterested. 'You wait in room.'

She withdrew again and Dayton negotiated the base of an uncarpeted staircase to reach the surgery beyond. Tossing his jacket onto the examination table, he peeled off the shirt, hung it over a chair and sat down to wait. Presently, a heavy tread preceded the doctor's appearance - a short man with thinning grey curly hair and beard, wearing an old lab coat over t-shirt and cargo shorts in a sop to his profession.

'You are early, Mr Dayton, no?' he asked in heavily accented English.

'Only a day. I'm assuming that's not a problem?'

'No, no. Of course no problem.'

Voros pulled open a domestic refrigerator, extracted a vial and took a syringe from the box above. Dayton saw the lack of care - the unlocked medicine store, no washing of hands, no checking of the label, no cleaning of the soft rubber cap with alcohol before drawing the fluid - and decided it was time for a change even though good doctors were not easy to find these days. Even so, he held his tongue and looked away as the thin metal shaft punctured his left shoulder and the plunger was depressed. Withdrawing the needle with one hand, Voros attached an absorbent pad with the other and dropped the syringe into an open bin nearby.

'Any problems, you let me know.'

'Uh-huh,' replied Dayton, shrugging on the still-moist shirt. 'How long would you recommend before the next course?'

'To achieve same outcome? You come back December.'

'OK. And payment's been made, yes?'

'Yes. There is no problems there, Mr Dayton. See you again maybe?'

'Maybe.'

After the claustrophobic, damp-smelling building, knowing there was no need to visit again for some time, if at all, he felt relief in turning left once again onto Smithy Street.

Ambling towards the prospect of a cold swim, a change of clothes and an air-conditioned apartment, Dayton paid no attention to the City's relentless activity. He thought instead of Sunita Malik, the image of her breasts and how much he would like to wipe the self-assured smile off the journalist's pretty face, preferably in bed. He thought of Fredrik Nilsson, whether he was indeed in contact with McGlynn-Lansing and how he could find out for sure. He thought of his father, then Eddie and then Fender Tang and again scrutinised his own judgement as to how far the man should be trusted. He thought of his son. He thought of Wynter McGlynn.

But most of all Dayton thought of himself. Swearing occasionally, almost inaudibly but with great intensity, he berated himself for the awkwardness of the photoshoot and the one-dimensional, inarticulate answers he had given to Malik's questions. He started the inevitable process of worrying about what she would write and how that might impact the respect of his staff and his peers. He remembered his encounter with the mouth-breather on the corner of Old Fleet Road, his indignation at being challenged in such a manner and his cowardice in response. He dwelt again on the coming days, carefully burnishing the glow of satisfaction he expected from impending success, all while developing plausible excuses in the event he should fail. What he lacked in imagination, he made up for in persistence and preparedness, in anticipating the impact of all outcomes such that none would come as a surprise.

He thought of his childhood, when he had fewer cares and hot days like these would last forever.

Dayton paid no attention to the City as he walked, and the City paid him none in return.

6

'H e's not here.'

McGlynn's heart sank. She had sent Matthieu over to the fashionable Willowborough district to see if Rohan Mehta had inexplicably chosen to spend the day at home.

'How can you be certain?' she asked.

'I've been banging on his front door for ten minutes. Nothing.'

'OK. In that case try the neighbours, tell them you're from the office and that we're concerned. Ask if they've seen him or his girlfriend since yesterday then send me a message rather than call because I'll be with Thom en route to the Nilsson meeting. Oh, and if you can get hold of Rohan's team tonight or first thing tomorrow, find out exactly when they last spoke to him, what he said and whether they have any other contact details for him or Wenling.'

'Will do.'

'Let me know what you find out. *Merci* Matthieu.'

Where the hell was he? McGlynn's earlier meeting with her old friend and advocate Jacob Wiesenberg had not filled her with confidence. He had said that Rohan seemed distracted during their rehearsal on Saturday, unable to concentrate and making small mistakes which could insinuate a lack of transparency in court, particularly under cross-examination. When Wiesenberg heard Rohan had failed to appear at work, the old man rubbed his eyes behind the small, frameless spectacles before peering at her and speaking with undisguised concern.

'Find him Wynter,' he urged. 'You knew how critical his evidence would be before we decided to proceed. You must find him or I fear we shall lose.'

Losing was not an option. Comparing the detailed ways in which their rival software functioned, Rohan had persuaded her that Dayton had somehow accessed their systems and taken their code. But McGlynn knew neither she nor anyone else in the team would be as eloquent in making the same argument again in court. The damage from a negative verdict would set them back years, publicly vindicating Dayton's position that she was acting out of jealousy and reopening the gap she had worked so hard to close. Wiesenberg was right, Rohan must be found.

Turning her attention to the laptop on her desk, she accessed his personnel record, thinking there might be an emergency contact number for Wenling. However, she was surprised to see he had instead given his father's details at an address in Amritsar. She glanced at the clock, making the mental calculations and weighing up whether she ought to trouble his parents so early. Deciding against it, she noted down the information and resolved to call over the next few days if needed. She then opened a drawer, retrieved the uppermost business card from a short stack, took a deep breath and dialled the number.

'This is Kenise Campbell.'

'Detective Campbell, it's Wynter McGlynn. Could you spare me a moment?'

'Ms McGlynn, of course,' said Campbell, sounding surprised.

'Hope you don't mind but I wanted to ask for your advice on rather a sensitive matter.'

'Go on.'

'One of my senior staff members, Rohan Mehta, has failed to come to the office today and we haven't been able to contact him at all, which is very much out of character. I know he's a responsible adult and it's a bit premature to register a missing person but I have it on good authority he was acting strangely when last seen on Saturday. I'm worried about his safety.'

'This isn't my area of responsibility, Ms McGlynn. You should log your concerns with the duty officers at Bay West police station.'

'Yes, I understand. But could you make some initial inquiries? Or perhaps help me reach his partner as we don't appear to have her contact details?'

'Like I say, this isn't something I can deal with, I'm sorry.'

'I do understand, thank you.' McGlynn closed her eyes and decided to gamble. 'I also wanted to tell you that I visited our dockside operations earlier and am hopeful there might be information relevant to the matter we discussed this morning. But I'm afraid that's going to have to wait until after I've found Rohan.'

Listening to the silence, she willed Campbell to yield.

'I see.'

'Yes.'

A sigh from the earpiece. 'OK, I can't promise anything but will take a look. What was his name again?'

McGlynn spelled it out to be sure Campbell had it correctly.

'And you say he has a partner?'

'Wenling. I've only met her once and don't have her family name.'

'Have you tried his social media accounts?'

'He's quite private and puts very little online I think.'

'Great,' replied Campbell drily. 'OK, leave it with me, I'll be in touch as soon as I can. If I can.'

'Thanks, I appreciate it.'

'I think we understand each other, Ms McGlynn. I look forward to hearing from you also.'

The line clicked off and McGlynn breathed out. She worked the problem around for another minute or two then, pushing it from her mind, shut the laptop and carried it through to her private rooms.

'Call Jane Hallam,' she said along the way.

The sound of an overseas ringtone started up after a slight delay. Just when she thought it would go to voicemail, the call was picked up.

'Wynter, what a lovely surprise!' came the unmistakably gruff, friendly voice. 'What can I do for you?'

Typical Auntie Jane, she thought, straight to business. Well into her sixties, not even McGlynn knew quite how far, Hallam showed no signs of contemplating retirement and still put in the early mornings and late evenings characterising her long career. Fiercely loyal, she was one of the very few people across the organisation who did not customarily address McGlynn as Director, despite not being family. Although family isn't always related by blood, she mooted.

'Morning. Sorry to call so early.'

'Nonsense, it's after five and I was just about to go out for a walk before breakfast. How are you, my love?'

'Fine thanks, busy as always but I wanted to catch you about Hugo. I'm worried about him.'

'Hugo Valente?' asked Hallam. 'Why? We spoke only a few days ago and he sounded right as rain. What's the matter?'

'I went down to the docks today and the warehouse isn't operating at the right standard. Inventory control's poor, there's quite a bit of litter and most of the staff had been given a day's paid holiday for no other reason than Hugo and Jonah Turner thought they might be tired. But Hugo looks like he's carrying the weight of the world on his shoulders.'

'I'm so sorry to hear this, Wynter, you shouldn't have to be the one telling me improvements are needed. Things can take care of themselves here for a while, I'll be on the next flight out and get to the bottom of it. Is there anything else I need to know?'

McGlynn loved the lack of ego. Rather than rebutting her views or making excuses, Hallam simply accepted her opinion as fact and moved straight to solving the problem. She contemplated telling her about Campbell's people smuggling suspicions but, on balance, chose to wait. It would be interesting to see whether Valente volunteered the information first.

'No, not at the moment. And I don't think you need to come across either. But could you talk to Hugo? I mean really talk to him, help him through an improvement plan and see if you can wheedle out what's causing him to seem so... so flat.'

'Are you sure? I need to visit soon anyway.'

'Yeah, I'm sure. Might need you on something else this week,' she added, for no more reason than a hunch. 'But call me once you've spoken with him. Leave a message if needed but ask Matthieu to get some time in for a longer session midweek.'

'Say no more, Wynter, I'm on it. And sorry again.'

'No problem, I know you'll deal with it. Speak soon.'

She hung up and headed for the bedroom. Sifting quickly through the wardrobe, she picked out a short-sleeved blue and green summer dress. Thom Dalkeith might have booked somewhere outdoors for dinner with Fredrik Nilsson and, if so, she wanted to be comfortable in the remaining heat of the day. After brushing out her hair and adding a balm to her lips, she selected a simple pendant necklace, beige wedge sandals and a matching clutch bag wide enough to carry her phone. There was no need for perfume, partly as a courtesy to her fellow diners and partly because she wanted Nilsson focused on the meeting, neither thinking of her personally nor that she had tried to impress or, God forbid, please him.

A cursory check in the full-length mirror and then she was back out of the apartment, through her office and onwards down the corridor, collecting Dalkeith on the way past his desk.

'Ready to go, Thom?'

'Ach Wynter, born ready, you know that,' he replied in his deep Scottish baritone, falling into step alongside.

A broad-shouldered young man with a ruddy complexion and square jaw, Dalkeith was her sister's eldest - and hence a potential successor for her job - but even he would normally avoid being so familiar other than the working day was done and few faces remained. McGlynn cocked her head upwards to see how prepared he really was, past the good looks and into his eyes where she found confidence mixed with a desire for the meeting to go well, no bad thing.

'Born ready you say? We'll see. Do you have a brief?'

'Of course,' he said, the grin widening as he proffered a buff-coloured folder. 'We've twenty minutes in the car and I can answer your questions on the way.'

'Good. Where are we going?'

'Saltwater. Fredrik's bringing his wife and I hear she's a seafoodie.'

'His wife? Isn't she going to be bored to tears when we talk business all evening?'

'His PA told me she's always wanted to visit the City and often goes on his business trips.'

'Mmm.' McGlynn jabbed the elevator button, wondering whether Mrs Nilsson had a penchant for sightseeing or was instead keeping an eye on him. Maybe he was prone to flirting too much, maybe more. 'I don't suppose you'd like to take her on a VIP tour while I sound him out on terms?'

'Can try if you like. But I got the sense she's non-negotiable,' chuckled Dalkeith.

'OK. Seriously though, if I give you the nod, try and get her to one side so I can talk to Fredrik alone.'

'Surely, no problem.'

The elevator slowed to a halt and they stepped into the basement not far from her private garage. McGlynn pulled open the door of a large black sedan parked immediately opposite as Dalkeith skirted around its rear. The vehicle moved quietly up the exit ramp and down to Foreshore Road, then bore right in parallel to the Esplanade on which she had cycled that morning.

Turning her attention to the folder on her lap, McGlynn found a two-page resumé of Nilsson, a copy of the executive summary from the investment case, a bullet point listing of negotiations to date and an overview of the remaining items to be agreed, ideally this evening. She read through the documents in silence as they crawled between lights, committing the detail to memory.

'Good work Thom,' she said at last, meaning it.

'Thanks. Questions?'

'Only a couple. What do you think his main motivations are in choosing an acquirer, especially us?'

'I think he likes our technology strategy, culture and ambition,' Dalkeith replied without hesitation. 'He sees us as one of the most innovative businesses in quantum computing and wants Malmotec to be associated with that.'

'But we haven't agreed to maintain their brand?'

'No, but there's kudos to be had in the tech community if he sells to the right party at the right time. He's spent a decade and a lot of his own capital building the silicon division and I think he wants validation that he made good choices.'

'Interesting. And you think we're ready to finalise a price this evening?'

'Aye. We've given an indicative range as you've seen but he asked to conclude negotiations with you.'

'How much do you think he wants?'

'If I were a gambling man, I'd say somewhere close to four hundred.'

'Jesus. And at what figure would he walk?'

'Not much lower. He's been tight-lipped about who else is involved but I reckon there's plenty of interest.'

McGlynn looked towards the sea and thought hard about that number. Four hundred million was more than she hoped and it would be nigh on impossible to persuade her own investors to agree a cheque that large at tomorrow's board meeting. But she needed Nilsson's silicon manufacturing expertise and his patents else it would take years to reach the same level of capability. She would have to find a way to reduce expectations, that much was clear.

'What about Anders?' she asked, naming Nilsson's son. 'What does he want to do next?'

Dalkeith's expression faltered slightly.

'I don't know. He's agreed to stay for six months after any transaction but I tried to get into his personal interests and was completely blocked. Seems he's been told to only talk about the business.'

'Sensible. I bet Fredrik told him to keep his mouth shut, but I wonder what his plans are.'

'It'd be great if we could find out. We're nearly there, any other questions?'

McGlynn turned to him, a glint in her eye. She loved this aspect of her job, the thrill which came from a battle of intellects, each negotiator trying to gain an advantage over the other, neither wanting to give an unnecessary inch but knowing it was in both their interests to find a way to win together, or lose together. Like an athlete at the starting line, she trusted her training and her ability and was eager to begin.

'Only one. Did you check whether the grilled sea bass is back on their menu?'

Saltwater overlooked Foreshore Road a quarter mile shy of the marina wall. The restaurant's lower level was old, the diamond-paned windows and heavy black lintels in stark contrast to the white stucco façade. Much more recently the slate roof had been removed and an upper terrace added with low glass walls affording panoramic views of the bay whilst shielding diners from the breeze. McGlynn could see a mix of tourists and businesspeople and thought she caught sight of Nilsson, a heavily tanned, slim man with collar-length grey hair, as they walked inside.

In the relative darkness of the entrance hall, they were warmly greeted by the maître-de.

'Miss McGlynn, Mr Dalkeith, I'm so pleased to welcome you back. I hope you have enjoyed fine health since your last visit?'

'Hello Henri,' she replied. 'I'm very well, thanks. How are you? How's business?'

'Always good. We are so lucky to have such customers.'

'It's not luck when you cook the way Jacques does, eh? What would you recommend this evening?'

'Ah, if I may, I would suggest the crab to start, followed by the red snapper with new potatoes and seasonal vegetables.'

'Is the snapper caught locally?'

'Of course, fresh this morning. Mr and Mrs Nilsson have already arrived. May I show you up?'

'No thanks Henri, we know the way.'

She and Dalkeith headed up the narrow staircase, doubling back at the halfway point before arriving in a glass cubicle atop the tiled terrace floor. From the open doorway she could see Nilsson and his wife, a woman who wore silver hair in a severe but fashionable bob, watching her rather than each other. McGlynn raised a hand in greeting and picked her way between the tables.

'Fredrik? I'm Wynter McGlynn, it's a pleasure to meet you at last.'

'Hello Wynter, yes indeed,' he replied, removing his dark glasses and squinting in the sun. 'May I introduce you to my wife, Annika?'

Seeing how far the smile ended beneath the astute blue eyes, McGlynn knew immediately that Annika Nilsson would need to be won over every bit as much as her husband during the course of the evening.

'Would you both enjoy some champagne?' she asked, testing the mood. 'The Toirlot Grand Cuvée perhaps? We bring in more than twenty thousand bottles a year through our warehouse at the docks over there.'

'That sounds delicious but I think I shall stay with the mineral water for now,' said Nilsson. 'And maybe a glass of wine with the fish. There's a lot of detail we need to discuss before any celebration, no?'

'Of course. In that case I'll join you. Could we have two more glasses with ice, and a bottle of the Riesling too,' she added to the waiter.

The four of them exchanged pleasantries about the City, the views across the bay and the Nilssons' wider travel plans as the remaining tables filled almost to capacity. Gentle music from invisible speakers supported the hum of conversation from larger groups and filled the silences of a few couples who lacked the desire or capacity to do likewise. Annika Nilsson was mostly reserved, allowing her husband to do the talking, but McGlynn noted she seemed highly attentive to the conversation in her own unobtrusive way. Dalkeith was the opposite to the point of a garrulousness she put down to excitement at finalising the deal. Henri's recommendation for the fresh crab and snapper drew universal approval although, somewhere near the back of her mind, McGlynn wondered whether the boats bringing in today's catch had been privy to any other kind of activity in that shielded stretch of water beyond Alber Cove.

With the sun slipping towards the placid surface of the sea, they emerged from the parasol's shade, not that it mattered so much in the waning heat, and conversation turned slowly towards the agenda for which she and Dalkeith had prepared.

'Tell me something of how McGlynn-Lansing came to be based here,' said Nilsson. 'I met your parents once, years ago, when we were all working in Brazil. I don't think you had your headquarters here back then?'

'Oh, we've been in the City for over a hundred years,' replied McGlynn, brushing past the reference to South America and the memories it evoked. 'My great-grandfather Iain arrived on a troopship after military service and never left. Took the first job he could find, as a deckhand on one of the trawlers, before asking for a community loan and leasing a stall at the fish market. Fishing was still the main source of regional income back then. In the first few years, he secured contracts with nearly half the fleet's captains by offering a profit share on their catch rather than the usual fixed price based on weight, then he borrowed against the future earnings of those contracts to expand into logistics. It was his idea to build the rail tunnels all the way down to the new port and his financial commitment which made the project viable. It's why we have the benefit of our warehousing being closest to the terminal to this day.'

'Did you ever meet him?'

'No, he died a long time before I was born. Only in his early sixties but he'd lived a hard life, both through the war and then in starting the business. From what I hear he was a heady mixture of charisma and ruthlessness, fairly typical of servicemen back then, and took huge risks to keep McGlynn-Lansing alive in the early days. Everything was mortgaged and remortgaged, a constant balance between creditors and debtors. Rumour has it he once sold his car to pay the wage bill, he was so close to the edge. But it worked and he set the foundations for what we enjoy today.'

'Indeed. Sacrifice and risk are always a part of any company during its early years.' Nilsson glanced at Annika, as if reliving harder times, and she warmed a little in return. 'Where did your great-grandfather see service?'

'All over the world, mostly Africa. He was honourably discharged at the rank of captain, Coldstream Guards, as high as a working-class man from Glasgow could expect in those days.'

'Ah, he was a proud Scot?'

'Depends on who was asking. We're not entirely sure but think the name McGlynn is Irish rather than Scottish, something to do with the colour red. Or maybe even Welsh if you go further back, meaning from the glens, or valleys, of Wales. But there had been at least a few generations of McGlynns working in the shipyards on the Clyde before he enlisted. If you asked my father whether he was American he'd likely agree with you. But if an American asked, he'd say Scottish, and if a Scot asked him, he'd probably say Irish. People can be so contrary about their heritage. Or maybe that's just my father.'

Perhaps knowing something of the strain between them, Nilsson moved on.

'And how about you, Wynter, is there a country you call home?'

'Ha! Well, I have an Irish, Scottish, American father and a French mother of colonial descent. I've lived across six of the seven continents for nearly as long as I've lived here in the City. But I guess this is where I'd call home. It's as good a place as any and there's a lot of family history in these streets.'

'Your mother has colonial ancestry? I wouldn't have guessed it from meeting her.'

'She has. The Moreau family emigrated from metropolitan France to southern Vietnam in the late nineteenth century, buying land near Saigon and building a farming and mercantile business to export rice and rubber to the western world. They were there for a couple of generations before the advance of the second world war forced them to leave, not for France which had just fallen to the Nazis, but for South America where the allies were heavily subsidising rubber production for the war effort. There was a third generation born overseas before they could finally return to Paris. Have the Nilssons always hailed from Sweden, Annika?' she added, trying again to bring her into the conversation.

Annika nodded politely but avoided being drawn and Nilsson resumed after a moment.

'And who was Mr Lansing? Was he your great-grandfather's business partner?'

'She was his wife.'

McGlynn never failed to enjoy the reaction this information tended to elicit. His was no exception.

'Yep, Jeannie-May Lansing was pure-blood American and daughter of the City's mayor at the time, Jim Lansing. The story goes they met as Iain was petitioning her father for help with the railway. Apparently he thought her influence might be what tipped the balance between investment in the tunnels and the array of other infrastructure projects Jim was being asked to approve. So Iain set his sights on Jeannie-May, even though she was barely out of school and he was in his mid-twenties, and ultimately won her hand in marriage. Little did he know she would prove every bit as strong-willed as he was. She helped him gain her father's agreement then took more and more interest to establish herself as a full partner well before my grandfather, Kenny, was born when she was only twenty-three. She insisted on keeping her maiden name though. Had it appended to the company's saying it would bring extra prestige given her political connections. She even persuaded my great-grandfather to write into our constitution that it was never to be removed.'

'She sounds like quite a woman.'

'She absolutely was. Lived just short of her hundredth birthday which meant I knew her both as a child and an adult. Sharp as a knife until the day she died, full of stories and a never-ending zest for existence despite the difficult times she and Iain had faced.'

McGlynn paused before leaving a trail she hoped Nilsson might follow.

'She told me it was her idea for McGlynn-Lansing to invest in computing, and even quantum computing at that, when the research was still in its infancy and long before the commercial benefits were known. She also taught me the importance of trust in a family business.'

After a moment, he did.

'Yes. I have been in business a long time and Malmotec is my life's work, Annika's too,' he added, although McGlynn was still unsure whether that meant her active involvement or simply as a support to Nilsson's own commitment. 'It's important that we are able to trust any new owner of our manufacturing division, particularly as our son will want to stay on after the transaction.'

'Wouldn't Anders take over from you one day, Fredrik? The silicon plant is now the largest source of revenue in the group by some distance I believe. He could run the company from Sweden and maintain family ownership for the next generation?'

McGlynn sensed Dalkeith tensing as she played out the reverse psychology but felt the need to draw Nilsson into the open. To her surprise, Annika spoke up in a quiet but resolute voice.

'My son is a gifted boy, Wynter. But to be clear with you, he is young, he perhaps lacks confidence and he is far more interested in how the technology works than how to make a profit from it. In this he has no, how would you say, no passion?'

'Of course, I see exactly the same in my girls,' replied McGlynn, noticing the indecision in Annika's eyes and intuiting the likely route to success. 'Even though they're much younger and alike as only twins can be, they're already so different in what interests them. Catriona buries herself in books, loves all things academic and wants to be a doctor, whereas Adeline detests her schoolwork and spends most of her time playing sports or riding her horse. Neither is showing any interest in following my footsteps, but I don't mind. As long as they're confident and enjoy whatever they choose to do with the rest of their lives, then I'll be happy for them too.'

Annika held her gaze for a moment longer but, with her mind apparently made up one way or another, volunteered nothing further.

'Parenthood is indeed both a joy and a responsibility,' resumed Nilsson, seeming to recognise McGlynn had made ground. `We have pursued several lines of enquiry for this transaction and narrowed these to a smaller number in which Anders' future can be assured. We would like to see how you might propose this contractually, alongside the other terms of the sale.'

'I think Thom's already laid out the details?'

'He has, but we're not yet agreed on the final value of the business. Isn't this for you to decide?'

'Yes,' she said, making up her mind how to pitch. 'I'd like to make you a firm offer but then, if you agree, delay completion for six months.'

She saw Dalkeith's face fall from the corner of her eye but kept her focus calmly on the Swede.

'Go on,' he said slowly.

'If you agree, then I propose Anders comes and works with us for that period. I'll ask him to sign a non-disclosure agreement and pay a fair salary but other than that, he's free to come and go as he pleases, to look into how we run our operation and get to know the software engineering teams led by Rohan Mehta. At the end of the arrangement, you can accept the terms or walk away with the benefit of knowing whether McGlynn-Lansing is the right home for both your company and your son. How does that sound?'

Nilsson recognised McGlynn's strategy at once, to delay completion and hence have him abandon or at the very least disrupt dialogue with other interested parties. Yet this was not a scenario which had occurred to him. He knew it would appeal to Annika and perhaps to Anders too. Far too wily to make an immediate decision, or to ask again for the price McGlynn had referred to, which was at least as important as his son's job security, he changed direction.

'I've heard good things about this Rohan of yours. I'd like to meet him.'

Wouldn't we all, thought McGlynn, hoping beyond hope that either Matthieu or Campbell had made progress.

'We can certainly arrange introductions,' she said. 'Maybe you could join us at ML One next week?'

'Perhaps, perhaps. But tell me this, will you win your case against Dayton Global Industries in the meantime? It is very important that we choose a long-term owner representing good judgement and prudent decision making. I'm aware of your litigation and, to be clear, I will not want to pursue any offer should they be successful in their defence.'

'Noted. But I assure you it's the Daytons who have displayed poor judgement here. McGlynn-Lansing will always protect its interests and the people who support them. And that would include Anders and your staff too should you choose to go with us. I've absolutely no doubt we'll prove the alleged malpractice.'

'Well, that is for the court to decide, no? But Annika and I may stay in the City until a verdict is reached before finalising our decision.'

Nilsson being prepared to remain in the locale before moving to completion suggested his preferred bidders were close, both physically and logically. And something in the way he had spoken corroborated a rumour heard by McGlynn nearly a fortnight ago.

'Should I understand you're likely to sell to the winner of this case, Fredrik?'

'This still depends on many other things as we already discussed. However, I am in the fortunate position of having several options available and yes, McGlynn-Lansing and Dayton Global represent two of these. As I understand it, there's a long and, ah, interesting relationship between you, is there not?'

McGlynn remained impassive. She badly needed Nilsson's organisation but losing out to Dayton was unthinkable.

'No more interesting than with our other competitors,' she said evenly, hoping the lie sounded more plausible to the Nilssons than it would to Dalkeith. 'It's true we've been rivals in the City for a long time, but Dayton's star is on the wane and their technology strategy is outdated to the point where they resort to plagiarising our ideas. And forgive me when I say that Julian Dayton in particular is not to be trusted. If you want an ambitious but secure future for Anders, then we're the better choice here, the only choice.'

Nilsson took a moment to drain the remaining straw-coloured liquid from his glass and dab the corners of his mouth with a napkin before replying.

'I respect your opinion of course, Wynter, but I do not share it. At least, not yet. We shall see how this case is concluded, and the value you place on the part of my company I spent ten years of my life creating. Only then, perhaps, will we decide whether to do business.'

7

At the end of the marina walls, solid green and red beacons shone through the dusk, both an invitation and a warning to anyone still out on the water. McGlynn leant against iron railings coated in generations of black paint and drew the salt air into her lungs. She and Dalkeith had barely spoken a word since leaving the restaurant. Light conversation had continued during after-dinner drinks but they all knew the evening was over and were simply nodding to tradition. Courteous handshakes and promises of further dialogue were exchanged before the Nilssons strolled away towards their hotel and the two of them had crossed Foreshore Road to compare notes.

'What do you think?' she asked, watching the last of the yachts run with the prevailing wind.

'Honestly? Not sure. I thought we were ahead and could have reached agreement tonight, but I have to admit I didn't see Fredrik's condition about winning the case coming. He hasn't breathed a word about it until now.'

'Mmm. We could do with finding out if Julian knows about our bid. If so, then he must realise we have a much better capability to absorb Anders' crew and extract value. He's just not in a position to leverage the deal like we are, not unless he has other acquisitions in the pipeline or is going into partnership for the software skills. I'm sure he stole our code but I'm equally sure he doesn't have a clue how to develop it further and I don't think he can spare the cash for an acquisition at this scale.'

'How come?'

'I hear his medical equipment distribution costs are through the roof as a result of trying to break into Asia. If rumours about new UK trade tariffs are true, he'll be left badly overstretched.'

'Then I can't believe he's willing to risk making Fredrik an offer just to spite us. It could ruin him.'

'He might have planted this idea about the litigation outcome. If he delays on the assumption we lose, then he might believe he gets a better price with fewer serious bidders involved. Or maybe he needs to know about the trade deal before committing to an offer. Maybe he doesn't intend to transact at all, just wants to stop us from completing. I wouldn't put it past him. He's an odious man but not stupid.'

'And what about Anders? I got the impression you think he's the key here but why offer him a placement?'

McGlynn turned towards her nephew, loving and liking him but knowing he needed more time, more experience before she might explicitly groom him as the next Director of her company. Lacking the guile to find his way through the kinds of negotiation veterans like Nilsson would instigate, Dalkeith would be gobbled up and spat out along with their commercial interests. That could not be risked. Whilst McGlynn had no intention of stepping down, there always remained a chance of being forced out like her father and, aside from her nephew, there were no other blood relatives yet offering themselves as candidates for succession. If anything untoward happened, the matter would become a serious cause for concern. But it isn't just yet, she thought, compartmentalising this particular problem once again. For now, she would do what she could to help him further along his way.

'Why do you think?'

'Aye, well, I know Annika seemed more interested in Anders' future than anything else. But why not just pre-negotiate a payoff if he were to leave?'

'Because I don't think she's worried about his finances.'

He evidently didn't get the point so McGlynn offered another breadcrumb.

'She and Fredrik are already wealthy and would be exceptionally so after the transaction. And she's his mother.'

'Ah, so you think this is about her looking after him, beyond the money?'

'Uh-huh,' she said, looking back out to sea. 'The clue was when she said he lacked confidence. Neither Catriona nor Adeline lacks confidence but I still try to shield them from things they might not be able to deal with yet. If she can find someone who'll watch over him and his career in the same way that she and Fredrik have done, then I think it's worth a decent chunk of whatever valuation we might otherwise agree. Besides, I thought stalling the close could help rid ourselves of the competition, and we could always propose an early completion before Anders' placement was up. At least, I thought it was a decent tactic until Fredrik threw in that point about the trial.'

'Understood, thanks.'

'Sure.'

They remained in their own thoughts for a while, side by side and comfortable in each other's company as only lifelong friends or relatives can be. Small waves lapped against the wall beneath the railings and the riding lights on the bigger ships became the only discernible objects ahead before McGlynn stood erect again.

'I can't find Rohan,' she said simply. 'He didn't come to work today, isn't answering his phone and isn't at home.'

'Bugger,' replied Dalkeith as the implications dawned. 'That's not good, not good at all. How can I help?'

'Can you put the feelers out. I'm working on it with Matthieu but can't be seen to know about a problem, not this week of all weeks. Be discreet and see if you can find anyone who knows where he might have gone or has spent time with him and Wenling recently. I want contact details for her if possible. Also, start planning for how we'd cover a meeting with the Nilssons without him. Get Zack and Paula up to speed on the quiet and have them prepare enough of a presentation to get Anders excited without giving away anything too confidential. I want them ready by the end of the week in case Rohan's not back and we can still catch Fredrik and Annika in town. We'll offer to fly Anders over if we have to.'

McGlynn doubted any such meeting would take place if Rohan remained absent but would not compromise on being ready for all eventualities.

'Got it. Anything else?'

'No, but we have to find him, Thom. By Wednesday at the very latest.'

'Leave it with me. Are you staying at the office tonight? Want me to drop you off?'

'Thanks but I'll walk back along the front. Don't worry,' she added, detecting his concern. 'There's plenty of people out and about. See you in the morning.'

Dalkeith headed off in the direction of the Blake Street subway. McGlynn watched him go, tall and confident with his easy stride, then turned and began the return journey along the Esplanade. Here, near the hotels and restaurants, there were couples sitting on the low walls and benches, the occasional late-night cyclist or jogger wearing reflective clothing on the track to her left. She knew their numbers would dwindle as she neared the business district, ML One and her bed but the thought was of no concern. She had no intention of going that far.

A couple of streets inland and half a mile to McGlynn's east, Eddie Dayton lounged across one of the Establishment's wide leather banquettes and dangled the remains of an eighth, maybe ninth pint of dark beer from his meaty right hand. Expensively converted from an old Lincoln Bank branch, the vast space housed several elegant bars. Warm light from the chandeliers created a cosy atmosphere despite the height of the ceilings and, although early in the week, the place was busy as usual with workers from nearby blocks. On the raised stage, a group of middle-aged men, the kind who could only secure an unfavourable Monday evening slot, were well into their set of original songs and being roundly ignored, much to Eddie's disappointment. He liked to watch people dancing. Specifically, he liked to watch women dancing, believing in a strong correlation between their rhythmic ability and their enthusiasm and expertise between the sheets.

To his left, Toby Milton-Jones and Jonny Havilland were involved in a heated discussion about the performance of their personal investments. To his right, Simon Fitzwilliam shouted at him over the amplified music. Having been in the bar since mid-afternoon, the other three, by his estimation, were more intoxicated than was fitting given the modest amount of alcohol involved.

'Brilliant to see you again, Eddie,' boomed Fitzwilliam for the umpteenth time. 'It's not been the same... round here... without you. You know?'

Eddie nodded sagely.

'You're staying until, um, next week right?'

Another nod.

'Brilliant, brilliant. Let's take the boat out at the weekend. Haven't had her out in weeks, months even. Jonny went out yesterday on his shitty little dinghy... thing's a fucking deathtrap... says he caught more, you know, more blue... fin... bluefin than he's seen in years.'

'Sophia's coming on Friday.'

'Oh, oh bugger... Oh... um, well, she ought to come out too! We'll take the... the girls and... and earn some brownie points while we're hard at it. What d'you... what do you say?'

Eddie could barely stand the man's wife, and had no intention of sharing his time with Sophia, but in truth had missed being out on the water. A day in the sun, pole and line in one hand and a chilled bottle in the other, appealed. Best to keep one's options open.

'Maybe.'

Fitzwilliam was trying to think of something else to say, probably rugby-related if he was to capture any interest, when the nearest of five or six men making their way past in the half-light tripped over Eddie's outstretched legs and nearly fell. He straightened, an accusatory scowl on his face.

Eddie looked sideways to determine what had nearly caused him to drop his glass and found nothing to worry about.

'Fuck off,' he rumbled, then lazily swung back to watch the band tune their instruments.

The man stood his ground, shoulders squared and fists bunched by his sides, evidently weighing up the odds as his friends stood close by, eyeing the group on the banquette. Not sensing the expected departure, Eddie turned again. Similarly dressed in a tailored suit, the fellow was much his own height and reasonably broad across the chest and shoulders. To an expert eye however, it looked like muscle built in the gym rather than hard earned through anything more hazardous. Eddie looked him in the eyes and saw indecision, concluding there was no excitement to be had here.

'Fuck off,' he said again, the lack of interest palpable. 'Or I'll kick your fucking head in.'

After a further moment's consideration, this new and improved invitation was accepted. The would-be assailant stalked off with as much dignity as he could muster, collecting the others along the way. Eddie watched them go, drained the last of his beer, deposited the glass on the table and yawned as he stood up.

'I'm off for a piss and then I'm going to bed. It's been a long day,' he said in Fitzwilliam's general direction.

Havilland and Milton-Jones broke off their debate and looked up at him.

'I'll see you gents in the office tomorrow. First thing.'

He wound his way between tables while contemplating the slow dissolution of such friendships. Colleagues who had become allies and drinking partners over the years, they seemed happy enough at his unannounced return but he sensed the idea of going to the Establishment was accepted more out of duty than enthusiasm. They were now married, Havilland and Fitzwilliam each had two children, Milton-Jones three, and priorities had changed permanently so it seemed. Eddie risked being the last man standing from a diminishing bachelor circle and, despite his earlier protestations, was slowly coming to terms with the idea of a more settled existence. The thought was depressing.

He barged through two heavily sprung, original slabs of panelled oak to the men's room. Like many of the Establishment's fixtures, the urinal opposite was an over-engineered affair - a beaten copper trough fed by a complex array of tubes from overhead cisterns. Stepping onto the low platform he banged a knee into a thick glass splashback and swore. Nevertheless, gratefully unzipping his fly, he loosed a heavy stream as his thoughts turned to, somewhat appropriately in his opinion, his brother.

The look on Julian's face had been worth the long-haul flight alone. Who did he think he was, packing him off abroad on the flimsiest of pretexts? He had to admit it was an astonishing place; the food, the architecture, the vibrancy of the culture and the high percentage of expats should have all combined to make it a perfect seasonal secondment. Fender Tang's welcome was gracious enough, but he also had a young family these days and Eddie had felt himself gradually becoming a burden. His need for a sense of connection, for the discourse and gossip and sheer serendipity that came from sharing a working space with others, had grown into a craving and driven him back to the City.

That his brother was upset about it mattered not a jot. Sensing the man's insecurity like a shroud, he knew Julian was suspicious of his motives and desperate to cling onto the perception of power. Ironically, Eddie was in no rush to replace him. It served his current lifestyle to keep Dayton weak, distrustful, timorous even, but nevertheless prepared to endure all the repetitive drudgery which came with the more senior position. Eddie had ambition for sure, but he already had plenty of influence and a much, much greater advantage - time.

He squeezed and shook the last drops into the trough then zipped his fly and left without bothering to wash his hands. Passing a row of semicircular wall booths, his subconscious registered two young women in close conversation beside an assortment of empty cocktail glasses. For fully three more strides he contemplated whether he had the energy or desire to suggest adding to their collection before ruefully dismissing the idea. He must be even more tired than he thought.

After several hours in the air-conditioned bar, the sweetness of the breeze was a welcome companion for the twenty-minute walk to his studio. Unlike McGlynn, he gave not the slightest consideration to being alone in the city's streets after dark. When it came to urban nightlife, Eddie was at the top of the food chain.

Dayton set down his book, a dense tale of human fallibility set in post-war Czech communism, and switched off the reading light, leaving distant windows in sharp relief.

His brownstone penthouse was a solid affair. The walls and floors, packed with heavy clay excavated for the foundations, acted as a supremely efficient barrier to sound.

He never heard his neighbours below and only caught the city's incessant buzz when the balcony door was open. Tonight though, the air conditioning kept the temperature to a comfortable level, the door was closed and the room was quiet.

By contrast, his mind remained stubbornly incapable of casting off the day's events. Too tired from the earlier gym work to form recognisable profanities, he lay naked, slack-jawed and open-eyed in the darkness, an occasional moan punctuating the silence as he fought an ineffective campaign towards sleep.

Turning her back to the sea, McGlynn cut up Cornhill Road, her step still light and energetic. The incline wound between small apartment blocks erected close to the pavement and much older houses set back in formal lawns and gardens. The latter were designed to be imposing, built by City grandees when land in this part of town commanded less ruinous prices than today. Glimpsing neoclassical designs down long driveways and through wrought iron railings, she walked upwards alone, her sandals making no noise on the slabs.

Since leaving Dalkeith, her attention had been mostly on her phone as she wished the girls goodnight. They replied independently of each other, Catriona with a prompt and simple response wishing her the same whilst Adeline took the opportunity to launch into a flurry of messages including videos of Maisie Smith's new dog, Eveline Dunne's split with her latest boyfriend and repeated requests for help in finding her sports kit. McGlynn sighed contentedly as she worked through the threads, suggesting a number of locations

Adeline would not have thought to investigate. With the mystery finally solved, she sent another, slightly firmer message about the need for a decent night's sleep, then left the road and crossed a courtyard to a cluster of modern apartments, her heart thumping pleasantly from both the gradient and a sense of rising excitement. The foyer was protected by plate glass doors with a brass panel containing the obligatory buttons.

'Hello?' A quick response, clearly someone expecting a visitor.

'It's me.'

'Hey, come on up.'

Choosing not to wait for the elevator, McGlynn climbed flights of carpeted stairs decanting into a top floor corridor. The second doorway on the right was already open and occupied by a figure leaning casually against the frame.

'Hi.'

'Hi. Sorry I'm late.'

'*De nada*. This is for you,' came the reply as a large glass of red wine was offered and accepted.

Now face to face, their eyes locked, each of them very aware that the width of their smiles, their unconcealed happiness at simply seeing each other again, bordered on the ridiculous. Younger than her, and of similar height despite being barefooted, Charlie Méndez had cropped jet black hair, brown eyes full of humour and an athletic, muscular build pleasingly outlined in a tight t-shirt and jeans, all of which served to remind McGlynn exactly why she had felt so strongly attracted when they first met at the Post's business awards. They had been seated at adjacent tables, Charlie's traditional black and white suit heightening McGlynn's feeling of femininity in her long green gown. After reciprocated glances, it had only been a matter of waiting until coffee was served and guests started to mingle before Charlie moved to a vacant chair at her side and extended a confident hand in introduction. That was nearly two months ago and they had been discreetly seeing each other once, sometimes twice a week since.

McGlynn took a sip of the wine without breaking eye contact, forcing herself to wait, savouring her sharpened senses and the basic desire flowing through her lower torso. Reaching the point where resistance was no longer possible, she crossed the intervening space and kissed Charlie full on the mouth. The reciprocation was immediate. Lips moving, opening, tongues probing, arms embracing as they turned as one into the hallway, nearly dropping the wine, depositing the glass and her bag clumsily on the wall table, kicking the front door closed. Each starting to undress the other, briefly losing contact, laughing, pulling at clothes, snatching brief kisses and touches, making it to the bedroom, peeling off underwear. Charlie's strength lowering McGlynn backwards onto the bed and the incomparable luxury of skin against skin along the length of her body.

They kissed more deeply now, in unison as their pace eased, wanting to remain in such sensory excess and no longer dominated by the near-frantic urgency which had marked their first few times. After a while, as was often the case, Charlie took the initiative and moved to McGlynn's neck, onwards across her breasts and down the smoothness of her stomach. Comfortably settled and firmly gripping each other's wrists on the cool surface of the bed, Charlie's tongue slowly teased her towards a first orgasm. She felt the definite edges of her physical and mental forms dissolve and gave herself willingly to the exquisite, overwhelming lightness into which she was guided.

In the dimness of the semicircular booth to which Eddie had considered returning, Becca Giordani and Sunita Malik continued their heart-to-heart. They had met in the Establishment shortly after six o'clock together with three of Malik's colleagues whom she had persuaded along. Conversation within the first hour was enthusiastic, the staff from the Post having been fully briefed on the parts they should play and what signal would be used when they were no longer required. There had been talk of how important and exciting the work of the paper was, of how they were bucking the trend of zero cost, advertising-led, low-grade journalism by investigating the truly vital stories of the day and demonstrating integrity, verve and the championing of the underdog. By the time Malik's colleagues said their regretful goodbyes, coinciding with the delivery of Giordani's fourth Manhattan, she was completely sold on the idea of abandoning Dayton Global Industries and taking any job which offered the opportunity to work with such a dedicated group of free thinkers.

Malik had carefully moulded that enthusiasm further over the subsequent couple of hours, the conversation slowly and gently widening like ripples from a stone pitched into a lake. While leading the way via possible vacancies at the Post, the identification of common interests and experiences and then shared values and beliefs, she ordered drinks from an attentive barman who recognised an expense account when he saw one. Giordani was now drunk, Malik was not, having switched to fruit juice several rounds ago, and there were no topics of conversation remaining out of bounds.

'She's such a snooty b... a bitch,' giggled Giordani with a quick snort of derision to follow. The Manhattans were having a significant effect on her accent, exposing the girl from the Marshside estate as they swapped gossip on one of the network anchors. 'You're much nicer, much. Lovely you are. You could definitely tekker... I mean, take, take... take her place if you wanted, you know.'

'Aw, thanks Becca, that's really nice of you,' the journalist crooned. 'But my face just wouldn't fit on Capital News. I don't have the right set of friends and I don't come from money like Nikki.'

'Yeah, but shouldn't matter, eh? Shouldn't matter if you don't have money... Work hard, not relying on no one. Be better'n everyone... get what's yours, eh?'

'It shouldn't matter, but it totally does and I'm guessing you know that too. Some people are born into money, some make it into money, but most of us just about make ends meet.'

'Yeah... yeah. S'not fair. Not fair at all. Worked my arse off to just get an interview with Dayton's. Still working my arse off in fact. Hate it. Every month... more... No overtime, no please, no thank you, spending all my money on fancy clothes and the commute... Just about staying off of the overdraft... need to choose which bills to pay... bills...' Giordani trailed off, smearing her make-up as she rubbed her face and tried to focus on the cocktail's cloudy liquid.

'I bet Julian Dayton's never struggled to pay his bills,' prompted Malik.

'Nah, loaded. I mean proper rich. But money can't buy class. That man's no class, none.'

'How come?'

'Just don't. Couldn't stop staring at me… Moment he met me. Seems to like it when my skirts are short but… but too chicken to say so, just stares instead. All scary eyes and skinny face… like a horror movie, you know… the old ones? Gives me the creeps…' Giordani practically shuddered. 'Never talks to no one that don't matter to him… Sulks most of the time… sulks like a little kid.'

Another snort.

Malik processed this latest piece of information as she had done all the rest, carefully adding to the model of Dayton building in her head, the model which would become the central focus of the column she was more determined than ever to write.

'What does he sulk about?'

'Anything. Everything. When something goes against him… gets in a proper, proper mood. Slams doors, cancels meetings, snaps at me… more'n usual that is. Royally pissed off after you met him today, I can tell you… And you should've seen the face first thing when he found out Eddie'd showed back up… fuckin' brilliant... Least Eddie buys me flowers once in a while.'

'Does he?'

'Yeah, I like Eddie. Always comes over and says hello… Keeps asking me out for a drink… Proper posh… too posh for me… but there's manners in that man… Not like Julian… Scared of Eddie, he is…'

'Sounds like Julian must be awful to work for. Shall we get one more for the road?' she added, noticing the nearly empty glass.

'Nah... better not... Work in the morning... for him. Bollocks.'

'OK. You were saying? What else makes Julian sulk?'

'Oh yeah. Dunno...' Giordani furrowed her brow until a new thought gave birth to an impish smile. 'McGlynn... Wynter Mer... Mrs McGlynn. You know, her from McGlynn-Lansing down the way? Know the one I mean?'

'Mmm. I know of her although we've never met.'

'She puts Julian in a right mood, more'n anyone.'

'Why's that do you think?'

'Dunno.... Just does. Seem to hate each other's guts if you ask me.'

'Well that's fairly normal in business isn't it?'

'Not like this... I've heard she's nice enough... Julian can't stand her though... Catch him all the time... looking at her building down the bay... just stands there, all weird like. Always wants the gossip about their firm... Loves it when there's bad news... And rumours... there's rumours too.'

'Rumours?'

'Yeah... Annabelle, Annabelle Crowley... know her? No? Such a laugh, I'll get her to come out with us... next time... Anyway, where... Shit, sorry, bit drunker'n I thought... Oh, s'right, Annabelle... she told me Julian once... you know... once tried it on... with her... no, not with her, not Annabelle... tried it on... with Mrs McGlynn!' she finished triumphantly, sure such information was worthy of her new friend's reputation.

From what Malik had already read, heard and observed first-hand about the man, this morsel was wildly inconsistent. He had no known romantic connections, seemed to be highly uncomfortable around women and the enmity between him and anyone who worked at McGlynn-Lansing, particularly its Director, was the topic of frequent conversation across the business district. Giordani's story was no more than office fiction and she dismissed it as such.

'Really? Doesn't he have a partner then?'

'Nope... always loadsa goss but nothing concrete... Reckoned he might be gay to start with... 'cept for the way he looks at me and... and the other girls. Maybe ... you know, goes both ways...'

'Mmm, probably. What will he say if you resign to work at the Post?'

'Won't care. Not a bit... Find a new one... Women like us... you'n me... easy, we're easy... to replace.'

'Have you heard anything about a man called Fredrik Nilsson?' asked Malik, letting the comment pass. 'Or his company, Malmotec?'

'Yeah, yeah... booked calls in with Julian... few times. Coming tomorrow... Nice man... funny accent.'

'What about his–'

Giordani's chin had slipped from the hand on which it had been resting, causing her to nearly headbutt the table.

'Oops!' she giggled. 'Better stop... stop drinking... Had enough... Let's go find something to eat, eh? Takeaway... up the road.... I know where...'

'That would be lovely but I'm afraid I can't tonight,' replied Malik, grimacing inwardly at the thought of a Monday night takeout. A figure like hers required a healthy diet. Even so, she could see the younger woman was increasingly in need of some nourishment and the opportunity to sober up. 'How about I call us a ride and you can make something at home?'

'Don't have to... do that... I can get home... my own... honest...'

'No, let me help. I'll get a car. Where's home Becca?'

Even in her drunken state, Giordani hesitated before replying.

'Rad–... Radbroke Esta–... Estate... Marshside.'

Poor girl, thought Malik, must be sturdier than she looks. Marshside had been one of the City's roughest neighbourhoods for a long time. There were rumours even City PD had unwritten rules about how and when they would respond to emergency calls there and the grey, cadaverous, near-derelict Radbroke tower blocks were notorious, even in that context. Dressing like a downtown office worker and walking through the estate every day would expose her to a gauntlet of catcalling, petty theft, assault and worse. Malik decided to make two bookings, one for Giordani and another for herself, justifying it on the basis the route home to her condominium on the outskirts of Willowborough took them in nearly opposite directions.

On stage, the band were beating out what was clearly the climax of their set. The drummer and bass guitarist were locked in pounding unison, faces raised and eyes closed as they drove along a staccato three-chord progression. Fighting to stay in lockstep with his own guitar, the vocalist was giving plenty of volume to the song's final lines but missing his pitch by enough to make Malik wince.

'Come on Becca, let's go outside and get some fresh air while we wait.'

'Mmm. OK… need go… toilet first…'

The journalist sighed. Nevertheless, knowing she was responsible for her companion's current state, she helped Giordani up and guided her towards the bathrooms, praying the girl would keep from vomiting before being safely deposited in the back seat of someone else's problem.

Later, McGlynn roused herself from the unconsciousness into which she had been drifting and gently lifted her head from Charlie's shoulder. The illuminated clock on the dresser showed nearly midnight. Careful not to disturb the sleeping figure by her side, she rose to collect her underwear from the floor then bag, dress and sandals from along the hallway, smiling in recollection as she made her way to the small bathroom. Once clothed she notified the car to collect her for the trip back to ML One. Although this part of the City was as safe as any, there were always risks and besides, she was now pleasantly weary and travelling by road would maximise the remaining hours of sleep. She moved back into the bedroom to wait, sitting on the edge of the bed and looking down at Charlie's relaxed, handsome face in the soft light from the window.

There was no doubting how much she valued their relationship. Still within that beautiful, breathtaking period of beginning where there were no expectations, no complications, no history - simply a heady feeling of unburdened happiness in each other's presence. Aware of McGlynn's situation, Charlie also understood what was able to be offered and had so far made no mention of anything more serious. However, two months could no longer be described as new and decisions would inevitably arise about what they might want themselves to become. McGlynn tested the depth of her affection, knowing if it became too profound she would need to have retained enough strength to back away, regardless of whether Charlie agreed. I've been here before, she thought, I know what I want, what I'm doing and where to draw the line. It's safe to continue, for now at least. In matters of business she placed total trust in her judgement. In matters of the heart, less so and she resolved to re-examine her feelings once she had more distance, more perspective.

A discreet vibration from her phone indicated the car was now waiting outside. She looked at Charlie one more time, paying close attention to every detail, imprinting the memory, then reached down and kissed her softly on the temple. Charlie stirred but did not wake from her sleep as McGlynn left, noiselessly pulling the door closed behind.

8

Her stomach lurched as she plunged downwards, skimming smoothly over the uneven ground with no apparent contact. She was sure this was the City, somewhere in *her* City, but nowhere she could recognise. The road was old, a shabby mixture of tarmac and cobblestone between buildings which seemed familiar but had been subtly altered - a new shade of brick here, fewer or more floors there, unbalanced columns and windows, oblique doorways. There was no traffic and it must have been evening because the sun was low and the street busy with people dressed for socialising. They walked alone and in groups and gathered together next to cinemas and clubs, behind velvet ropes and under illuminated street signs, overshadowed by giant hoardings advertising the latest and greatest in convenience products. She tried to look at their faces as she flashed past but they were blurred, indistinct, featureless.

Up ahead was a junction where the road bottomed out and turned sharply to rise back uphill, out of sight around a corner. Making the turn would be impossible at such speed. She would career instead into the face of the building opposite to be crushed upon the tan brickwork. With no time for evasive action, there was seemingly all the time in the world to wonder what it would be like to be gone, her work unfinished, her existence meaningless.

Would she know of the futility of her earthly life, her *unbeing* once the agonising moment of collision had passed? Given all the millennia which came before and all that would come after, it seemed inconceivable she would lack any form of awareness. How could it be probable, or even possible, for human consciousness to spark into being within a tiny fraction of all eternity and then be permanently extinguished? A unique species within an otherwise empty universe whose sensory memories, ideas, emotions, relationships, failures and triumphs lacked any kind of perpetuity, or wider frame of reference?

She did not believe, not in that at least.

Neither did she believe in a benevolent deity incomprehensibly remote from the world's atrocities, or the collective religions conceived and cultivated in times when their explanatory stories could not be disproved. Underpinning concepts smacking too much of patriarchal coercion, an indisputable method of controlling a population to the advantage of the storyteller, the genesis of so many human rights violations, centuries of warfare and the most misguided use of valuable time since the very earliest days of humankind.

Nor was she convinced by the logical reasoning of the philosophers. How could they unravel the mysteries of existence any more effectively than their religious counterparts when they shared mostly the same knowledge and capability? She found *cogito ergo sum* persuasive, the remainder less so.

So what did she believe? What should she choose to comfort her in this final moment? What reality awaited following her imminent demise?

Put simply, she believed in all which remained. That consciousness would be restored, with or without any memory of the life she was leaving. That whatever she found next, wherever she may arrive, was simply the start of the next period of awareness and therefore death itself was not to be feared. That human existence was part of something bigger, currently unknown and unknowable, but *something* nevertheless. That this was not to be the end.

Then it was too late for further thought as the corner arrived and she banked like a speedskater, the angle impossible, leaning near to the horizontal at the apex yet somehow feeling supremely balanced and sure-footed and in control. The forces generated by the turn pulled at the mass of her body but the movement maintained itself and suddenly she was away from the wall, through the bend and accelerating upwards in a new direction with no discernible effort or movement of her limbs. Upwards towards a crest where the road and the buildings disappeared out of view and only the golden clouds remained, swimming languidly across an endless sky. Reaching the summit, the cobbles dropped away below and momentum carried her high into the air, high enough to see all the districts fanning outwards away from the ocean. Miles and miles of rooftops and streets dotted with rectangular green parks near the shoreline and larger, more irregular areas of open land further away. Sports arenas, shopping malls, commercial buildings with their unmistakable air conditioning units, even cars and individual people going about their everyday business were visible in microscopic detail. She gloried in this unpredictable freedom until gravity reasserted itself and began to drag her earthwards, the fall accelerating, her gut lurching again, the ground rushing upwards to meet her, the growing comprehension there was no way of cheating death this time. Closing her eyes just before impact, she felt at peace.

McGlynn jolted awake, disoriented by an abstract threat, and lay still for a while - not chasing the dream but hoping to catch it unawares by allowing it to return of its own free will. Frustratingly, the memory slipped away and she yawned and stretched and allowed her mind to focus. Her first thoughts were of the time spent with Charlie and when they might see each other again. Perhaps on Thursday but otherwise the following week. She wanted to exert no more energy than necessary on Friday evening because Saturday was race day.

The City Triathlon was an established event. Attracting thousands from across the country, it took place over the standard Olympic distances - a one-and-a-half kilometre swim across the bay, a forty kilometre bike ride into the surrounding countryside and finally a ten kilometre run through the streets and parks to finish in Merchants Square. She had first decided to enter as motivation for regaining full fitness after the twins' early childhood, enjoying it so much she had returned every year since. Then, at her fourth race, Dayton appeared unexpectedly at the starting line. The elite athletes had long since departed but her age grouping and his were to be released together. She remembered the conflicting emotions at seeing him; annoyance he had encroached upon what was personally valuable mixed with the anticipation of testing herself and beating him in a new arena. Losing sight of each other during the melee of the swim, she only discovered he had won by some distance after the results had been published. She trained harder over the following months in case he returned. He did and beat her for a second time and then again in the following two events. However, his margins of victory were diminishing, less than three minutes separating them last year, and she was sure of holding the advantage this weekend. Training had gone even better than expected under Brookes' supervision and she felt fitter than ever whilst Dayton, in his fifties, was inevitably on the wrong side of his physical peak. She would wait at the finish this year and watch him realise he was no longer in the ascendancy.

McGlynn swung her legs over the side of the bed and stood, thinking there was still much to be done before Saturday. The view from the window was identical to the previous morning - blue sky, blue sea and the promise of another hot day. Setting the covers straight, she picked up her phone and checked her diary - coffee with Christopher Boland followed by the wider board meeting until lunch, then it looked as though Matthieu had confirmed a mid-afternoon appointment with Mayor Santoro. Switching applications, she scrolled through the many messages received overnight. None required immediate action so, heading for the bathroom, she compiled a mental checklist of other tasks. Reviewing her notes for the board meeting ought to come first, then a lunchtime conversation with Brookes about progress at the docks. Somewhere around those she would need to ask Detective Campbell for any update on the search for Rohan, talk with Wiesenberg to formulate a plan in the event he could not be found, check Matthieu had booked a catch-up with Jane Hallam and make arrangements for the follow-up meeting with the Nilssons. That would do for a start.

She showered a full four minutes under cold water, maintaining a controlled breathing pattern and forcing an increase in her heart rate, then roughly towelled herself dry. Feeling invigorated, dressed in the usual shirt and trousers, a cup of steaming coffee from the machine on the kitchenette's stone worktop in hand, she was about to walk through to her office when her phone rang.

'*Bonjour Maman, ça va?*' she said, dropping onto the sofa.

'Good morning. 'ow are you, my beautiful child?' said Cécile McGlynn, her heavy accent full of Parisian chic and warmth.

The pair had conversed in nothing but French until McGlynn was within a year of going to school but then her mother insisted they must talk only in English "for practice, which is good for me, and for you too *ma chérie, hein?*". The habit had stuck although the languages sometimes intermingled into a patois only they understood.

'Are you at the office? I thought I would call early so that you might be free to talk to me.'

'*Oui Maman*, it's a busy week so I'll probably be here until the weekend.'

'Oh, but that is no good for you, Wynter. All work and no play. I was hoping to come and see you for lunch one day. Can you spare some time for a poor old woman? I haven't seen my daughters for so long. Maybe Sylvie could come too, if only the boss would let her have time away,' she teased.

'Um, I think this week might be difficult, sorry. How about next?'

'Let me look at my diary. Oh, yes, it looks as though I might be free on, now let me see… let me see… oh, it looks as though I can make time for you any day you wish.'

'Point taken. Let me check with Sylvie and then Matthieu. One of us will fix something up.'

'Very good. I have always liked that boy. But I am sorry to say that Eloise seems to have taken a turn for the worse.'

'What have you heard?' asked McGlynn, wanting to know whether she ought to send him home sooner than Thursday.

'We spoke on the phone yesterday and she sounds very weak. We have been friends for a long time, you know, and I can tell when she is lying to me. She says everything is fine but of course it is not. I was supposed to visit next month and she has put me off again, another excuse, always excuses. I think she doesn't want me to see her when she is so ill, as if I would care. All I want is to see my friend. She is too young to be going through such a difficult time. It isn't fair.'

'I know *Maman*, I know. I've arranged for Matthieu to be at her next appointment.'

'You're a good, kind person *Chérie*, thank you.'

'It's the least we can do. Is there anything else Eloise or Olivier need?'

'I don't believe so. They want their privacy and I understand that. Your father and I will send some more flowers and try to keep in touch.'

'OK.' A pause. 'How is *Papa*?'

'The same as always my child. He pretends not to be interested but I still catch him reading about you or the company on his phone or in the Post. He wants you to do well and beat the Daytons, even after everything.'

McGlynn wondered which of these was more important to David. His personal hatred of Richard Dayton extended to the man's two sons, through whom damage might continue to be inflicted by proxy.

'If you like, I can ask him to lunch too?' added Cécile, hope in her voice.

'I don't think he would come,' said McGlynn wistfully. 'But of course, Sylvie and I would love to see him.'

'Very good. Now, are you eating well? You are always so thin. Do I need to bring you any food?'

'Ha! I've been able to feed myself for a long time. And I've been in training for the triathlon so I'm eating like a horse.'

'Ah, that's right. Maybe I can persuade your father to come and watch. I shall do my best. And how is Charlie?' The softness of the pronunciation made it *Sharlee*. 'Are you having good sex?'

'Christ *Maman*, is nothing sacred?' exclaimed McGlynn, rueful of keeping no secrets from her mother but laughing nonetheless.

'Of course, *ma chérie*,' came the casual reply. '*Mais seulement le féminisme et la féminité.*'

'Well…! In that, we can agree. And, yes, we're having… getting along just fine, thank you for asking.'

'Don't mind me. I think you are being very sensible. As long as this is not of the heart, *hein*? You must always think of my granddaughters. It is easy for children to be hurt by the actions of their parents if we are not careful, no?'

The irony was not lost on McGlynn.

'I'm being careful. Don't worry.'

'Mothers always worry Wynter. It's what we do best. Now, go and do your very important work but don't forget to tell this poor old woman when I may come and see you, OK?'

'OK. I love you *Maman.*'

'I love you too my child.'

McGlynn drained her coffee, smiling from the conversation and reflecting on whether the experiences of her mother's antecedents, the relentless labouring and risk-taking in the hope of a better life overseas, had been the crucible from which Cécile's temperament had been forged. The pioneering spirit, unending pragmatism, humility and humour reinforced by a backbone of steel - she felt lucky to have such a wise confidant. Her mother certainly felt no obligation to share anything they discussed with her husband, understanding the differences between discretion and disloyalty, leaving McGlynn free to vent her emotions and seek counsel whenever she wished.

A few hours over lunch with her mother and sister were well overdue. She could even ask Michael if he would like to join them now that his university commitments were sure to be winding down towards the summer break. Something else for the tasklist.

In her office, she picked up the budget review again. She and Damian Bailey would be the only McGlynn-Lansing executives at the board meeting and needed to be completely aligned in their understanding of the company's performance. Any inconsistency in answering the investors' innumerable questions would be taken as a lack of understanding, leading to swathes of follow-up actions. The format was familiar and she skimmed much of the content to focus on the key metrics. Other than the shortfall in computing revenues, the only contentious point she could foresee was Dalkeith's assessment of the purchase price for Malmotec.

Nearing the document's end, she heard soft footsteps beyond the doorway followed by a polite clearing of the throat. Realising it was too early for Matthieu and praying any visitor was not bringing further problems, McGlynn was relieved when a short, elderly man appeared. Immaculately dressed in a dark grey suit, he carried a small briefcase and an air of quiet authority.

'Jacob! Come and have a seat. What are you doing here at this hour?'

'Good morning Wynter,' said Wiesenberg, his elocution calm and precise. 'I thought I should take a chance on you having stayed in town and drop by on my way to court. Perhaps we might finalise our plans on the assumption Rohan is yet to be found?'

'There are a few lines of enquiry but I'm not optimistic. He's either unable to contact us or doesn't want to but, either way, I don't think we can expect to hear from him in time.'

'Mmm, quite so. Well, there are one or two arcane devices I can employ to force a recess today, but the justices will take advice and see through those in no time. I think we should expect an order to reconvene no later than tomorrow morning. Have you made your decision on taking the stand in Rohan's place?'

'Would you still advise against it? I know he's the expert but he took me through the proof points again only last week. I should remember enough to give credible testimony?'

'I don't doubt it, Wynter. But instinct tells me the defence are not expecting him to appear either, in which case they're likely preparing for you instead. I think you should expect very technical questioning under cross-examination. Any hesitation in your answers, any confusion in the precise details, will weaken our argument quite quickly.'

'How would you assess our position if we call no further witnesses?'

'Mmm, I thought you would ask. As always, I'm unable to give an exact answer and I can't read these expert judges as well as I usually can a jury. But I would say we're probably neck and neck. If you testify and it goes well, the balance will tip in our definite favour. If not, then clearly the reverse is also true. Given our acknowledged specialist is unavailable, it might be better to, ah, avoid the risk altogether.'

McGlynn weighed the odds, ultimately deciding they were unfavourable and backing herself to make the difference.

'I'll testify.'

'Very well,' said Wiesenberg. 'In that case, please ensure you're fully versed with Rohan's prepared scripts. And if time permits today, have his team ask you as many awkward questions as possible about your understanding of the software. We've worked together often enough that I don't need to brief you on the right etiquette, body language and phrasing but you should know these judges seem to be towards the more conservative end of the spectrum and, from what I've seen, value brevity over detail.'

'Understood. I'll be as ready as I can.'

'I'm sure. I'll provide young Matthieu with the court schedule but contact me if there's something you would like to go over in person and I'll come back once we're in recess. In the meantime, let us hope for some luck and Rohan's return.'

'Hope is a fickle mistress Jacob, we both know it,' replied McGlynn. 'But I'll be in touch later regardless.'

Alone again she returned to the budget but, atypically, the need to locate Rohan overrode her concentration. His continuing absence meant she was now at least as concerned for his safety as wanting him available for the trial. Looking back through her notes, she checked the clock, calculated the time difference and dialled the number found the previous afternoon.

'*Namaste?*' said a young female voice.

'*Namaste.* Do you speak English?'

'Yes, of course, may I please ask who is calling?'

'This is Wynter McGlynn and I'd like to speak with Mr Rahul Mehta if possible. I work with Mr Mehta's son, Rohan.'

'Thank you, I will see if he's available. One moment.'

McGlynn waited as the line was muted and whoever had spoken went off to find Rohan's father. After less than half a minute, the hiss on the line returned along with an older, more authoritative voice.

'Hello? Mrs McGlynn? I've heard much about you. Is everything all right?'

Mehta's English was excellent and she would have wagered from his accent that he had spent time at a British school or university.

'I'm sure it is, Mr Mehta. But I was hoping to ask if you'd heard from Rohan recently?'

'We've exchanged messages but haven't spoken in person for a while. Why do you ask?'

'As I say, I'm sure everything's fine but I was expecting to see Rohan yesterday and he didn't come into the office. We have some important meetings together this week and I'm keen to get back in touch.'

'Have you tried him at the house?'

'In Willowborough? Yes, unfortunately there's no sign of him there either.'

'In that case, Mrs McGlynn, it doesn't seem I'm able to help. Although we brought all of our children up to have a strong sense of responsibility so I'm sure he'll be in touch. I have to say that I'm surprised you're calling so soon if there's nothing to be concerned about? After all, it has only been one day?'

'Please don't worry. If it's not too personal a question though, may I ask whether there was anything unusual in his messages?'

'Everything seemed normal to me. He said he'd been working on Saturday but was planning to head out of town. I assumed that meant for the remainder of the weekend but perhaps he intended to be away longer?'

'I don't suppose he mentioned where he was going?'

'He didn't, I'm sorry.'

'In that case I apologise for disturbing you. But if you hear from Rohan soon, would you mind asking him to contact me on this number? Or perhaps you could even call yourself if it's not too much trouble?'

'Of course. I'd be happy to.'

'Thank you. And one last thing if I may, do you happen to have contact details for Wenling?'

'Who is Wenling?'

'Um, she's a mutual friend,' said McGlynn, feeling as though she had been indiscreet in some way. 'I've met her once or twice.'

'Sorry, but I don't know who that is.'

'No matter. I shan't take up any more of your time. I'm sure we'll hear from him soon and I'll be in touch.'

She hung up, unsure what to make of the conversation. Rohan telling his father he was going away meant he had at least given some thought to his departure. This was good news in terms of his wellbeing but made his absence from work all the less understandable. Knowing how central he was to the trial, why would he not have told her? And why would he have spent time preparing with Wiesenberg on Saturday? Then there was his father's reaction to Wenling's name. McGlynn was under the impression they were in a reasonably serious relationship but it was clear she was yet to be introduced to his family. Why would that be?

This information could be useful to Campbell's enquiries but she was reluctant to risk a phone conversation. An update concerning the docks would be expected and Valente's report was not due until the end of the afternoon. Also, if Rohan had indeed left the City voluntarily, then there was no missing person's case to investigate and retaining the detective's help would become even more difficult. Regardless, he still had to be found so, rather than calling, McGlynn typed a short message to the detective asking for news.

The budget document secured her attention for another twenty minutes prior to Matthieu's arrival.

'Good morning Director. How was dinner with Mr Nilsson?' he asked.

'Fine thanks. Although Thom's going to need your help in arranging a follow-up. Did you make any further progress at Rohan's last night?'

'Not really. One neighbour said they'd seen a couple living next door but the others didn't even know that. Sorry but I didn't think it was worth messaging you.'

'Fair enough, worth a try. And what about his team, any luck?'

'Those who got back to me said they don't have any extra contact details and hadn't met Wenling. I'll chase the rest this morning.'

'Please. Jacob was just here. We're having to make a back-up plan and I'll probably be at court tomorrow. That means I need time with Rohan's team today, at least an hour, preferably longer. Can you rearrange my schedule? I should be back from the mayor's office at what, around four-thirty? And I'm OK to work until late.'

'No problem.'

'Can you also ask Damian to come and see me, there are a few more points we need to discuss. And I'd like to have lunch next week with Sylvie and my mother. Ninety minutes.'

'Got it. There was one other thing Director. You asked me to mention anything I thought you ought to know about?'

'Absolutely,' she said, interest rising.

'I had a call last night from someone saying they worked at the warehouse, asking for a meeting with you.'

'Hugo's looking at a few things for me. I wouldn't be surprised if he wants time to follow up.'

'It was the way this guy talked, as if he didn't know where you normally worked, and I didn't recognise his name. I think he said Ben, or maybe Ken. The call was kind of muffled right at the start and came through reception rather than direct.'

'Hmm. Did you give him any details?'

'I just said your calendar was very busy, that you were out this afternoon and probably tomorrow morning but then in the office for the rest of the week. He wanted to check the address so I asked for his name again and we got cut off.'

'Did you say where I was going?'

'No. But I thought about it overnight and, like I said, it seemed strange he never called back if he'd been told to organise a meeting.'

'Agreed, no harm done though. When you get the chance, give Hugo a call and check it out. Or try Andrew - he's over there this morning too,' said McGlynn, looking forward to a lunchtime swim and thinking she could also ask Brookes about anyone at the warehouse with a name like Ben or Ken. 'Door closed thanks, but send Damian in once he's free.'

With Matthieu gone, her thoughts returned to the board meeting for a fourth time. Boland would be arriving soon, ostensibly to discuss the hiring of Zhao, but she also wanted a better sense of his attitude towards the wider session. She had worked with him, Stratton, Hounslow and Turnbull for long enough to know how they operated, individually and collectively, and become used to their support for her running of the company. However, the previous morning's call had done nothing to help her normal confidence.

There were also the delicate questions of whether she should inform the board of Rohan's disappearance or Fredrik Nilsson's new proviso. Neither would be welcome news and she was increasingly starting to feel as though she might have a fight on her hands.

9

Dayton's mood lurked in stark contrast to the fine morning. A worsening headache had kept him awake since the early hours. Rather than making the effort to find medicinal relief he had tossed and turned in the vain hope it would simply go away.

Age might be a privilege but his body had begun to disagree. Each day arrived with a moment of misgiving as he checked for signs of new discomfort - headaches, perhaps a crick in the neck or an aggravated sciatic nerve, possibly a frozen shoulder - an expanding assortment of ailments apparently lay in wait. Grandmother warned him getting old was no fun but he had ignored her with all the conceit of youth. Yet she had been right, of course, and he missed that feeling of glorious vitality, the knowledge he could bounce back from anything with no more than a decent meal and half a dozen hours of sleep. Elderliness had ceased being a distant and abstract concept and now had definite, unappealing form.

As the sun doused the streetlights and unveiled the greens and browns of Valiance Park, he had finally admitted defeat, risen and made his way to the office even earlier than usual. The last three hours were spent wading through messages accumulating unread since the previous afternoon. Now past nine o'clock, there was still no sign of either his brother or his assistant and the internal narrative of him being the only person to give a damn about the company was in full voice.

A knock on the door and a nervous face appeared around its leading edge.

'Excuse me, Mr Dayton, would it be OK for you to approve a couple of contracts?'

'What are they for?'

'The facilities management renewals.'

'Can't Sandy approve them? I'm busy.'

'Sorry but he's out this morning. I've been told to ask you because the costs have gone up. They're nearly a month overdue.'

'Why are they overdue?'

'I don't know.'

Dayton blew loudly through his nose, despite the nagging feeling he had seen and ignored correspondence from Sandy White on the topic.

'Right, OK, come in. How much have they gone up by?'

'About fifteen percent I think.'

'You think? You're not sure?'

'James has been dealing–'

'I don't care who's been dealing with them. It's you who's now asking me to approve them. Why have the costs increased?'

'Um... well we ran competitive bids with three other suppliers and this one's still the cheapest.'

'Cheapest? Who cares about the cheapest? I want to know about the increase in costs, and if they're still the best value for money.'

'I'm sorry but I'm not–'

'Yes, yes, I know, James has been dealing with them. What about changes to the terms and conditions? Anything material?' In the ensuing silence, Dayton's disapproving expression progressed to a sneer. 'You don't know, do you.

Incredible. Are you stupid? Do you know anything about these contracts? Anything at all?'

'S–sorry, Mr Dayton. Sandy said he'd booked some time with you yesterday afternoon but you'd had to cancel.'

'That's right. Something more important came up.'

'Sorry, sorry. I'll… I'll go and ask.'

'Do that. Disappear and come back once you've done your job properly. You can't just leave everyone else to do all the work.'

He noticed Giordani arriving at her desk and promptly switched his attention.

'Becca,' he called to no avail. 'Becca!'

Giordani had heard the first time but took a guilty pleasure in making him ask twice. Like Dayton, she was tired and had a violent headache but with the added jeopardy that she might throw up at any time. She took a couple of steadying breaths, fixed something resembling polite interest on her face and walked into his office as her crestfallen colleague hurried out.

'Morning Julian. Sorry I'm late. Delays between Marshside and Valley Bridge.'

'Nice of you to join us,' he said, determined to use the line regardless and resisting the immediate urge to check the traffic news. He looked her up and down in his usual intrusive manner. 'Are you ill? You look terrible.'

'Thanks. I'm OK, probably just a virus.'

'A virus eh? Have you been getting too close to someone you shouldn't, young lady?'

Swallowing hard to suppress the rising vomit, Giordani said nothing leaving Dayton to grunt in disappointment.

'Anyway,' he continued. 'Keep your distance, I can't afford to catch anything this week.'

'Not a problem.'

'Get me a coffee and then go find Eddie. I need to talk to him first thing.'

'Sure. Anything else?'

'Make sure you wash your hands first.'

Dayton's eyes were already back to his desktop screen. Rather than concentrating on his inbox however, he was thinking about whether it might be time to find a new PA. In offering her the job, despite him having seen twenty candidates with stronger experience and having twenty more only a phone call away, she was so grateful for the opportunity, so willing to please, he had felt almost philanthropic. There was no denying she worked hard, all the extra hours without complaint and not a single day of absence, but he was starting to notice a lack of respect and no longer felt any satisfaction in having this attractive young woman at his beck and call. Life was otherwise too dull to deny oneself beautiful things but they all lost their lustre eventually. Keen to avoid an unpleasant sacking he decided to offer her to Eddie first, the opportunity presenting itself only a few minutes later.

'Morning Jules.'

'Ah, morning. Close the door, lots to discuss. Where were you yesterday afternoon? Couldn't find you.'

Landing on one of the sofas, Eddie lay back against the cushions, hands behind his head.

'Team meeting. Offsite.'

'Whereabouts?'

'The Establishment.'

Dayton elected not to waste time by enquiring further. How Eddie maintained business relationships was up to him, although the thought of him spending the working day drunk with his friends was yet another reasonable irritant.

'Very good,' he said. 'What about tomorrow night, are you free?'

'Possibly.'

'I'm sure you haven't filled your week already. After all, this was an unplanned visit, wasn't it?'

'Probably then. What's up?'

'It's the Mayor's Ball. I think you should come.'

'Mmm. How many tables do we have?'

'Four, with eight places apiece. They're even more expensive than last year, three hundred a head. McGlynn's have only shelled out for two.'

'Well it's all for a good cause. Who's the beneficiary?'

'You mean apart from that fat bastard Santoro? The money's going to the new treatment centre at Woodlands.'

'Smart move given he must be kicking off his campaign soon. A few pictures of him handing over a big cheque make him look like a man who gives a shit about the community.'

'My thoughts entirely, not an ounce of shame. But I bought the extra tables because we should be in pole position to equip the new centre once it's commissioned. Are you in?'

'Alright. But I'm choosing where I sit. Are we taking the Nilssons?'

'I wasn't planning to but that reporter from the Post hinted they're talking to McGlynn-Lansing and possibly others. I'm meeting Fredrik later so I'll probably have to ask him to come - better they're seen in public with us than anyone else. And as for place settings, I'm down to host one of the tables but you can take your pick of the others. Let Becca know will you? She's organising and can bump someone to make space. You'll need a plus one.'

'Not a problem. How did it go with the Post?'

'Ugh… they sent Sunita Malik. Burdened by self-importance, that one. Turned up with a half-arsed list of inflammatory questions, clearly wanting to sensationalise a perfectly straightforward advertorial. But I tell you what Ed, if she goes too far off-topic, I'm going to have Rutter fire her, or at the very least replaced for this piece. She's no fucking clue.'

'I quite like some of her stuff. Did you see the article on Vince Evesham? Very amusing.'

'Unless you're Vince, I hear he's preparing to sue. Listen, about Becca…'

A knock on the door and Giordani returned, placing a steaming mug on the table in front of Dayton but with eyes only for his brother.

'Are you sure I can't get you something too, Eddie?'

'Not unless you're going to share it with me, Miss Giordani. Have to say you're looking gorgeous as always.'

'Ha! Thank you very much, Mr Edward Dayton sir,' she giggled. 'Give me a call if you change your mind or want anything else. To drink, that is.'

Watching the exchange, knowing his use of the same compliment would result in nothing but mutual embarrassment, Dayton felt a stab of envy.

'What about her?' asked Eddie once the door had closed.

'It's time for a change. She's been with us a couple of years and learnt about as much as she's going to under me. Do you fancy taking her on?'

'Eh? Um, not really. You know I don't like being distracted in the office, except when I want to be, and I'll be overseas for the next few months anyway.'

'Are you sure?' said Dayton, trying hard to be enthusiastic, desperate to avoid having to fire her himself. 'She's quite bright, you know. Helpful, reasonably capable.'

'If you really want rid, why don't I ask Fitz?'

'Does he need someone?'

'Yeah, I think he'd be interested.'

'OK, but not a word to Becca. She likes working for me and I don't want it affecting her output until we have a definite plan.'

'Righto. Should we expect a similar replacement? Blonde this time?'

'Depends on who applies, doesn't it. Now, I have another opportunity for you. How m–'

'Really? Must be Christmas.'

'Whatever. So, McGlynn's, how many people do you know there? People who'd give you information, confidential information, if you asked?'

'Not many,' admitted Eddie.

'None is my guess.'

'Well how many do you have?'

'Not enough. Never enough. But I think we have a chance to expand our network.'

'You mean recruit a spy?' Eddie replied, his surprise genuine. 'In McGlynn's? Are you serious?'

'The enlightened ruler and wise general uses the highest intelligence for the purposes of spying, and thereby achieves great results.'

'Well, well, brother mine. I'm assuming that's a quotation you've stolen from somewhere?'

'Sun Tzu,' replied Dayton, pleased he had memorised something appropriate with which to impress.

'Indeed. This sounds like it belongs in the dark ages. Are you sure it's not just an ego trip?'

'Wake up and don't be so naive. This is about winning. Information's king in this business, in any business. Not you, not me, not cash, not customer. Information. Without it we end up making lousy decisions and put the company at risk. Sometimes a little, sometimes a lot.'

'Don't lecture me on the bloody obvious. We're awash with data, I spend half my life trying to make sense of it. But you're talking about persuading someone at McGlynn's to leak trade secrets? That's industrial espionage, it's illegal and you... sorry, we... could go to jail for it.'

'It's actually rather a grey area according to the law which is why she's taking the current action through the civil courts. But how do you think we were able to copy her code in the first place?'

'What? I thought the labs managed to reverse engineer it from a commercial access point?'

'They did. But they couldn't have done it without an insider to solve a few teething problems.'

'Are you having me on?' Eddie leant forward, a look of astonishment turning to anger as he worked through the connections. 'Rohan fucking Mehta. I knew it. No wonder, no sodding wonder. He could have us over a barrel if we're not careful, Jules.'

'No, not Mehta. Unfortunately,' said Dayton, thoroughly enjoying himself. He rarely had such attention from his brother, or such an advantage. 'He'd be able to identify the code but the person who helped used to work in his team.'

'Who?'

'The whole point of this kind of activity is that you shouldn't ever reveal your sources. The fewer people who know, the better.'

'Oh piss off then.'

'I'm serious, Ed. These are the kinds of things which have to be limited to two people if at all possible. Which brings me back to the opportunity I mentioned.'

Eddie sat in silence, unsure whether he wanted to hear what was coming next.

'Do you know who Matthieu Gautier is?' continued Dayton. 'No? He's McGlynn's exec assistant. Young lad, been with the firm a few years and now works for her directly. She's obviously grooming him for a senior position which means he'll be close to what's going on and have decent access privileges. I think we can obtain his help and I want you to be the one to ask.'

'Why me?'

'Experience. As in, you need some. And there's no better place to start than McGlynn-Lansing.'

'Why would this Gautier chap tell me anything?'

'Leverage.'

'You mean bribery? Does he need money?'

'No idea, although it's often a useful way of getting information. But it's generally not money that motivates people beyond a first transaction. No, I found out recently that his mother's ill. Stage four stomach cancer with second-stage spread to nearby lymph nodes.'

'So?'

'So…' Dayton let the word hang, waiting for the mental leap required, running on when it failed to materialise. 'So who makes the most advanced targeted radiotherapy equipment in the world and specialises in gastric cancer treatment?'

'You're suggesting I tell Gautier that we do?' asked Eddie incredulously. 'That we offer his mother access to our prototypes in return for him selling out McGlynn? For Christ's sake, it's not even true, the first machines have only been operating in Bangkok for a couple of months. We have no data yet about their clinical efficacy outside the trials. And we're not expecting better results for gastric tumours than for any other.'

'We don't need it to be true. We need it to seem credible to Gautier.' Dayton paused. 'You want to know what the most powerful motivator is for a potential recruit in this game?'

'Fear?'

'No Ed, not fear. It's hope.'

Eddie sat back again, nowhere near as relaxed.

'Does Richard know about this?' he asked eventually.

'Who do you think told me about Gautier's mother?'

'You're joking.'

'I'm not. It was the old man who introduced me to this kind of work in the first place. He met her a few times apparently, back in the day, and they still have people in common. So yes, I think you can assume he's fine with the idea.'

'Jesus.'

'Look, this isn't much different to any of the other tactics we use to stay ahead. But I do need you on board, and quickly

- I hear the mother's not going to last more than a few more months. My bet is that Gautier will be at the ball tomorrow. If so, take him aside, talk about the treatment we could offer and be non-specific about what we want in return. We'll get to the form of payment once he feels as though he owes us.'

'Jesus,' said Eddie again. 'I'll, uh, think about it.'

'Good man.'

The more Eddie could be involved in such activities, the more Dayton bolstered his own leverage and therefore the stronger his position in their inevitable future arguments. Eddie had agreed to accept his leadership seven years ago but their respective seniority needed constant reinforcement to maintain order. It's not who you know, he thought, it's what you know about who you know which gave one the upper hand.

'Anything else? I need some air,' said Eddie.

'What are your plans for the day?'

'Thought I might sit in on the trial. I want to be there if McGlynn takes the stand and listen to what her lawyer says if she doesn't. Are you coming down?'

'Probably not. Me being there would suggest I'm giving the case a status it doesn't deserve. Franklin thinks it's going as expected and I'd be surprised if she dares to testify, but it could be a Hail Mary. No issues at our end I need to know about?'

'None. I checked last night and they're OK. Nervous, but OK.'

'Keep reminding them what's at risk and they'll be fine. And let me know if she does show up. I may decide to come and spectate after all. Just for fun.'

10

The glass and steel shell of ML One contained hundreds of rooms, none of which were dedicated to the company's board meetings. McGlynn had strong egalitarian views and wanted as much of the building as possible to be used by her staff, even to the extent she had ordered a reduction in her own office and living space within the architect's plans. Given the simplicity of the private investor structure, few people were expected to attend the quarterly events in any case. For today's, Natalie had booked a room overlooking Cornelian Lane and the six people involved were spaced at regular intervals around the table positioned at its centre. Even with the circular seating arrangement, McGlynn felt as though she and Damian Bailey were on one side with the four non-executives on the other.

The preceding conversation with Christopher Boland had been far from satisfactory. Arriving in the preferred uniform of the super-wealthy British investor - chinos, patterned shirt and gilet - he looked tanned and fresh despite the early flight from London. Natalie brought tea and a light breakfast to the roof garden and they had begun by talking about current economic conditions and how the technology markets were faring. After hearing of Danny Zhao's move over the weekend, McGlynn had skimmed the latest set of results for Boland Technologies and was surprised to find both profits and revenues in decline, but he was relaxed in response to her tactful questions, saying this was an expected period of transition as the company continued its metamorphosis from traditional hardware manufacturer to a more specialised services provider. It was for this latter purpose that he had seen fit to hire Zhao, believing there was an opportunity to focus on software research for the quantum computing market. McGlynn pointed out she invested heavily in the same field to which he had laid out a potential commercial arrangement, suggesting it made better sense for her to buy in the results that Zhao's team would produce than allocate further funding well ahead of the payback. She had not been convinced by this argument, ambushed by the expectation of paying handsomely for exclusive access to Zhao's work and, if Boland's suggestion was rebuffed, that it could be offered instead to her direct competitors. The ensuing debate resulted in them running out of time before reaching the matter of the trial, meaning he was still unaware of Rohan's disappearance.

With the usual review of the company's trading figures, the wider board meeting had started well enough but Boland then opened a discussion on their computing strategy, citing the lower-than-expected sales performance as driving a need for change. The intent of his examination - to infer a lack of expertise in her product design team, something which could be addressed via the contract he had offered - may have been obvious to McGlynn but the others so far seemed unaware of an ulterior motive. He was the acknowledged expert on the topic and had the right to probe.

She glanced around the table. Bailey was on her left, staring intently at his laptop while working through the latest question on development cost capitalisation.

Next to him was Brendan Stratton, a short man wearing an unfashionable suit and a permanent air of mourning.

Stratton's father had been friends with McGlynn's grandfather, meaning he and David McGlynn had grown close during the many shared holidays of their childhood, skiing in the Cairngorms during the winters and spending long summer days climbing in the mountains near their lakeside estate. Once Stratton had inherited his stock in McGlynn-Lansing, his interest was therefore almost entirely social, using board meetings as good reason to meet and break bread with his friend while otherwise concentrating on the family's oil and gas exploration interests in Aberdeen. Other than Aaron Castellane, he had seemed the unhappiest with the coup resulting in David's departure, but not so unhappy as to have considered parting with his thirteen percent, she noted. Passive by nature, he was generally content to let the others lead and appeared disinterested in the current dialogue.

After Stratton was Nick Turnbull who by contrast was listening closely and seemed frustrated at Bailey's delay in answering. Immaculately attired, hawkish, restless, Turnbull was educated in economics at Yale before pursuing a highly successful career as a New York financier and then semi-retirement to the Hamptons. He had owned the least amount of stock prior to the reinvestment round and had hence supplied the biggest injection of cash to bring his shareholding up to the same level as the other three. With increased authority from that transaction and the related shift in power, he had become much more vocal, taking David to task and clashing several times over what he saw as profligate use of the company's resources. McGlynn suspected it was Turnbull who had been the first to lose faith and patience in her father, initiating the events leading to his downfall.

Then came Boland, sitting erect with a self-assured smile as he waited for Bailey's reply.

Last was Elliott Hounslow, to his left and her right. Hounslow was the oldest of the four and retired from all other professional commitments. He had spent nearly a decade on the board with old Kenneth McGlynn and brought wisdom and calm to the group with his conventional, avuncular style. From what she could glean, Hounslow had reluctantly supported the decision to have her father replaced, torn between loyalty to Kenny and the recognition of David's terminally damaged authority. During her years as Director, it was Hounslow to whom she had grown the closest. He would help in navigating a particular issue or hint at what the others might be thinking and she had come to rely on his advice. However, the computing division was his weakest area of understanding and McGlynn could tell he was struggling to keep up while making copious notes in a leather-bound journal.

Five men and one woman. Hardly a poster for gender equality but the kind of ratio to which she had long been accustomed. When Aaron Castellane made the decision to sell his stake in the company, Turnbull, Hounslow and Stratton had each put forward possible replacements, all of which had been men. McGlynn shied away from these anyway given alliances between the non-executives would increase the chances of a consolidated vote. Instead, she asked for referrals from her own network and was again disappointed to find all the nominations had been male. Up to that point, she was involved in the expected activities of any influential businesswoman - mentoring other women in the company, speaking at local schools, acting as figurehead of the various diversity programmes within McGlynn-Lansing and beyond. However, the search for Castellane's replacement led to her rethinking this strategy and she now invested much more of her time supporting young female entrepreneurs. As was always the case when faced with an undesirable situation, she was actively working towards change, determined that any future replacement for her board would bring a different perspective.

'Eighteen percent,' said Bailey, finally looking up.

'Precisely,' replied Boland, as if merely confirming a figure he already knew. 'I'd like to see some follow up work here, specifically an action plan for additional cost control measures.'

'Do you have any initial suggestions, Christopher?' asked McGlynn.

'Of course, and I'd be glad to join the team in thinking them through.'

So, he would rather not have the discussion about Zhao's appointment in public yet, she thought, which was interesting given it would surface soon enough. I wonder what he's waiting for? To follow up now, with Boland having warned her off, would be a declaration of hostilities and she wanted more time to investigate his strategy before bringing him to battle on her own terms. Accordingly, she changed tack.

'I'm sure they'd appreciate that, thanks. Shall we move on to the Malmotec acquisition? I'd like to confirm our agreement to complete contracts as and when I see fit.'

'Yes, let's move on,' said Hounslow, pleased to be covering more familiar ground. 'Weren't you meeting with Fredrik Nilsson yesterday?'

'That's right. Thom and I joined Fredrik and his wife Annika for dinner. My sense is they're both involved in selecting an acquirer, and it's not just about the value of the offer.'

'Remind me of our current valuation?' asked Turnbull, straight to the only point which interested him. Once a banker, always a banker. 'Three fifty, wasn't it?'

'I think we should propose an indicative range at this time,' replied McGlynn. 'We talked about–'

'Yes. But what's your expectation in terms of a figure he'll agree to?'

'As I was saying, I want to provide only enough detail to secure Fredrik's sole interest before finalising in the coming months.'

'But you previously made the case for completing as soon as possible, didn't you, Wynter?' said Hounslow. 'What's changed your mind?'

'Annika Nilsson. Their son comes across as part of the deal. I think she wants Fredrik to transact with a buyer who'll look after him properly.'

'Did she tell you that?'

'No, but that's my strong instinct. I suggested Anders come and work with us while we conclude terms. I'm sure Rohan and his team can build a good relationship and make him feel at home here.'

'That's not something we've approved,' put in Turnbull sharply. 'And I don't like the idea. Too much could go wrong, leaving us with no contract and more months of lost time when we should have been investing in our own silicon plants. We should take the deal off the table now or not at all.'

'With due respect, Nick, you know opportunities like Malmotec don't come to market very often and we ought to act flexibly when they do. We agreed to acquire the production capability rather than grow it organically and I don't need your help on the negotiation.'

'We agreed you could go ahead but only at the right price. And I note you haven't answered my earlier question. How much?'

Bailey had been hugely resistant to Dalkeith's estimate of four hundred million when she raised it with him earlier. Nevertheless, there was no point in maintaining too low an expectation now only to necessarily come back and debate it again.

'I'm going to propose a completion range of three seventy-five to four twenty-five.'

'No chance! Not a fu– not a chance!' Turnbull nearly shouted. 'Are you kidding me right now? Three fifty was already a stretch given the substandard performance of the whole division and we're not paying not a red cent more! How the hell would you expect to justify an increase like that to the lenders, or even to the people in this room?'

'We've got competition,' said McGlynn evenly, paying close attention to the others in her peripheral vision. Even Stratton was more alert, a look of dull interest on his morose face. She was ready to provoke a full-scale argument, calculating a release of emotional energy now, over a theoretical issue like an acceptable price for Malmotec, would result in a more rational conversation when Boland raised the subject of the trial and she was forced to reveal news of Rohan's absence. 'Fredrik confirmed my suspicions last night. He's no fool, he knows he has a premium asset and knows what it's worth.'

'It's not worth four hundred and twenty-five mill, that's for damn sure. Not to us leastways.'

'It's worth whatever someone will pay for it, Nick.'

'Damian, how do you feel about this?' said Hounslow quickly, noting Turnbull's reddening neck.

'I've run the numbers and, er, believe we can extend if the Director thinks it's necessary,' said Bailey.

'And I'm not suggesting it is,' continued McGlynn without missing a beat, shielding him from the room's scrutiny. 'Not yet. But I need exclusivity with Fredrik, then some time to get Anders comfortable and only then can I propose completion at a lower amount.'

'I can't believe I'm hearing this, this… craziness,' said Turnbull, still furious. 'Based on no more than what your gut is telling you that Nilsson's wife may or may not want and what level of influence she may or may not have? Once you put a number like that in his head, you won't be able to back him down and you'll be stuck miles above the market price. I strongly, strongly recommend you call him back today and tell him the price is three fifty and we want contracts signed before the weekend or we walk. Christopher, perhaps you can talk some sense into our young friend here.'

Boland paused before replying.

'On balance, I'd be inclined to advocate for Wynter's proposal, at least conditionally. Provided we're able to manoeuvre as she suggests, then it's unlikely for the sale to proceed with another party and the delay benefits us alone. As to whether we end up at too high a price and are unable to retrench, Nick, then I suggest we rely on the Director's judgement here. Wynter, if you're sure Annika's blessing helps secure a lower figure at the cost of a few extra months, then you have my support.'

The whole room seemed wrongfooted by this response, none more so than McGlynn. Why was Boland suddenly making himself an ally?

'I appreciate that, Christopher. You mentioned some conditions though?'

'Perhaps. Who else do you think is in the running?'

'Fredrik confirmed he was talking to Dayton's but didn't budge on any others. Julian's sure to be as keen as we are and, if he won, we'd have find an alternative supplier.'

'Hmm, which would be inconvenient to say the least. I think it would be prudent to keep the four of us much more closely informed on progress, perhaps a weekly update until the next board meeting? In the meantime, let's use our personal networks to help identify the other names on Mr Nilsson's list.'

'Of course. Anything else?'

'Not at the moment. Elliott, what do you say?'

McGlynn noted the older man's relief at avoiding a major altercation. There would be no need to ask for Stratton's opinion given he would inevitably be led by the majority, meaning Turnbull was marginalised and would have to follow suit, like it or not.

'All seems very sensible to me,' agreed Hounslow. 'Wynter, are you happy to proceed on that basis?'

'Yep, that's fine.' She saw a still-annoyed Turnbull drawing breath and moved on, wanting to use her temporary advantage as a head start on the next issue. 'And as we've just mentioned them, this might be a good time for an update on our suit against Dayton's?'

'Yes please,' said Boland. 'And I think I speak for us all when I say we're particularly keen to know how you're preparing for the outcome, positive or negative.'

'OK, let me recap and I'll come back to that. As you'll remember, we conduct regular competitive analysis and found the latest release of their software includes features clearly copied from our own. At our December meeting, we therefore agreed legal action was required to protect–'

'I think you're overstating our level of commitment here,' cut in Turnbull. 'If I recall correctly, we discussed this in great detail and advised you against going to court.'

'And if I recall correctly, Nick, you were as convinced by this analysis as anyone and gave me sole discretion as to whether to proceed, discretion which I subsequently exercised. We're now in the fourth week of the hearing and expect to finish laying out our case later today or tomorrow.'

'What's your sense of our position?' asked Hounslow.

'You know Jacob Wiesenberg don't you, Elliott. For the rest of you, he's our lead counsel and not generally prepared to commit one way or the other. But in his view, it's looking favourable,' she said, stretching the truth. This was no time to display a lack of confidence, or mention Nilsson's ultimatum about winning the case, given more difficult news was yet to come.

'Good, good. And what do we stand to recover assuming Jacob's correct?'

'I'd expect Julian to appeal immediately which would delay payment of damages. He could yet try and settle during the appeals process but knows our asking price will go up accordingly. In addition to a public apology and removal of the disputed features, we're seeking sixty million in restitution. But that'll be subject to assessment once we've won.'

'If you win,' said Boland.

'When we win. And the cash will more than cover any extra costs for Malmotec,' she added, glancing in Turnbull's direction.

'Has Rohan testified yet?' continued Boland. 'He struck me as having both the charisma and the expertise to take the jury with him.'

'It's not a jury, it's a panel of expert judges and no, not yet.' McGlynn took a deep breath, rested her forearms on the table and interlocked her fingers, keeping her expression neutral. 'He was due to take the stand this afternoon but has been absent from work and out of contact with us since the weekend.'

She watched as reactions flowed around the room. Mild surprise from Stratton, horror from Bailey and Hounslow. Turnbull, having somewhat recovered his equilibrium, promptly lost it again. Only Boland managed to remain inscrutable.

'I'm sorry,' he said. 'Did I just hear you correctly? That Rohan Mehta, our head of technology and the key witness in this case, is nowhere to be found on the day he's due in court?'

'That's right.'

'Perfect,' said Turnbull, emphasising his derision with a wave of the hand. 'Just perfect. How in the hell could you let this happen?'

'I'm not Rohan's guardian, Nick. He seemed fine at work last week and even spent time with Jacob on Saturday preparing his testimony. As far as I knew, everything was on track.'

'Where do you think he is?'

'Unfortunately, I don't know.'

'Why would he have decided to leave?'

'Again, I don't know. He was as outraged as anyone by Dayton's use of his code, more so in fact. I'm pursuing a number of actions to re-establish contact but, if they're not successful, then I'll take the stand tomorrow instead.'

'This is very disappointing, Wynter,' said Boland. 'If you were the best choice to explain the more technical aspects of this issue, then presumably you'd have already been prepared and expecting to do so. What will the extent of the damage be if you lose?'

'I repeat, we're not going to lose.'

'Humour me. Us.'

McGlynn contained a sigh, not wanting to put into words what a negative outcome would mean but knowing it was her responsibility.

'I'd expect Julian to issue a counterclaim for defamation and costs. I would if I were him.'

'And what figure would that entail?'

'We'd have to take advice, but I'd probably want to settle out of court rather than allow it to drag on.'

The atmosphere in the room was becoming oppressive. Bailey looked stoically into the middle distance but the others were all staring at McGlynn - Stratton with curiosity, Hounslow with what seemed like a mixture of concern and regret, Boland and Turnbull with outright disapproval.

'Yes, and regardless of the financial implications, the reputational damage to the company would be significant,' said Turnbull, cold hostility dousing his anger. 'Damian, could I ask you to step outside please.'

Bailey looked to McGlynn. Once it was clear no counterviews were forthcoming, she gave what she hoped was a reassuring nod and he withdrew, closing the door much too quietly.

'Following on from Christopher,' continued Turnbull, 'I have to say your handling of this issue has been entirely dissatisfactory. We explicitly advised you not to proceed given these cases pivot heavily on the witnesses and, even then, verdicts are unreliable. Yet you chose to go against that advice likely, I suspect, because of your personal enmity with Julian Dayton.'

'That's not fair, Nick. This has nothing to do with Julian and me, this was about protect–'

Turnbull raised his hand to forestall her.

'I know you'll say that you've acted in the best interests of the company, and hence in ours too, but I think it's increasingly clear that your history with the Daytons, and that of your father and even your grandfather before you, clouds your judgement. You were far too eager to launch this case and now that Julian's in the running for Malmotec, you seem desperate to bid far more than it's worth. It goes without saying that Christopher, Brendan, Elliott and I rely on your judgement to deliver the best possible results for our investment. And I, for one, am losing conf–'

'Nick…' began Hounslow, seeing Boland start to nod.

'And I'm losing confidence in your ability to do that objectively,' concluded Turnbull.

In the ensuing silence, McGlynn fought to remain outwardly calm amidst a rising tide of emotions. She had inherited at least some of her father's temperament, especially when she felt she was being treated unfairly, and was livid at Turnbull's apparent willingness to threaten her in such an overt way. Although fully prepared to be judged on the success or otherwise of the calls she made, understanding such judgement was inescapably bound up with the authority she held, any criticism should be levelled after the fact, not before. The bid for Malmotec was still some way from being finalised and the case against Dayton's yet to be decided. These were everyday problems for someone in her position and unquestionably minor when set against the years of leadership, stability and financial returns she had delivered. Turnbull had no right to suggest otherwise.

Was he right to question her impartiality though? How much did she allow herself to be influenced by past events in making decisions where Julian Dayton was involved? Was she being fair in telling others or even telling herself she could be entirely rational as far as Dayton's company was concerned? Like her temper, McGlynn's self-esteem was underpinned by a solid foundation of fairness. If her personal agenda was indeed interfering with her duty to the company, then she ought to, and most certainly would, feel ashamed.

Anxiety stole like a rare predator into the pit of her stomach. The position of Director was untenable without the investors' confidence and the thought of being forced to hand over control to someone less proficient sickened her, knowing the years of meticulous planning and relentless execution would likely come undone. Feeling the weight of her predecessors, of their labour and sacrifice, she understood this could not be allowed.

Turnbull had placed one foot over a line beyond which there was no return but was too clever to risk isolation, suggesting he knew or at least firmly believed the others would lend him support. Which was it, the oldest, deepest part of her brain cried out – did he believe or does he know? Was he operating independently or had her position already been discussed behind closed doors? Boland would surely be his most likely collaborator but what about Stratton, even Hounslow?

To consider launching a coup, he or they must be convinced a replacement could be found. However, with the company's constitution clear on the prerequisites, any succession would require a McGlynn blood relative capable of assuming office. As far as she was concerned, there was no such person available, not yet at least, and this gave her an opening.

'I'm very sorry to hear that, Nick,' she began, choosing her words with exceptional care. 'I assure you no one takes their responsibilities towards McGlynn-Lansing more seriously than me. It's true we share a colourful history with the Daytons but wanting to beat them over and above any other competitor is a catalyst, a lightning rod if you will, which keeps us driving towards our full potential. They've been number one in most of our territories for a long time but we've moved clear of them in global computing and are closing the gap elsewhere. In my opinion, they're a useful and necessary evil and Julian is simply the figurehead in this endeavour, in no doubt the same way that I am to him and his staff. As such, I will not fail to act with the full power available to me if it prevents Dayton's or any other competitor from gaining an advantage and hence my interests are completely aligned with yours. All of yours,' she added, looking at each of them in turn. 'I believe I've proven beyond doubt over the last seven years that no one is better equipped to lead us to success, and I believe I deserve your ongoing confidence.'

She stopped and waited to see which of the four would speak first, knowing the answer could indicate how widely any conspiracy had spread. Unexpectedly, Stratton cleared his throat.

'I don't doubt your track record, Wynter,' he said in his melancholy brogue. 'But I think Nick's point is that it's difficult for us to believe you can be unbiased when it comes to dealing with Dayton's. Somewhat understandably, I should add.'

'I agree with Brendan,' said Hounslow. 'I think all we're requesting is for you to give consideration to our thoughts and allow us to help when the situation requires it.'

So, they had discussed her in private and as she suspected the power lay with Boland and Turnbull. The two men sat opposed, across the table, the others now outside her line of sight. Did they have enough influence to consolidate a vote against her if it came to that? Or would she be able to convince Stratton or Hounslow of their folly beforehand?

'I like to think I'm always open to advice, Elliott. But are you offering help or are you asking me to follow your instructions?'

'Let me be plain,' replied Boland, resuming control. 'Sometimes we're doing both. This company is not your private fiefdom Wynter, despite it bearing your family name.

With our guidance, I think you've done an acceptable job in sorting out the mess your father left behind. But we're not willing to allow you continued free rein when it comes to decisions carrying so much risk, especially when you're not getting them right. In future, these decisions will be made by us and implemented by you.'

Only an *acceptable* job in restoring the company's fortunes? McGlynn seethed at the lecture. Had he really used that word to describe all she had achieved? And to reapportion the credit to himself and his peers when he had joined the board with her personal approval long after she became Director, when these wealthy grey men with their abacus minds and dispassionate eyes flew in once every three months, to pick over her efforts and pronounce their findings in sombre tones.

'And if I disagree?'

'I think you know the answer,' said Turnbull.

'I'd like to hear you say it.'

'Then you will be replaced as Director.'

'By whom?'

'I know you believe there are no other options but, if it comes to it, we will find and appoint somebody who fulfils the bloodline requirements and who better understands their position.'

Transitioning into detached ruthlessness, McGlynn considered the problem. The non-executives could be bluffing, she suspected they were not. However, to continue enduring their will and decree would be to lessen the trust and potential of the thousands of people whom she and McGlynn-Lansing represented. The status quo would no longer do and she would have to find a way of changing the balance of power. But in the interim she would not, could not submit.

'Then I disagree,' she said. 'Once the case against Dayton's is won and I've signed Malmotec at a reasonable price, we'll talk about this again. And I look forward to a more open, more constructive discussion at that time.'

'Wynter, I would encourage you–...' said Hounslow, looking glum.

'No, Elliott. I don't need your encouragement. I need and expect a supportive board.' McGlynn rose from the table. 'Gentlemen, I believe we've finished earlier than anticipated. Natalie has ordered lunch which will be served in about half an hour. I regret that I'm unable to join you.'

Head held high, she turned on her heel and left.

11

'm sorry, Bill, and I know you're friends, but the man's a weasel,' said Malik, leaning against the edge of the editor's desk.

'We're not friends. But he is a friend of the Post. I've spoken with him several times and I can't say I recognise the person you've captured.'

Rutter, an untidy man with several chins, a receding hairline and a voice like whisky-soaked gravel had finished reading a first draft of her article and was slowly pacing back and forth, looking distinctly unhappy.

'I have multiple sources for everything, as usual. I promise you it's correct.'

'I'm sure, but the problem is that it's incomplete. You've put forward such a one-dimensional view of Julian himself that it's become an opinion piece. I only asked you to cover the job because Phil was away but this isn't what I commissioned you to write. Not in this case.'

'You've never worried about it before. You know I'm always well-researched. And I'm popular. My work gets eyeballs and commentary and delivers revenues. I'm still the highest trending writer on staff.'

He knew she was right on all fronts but Malik's personal popularity could not be written into their accounts, only the modest increase in sales and advertising revenues specifically attributable to her work.

'Maybe I should have paid closer attention. I heard from Vincent Evesham's lawyers last night.'

'Oh.'

'Oh, indeed. He wants an apology in the paper and online before the end of next week, or else.'

'He must realise there'll be a tonne of further exposure if he takes us to court. He can't seriously believe that's in his best interests. Or his wife's.'

'Who knows what drives a man like that? Maybe he's already had it out with Donna and she's leaving him. Maybe he never liked her in the first place and doesn't care what's said about them in public. But sooner or later, if you push someone too far, they'll take a stand just because they have less to lose than gain. The fees alone would wipe out our extra sales, let alone any damages.'

'We're insured aren't we?'

'Hardly the point. Our policy assumes we act in the public interest and try to stay on the right side of the law. If we become a regular litigation target, our premiums go up. We're going to have to be more careful.'

Malik exhaled slowly, tired after her long evening's work at the Establishment. Gone were the days when she could carelessly take to her bed after midnight, particularly on a Monday, and then be into the gym before six without it affecting her concentration at work. She inspected her French manicure with some small satisfaction and resolved to have an early night.

'Look Bill, I know this was supposed to be a PR piece but there's not enough core material to make it interesting. If all I can talk about are Dayton's new jobs and their basic trading stats, then it's going to be less than five hundred words buried in the business section somewhere. What's in it for us? We might as well not bother.'

You mean what's in it for you, thought Rutter, stopping and turning to face her. He remembered the day she interviewed for an internship during his first months as editor-in-chief. The oldest of the applicants by a couple of years, with the extra life experience and confidence to show for it, she had marched like Kashmiri royalty into this very office and told him, not asked, *told* him that he was going to offer her the placement despite a lack of relevant qualifications. To demonstrate why, she had given a ten-minute critique of the Post's underlying problems, illustrated not only with examples of shoddy penmanship and lacklustre graphics but, and this is what really impressed him, also with well-researched suggestions on how to improve the paper's cost base and morale. These were the traits he needed and which were almost impossible to teach - the wit to translate complex topics into digestible soundbites and the ability to extract more information from people than they might normally want to give.

She had since rewarded him by working like a Trojan, taking not a single day of holiday and spending so many hours in the office there was a running joke about her moonlighting as a security guard. After three months he managed to make her position permanent but could not begin to understand why she stayed. Not for the money. Like all his staff, she was paid in line with the dwindling rates of a declining industry although somehow still managed to dress well and live in an up and coming if rather bohemian part of the city. Nor for the glamour of a job which had personally cost him two marriages and the better part of his liver. And bizarrely, given her self-motivation and clear ambition, not for the career opportunities either. With her mental acuity, looks and poise she was a shoo-in for roles in front of the camera. He knew the big networks had tried to lure her away but apparently she had no interest in working in television or anywhere else.

From a professional standpoint, Malik was impressively selfish, always pushing to work on difficult, contentious pieces and wanting an unreasonable share of the Post's resources. Yet she was a closed book on a personal level and he knew nothing about her family background, personal relationships or outside interests. She remained a mystery - an industrious, beautiful and aloof enigma. Rutter generally tried to avoid thinking too hard about why she stayed and only remind himself to be grateful that she did.

It was no surprise she wanted to develop this straightforward assignment into a character assassination. Big business and especially the people who ran it seemed to fascinate her above all else, although provoking Julian Dayton was a dangerous step up from the likes of Evesham. Not only did he control one of the largest firms in the City, with the financial and litigious clout that involved, but Dayton Global Industries also maintained healthy marketing budgets and regularly bought premium advertising space. Rutter had no wish to make an enemy of the man, but neither did he want to shy away from pursuing news in the public interest or have the argument with Malik about backing off. He began to pace again while attempting to come down on one side or the other.

'Come on, Bill,' she resumed in her most persuasive tone. 'Let me run with this. The way they've offshored staff is nothing short of scandalous, as much for the use of cheap labour from oppressed countries as for the impact on the local economy. They've put at least two smaller City suppliers out of business because of chronic non-payment of invoices. And the culture towards the top is so toxic that pretty much everyone is frightened to speak out, particularly the women. I can see why having met him in person. I've heard of other malpractice too, I just can't prove it, not yet anyway. Their suit with McGlynn-Lansing is only one example and don't tell me it's baseless because I won't believe you. People deserve to know what it's like over there, what he's like. He's in complete charge, there's no one to hold him to account - no shareholders, no single regulator, nobody but us.'

'Ah, spare me the sermon, Sunita. And the suit with McGlynn's is coming to a close so there's no point in speculating on the result, we'll know whether it's baseless in the next day or so.'

'I'd bet you a week's wages he's guilty.'

'Mmm. And I suppose you'll claim it was a miscarriage of justice and not pay up if he's cleared, eh? As I said, I don't entirely recognise Julian Dayton from your draft. Can't say I particularly like him but nor do I get the sense he's a misogynist, double-dealing tyrant either. So how about this. I want you to write the piece that I asked for, just as Phil w–'

'But–'

'Wait a second. You can even attribute it to him if you want to protect your reputation as the guardian of City morality. In return, I'm OK with you spending more time on the man himself, but I want a balanced opinion. *Balanced*, yes? So, if I was you, I'd go down to the courts and listen to the verdict, see who's there and who cares whichever way it turns out. Speak to more people in Dayton's circle, get a view on him from his friends.'

'Huh. Far as I can make out, he doesn't have any.'

'Well talk to those who've known him the longest then. There are plenty of people across this town who–' Rutter had a thought. 'Listen, are you going to the Mayor's Ball tomorrow night?'

'Give me a break, who do you think I am? Cinderella? The mayor doesn't give out tickets to people like me. I'm not going to fund the new hospital or his campaign, am I?'

'Then find a way to get one. I couldn't afford a whole table and I'd imagine they're sold out now anyway. Julian will be there along with the great and the good from the business world. Work the room and I bet you can find a dozen or more people who are long-time friends with his parents and have known him since before he could walk. Get a backstory, figure out if the human being is as unlikeable as the businessman. Talk to his brother if he shows up too.'

'Eddie? Isn't he overseas?'

'I hear he's back in town and I don't think you'll have any difficulty in persuading him to spend time with you. Do the extra legwork and I'll consider running a story if you come up with a more open-minded portrait. Or if you can get proof he's acting illegally rather than just unethically. OK?'

'Yeah, alright. I'll look again but I can't see it changing my opinion. And I'll be back to get sign off sooner than you think.'

Don't I know it, thought Rutter, already looking forward to a lunchtime drink.

The bay's blue water was yet to be warmed by the longer days of summer and McGlynn shivered as she and Brookes made their way up what remained of the beach, swapping feedback on the session. She had swum parallel to the shoreline for thirty minutes in the swell of the arriving tide with Brookes, immersed up to the waist, calling out encouragement and instructions. Back and forth, back and forth, breathing on alternate sides every three strokes and lifting her head to check direction every nine. Exposed by the short wetsuit, her face, hands and legs stung like they had been sandblasted but she felt refreshed, clear-headed and rid of the board meeting's grime.

At the old boardwalk, close to where the banners and flags of the triathlon's starting line would be erected, the discussion moved on to tactics for the first segment. As they talked, McGlynn peeled off the suit and towelled vigorously before shrugging an old t-shirt over her damp swimwear, pushing her hair back with her fingers and slipping on some sunglasses. She sat on the bleached planking to soak up the heat, bare feet dangling over the dry sand. ML One stood three quarters of a mile away and she could see her tower's metalwork glinting in the brilliant sunlight.

'A thirty-two, thirty-three minute swim would be a good result,' repeated Brookes, as if trying to ingrain a mantra in a recalcitrant pupil. 'Don't forget the tide will only just have turned so there'll be more of a run down to the edge and the water will be much slacker once you're in. Use your speed, get to the front if you can and off your feet before everyone else. It doesn't matter if the faster swimmers go past you one at a time, you're much less likely to get a foot or an elbow in the face once you're away from the group. Focus on your stroke patterns, remember the bigger picture and don't waste energy thrashing around trying to go sub-thirty, you'll need it later on.'

'Gee thanks Andrew, you're full of positivity,' she laughed, nevertheless making the effort to commit his advice to memory. Brookes had dipped under two hours twenty on more than one occasion and knew what he was about. 'I'll be fine.'

'I'm not worried about you, Director, I just want to make sure I get the big bonus you're going to surprise me with in return for my superb coaching.'

'Ha! Now, fill me in on how's it going at the docks. Is Hugo close to finishing the report I asked for?'

'Yeah, but it probably won't be the one you wanted.'

McGlynn steeled herself.

'Go on then, what have you found?'

'It's what I haven't found that's more worrying. The physical security logs are incomplete for much longer than three months – there are entries without a proper signature and some missing altogether across site access, building access and container handling aboard and onshore.'

'Not good. What about the cameras?'

'Mixed. According to the ops manual, there are a total of sixty-three in the warehouse, in the compound, around the perimeter and on the dockside itself. I could only find fifty-four working, and the others–'

'What?' interrupted McGlynn, not believing what she had heard. 'How many?'

'Fifty-four. The other nine were disconnected at either the camera or the control unit. Carefully enough so you wouldn't notice unless you removed the casings.'

'When was the last security audit?'

'Last September and they were all signed off as operational back then. Each camera records twenty-four hours a day. Motion detection's enabled but if we really wanted to be thorough, that's over forty-thousand hours of footage a month to go through.'

'Which cameras were defective?'

'Warehouse doors one through four and the west side of the compound, both perimeter and internal.'

'But that section includes the gatehouse, doesn't it?'

'It does.'

McGlynn cupped her palms over her mouth and rubbed the sides of her nose with her fingertips to stifle the rising expletive.

'Who signed off last year's audit?'

'Hugo.'

'Right. Can you include a copy of it later please. What do onsite security have to say for themselves?'

'I've only talked with the morning shift so far but I'll get to the rest. There's a mix of excuses but I think it's pretty clear they've been told to keep quiet.'

'Who's the team lead?'

'He was let go a few months back. They kinda loosely report to a big guy, name of, um…'

'Jonah. Jonah Turner.'

'Yeah, that's him. He's following me around like a sick puppy.'

McGlynn sensed rather than heard a vibration and pulled out her phone, finding a message notification from Campbell. Hoping the detective had good news about tracking down Rohan or Wenling, she tapped into the application only to be disappointed by the reply - *Nothing yet*. Should she call her later in the day, the urgency with which she needed to talk with Rohan now outweighing the risk of the detective's own questions? Maybe. She certainly needed to make something happen rather than trust to luck and time.

'Do you want me to tell Turner to back off?' she asked, forcing her mind back to the immediate issue.

'Don't think so. The *Santa Rosa* docked a couple of hours ago. Reckon he's going to have his hands full right there. The thing's a floating mountain.'

'Twenty-thousand units, give or take. I told Hugo that I want every container double checked as it's brought ashore so unloading is going to be much slower than usual, even with the dogs and the multi-modal scanners. Can you make sure Turner and the team are kept on their toes please. Do some random process checks this afternoon, feel free to demand a few units are opened and inspected in front of you. And go aboard too, you can pick up a pass from the admin block, take a look around the holds and the superstructure. Let me know what you find.'

'Will do.'

'How about Hugo, is he being helpful?'

'When I've asked. But mostly he's just sitting in his office and leaving me to it. I've kept him in the loop with issues as I've found them. That OK?'

'Totally,' she said, wondering if he was drafting a letter of resignation instead of cooperating with Brookes. 'It's his job to fix them. I assume that's in progress?'

'Yeah. Want me to keep checking in with him for the rest of the week?'

'Uh-huh, please. I might need you to stay until we have a new security supervisor on staff, perhaps a whole new team if there's a real cultural problem. And tell Hugo to book a meeting with me tomorrow to discuss his report. At least an hour. I'm going to be out in the morning so it'll have to be after lunch.'

'OK. That's fine.' Brookes hesitated. 'There's one more thing though.'

'I'm not going to like this, am I, Andrew?'

'Nope.'

'OK, let's hear it.'

'You asked me to keep an eye out for anything to suggest we've had unauthorised access? Well, in the compound yesterday afternoon, I found discarded clothing and food in two of the empty containers. They'd been cleared out first thing this morning.'

'Oh fucking hell,' said McGlynn quietly.

Any remaining hope of Campbell being wrong was rapidly disappearing. She was going to have to start approaching the problem from the opposite angle, from the standpoint that McGlynn-Lansing staff were complicit in, or at least negligent of, stowaways making use of their vessels and premises. What was she going to tell the detective when they next spoke, or the mayor for that matter?

'Sorry Andrew, not your fault. Did you get pictures?'

'Of course. I'll send them over in the report.'

'Do you need any more people to help?'

'Not at this point. The rotas look fine so Turner and I just need to make sure they're being properly followed.'

'Do you think you can trust him?'

'No,' replied Brookes immediately. 'But I'm going to say that I'll be checking the video feeds at random. That should be enough until we can get someone more reliable. I've already put a few calls out.'

'OK. I'm free later if you want to talk but, if you can't reach me, try Jane Hallam. She's in Australia so just be aware of the time difference. We'll catch up again tomorrow lunchtime latest. And not a word to anyone about your findings until I've spoken to Hugo, clear?'

'Crystal.'

'By the way,' she added, remembering her earlier conversation. 'Matthieu says he had an odd phone call with someone claiming to work at the warehouse yesterday, name of Ben or Ken perhaps. Ring any bells?'

'Can't say it does. I can get a copy of the staff list if you like?'

'It's not a priority. Stay focused on the job in hand and I'll see you tomorrow.'

Much warmer now but hardly noticing the difference, McGlynn picked up her bag, wetsuit and sandals and set off for ML One.

The idea of Valente becoming a passive observer to his own responsibilities was another concern to add to her growing list. Once the security report had been delivered, she would make a second call to Hallam and see if she had been able to speak with him directly. Comparing Auntie Jane's feedback with that from Brookes should give her enough information to decide whether to relieve Valente of his duties at the port. If so, then McGlynn would have to ask Hallam to come over and cover the position herself - there was no one else who had the relevant knowledge and whom she trusted enough to step in at short notice. Such a scenario was highly inconvenient given the business development work in Brisbane, but leaving the man disengaged in role with Campbell's visit to the warehouse imminent was the bigger problem.

The temperature on the Esplanade was relentless, the hot concrete and stone making the air boil. Seagulls landed only to launch themselves skywards again as the sun sustained its attack from every angle. She rechecked her phone and saw time was running short to shower, change and find something to eat before heading across to City Hall. Briefly, she mulled whether to ring Matthieu and ask him to rearrange the appointment with Nathan Santoro for later in the week, thinking she could usefully spend the afternoon at the docks, but ultimately decided to leave things as they were. Brookes could be trusted to do a thorough job and she would have to meet the mayor soon come what may. Who knows, perhaps yesterday's unexpected invitation meant he had assistance to offer.

Quickening her step, McGlynn remembered her gentle chiding of Wiesenberg early that morning and a wry smile appeared. Hope was indeed a fickle mistress, but beguiling all the same.

12

C ity Hall was a fitting monument to the long-standing wealth and power of its surroundings, dominating the northern skyline of a busy Merchants Square. Massive Neo-Baroque architecture erected in pale grey stone, the colonnaded dome held a twelve-ton bell which chimed every quarter-hour and could be heard all the way to the old city limits. Twenty columns stretching the length of the frontage supported a triangular pediment with a frieze depicting the city's main activities at the time of its construction - fishing, finance, manufacturing, shipbuilding, trade. Ornately sculpted lions on cubic plinths guarded the steps up to the portico, the largest of which issued its snarling challenge dead centre.

McGlynn stepped from the car at the plaza's south-eastern corner and zig-zagged between long benches where shoppers and labourers, office workers and day trippers all rubbed shoulders alike. Younger children queued impatiently at the ice cream vans or played in and out of the fountains, their laughter as bright as the sunshine. She looked up at the building as she approached, feeling their shared history. Sitting upright in the chair next to her bed, McGlynn's great-grandmother had recounted the stories of how her own father had been in the crowds at the laying of the foundation stone and of his vow there and then to one day achieve the highest office the booming, bustling town offered. Her roots had become intertwined with the City's long before anyone heard the name Santoro.

Winding her way through groups of lolling students, she climbed the steps and into the shade of a grand entrance hall smelling of wax polish and age. The queues at the security arches were mercifully short and she arrived at the front desk with several minutes to spare.

'Good afternoon. I'm here to meet Mayor Santoro,' she said. 'Wynter McGlynn.'

'Thank you ma'am, just a moment please,' said the middle-aged receptionist. He examined her ID then tapped at his keyboard, printed a name badge, stuffed it into a plastic sleeve and passed it across the counter. 'The mayor's office is directly behind me, at the rear of the building. You can use the hallway at either side. Scan the code on the badge to get through the turnstiles.'

'Thanks.'

McGlynn let herself through the barrier on the left and walked along the panelled corridor, heels clicking on marble flagstones, browsing the oil paintings on the western wall until she came, exactly as she remembered, to the picture of her great-great-grandfather. Looking much the same age as she was now, Jim Lansing had been depicted hard at work behind a large wooden desk wearing a dark jacket and tie, the hue of his moustache a shade deeper than the fair hair swept back from a high forehead. He was reading a document with a serious expression seemingly at odds with the charismatic figure of her bedtime stories, the self-made man who drove the City's progress faster and further during his term of office than many others who held the post before or since. Although there was little by way of family resemblance, the few times she had seen Lansing's portrait always brought her comfort and inspiration, an enduring reminder of the potential that ran in her blood and reinforced her determination to succeed. Passing by, she wished him a silent, thankful greeting.

The reception area at the end of the corridor was smaller than at the front but no less opulent, evidently designed to impress those lucky enough to be granted an audience with the incumbent. A stern-looking woman in a scarlet cravat sat behind the countertop, guarding floor to ceiling double doors.

'Mrs McGlynn?'

'That's right.'

'Welcome to the Mayor's Office at City Hall. May I offer you some refreshment?'

'I'm fine thank you.'

'Then please make yourself comfortable and he'll be right with you.'

McGlynn initially stood, expecting no more than a short delay given her arrival at the prearranged time, but crossed the antechamber and sat on an overstuffed chaise longue beneath a seascape when it became clear she would be kept waiting. At nearly ten past the hour, a brass handle opposite jerked downwards and the door swept inwards to reveal none other than the mayor himself.

'Wynter! So great to see you! So sorry I kept you, come in, come in!' he enthused, breathless with the career politician's bonhomie.

'Hello Nathan,' she said with a smile as genuine as she could muster. 'Good to see you looking so well.'

Mayor Nathan Santoro, known as Nathaniele to his family and Nate to his friends and donors, did indeed look surprisingly healthy given the gross corpulence which was as much a part of his public image as the loud-mouthed, bombastic rhetoric. No grey in his hair, no bags beneath the beady eyes, no wrinkles in the fleshy, unctuous face radiating self-confidence and excitement and goodwill in equal proportions. Though noticeably shorter, he easily weighed twice as much as McGlynn but trod so gracefully he almost danced over the carpet. Crossing the threshold, she felt him place a welcoming hand in the small of her back - low enough to be suggestive, high enough to avoid reproach.

The mayor's office was expensively appointed, the decor fresh and tasteful. Paintings of racehorses and sailing ships in golden Rococo frames offset dark wooden panels shining with new oil. Half the spotless cream carpet was covered by a burgundy Chinese rug, perhaps a gift from a visiting ambassador, on which lay a horseshoe of upholstered sofas capable of seating twenty or more around a huge fireplace. Supplementary lighting had been hidden within the alcoves and above the cornices to help the old wall lanterns banish the gloom and she could see neat lawns and shrubbery through the French doors to the rear.

Santoro returned to sit behind his desk, different to the item in Lansing's painting but still solid and imposing amidst the trappings of civic authority. Unsure whether to be grateful for their physical separation or wary of his psychology, perhaps both, McGlynn chose the centre of three wood and leather captain's chairs opposite. Despite being seated, the mayor still seemed as tall as he was wide and she idly speculated whether his toes reached the floor with the chair cranked to such an elevated position.

'I'm so pleased you were able to come and visit!' he gushed. 'It's been far too long!'

'I'm sure you're a busy man. How are things?'

'Very good, excellent in fact! Knife and gun crime are down, unemployment down, local taxes down. Better grades for the majority of school leavers than ever before, more hospital beds within ten miles of the City than ever before. We're making a difference, Wynter, that's a fact, making a difference!'

McGlynn stayed abreast of local issues and recognised the select statistics masking a much more variable picture of Santoro's achievements. Even so, she grudgingly admired the fluency of his delivery. These succulent soundbites no doubt found their way from interviews and speeches into news bulletins and papers, from there syndicated without critique across social media to osmotically become the overriding truths of a torpid electorate.

'Well, congratulations. The City deserves a strong and effective administration. Do you still plan to improve corporate taxation before the end of your current term?'

'Ah ha! Always loved that about you, Wynter, straight to the point! Great question! I'm pleased to say we're still consulting with the relevant parties but will be issuing a new whitepaper in the coming months. Can I get a copy sent to you?'

'If that's no trouble. And I'd be very happy to contribute to the process too. Several areas haven't been touched for decades and need a lot of attention.'

'I'll have one of my team arrange a follow up meeting,' he said with plausible sincerity, making no move towards the jotter on the desk's leather surface. 'And how about you? Business is booming I trust?'

'Yes, we're doing very well.'

'Fantastic to hear! The treasury remains exceptionally grateful for your success. Although, ahem, on a slightly less positive note I was disappointed to read that you've found yourself in court with Julian Dayton?'

'Disappointed because you believe our case is misplaced?'

'No, no, not at all. That'll be for the court to decide, I'm sure. But it's always unfortunate to see two of my largest employers having to settle their differences in public.'

'Always, but I'm sorry to say I was left with no other choice. I'm sure you understand.'

'Indeed I do, Wynter, indeed I do. We must always protect our legitimate interests while serving the wider needs of the community, particularly when the two coincide, no? I had the pleasure of discussing exactly this at lunch with Commissioner Petrucci. He's doing a fine job under the most difficult of circumstances, don't you think?'

'The police certainly seem to have their work cut out at the moment,' she said, trying to balance the close relationship between the two men with the truth.

'Regrettably so. The devil makes work for idle hands and the masses have become restless. It's a cyclical thing, you know, like the seasons but over a much longer timeframe, and has always been a downside of self-governing communities. An incontrovertible by-product of democracy is the illusion that life should always be better than it is today, will always be better, simply through the power of casting a vote. Now don't get me wrong, I'm a true, flag-waving believer in the beauty of the democratic process, living proof in point of fact. But after too long in the same situation, even if that situation's one of freedom and peaceful prosperity, the hive mind begins to crave change. But the pursuit of change by one portion of the population creates resistance in the other, you see, and that resistance creates unrest. Change has become the right of the people whether they're choosing a new government, a new mayor or simply new circumstances and a lack of change therefore becomes equally unsettling after a time. I tell you Wynter, the masses are restless, their hands are idle and they need a distraction. They need to be entertained, they need to feel as though they've exercised their right to self-determination, their right to choose.'

'Well, um, I guess there are the local elections next year and the national election the year after that. Plenty of opportunity for people to exercise their democratic rights?'

'Absolutely, absolutely. And I hope to persuade my fellow citizens that I deserve their trust for another term. Of course, there are a number of key issues which I believe ought to be of paramount importance for the people when they make their choice at the ballot box. One such issue, an ongoing challenge for us all as I'm sure you'd agree, is the seemingly unstoppable rise in illegal immigration we're witnessing.'

McGlynn saw little point in trying to sidestep what was coming.

'I'm sure that's true, Nathan. Nobody wants immigration to be undertaken through anything other than the proper channels. I had a visit from the police yesterday on this very topic.'

'I have to admit I was aware of that being the case,' he replied, making a convincing attempt to look sheepish. 'Yes, very unfortunate, but it's nonetheless of vital importance for the Commissioner to leave no stone unturned in closing off the entry routes used by those trying to enter the City illegally. May I, ah, ask your views on the likelihood of them finding any evidence of your involvement?'

'McGlynn-Lansing makes every effort to comply with both the letter and the spirit of the law wherever we operate around the world. Never more so than in our home port. If any evidence of our involvement is found, knowingly or unknowingly, I will take the swiftest possible action.'

'I would never doubt it.' Santoro's companionable demeanour was now gone, replaced by a more serious tone. 'But I'm sure Commissioner Petrucci would be interested in your views. The police have a very long list of possible areas to investigate and would no doubt prefer to concentrate on those most likely to yield the best outcomes.'

McGlynn shifted slightly in her chair, her thoughts alive at the implications of these words. Had she just heard the City's highest ranking official correctly? That the second highest ranking official could be persuaded to divert police attention away from her company and look elsewhere? A few weeks to finish her internal review and fix the problems it was uncovering before Campbell's team began could be enormously valuable. But why would Petrucci be open to such an idea? Was he or Santoro offering a deal and, if so, on what terms?

'Thank you for the kind suggestion, and I'd be grateful for the opportunity to speak with the Commissioner.'

'Excellent. I'm sure I could arrange it for you, sooner or later. It's such a shame his hands are tied by the federal legislation in this area.'

'It is?'

'Yes. I happen to know he would rather attend to other, more important concerns than devote further man hours trying to meet the unachievable targets set by the Capital.'

'I see. And which other areas do you believe he would like to prioritise?' she asked, probing for the conditions which would clearly govern any introduction.

Santoro leant back in his chair and steepled his stubby fingers.

'Oh, there are so many local issues more deserving of attention, however mundane they may sometimes be. Old fashioned neighbourhood policing, domestic and online abuse, burglary and fraud to name but a few. These are the things which I believe matter most to the good people and the businesses of this fine city, of the whole region in fact. I'll be doing my best on the campaign trail, on the doorsteps and in the hustings, to explain how difficult it is for City PD to balance the competing local and national agendas but I fear neither I nor my rivals will be able to make a full and proper justification. I know policing is only one example but perhaps that's the point, that the wider issues aren't justifiable, that the agendas can't be reconciled.'

McGlynn wondered why the mayor had returned for the third time to the friction between the city's police and the state's priorities, knowing tension between the holders and executors of power in a shared environment was inevitable and unlikely to materially change. At least this was her assumption. Regardless, there was little enough she could do to persuade the Capital to devolve more of the national budget or decision-making to the regions, if indeed that was his objective.

'I suspect such agendas will always overlap and therefore compete to some extent?' she asked, probing again. 'It's an unavoidable by-product of the relationship between local and national government, no?'

'Exactly right, precisely right, couldn't agree more. But... what if there was no relationship? What if I was able to offer the people their democratic right to make *that* choice?'

The mayor's true intent hit McGlynn like a freight train, her jaw almost dropping in surprise. Santoro was renowned for his greedy ambition but even so, it seemed she had vastly underestimated its proportions.

'Sorry, help me out here, Nathan. Am I correct in saying you propose to stand for re-election on an independence ticket? Is that what I just heard?'

'As I say, I propose to stand on the issues that matter most to the people I represent,' he beamed. 'But yes, I believe their interests, our interests, are best served by a future of self-determination. It's a fact that the City and the wider region, from Six Hills all the way to Newstead County, have been on a diverging course from the Capital for years, decades even. We have always had, and I believe we always will have, a fundamentally different outlook on virtually every topic imaginable. Moral and social values, healthcare, foreign policy, maritime jurisdiction, religion, economic and environmental responsibility, the list goes on and on. Our economy already represents more than fifteen percent of national GDP and is growing at nearly twice the national rate but all that effort - our work, our innovation, our increased productivity - is diluted by federal statute and leached away to the short- and long-term benefit of others many miles away. These distant lawmakers are the kind of people who prefer to look down instead of up, socialists who find it inconvenient to admit their reliance on our successful capitalist culture. They represent communism by another name and the time when we needed a marriage of mutual convenience with them and the rest of the country has long since passed. We're being held to ransom, strangled by an unfair tax model while we continue to waste our time and fritter away our resources on irrelevant national projects. Now is the time for change, Wynter, the polls are irrefutable, now is the time for independence.'

Her mind reeled. How had she not anticipated the mayor's plans? There had been no hint in the media, nothing during their previous meetings or via her social or business networks but some of the recent publicity coming from City Hall made much more sense in this context. What could he possibly want from her?

'It would be an incredibly bold move. But I'm slightly at a loss as to why you're giving me a preview of your campaign strategy.'

'It's obvious isn't it? I want you to join me.'

Now there were two types of career politician by McGlynn's reckoning. The first were the well-meaning souls who possessed near endless patience and had made peace with the need to occasionally compromise their principles in the pursuit of their goals. Such do-gooders tended to endure long stints of prosaic but essential service and short bursts in the spotlight where, in their rare exposure to the public's gaze, they looked harassed but quietly determined. The second group were those who lusted after power for power's sake, driven by nothing other than ego. These were the energetic and polished leaders who unapologetically clawed their way to the top and spent at least as much time in developing their media persona as they did on their citizens' behalf. Each produced wildly different results and identifying one type, for example Nathan Santoro, from the other was no more than a moment's work. McGlynn knew she lacked the underlying qualities of either and had therefore never entertained the idea of joining their ranks.

'I don't follow. I'm not interested in a political career.'

'Ah ha,' chuckled the mayor. 'Forgive me for not being clear. I'm not suggesting you join my staff, absolutely not in fact. Between you and me, I much prefer to work with people who are slightly more, um, obedient. But I am seeking the support of the brightest and best in City society, those upstanding citizens who already shine as examples of what we would collectively become within a successful, vibrant, independent nation. I don't know your political persuasion or whether you even took part in the previous election and honestly, I don't really care. But what I would like this time around is your vote. And I would like it in public.'

So, the mayor's price for redirecting the police was her support for both his campaign and the idea of an independent City. Her first instinct was to decline, but then she had never really contemplated the pros and cons in detail before - the likelihood of such a vote had always been so remote as to not be worth her time. What was the right thing to do? What was the best choice for her and her family, for McGlynn-Lansing, the population of the City, the country? She wanted space for reflection but Santoro would no doubt demand an answer soon, maybe even today.

'Do you believe you have the ability to secure the Capital's agreement to a popular vote?'

'I do indeed. The Assembly is split as never before with more than two years yet to run. No one believes the current party leaders will survive for long after the next election, no matter who wins. There are reputations to be made, ambitions to be secured, platforms to be built. The Capital is divided and we have an unprecedented position of strength from which to negotiate terms. We can be a strong ally for the leader of a new government when the time comes, or a fierce critic beforehand.'

'What about Weissmann?'

'Weissmann? That old fool? He's become weak, intimidated by the minority voices in his own party and beyond. His opportunity is still there, to consolidate the centre ground and stand up for what's actually a majority view if only he would take the necessary action, but his views are unfashionably out of sync with media hysteria and I believe he's lost whatever *cojones* he once had to risk or endure the initial vilification. Weissmann's done. He and his cronies need to move aside and allow a new generation to come through.'

'Mmm, you're probably right. But whoever leads the future government, they're going to need the City's economic contribution. They won't be able to deliver on the existing social and infrastructure programmes without us, never mind taking on some of the bigger problems still to be addressed.'

'They're not our problems to fix, Wynter. Why should we bankroll an inefficient, lazy nation?'

'Because if we vote for independence and break away from the country, there might be a short-term improvement for us, counterbalanced by a short-term deterioration for them, but what happens beyond the first few years? Would we really stand idle as our former compatriots, the only nation with whom we would share a land border, suffered? There's already too big a gap between the richest and poorest in this country, actually in most countries, and our independence would widen it further. The Capital's problems would inevitably become our problems again due to geography or conscience or influence from our trading partners and allies around the world. Our mutual problems would still need to be solved and hence arguments would still need to be won. I suspect both of us would rather we were on the inside of those debates, not on the outside throwing rocks or meekly offering unwanted help. An independent City would become a peripheral, relatively unimportant stakeholder.'

'We'd be focused on our own agenda. That's not a bad thing.'

McGlynn worked through the underlying argument for a moment.

'Look, if you wind it all back to the fundamentals, never mind what you and I might think, people generally believe in collectivism and in the humanitarianism which borrows our family name. The–'

'Let me stop you right there. You see I don't believe that's the case at all. Self-determination, individualism, that's what the people want, what they believe in, the ability to stay in control of their own destiny. The self-reliance and freedom of action which makes our culture so strong, so flexible.'

'Sorry Nathan, but I disagree. Freedom of action might be what people want on a day-to-day basis, me included, but the ability to cooperate effectively and the desire to help each other are two of the principal reasons we've thrived beyond all other species. They're what took humanity from primate groupings through tribalism and into nationalism. That evolution was probably motivated by our core personal and social needs which are now more or less guaranteed, I grant you, but just think about all the communal progress we've been rewarded with along the way, all the shared knowledge of which you and I are the beneficiaries. The creation of the internet proves my point. In less than a decade it overran national borders and conventional organisational structures, allowing communities to form organically and work together on the world's biggest problems. It achieved all this by simply offering people what they wanted, what we've always wanted - the opportunity to work and play nicely with others. If we reverse that trend, if we subdivide and classify ourselves into ever smaller societies, we weaken the ties that bind us and slow down the future progress we absolutely have to make. It's not in anyone's long term interests to do that, least of all those of our future generations. For example, if I took your argument for self-determination to its next logical iteration, I could declare McGlynn-Lansing as an independent state and claim our property and our people as my own. I'd stop paying tax and my GDP per capita would far outstrip yours but would that be a good thing? Would you support our right to independence?'

'It's not a valid argument. You wouldn't have the resources necessary to sustain yourselves as an independent entity. We do. We should.'

'I'm not sure that's true. An independent City would still have to be a net importer, more so perhaps. The national economy and natural resources are much better balanced right now.'

'No, you're wrong. Our economy is well-balanced. We have a healthy mix of skilled, professional services workers alongside mature manufacturing, agriculture and fishing industries. We make a fiscal surplus and have the financial muscle to mean we'd always be negotiating from a position of strength. And we have enough people to effectively operate the machinery of statecraft, essential for any nation who would otherwise be bullied by larger blocs. We'd be able to agree on our own legislature and trade on our own terms rather than have to drag the rest of the country with us.'

'Isn't that to the point of my hypothesis?'

'Well, what if I took the counterargument, your argument on collectivism to its extreme? Does the human race really want to aggregate into larger and larger entities? I don't think so. None of the various empires have ever lasted - Mongol, Roman, Ottoman, Spanish, British - they all failed. People don't want to work together at that kind of scale.'

'All of those were built through force. People don't want to be coerced into working together, how they should behave, what they should believe. We want to work it out for ourselves. What is a country, a state? It's not a landmass, not arbitrary lines drawn on a map, it's a largely stable collective of people who for whatever reasons have come to believe in mostly the same things and want to live and work and simply exist with others like them. You can't build an empire or even a long-lasting country through coercion, you have to build it through peaceful argument, through influencing hearts and minds, and that takes time. And you have to carefully dismantle centuries of cultural memory, all that bad blood and jingoism, and have some luck along the way - the situations, convenient or otherwise, which make people realise it's better to cooperate than isolate. Various continents are already on the same journey and just look at the mountain of problems yet to be climbed. So instead of empires built through consensus, and in place of the wider collectivism they would represent, we currently have to use internationalism as a proxy to achieve the same end result. To that point, I agree with you about the associated bureaucracy, it's all horribly inefficient. All of those interminable negotiations, the management of day-to-day processes, tit for tat sanctions, resorting to wars when diplomatic disagreements become too profound. It's a necessary evil given our process of global civilisation still has centuries, maybe millennia left to run. But it's a waste, an unforgivable waste of our time and potential. And a vote for City independence is a vote to make it worse, to erect new boundaries and create unnecessary work whilst only prolonging the inevitable.'

'I'm telling you, Wynter, you and I have a once in a generation opportunity to help deliver the freedom this exceptional City deserves. We're one people, united by a common cause and ready to step into our rightful place in the world. You have as much to lose as everyone else if things remain as they are, more perhaps. But it sounds like you've already made up your mind? I have to say I'm very disappointed if that's the case.'

McGlynn thought about this. She recognised her own deep-rooted values and beliefs in their discussion so far but was her mind truly made up? Not yet. Despite her principles, she was still subject to human nature, to selfishness, to

Darwinism, perpetuating her own survival by whatever means necessary. If she accepted Santoro's proposal, her immediate interests would be aligned to his and a call to Commissioner Petrucci presumably forthcoming. To deny she was tempted would therefore be to deny her own humanity.

'At this point, all I'm saying is that we have much more to unite than divide us. But what would happen if we voted yes? Who's in charge and where does an effective opposition come from?'

'Well naturally there would have to be a short-term government to maintain stability. And on the basis of my manifesto, I would have the mandate to lead it. But it wouldn't be a dictatorship if that's what you're hinting at, you know as well as I do there are plenty of people desperate to take my place. We'd organise free and fair elections in due course.'

This is another part of the problem, she thought, and the real reason why Santoro would not debate a hypothetically autonomous McGlynn-Lansing. Egotistical leaders required individualism to stop at their level in a hierarchy defined on their terms. A separatist conveniently promotes independence and freedom of action, knowing it supports their personal agenda and appeals at face value to the electorate, but only to the point where their position of leadership is retained, otherwise the leader's own authority and their vision of the independent state is further delegated and lost. The status quo exists solely once their personal ambition has been fulfilled and prevails only until a new challenger emerges with different opinions and the ambition to take some or all of that society in yet another direction.

Equally, whether a democracy or a dictatorship, protecting and fomenting every nation's self-identity through the fallacy of patriotism must be a primary focus of its leader as, without distinction from others, national borders dissolve and positions of leadership become redundant. Independence, Santoro and his personal vision of an independent City therefore all came as a package and the mayor - as what, president? - would immediately assume and attempt to retain executive powers lying a long, long way outside his current remit. Yes, there would be elections but they could be years away. What damage would a President Santoro inflict in the meantime?

'There's a lot to be thought through here, Nathan.'

'Unfortunately, time's not on our side. Not for me given my re-election campaign launches in less than sixty days and especially not for you. So I suggest you think fast.'

He stood, having evidently achieved his objectives for the meeting and ready for McGlynn to leave.

'Should I expect the pleasure of your company at the Portland tomorrow evening?'

'Yes,' she replied, also rising. 'We've a couple of tables.'

'Then I'll come and find you after dinner perhaps and introduce you to my campaign manager, Kip.'

'Kip Cox? I thought he was in Weissmann's camp?'

'Like I said, Weissmann is done. Kip's reputation is built on winning which means he only wants to work for people he knows are going to get elected, or re-elected. Like me. He'll outline the event plan and timings for you. I can't promise anything but I'll also see if I can talk to Commissioner Petrucci, and find out if he's free for your call before the weekend. I'm not asking for much of your time here, just your willingness to support a better future, a future in which you and your company would continue to prosper.'

Santoro took McGlynn's hand and held it firmly, full of geniality and good intention once more.

'It's been so wonderful to see you again, Wynter, it really has, but now if you'll excuse me, I need a few minutes to prepare for my next meeting.'

McGlynn was grateful for a dismissal which avoided further contention and, in particular, further commitment. As the mayor closed the door behind her, she said goodbye to the stern-looking woman and slowly made her way back towards the main concourse, lost in thought until reaching Lansing's portrait on the wall.

What would you do Jim, she wondered, stopping to look up at his picture. You certainly faced your fair share of challenges and would have fought and cajoled and compromised on all sides to get what you ultimately believed in. Would you take the mayor's deal?

No doubt contemplating the important issues of an evolving municipality, Lansing's handsome face remained focused on his paperwork but she heard his reply all the same. Do your duty Wynter, he said from across the ages, that is all any of us can do, what we must do.

She walked on, wondering to whom her duty lay.

13

Fredrik Nilsson looked at his wife, unsure how to respond. They had been held captive for nearly two hours now, attempting to answer endless questions from one dour, inflexible man while another looked on.

'I mean, Anders wouldn't want to relocate, would he?' asked Dayton in follow up to Sandy White's query. 'So a fixed transition period would make sense before terminating his employment? If three months isn't enough, we could perhaps stretch to six, maximum?'

'And what would you suggest my son does then?' asked Nilsson.

'He'd need to observe the non-compete clauses in the contract but other than that, I'd imagine it's up to him. He must have other interests, hobbies.'

'He's not yet thirty. I do not think a man should consider retirement at such an age.'

'Well then, he's certainly old enough to look after himself. I'm afraid we don't see a place for him here.'

'I think that's very different from what we already agreed but yes, I believe we now understand your position completely. And this figure here,' continued Nilsson. 'What is this?'

'Those are the cost savings we expect to realise in the first twelve months post-completion, the synergies we'll want you and Anders to help us identify. We have some ideas of course.'

'Which are?'

'The first thing is to move production to a cheaper location, one with capacity for growth without a straight-line increase in cost. We already have several offshore sites which could accommodate a new plant considerably larger than yours. We'll keep research and design in Sweden for now and move remaining roles here. These changes alone should save about sixteen million a year.'

'What happens to the staff in Lund?'

'Once the new facility's ready, a few will be offered relocation and the rest will be given severance.'

'And what level of attrition is represented by this number, these synergies? How many people do you plan to let go?'

'Not sure. Sandy?'

'We've assumed a ninety percent reduction in factory staff,' said White in his dry monotone. A quiet, unimaginative man, he was nevertheless dogged and detailed, the two qualities which had kept him above the cannon fodder but below the parapet during his long service. 'About three hundred give or take.'

'Eh? Three hundred? But our factory is the area's largest employer. To simultaneously remove three hundred jobs would be a disaster for the local economy, and for the families involved.'

'All very unfortunate,' said Dayton. 'But we can't make our offer work unless we reduce costs immediately. Luckily, not many of your staff are union members. As I understand it there's no legal requirement for redundancy pay beyond their normal notice periods.'

'The law may not require this but most of them have been with us for years.'

'And I'm sure such loyalty will go down well on their job applications.' Dayton was keen to move on from such a distasteful topic. 'Now, I think Sandy and I have covered all our questions but do you have any for us, Fredrik?'

Nilsson glanced at Annika again. Invariably, when visiting their summerhouse on the beach at Öland, they would renew old friendships over a few hands of bridge and several glasses of the local wine. However, no one would play them for serious money anymore. To the two men opposite, Annika appeared impassively neutral. To her husband and long-standing bridge partner, her opinion of both the conversation and these men was unmistakable. But, *vid Oden's kuk*, four hundred and twenty million was a lot of money in anyone's language and he was not yet ready to dismiss Dayton's from his carefully curated shortlist.

'Thank you but no, I don't think so, Julian. We need some time to ref–'

'In that case I'd like to move to contracts as soon as possible,' said Dayton. After Malik's rumours, he was increasingly anxious to secure a written commitment before anyone else could cut in, *her* in particular. 'Shall I have an exclusivity agreement drafted for this afternoon? And, er, I'd also like to invite you both to join us at the Mayor's Ball tomorrow evening. To celebrate.'

Truly an unpleasant man, thought Nilsson. How vulgar to assume a high bidding price outweighed all else and to consider celebrating the loss of three hundred of my countrymen's livelihoods. What an anticlimax it is to find someone of his calibre running a business the size of Dayton Global Industries. Perhaps the City wasn't a suitable place to sell the lion's share of the company after all, even though it might be very entertaining to stay while the remainder of the lawsuit with Wynter McGlynn played out.

'Thank you for your kind invitation,' he said, knowing without looking what his wife's view would be. 'But I'm afraid we have to decline. And now, I'm sorry to say, we really must be going.'

'But it's held at the Portland,' said Dayton feebly, unsure what to say next which might secure another meeting, another chance to press for a signature. 'It's the best hotel in the City. Everyone who's anyone will be there.'

Hearing a slight noise, he saw the boardroom door opening in his peripheral vision but desperately maintained eye contact with Nilsson.

'Not now. I told you we were not to be disturbed,' he barked. 'Not now.'

'I'm sure Mr and Mrs Nilsson won't mind, Julian,' said a calm and cultured voice.

Not believing his ears, Dayton's head snapped to the side and came face to face with his brother, only thirty years older. The same features, same build, same solidity of movement but with greyer hair, deeper lines and the gravitas which comes with long experience. Radiating goodwill, the man advanced into the room and shook hands with each of the Nilssons in turn.

'Hello Fredrik, hello Annika. I'm Richard Dayton. It's an absolute pleasure to meet you.'

'Da– Richard, what are you–' blustered Dayton. 'I didn't know you were due. Fredrik, this is my fath–'

'That's quite alright,' interjected the older man, drawing up a chair alongside the visitors. 'When I heard we had such important guests, I immediately cancelled my plans and caught the next flight. Have you enjoyed your trip to the City so far, Annika? I hope our hospitality hasn't been found wanting?'

'We have very much enjoyed the last few days,' she said carefully. 'It's a beautiful stretch of coastline and reminds us both of the Øresund, the strait between–'

'Between Sweden and Denmark,' he finished for her, his interruption somehow welcomed as a compliment. 'Yes, I know it well. I've driven across the bridge many times in visiting Stockholm and you're absolutely right, we're both lucky to be based in such picturesque parts of the world.'

'You live here too then, Richard?' asked Nilsson politely.

'Ah, sorry for the confusion but I meant the company. No, not anymore, alas. My wonderful wife Vanessa and I have a house on the Thames just west of London. It's not exactly a hardship but we miss spending time here, especially the summers. Oh dear,' he added. 'It looks like we're lacking any proper refreshment. Could I offer you some afternoon tea? Coffee if you prefer?'

'No thank you,' said Nilsson after a moment's reflection. 'But some mineral water would be welcome.'

'Sandy, would you mind?' asked Richard affably. 'Now then Fredrik, Annika, I believe you're still considering whether we're a suitable home for your potential divestment, is that correct? If so, I'm very interested in your thoughts regarding Julian's offer, particularly any areas of concern you might have.'

'I've already asked if–' began Dayton.

'The headline offer is a good one,' interrupted Nilsson. He and Annika had turned to face Richard, leaving Dayton himself stranded on the other side of the table. 'But a few drawbacks remain.'

'Oh dear, these should have already been addressed. Please, tell me what's on your mind and if I can reassure you of our commitment, then I certainly shall.'

The two men began to discuss the structure of the bid, Nilsson quickly warming enough to raise topics he had previously withheld, including his intention to delay a final decision until after the outcome of McGlynn's litigation. Dayton tried repeatedly to join the dialogue but his arguments, the succinct and pertinent points which demonstrated his thorough understanding of the proposal, were ignored like flies dancing on a windowpane. Eventually he capitulated to become an impotent spectator, then was demoted further to the role of waiter when the mineral water arrived. He ended up forgotten entirely, slumped in his chair and blowing out his cheeks like a sullen teenager.

That Richard had come unannounced within a day of Eddie's return bothered him almost as much as the fact someone must have tipped him off about this meeting. Dayton generally chose not to believe in coincidence and his father's obvious and unending mistrust of his ability remained an open wound. Why was he really here? Did he not have confidence in these negotiations concluding successfully or had he heard they were actually at risk? If the latter, then from whom? Was Richard here solely to meet the Nilssons or were there other reasons for his decision to travel? Had he spoken to Eddie? He churned through possible scenarios, retaining the more feasible while discarding those even he recognised were probably a result of paranoia. After a time, a subtle shift in the conversation's rhythm dragged his concentration back to what were evidently the closing points.

'I understand your views completely,' his father said as the three of them rose. 'Let me work through the issues you've raised and perhaps we can follow up once the case with McGlynn-Lansing has been won. Would Monday be convenient?'

'That would be most kind of you,' said Nilsson. 'Our flights are booked for Saturday but we may stay longer.'

'Not at all. I wouldn't like to be presumptuous but does that mean you're at a loose end tomorrow evening? If so, then Vanessa and I would be delighted if you joined our table at the Portland's summer ball as guests of honour? We can get to know each other better and perhaps introduce you to some of our local entrepreneurs, maybe even Mayor Santoro. I dare say Wynter McGlynn will be going as well.'

'We're staying at the Portland so yes, if it's not too much trouble, I think we would very much enjoy such an occasion.'

'Excellent, we're there too so let's meet for drinks in the Venetian Bar on the mezzanine at seven. Black tie of course, and there's a rule we don't talk shop although I have to admit it's mostly ignored, thank God.'

'Forgive me, talk shop?'

'Talk business. But given the crowd who come along I'm afraid it's rather like telling overstimulated toddlers not to throw tantrums.'

They shared smiles as goodbyes were said. Having joined the group at the door, Dayton felt obliged to offer an unenthusiastic handshake. Annika submitted with equal antipathy whilst Nilsson simply grasped the outstretched fingers without so much as a glance in his direction.

'Allow me to see you out,' said Richard. 'Julian, wait here for me please.'

Their pretence at friendliness might fool strangers but the lack of attachment between father and son was laid bare in that moment of instruction. Once alone, Dayton wandered to the window, very aware they had not always been so distant. Thrusting his hands into his pockets, he tried again to identify exactly where their relationship had soured.

From his earliest memories he could distinctly recall lying in wait on the porch for his father to return from the office or a business trip. The preceding day or days would have seemed an eternity, but then there was overwhelming excitement as the driveway gates opened, him racing across the lawn to stop the car and being swept up and around by a man as tall and strong as the oak trees bordering the grounds. There had been birthday parties with gifts and candles and cake, trips to the beach or the parks, kicking or catching or throwing of balls in assorted shapes and sizes, bedtime books and kisses goodnight. Surely his father must have loved him then, or liked him at least?

Maybe the cracks opened as early as his seventh summer when, flanked by his parents, they told him he would be changing schools in September. Too young to understand the benefits of a private education or why entry to Richard's alma mater was more important than remaining with his friends, he was desperate to be pleased at their apparent generosity. Even so, he had begun to cry and turned to his mother for comfort, realising this was his father's decision and unsure what he had done to deserve being sent away. All these years later, he still remembered the long drive to the gothic Rovingham Preparatory, the rising panic as he stood alone in the courtyard next to his heavy trunk, adrift amidst a sea of grown-ups and identically uniformed but unfamiliar boys. He had tolerated the school's formal curriculum easily enough, the lessons delivered in draughty classrooms by old-fashioned staff, but less so its pastoral traditions which gave him his first experiences of vulnerability. As the senior boys avenged their own initiations, he and the other homesick first-formers had learned how to weep silently in their narrow beds while counting down the remaining weeks of term. The holidays brought only a transitory respite and then, no matter how hard he fought them, the tears always returned. Those tears and Richard's embarrassment at his son's sensitivity taught Dayton a longer-lasting lesson than any of his teachers, they taught him the shame of self-pity.

By thirteen, he had hardened his heart enough for the crying to stop permanently. He even formed nascent friendships and grew excited at the prospect of joining the distinguished academy attended by several generations of Daytons and where his name had been registered since birth. Regardless, Richard's opinion was that six years of private education had so far failed his weakling child and decided to send him instead to one of the City's non-selective secondary schools. The boy would have no choice but to toughen up and earn his manhood. Dayton's existence, largely unhappy but at least manageable at Rovingham, became unrelentingly miserable at Shardwell High where his privileged accent and lack of physicality marked him out as a daily target for the playground bullies and the streetwise gangs outside the gates. The few teenagers not actively involved in his persecution stayed well clear of his attempts at friendship, leaving him isolated at home where he could watch his younger brother develop into his father's favourite at first hand. Five-year-old Eddie was a boisterous child, full of fun and energy and already very different to an elder sibling who had inherited his mother's delicate, introspective nature. To compound Dayton's sorrows, Eddie then took to prep school like a duck to water, building a wide circle of friends, establishing a starting place in the rugby and cricket first teams and coming home at the end of every term brimming with trophies and anecdotes. Their father chose to spend less and less time with an older child who could not help but notice the relief in his eyes. After a failed first attempt, Richard finally had a son who lived up to expectations.

To survive a progressively introverted adolescence, Dayton dumbed down his scholastic ability, allowed his accent and vocabulary to coarsen and diligently buried his emotions under thickening layers of self-loathing. But then, after serving out his time at Shardwell as unobtrusively as possible, came a chance at reconciliation. With Eddie still away at boarding school, he sought to curry favour and monopolise more of Richard's attention by joining the family firm. Hopes of the two of them working side by side and reforming bonds, if not of love or even friendship then at least of respect, were quickly dashed, however. Although Richard kept enough of an eye on his son to ensure his career was progressing, he was a largely distant figure whose time was preoccupied elsewhere. As far as Dayton could tell, his work had done their relationship no harm but neither had it helped in any material way.

What had finally destroyed any remaining esteem were the interventions in his adult relationships. Rarely finding the courage to oppose his father, twice they had quarrelled about women whom Richard deemed wholly unsuitable for his son. After the first of these he had backed away, questioning his own judgement. After the second, he had proposed out of little more than spite only to endure recrimination and bitterness through a desultory engagement, a strained wedding and a short-lived marriage. His relationship with Richard had since been courteous at best - he was treated like any other employee and seldom spoken to otherwise. Perhaps there was no single moment which had initiated their divergence, he concluded, but a gradual and inevitable decline for a son who was simply too different from a man determined to perpetuate the family line in his own image.

At least it sounded as though his mother had also travelled to the City. She was the yin to his father's brutish yang and he had missed her gentle, reassuring presence since she moved to London. He would find them an opportunity to spend time together, knowing she would offer what he permitted from no one else; sympathy and comfort.

Through the glass, ML One rose from the rooftops like a sharp-edged blade thrust upwards into the blue. Maybe McGlynn was there, maybe not, but there was one thing of which he could be reasonably certain, she was unlikely to be having any sort of conversation with her own father today. Like most of the people moving in their circles, Dayton knew the story of David's removal from power and the consequent blame placed on her shoulders. He had tried and failed on a number of occasions to determine which of their paternal situations was the less preferable.

The door opened and Richard returned alone.

'Please sit down,' he said evenly.

'It's nice to see you too.'

'I'm not here for pleasantries, Julian.'

'Then why did you come? Did you need a break from all the grandstanding?'

'I didn't come to fight either. I came to help with Malmotec and perhaps the court case.'

'You came because you think I need your help. Because you don't trust me to deal with Fredrik on my own. Or McGlynn.' Dayton paused for any sign of denial. 'Thought so. And you turning up unannounced today just confuses the situation. I mean, he's not going to know who to work with, is he? What's the point in me running the company if you're just going to waltz in and take over whenever you feel like it? It's been seven years for Christ's sake. Seven years and you still think you have to constantly watch over me in case I make a mess of things.'

'There's no shame in asking for help.'

'I didn't ask for your help though, that's the point. We're fine, I'm fine.'

'Unfortunately I disagree. Fredrik and Annika just made it quite clear that negotiations were coming to an end before I got involved.'

'What? Nonsense. We're getting down to the short strokes, that's all. He's playing hard to get, just like I would if I was him.'

'There's a difference between him playing his cards close to his chest versus withdrawing from the table altogether. If I've told you once I've told you a hundred times about the importance of building good relationships. If you want to win the game, then common sense dictates that you have to stay in it, generally by observing the rules and making friends.

With Annika as much as Fredrik. Can't you see how much influence she has?'

'She hardly said a word and if I'd have buttered him up too much he'd only see it as weakness. He's the kind of guy who wouldn't respect someone who rolls over.'

'Really. Even so, and despite me having to touch my toes to try and charm him back into a dialogue, I'm reasonably sure he respects me. And I can assure you that I have no intention of rolling over on the terms of the contract.'

'It's not yours to negotiate though, is it.'

'It rather looks like it is, I'm afraid. He doesn't want to continue working with you, which is unfortunate given I'm supposed to be back for a debate on Friday.'

'You've got to be joking. I've spent months on this and you've persuaded him to negotiate with you instead?'

'Not me. You, my boy, did that all by yourself.'

'I am not your boy,' retorted Dayton, voice shaking as the old, familiar sensation began to constrict his throat. 'If I was, then you'd let me get on with the job. My way, not yours.'

'Enough. I'd like copies of the latest proposal documents, revenue and cost models, organisation charts and anything else relating to the bid by this evening. And could you follow up on those actions we agreed at the end.'

'What actions?'

'Really Julian? You were still in the room weren't you? Or had you decided to stop listening by then? Of course you had. As you leave me no other option, I'll drop a list off with Rebecca. Please see they're completed by tomorrow afternoon. I'll want an update before drinks at the Portland.'

'There's no room on our tables.'

'Then make some. I hear you're hosting one and so is Edward. Add the Nilssons and your mother and me to one of the others.'

So he knows Eddie's in town, thought Dayton. One coincidence off the list.

'I'm afraid that's not convenient,' he said peevishly. 'You should have checked with me before inviting them.'

'I do not need to check,' said Richard, grinding out each syllable, face mottling. 'Just as I did not need your permission to join the meeting today. I will do exactly as I see fit when it comes to the best interests of the company. Do I make myself clear?'

Dayton tested his own resolve, found it wanting and breathed out heavily.

'Yeah, OK, I suppose so. I'll talk to Ed and find space.'

'That's better. Now, the McGlynn case, what are the chances of them winning?'

'Not high. I've taken–'

'Spare me the details,' said Richard, holding up a hand. 'I don't want to know for sure what I only suspect. Plausible deniability. All I want is your assurance they're not going to be proven right in their claims and to ask if there's anything I can do to help.'

'No they won't and no there isn't. It's under control.'

'Very well, but do not let me down. I won't have us losing face in front of McGlynn, never mind the costs if you were to lose.'

Obviously his father had been talking about David McGlynn. Even though David had dwindled into retirement whilst Richard had his peerage and societal influence, it was still remarkable how he would not cede even the slightest ground to his generational rival.

Some of the stories from their conflict were legendary, even upstaging those of their children. Although, reflected Dayton, they had fought for two long decades rather than seven short years. Plenty of time to write further chapters of my own, including the last where I finish off McGlynn and her godforsaken line for good.

Richard's enduring scepticism only reinforced his determination to reach that goal. He was desperate for the achievement to be his and his alone, one which neither father nor brother would ever be able to replicate, or misappropriate.

There was no doubt about it - handing over the reins to Eddie would have to wait.

14

The space beyond her doorway, bathed in blood orange by the rays of a dying sun, was now perfectly still. Even the cleaners had finished their rounds and were somewhere below as they worked their way floor by floor down ML One's structure. McGlynn stretched backwards in her chair, away from the screen and the scattered papers, to rub her eyes.

On returning from City Hall, she had spent nearly two hours talking to senior members of the development team about the similarities between Dayton's software and their own. Confused and embarrassed by their manager's absence, they had been eager to help but nowhere near as persuasive as she had found Rohan to be. Their explanations were a much paler imitation and she had needed to ask countless questions and make copious notes to tease out the detail with which she might convince herself, let alone the judicial panel to be faced tomorrow. When at last a halt to the grilling had been called and the team allowed home for the evening, McGlynn retreated to her office and carried on. She worked to further reduce and refine the key points, cross-referencing them to the piles of written documentation already submitted to the court, and then attempted to form a cohesive argument she could weave into testimony under questioning. The neatly structured bullet points on the screen had been paid for with mental fatigue, cramp and hunger but she was satisfied with the results. All that remained was to commit their essence to memory before the rehearsal arranged with Wiesenberg at six o'clock the following morning.

Having loosened the tension in her upper body she checked her phone. So absorbed had she been that there were two missed calls and a voicemail from Brookes, saying the security report was in her inbox and that Detective Campbell had arrived at the warehouse.

Had Santoro sent her across for the final hour of the day to ratchet up the pressure after their meeting at City Hall? The timing was surely suspicious. In any event McGlynn would have to decide whether to agree to his demands before the ball, maybe earlier if she wanted the police called off before they spent more time at the port. She leant forward and switched applications to find the report from Valente was over a hundred pages long. Switching again, she saw Matthieu had booked a call with Hallam to review the document last thing tomorrow, immediately before leaving for the Portland. That was going to be too late to discuss the contents and take any action prior to being cornered by the mayor and his campaign chief.

She scrolled down the list of contacts in her phone, tapping a name and waiting for the connection.

'Evening my love, thought I might hear from you,' said Hallam. 'It's getting late over there so I hope you're not still working?'

'Is the pot calling the kettle black, Jane?'

'Touché. I assume you're calling to see if I spoke with Hugo?'

'Yep, and to give you a few updates. You first though, did you get to him?'

'Briefly. He seemed keen to get off the phone. Told me unloading the *Santa Rosa* was already behind schedule with extra inspections and he was struggling to deal with that plus questions from Andrew Brookes and working on some other reporting for you?'

'Uh-huh, I'll come back to that. Do you think he's OK though?'

'He sounded so flat I asked him straight out what the matter was. Puts it all down to being so busy. I told him I wanted to help with a recovery plan and he tried to fob me off until next week, which is a nonsense if there are problems to be solved today.'

'Did he tell you why I'd asked for the report?'

'No. But I know something's up so, come on, spill the beans.'

Along with her court appearance, the ongoing search for Rohan, Santoro's ultimatum and the need to find a way of bringing her investors back in line, let alone the hundred or so unread messages in her inbox, McGlynn knew she was out of capacity. She needed help and saw little point in waiting any longer to reveal the real problems at the docks.

'I've asked him and Andrew to pull together a full operational security review. I had a visit from City PD yesterday morning. They seem to think people traffickers are using our vessels and premises so they turned up at the warehouse this afternoon to take a look around.'

'Bloody hell, Wynter! Why on earth didn't you mention this? I could've been on last night's flight and made sure I was there to take care of it.' There was no malice in Hallam's outburst, only frustration born of good intention. 'Do you think there's any truth to their accusations?'

'It's not a formal accusation, not yet. But I've had Andrew on site running interference and he's found a bunch of things that worry me. Sabotaged cameras and discarded food and clothing inside the compound to start with.'

'I'm so very sorry, this should never have happened on my watch. Right, I'm coming across to look after Hugo, manage the police and get things fixed ASAP. I can be there by the middle of the day if I hurry.'

McGlynn hesitated. Did she really need Jane to travel thousands of miles when a simple conversation with the mayor could make the problem disappear? And something stirred again at the back of her mind.

'No, stay where you–'

'You can't just expect me to sit on my hands. This is my problem, not yours.'

'It's a problem for both of us Jane. I'm already here, you're not, and I know the lead detective from that suspected false accounting case a couple of years ago. We have a decent enough relationship and are–...' And are trading favours, she had very nearly added. 'Listen, I have the draft report. I'm going to skim it tonight but won't have time to read it in detail until tomorrow afternoon at the earliest. If I send it across, could you take a proper look and let me know what's missing and what immediate actions should be taken?'

'Of course. But I can do that and still be on a plane.'

'Give it one more day and you can come over then if needed, OK?'

'I really don't like being at arm's length but alright, if you're sure. Is there anything else I can take off your plate, my dear? You sound tired.'

'Ha! Nothing I'm not used to. Are you worried about me?' asked McGlynn, touched by the concern.

'What's the point in you all calling me Auntie Jane if I'm not allowed to worry?'

'And here's me thinking you didn't know. But no thanks, everything else is under control, sort of.'

'Good, now go and get some sleep.'

The idea was highly appealing but McGlynn knew there was more work to be done first. She switched on the lamp to counter the deepening darkness and looked at the paperwork strewn across her desk. What should be prioritised when everything seemed important and urgent? Fight the nearest fire first, she counselled herself, and the nearest fire was going to be taking the stand under oath in a court of law. She stood and touched her toes for a full minute then slipped through to her apartment, sending messages to Jack and the twins while making a sandwich. Back in her office, she took a bite and gathered the papers into a neat pile, flicked the screen over to the list of bullet points and settled down again to concentrate on the task in hand.

Rutter stared moodily into the remaining amber liquid, ruminating on the pity of so rarely achieving inebriation anymore. Like so much else in his life it was his own fault given the significant investment he had made in increasing his tolerance to alcohol. Journalism had a reputation for breeding hard drinkers and he had succumbed without protest. His first job as a cub reporter in Dallas felt like a lifetime ago, more than a lifetime ago, but he remembered working with the experienced pressmen on some of the stories which made the Garland Herald's main pages in those days. Lawson, Cronsky and another guy whose name escaped him, a generation older and a tight-knit group well before he walked through the doors on South Seventh Street, had been curious about new blood in the dusty bullpen of the Herald's low-rise offices. Relentless baiting aside, they had shown him the ropes, telling him where to go and who to find, how to look and listen and how to filter truth from lies, then criticised his efforts at interpretation until the unwieldy drafts began to coalesce around his own authentic style. More importantly they had taught him how to hold his drink. There was a long Herald tradition of decamping to the Tap House over on Fourth every night once the submissions deadline had passed, everyone throwing in a couple of twenties to buy pitchers of beer until the money ran out. A carefully observed minimum of four refills each per hour with independently purchased shots of bourbon for seasoned drinkers like Lawson and Cronsky. And Tyler, that was his name, Tyler Higgins, tall guy in checked shirts and faded jeans. Rutter sorely missed those irresponsible, inexpensive nights. They had been some of the funniest, warmest and most enlightening of his adulthood.

He lifted the glass to his lips and emptied it, debating the merits of another against the backdrop of his growing sentimentality. The Guardsman was less than half full but still offered more atmosphere than the deserted apartment around the corner. A proper bar, a mile and several income brackets away from the Establishment, with a single mahogany countertop running the length of the room, clusters of polished, hand-pulled taps and neat rows of spirits arranged on thin shelving against the mirrors. There were a few regulars whose company he enjoyed at a distance, as respectful of their right to solitude as they were of his, and Angelique was working alone, no need for any help on a Tuesday. She made his decision an easy one and Rutter heaved his bulk upright from the corner table and ambled over.

'Same again?' she asked good naturedly, reaching across for the empty.

'Please.'

Rutter watched her pull the tap handle of his preferred ale, half his attention on the velvety pour and half on the curve of her exposed upper arm, the firmness of the limb redolent of his distant youth. The muscles contracted and slackened three, four times, the delicate interplay between light and shadow on smooth skin encapsulating her wholesomeness. This was not sexual desire, he would have been mortified if she mistakenly thought he wanted to bed her, but an aesthetic appreciation of beauty. Her arm made him happy and sad, lonely, maudlin.

She carefully placed the brimming pint on the bar and he waited for it to settle, fascinated by the whorls of the tiny hurricanes migrating up the side of the glass. Maybe he would have liked to bed her if he was honest about it. Such a thought made him ashamed and he dropped his eyes.

'Thanks Angel.'

Taking a large enough swig to remove nearly a third of the contents, he returned to his table by the wall. He would pay when he left as always.

Further along, a couple in their late fifties or early sixties rose gingerly to their feet next to a tabletop besieged by glassware. The man staggered slightly and nearly lost his balance causing the woman to tut and laugh at the same time. She might have resembled Rutter's first wife at a similar age and he envied their easy familiarity. Regaining most of their composure, they linked arms and meandered to the front of the room where the door was pulled open and held for them by someone entering from the street. Two older men, casually but expensively dressed, came inside and headed for the bar. As they passed beneath the first of the overhead strip lights, Rutter's cursory interest turned into a double take and he nearly choked on the fluid halfway down his throat. He was sure of it, the man at the front now talking to Angelique was Richard Dayton.

What would bring Lord Dayton, the Baron of Inverlochy himself to a slightly grubby bar like The Guardsman? And who was his companion? The reporter's instincts kicked in and he tried to shrink into the background, no easy task for a man his size, to watch as drinks were served and they selected wooden chairs directly across the narrow walkway.

The two men were too far away for their muted conversation to carry, particularly as Richard had his back to him, so Rutter narrowed his eyes and focused on the other man's face. Lip reading was a skill at which he had gained some modest ability back at the Herald and his evening, which would have otherwise faded towards an empty, unkempt bed like so many others, now held unanticipated interest and purpose.

On the dashboard of a minivan parked close to the central bus station, a phone emitted a thin ringtone. The driver's big hand reached out to key the answer button.

'Yeah.'

'Progress?'

'Today was a no-show.'

'Go again tomorrow then.'

'Yeah.'

Three soft beeps indicated the end of the call.

The scented water in which Malik lay was noticeably starting to cool. Five more minutes, she promised herself, fighting off drowsiness after a busy end to another long day.

Securing a ticket to the Mayor's Ball had been harder than Rutter probably anticipated. Most were purchased on company expense accounts and her reputation ensured there were few who wanted her sitting beside them for an evening where tongues wagged looser than usual. After a fruitless afternoon on the phone, one of the PA's she knew from the gym had tipped her off to the charity liaison officer from Woodlands Hospital itself who, as this year's good cause, had been given a complimentary allocation. She called the man and laid on the charm as thickly as she dared, persuading him they had met previously and that she was covering the event from an angle of patient benefit. As luck would have it, the wife of one of the attending surgeons had declined only that afternoon due to sickness - would she like to accompany Mr Sharma if he was amenable? Malik readily left her details, wondering how Mrs Sharma might feel about the idea, or whether she would even be consulted, and received written confirmation within the hour. Some perfunctory research revealed a biography of the urologist which left her unfazed.

She had collaborated with much worse in the pursuit of a story before now.

With a means of entry organised she had taken the subway home, alighting at the first of two stops which straddled the boundary between Bishop's Cross and Willowborough. Her tiny apartment was one of twelve high-specification conversions within the brickwork of an old shirt factory - a kitchen diner with a sofa opposite, one bedroom, one bathroom and far enough off-street level to escape most of the noise. Pushing the front door closed with her foot, she restarted the still-warm laptop on the kitchen counter, stir-fried some fresh vegetables and swallowed them with microwaved rice, all the while methodically adding to the growing body of research on Julian Dayton. In particular, she had identified thirteen people in his network not employed by Dayton but whom she believed would nevertheless be likely to attend the ball. Each represented an opportunity to extract more personal information about the man and the prospect of persuading them to talk filled her with excitement and unease in equal measure. With her tired concentration finally stalling to the point where she realised little headway was being made, she returned the laptop to its charging cradle, cleared away the dishes, checked her planned outfit for tomorrow was in a fit state, then drew as hot a bath as her skin would tolerate.

The promised five minutes were gone. Malik summoned enough energy to leave the water, patted herself dry with a warm white towel and slipped on a clean set of silk pyjamas. With her head gratefully resting on the pillows, she closed her eyes and thought again about the names on her list, what perspective they might have and how she could strike up a conversation. A general sense of fulfilment cushioned her journey towards sleep.

This is all a bit squalid, thought Eddie, time to get going. As soon as they had crossed the threshold, he noticed the tired wallpaper, the thin curtains barely covering windows overlooking the road outside, a trace of dampness lingering from the winter months. Her room - with its frayed carpet and mirrored wardrobes and cheap dressing table covered with the detritus of a teenager, despite her profile saying she was twenty-nine - had proved no better.

Slowly and softly, he lifted the sheet and padded to where his clothes lay draped over a corduroy armchair. The pretence at quietness was more for good form than necessity, he was sure the woman was only feigning sleep which suited him entirely. Their evening had been mutually adequate, transactional and functional, and he saw no reason to spoil it with unnecessary awkwardness.

Carrying his jacket and shoes, he crept downstairs and from there fully clothed into the street. He realised he had no idea where he stood, too preoccupied on the way over to worry about where they had been going, so pulled out his phone and cursed when his location showed as out beyond Flawsby, much further away from the comfort of his own bed than anticipated. With a car ordered he decided to walk in the general direction from which it would arrive, keen to be away from the depressing house and to shorten the expected half-hour wait, even if only by a few minutes.

A full moon, surrounded by stars and the crawling navigation lights of high-altitude aircraft, hung high in the southern skies and cast silver shadows into the street's unlit spaces. The semi-professional workers who lived in suburbs like these were evidently asleep, recharging exhausted bodies and minds before being jerked awake to shower and dress and fill a go-cup for the beginning of another twelve-hour shift. Eddie thought about how dispiriting it must be to reside here and submit to such work. Flying back to an empty apartment next week was certainly preferable, but by how much? He found it increasingly difficult to deny evenings such as these and even the occasional parties were losing their attraction to his growing sense of malaise. Maybe these good people had it the right way round after all, with their long hours and hopeful attitudes. Maybe their early starts and late finishes kept them occupied enough to forget about their lot, perhaps even enough to be happy. Unable to decide, his thoughts returned to his own early start and breakfast with father and brother, a rare enough occasion since Dayton had left home. Richard's arrival in the City had been unexpected, his message to convene an early meeting at the Portland doubly so. With his leather-soled footsteps echoing off silent brick and glass, Eddie wondered what tomorrow would bring.

15

As much to his own surprise as anyone else's, Julian Dayton was in a nightclub, although not a particularly sophisticated example so it seemed. Aeons had passed since he was last in a place like this and even then slumming it to this degree had been a rarity. Dark, pitted architraves and dado rails contrasted with scuffed beige walls, institutional signage glowed green above double exit doors fitted with panic bars, foam stuffing protruded through ripped black vinyl benches and the bare floorboards were sticky with old varnish dissolving under a thousand spilt drinks. At the far end of the space, a lighting rig threw a rainbow of shooting stars off the rotating glitterball and deafening music reverberated from huge speaker stacks. The venue looked and sounded more like a school disco than a nightclub but, corroborated by the half full beer in front of him and the couple of hundred adults milling around or gyrating on the dance floor, the distinction seemed justifiable.

In spite of the assault on his senses and the number of people in high spirits, including those amongst whom he was sitting, Dayton felt sober and alone. Omitted from conversations on both sides, there was no choice but to face forwards and pretend to be interested in the writhing horde. To give the impression this exclusion was at his own preference he nonchalantly picked up his drink and took a mouthful, only to gag and replace it swiftly on the table as the sour taste evoked memories of a campfire doused with urine. He turned to see if anyone had noticed. To his immediate left were two men and a woman yelling to be heard above the din. They seemed oblivious to him and very young, perhaps only nineteen or twenty, the animated childish faces above full-sized bodies striking him as peculiar, almost grotesque as he strained unsuccessfully to catch the gist of their shouting. Two girls of a similar age were conducting a heart-to-heart of some kind to his right. He knew instinctively that he was a part of these social groups, and each was part of a larger whole, yet no one was any more than faintly familiar and their youth confused him further - why was he keeping the company of a different generation?

Puzzlement held him for a time, the background light and noise unabating, until a downward glance offered an unlikely solution. The backs of his own hands and the long shapely fingers looked remarkably as though they belonged to someone much younger. Gone were the veins and tendons beneath shallowing, puckered skin. Gone too were the liver spots and the white half-inch scar where he had accidentally sliced the joint of his left thumb with a kitchen knife. Even the ache and persistent stiffness in his knuckles had disappeared. Dayton brought his hands up, turning them slowly back and forth, clenching and unclenching his fists and staring at them in amazement. They felt rejuvenated. Come to think of it, *he* felt rejuvenated, of an age with those around him, roughly the age at which he would have enrolled in college had he not chosen to start working full time instead. Knowing he was young again, which he now accepted as fact without the slightest suspicion, made his surroundings instantly more vibrant, the lights brighter but less blinding, the music more recognisable, the atmosphere more enjoyable.

Three girls off to the left were making their way over, stopping at each table to exchange a few words with others who would typically then stand and hug them in turn before they moved on to the next group. In Dayton's limited experience such behaviour on the journey between adolescence and adulthood was not unusual. Perhaps they had taken a substance which made them overly affectionate or perhaps they were simply having a good time and expressing their rights to free love. Either way, he was heartened by such an innocent act and grew nostalgic. They came closer, only two tables away, and he saw each of them was very beautiful - lithe and demure in her first flush of womanhood. Being offered or receiving their embrace would be out of the question had he been older but, given they were now of the same age, he realised the gift could be accepted without fear of censure. The idea of such intimacy was intoxicating, causing his heart to beat more strongly as they duly completed their ritual and moved on again.

On arriving at his table with somewhat vacant smiles, a tall and willowy blonde mouthed words of introduction. These should have been difficult to catch above the clamour but were lost altogether as his hearing faded into silence. Nevertheless, feeling himself rise from the bench as expected, he moved effortlessly round the table and into her arms where she held him as a lover would - gently, respectfully, without inhibition. His rigidity began to weaken under the soft touches of her freshly washed hair and the warm smooth cheek against his neck. Time slowed and without conscious thought he became aware of being hopelessly lost in love.

Long before he was ready, he sensed her arms slackening in preparation for withdrawal. To her, their connection was one of many and there were strangers sitting away to his right awaiting friendship. Not to him, however. To him, she offered a way back from the hatred and the shame, a chance of rescue from all the painful things he had done and had done to him. She would be so tolerant and kind and free from judgement that he might even come to accept her compassion someday. He held on desperately, prolonging the moment, delaying the familiar sting of abandonment but, to his utter disbelief, this unique and perfect girl understood the greatness of his need and subsided back against him, content to hold and be held. For a while he exulted at this victory, at the mere possibility of salvation, until she began to withdraw once more, not pulling away this time but dissolving in his arms as the whole nightclub blurred and slid sideways like a ship rolling in heavy seas. Despairingly, he retightened his grip but there was nothing tangible to which he could cling. The nightclub and the girl and the redemption she embodied were being rendered immaterial, untouchable and then, as he tried to cry out in panic, they were gone altogether, replaced by the whiteness of the ceiling above.

Dayton yawned in disappointment and sat up, smoothing the tiredness from his eyes and blinking as his vision adjusted to the City's sharp lines beyond the balcony window. The remnants of the girl remained lodged in his memory, the feel of her skin and the scent of her hair, but the hope was gone, replaced by crushing reality and the imminent prospect of a family breakfast. Rolling to the edge of the mattress he put his feet flat on the floor and cautiously tested the nerve endings before bearing any weight. Today was a good day and he made for the adjoining bathroom.

Thirty minutes later and wearing a pinstriped suit, he emerged from the brownstone block and strode northeast through the complicated maze of winding roads and alleyways he knew by heart. Walking in the city before the flood of commuters was always more pleasant, especially so during the bright but cool summer mornings. Other early-risers carried coffee or jogged or accompanied small dogs, occasionally all three, but the relative quietness gave him time and space to appreciate the built environment in which he lived. Most of the properties stood on plots sold onwards many times during the city's evolution, an eclectic array of buildings rising skywards on foundations packed with the rubble of smaller predecessors. He liked the neatness of their almost universally perpendicular lines, the textures complementing or jarring with their surroundings by thoughtful design, the careful configuration of every inch of available land. With an admiring glance at the frontage of Fentimans Theatre, a hulking art deco masterpiece resembling the upper half of a Fifties jukebox, he turned left along Lockmakers Lane and ascended The Portland Hotel's granite steps.

Other than three weary-faced receptionists the double-height lobby was unoccupied. The Portland's main clientele of rich tourists, who tended to sleep in later than the business travellers staying in chain hotels further towards the waterside, were yet to venture down the sweeping staircase for breakfast let alone be ready to check out from their suites. Ahead of him was the Grand Ballroom's foyer where the

Mayor's eight hundred paying guests would gather but Dayton knew the layout well and bore left without hesitation, toward the sounds of muffled crockery, past an unmanned pedestal with a sign asking diners to wait and into the restaurant, scanning the few occupied tables for his father or brother. With neither apparent, he took a copy of the Post from the nearby rack and chose a corner table overlooking the gardens and from where he could keep an eye on the doors.

Flicking straight to the business section, he checked that Malik was yet to publish her article and resolved to call Rutter as threatened if no draft had been received by midday. Returning to the front page, the main stories of the day appeared mundane enough - rising property prices, the opening of two new railway platforms and refurbishment plans for the Pennygate shopping district. Tonight's ball was mentioned in the social column but with no more than the promise of a four-page spread in tomorrow's edition and he was about to turn to the sports news when Richard materialised.

'Morning,' said Dayton, still guarded. 'Sleep well?'

'Reasonably,' came the reply with no hint of concern. 'Always prefer my own bed but at least the Portland can be relied upon for some peace and quiet.'

'Is Mum here too?'

'Not yet. She's up at the house. Wanted to make sure everything's alright, you know how she is.'

'It'll be nice to see her again. So what brought you into town?'

'I had some things to take care of, including that opportunity we discussed.'

'Ah, good. Progress?'

'Yes. He signed the papers, so can you countersign this morning please. Remind me, when's the verdict due?'

'Depends on the remaining testimony but probably before the weekend.'

'Fine. We need that to go in our favour for this to fly, obviously.'

'We'll win.'

'I hope so. I really do. It's a sorry state of affairs to find ourselves in this position.'

Dayton bit back an oath.

'How's London?' he asked instead.

'Busy. Glad we're in Bray, it's a lovely spot and the garden's glorious, but the commute alone is a couple of hours and there's a lot going on in the Upper House, more than there should be this time of year. This bloody government's obsessed by a populist agenda which doesn't remotely solve for long-term economic growth. But they're still trying to ram the legislation through before recess and we're having to push back harder than we ought. And that idiot Huddlestone, well, dropping off slightly in the polls has caused him to lose his head completely. I should think he's rather more suited to some kind of celebrity work than attempting to be prime minister. Vacuous, spineless little man.'

'Certainly seems that way.'

'Count yourself lucky you don't have to deal with him and his cronies. Can't make any kind of a decision unless it's gone through their communications team first. Bloody ridiculous. Ah,' said Richard, setting down his cup and rising. 'Here's young Edward. Good morning, good morning, how are you my son?'

'Morning Ed,' said Dayton, jealous at his father's language and embrace, despite Eddie's late arrival. 'Will you want breakfast? We've ordered.'

'Sorted on the way in thanks, best full English in the City. But I'll have some of that coffee.'

'Help yourself. Late night again?'

'Not especially. How was yours?'

'Quiet.'

'Surprise. Never mind, Jules, big night out tonight.'

'Indeed. Should be fun,' lied Dayton. 'Found yourself a date?'

'Yeah. Have you?'

Fuck you Eddie, he thought, you can just fuck off with your petty insinuation and insults, especially in present company. Nevertheless, he fixed a smile on his face before replying.

'My table was an odd number anyway so no, rather than concentrating on my libido, I'll be ensuring our guests have an enjoyable time instead. I trust you'll be doing the same.'

'Ha! Good one and yeah, no problem in that department, Suze is a social goddess.'

'Suze? Tell me you're not bringing Suzanne Connaughton?'

'None other.'

'But she's married? Clive's lot will have a table or two tonight. He's more than likely to be there himself?'

'Won't be a problem. They've separated because he's screwing the nanny. Think she quite likes the idea of flaunting herself on someone else's arm.'

'It's still a bit vulgar, isn't it. Just try not to cause a scene.'

'Heaven forbid. I hear you're coming too?' added Eddie, turning to Richard.

'That's right, your mother and I are bringing the Nilssons, see if we can't get this deal back on track.'

'It doesn't need bringing back on track, it just needs closing out,' groused Dayton, needled by the implication he required any help and his own suspicion that he probably did. He lapsed into awkward silence, pretending interest in the steady flow of newcomers while breakfast was served. Eddie and Richard struck up small talk on the state of English rugby and his eggs Benedict was nearly gone before a lull gave him an opening.

'So Dad, why the invitation? Something we can help with?'

Finishing his mouthful, Richard washed it down with the remains of his coffee before leaning back in the chair.

'Given I was in town, it seemed like too good an opportunity to miss. Can't a man enjoy a meal with his children?'

'Of course. But it's not exactly a family tradition anymore. What's on your mind?'

'A few things actually. Let's start with the trade negotiations shall we? My sources in the Civil Service tell me the timetable is going to slip. What preparations have you made?'

'We've modelled costs for transferring production out of the UK, either to the existing site in Sri Lanka or nearer shore to Hungary. Sri Lanka's probably better. It's closer to our intended markets for at least the next decade, improves margins by nine percent and breaks even in about four years although we'd need to ramp up distribution.'

'And Hungary?'

'Margins improve by six percent and payback is longer as we'd need to build distribution from scratch.'

'How long?'

'Difficult to say. The exchange rate's volatile and their labour costs are rising faster. Not much less than six or seven years although it's more convenient for existing customers.'

'What do you think, Edward?'

Dayton brightened at the question. Eddie was rarely consulted in this type of exercise, having shown little previous interest, and his attempt at an informed opinion should be entertaining.

'I think we should switch production to South Korea, maybe Japan,' said Eddie promptly. 'They're both friendly with strong independent demand alongside well-established trade with the Chinese. They're also less likely to be affected by political squabbles than other Asian countries for the foreseeable.'

'But their labour rates and laws are prohibitive,' interposed a startled Dayton. 'We'd end up making a loss on every machine.'

'Not necessarily. We could improve budgeted sales if we had better access to the Far East and drive efficiency as a result of volume. I think we're currently too pessimistic if the trial in Thailand goes well and we secure first mover advantage.'

'What's your view on that, Julian?'

'I disagree. Our forecasts were modelled using real data whereas I suspect Ed's relying too much on the optimism of our distributor there.'

'I'm not. I haven't talked to Fender about this yet. But I have spent time with local procurement and there's definitely an appetite to switch out older units.'

'Have you done that?' asked Richard, turning back to Dayton with a trace of amusement.

'No. No, we haven't. Didn't seem to be much point given we already have two viable options.'

'But this is an opportunity to up the sales forecast, isn't it? Sounds to me like it'd be worth exploring.'

Dayton still disagreed but could not prove Eddie wrong without replicating the cost models and doing similar market research. Much as he hated the idea of the extra work, or the prospect of increasing sales forecasts for which he would ultimately be held accountable, he was cornered.

'Alright. I think it's pointless but I'll talk to Sandy.'

'Good. By when?'

'I'll get back to you later,' he said, unwilling to commit without sizing the effort first. Noting Eddie's smugness at blindsiding him, he resolved to delegate the exercise in his direction as soon as their father was out of earshot.

'Please do. And there's a related issue to be modelled in each scenario - the impact of the City becoming an independent state.'

Both brothers were taken aback by this.

'Waste of time,' said Dayton, recovering first. 'The Capital's always rejected independence out of hand. There's no chance of the City administration obtaining a mandate.'

'Isn't there? The whispers in London are that Mr Santoro is canvassing support for a popular vote. The CS have been told to be ready for a new partnership inside two years.'

'What? He's never struck me as pro-independent before.'

'From what I hear he's exceptionally ambitious though, so I don't think we should be overly surprised. What's he like in person?'

'Loud-mouthed, big ego, bit smarmy. Always been pro-business but hasn't achieved much in office. Got in by spending millions on social media although I don't think he's independently wealthy. Managed to mobilise the illiterate, disenfranchised masses who then don't bother keeping tabs on whether he's actually doing anything for them or not. A bit like Huddlestone I expect.'

'Hmm. How well do you know him?'

'Not well,' admitted Dayton. 'Met him a few times in passing but no more than a hello. Works a room like every politician and is already moving on to the next voter or donor before he's let go of your hand. Ed?'

'Me either.'

'Nor do I,' said Richard. 'However, I invested energy in his predecessors and you two should do the same. Let's try and get him alone this evening but, in the meantime, put our people to work on identifying his main funders. Follow the money and we'll have a better idea of where his priorities lie. If the rumours are true, the foreknowledge could make or save us millions - it's the main reason I came over.'

'How reliable is your source?' asked Eddie, topping up his cup yet again.

'We certainly can't afford to ignore the tip. You'll remember I accepted my peerage entirely for early access to this kind of information.'

'Mmm,' said Dayton.

And for the titles, the bragging rights and the name-dropping which all go down so well at the golf club, he thought. That Richard had come back to share the news mollified him a little, however - it meant him turning up to the meeting with the Nilssons was not solely down to a lack of confidence in his elder child.

Liveried staff cleared their plates as he worked through the possibilities of his father being correct. If Santoro finessed a referendum from the Capital, then his force of personality and inflammatory, one-syllable soundbites might sway the proletariat who, depending on the threshold set, could be enough to propel him over the line. That would mean significant upheaval for Dayton's as a result of changing laws, taxation, currency movements, workforce access, export and import controls - the list would go on for years. Trying to predict whether the long-term outcome would be positive or negative was nigh-on impossible. At the very least, local government would be strangled for decades by the unpicking of shared infrastructure leaving the business community to operate with much less oversight than today. What could they get away with as a result?

'Alright,' he continued once the waiters had left with instructions from Eddie for more coffee. 'Our tables aren't far away this evening, I should be able to reach him at some point.'

'Leave it to me please,' said Richard. 'You'll remember I promised Annika and Fredrik I'd try for an introduction. The Malmotec investment's a decent pretext, especially if I pitch the idea of him getting involved in the announcement.'

'Are you sure I shouldn't make first contact?' asked Dayton, insecurity over his father's opinions promptly resurfacing. 'As head of the company?'

'Quite sure. You and Edward should focus on our own guests.'

'Ed's going to be busy finding this Gautier chap from McGlynn's, but I'll make sure I'm nearby.'

'No need. But let's gather before dinner and compare progress. How do you feel about co-opting Gautier?' asked Richard, turning to Eddie.

'Honestly? Not great. I dislike that crowd as much as you–'

'I doubt it.'

'– but using this kid's mother as a bartering chip, well, it's beyond immoral isn't it? I mean, what if it was Mum?'

'All's fair in love and war and…'

'And business. I know. But still.'

'But nothing. We have leverage and have to use it. Who knows what he'll be able to tell us. McGlynn would do the same if he were in our shoes, I guarantee.'

Eddie had no reason to disagree but was less sure about whether Wynter McGlynn should be burdened with the sins of her father. For all that he wanted her company dead and buried, it ought to be done the right way, within the rules of the game. Yet beyond the extensive but blunt legal and regulatory frameworks, such rules were self-defined, pegged to a sliding scale of morality down which he had already taken several strides. He nodded, more to himself than anyone else.

'Good,' said Richard. 'Now, as I'm unlikely to be back this year, there's one more thing I wanted to discuss.'

'Go on,' said Dayton, wary of his father's premonitory tone.

'It's time for us to speak about you passing on control of the company to Edward.'

Dayton froze. Difficult conversations were best avoided if at all possible and subject to sufficient notice if not - how else could he be expected to prepare a suitable argument? This was a topic for the future, solely for him and Eddie to agree, and his father had no right to bring it up let alone interfere. The one saving grace was that his brother appeared equally taken aback.

'Um, I don't think now's the right–'

'Don't be squeamish, Julian. Succession planning is good practice and it's obvious Edward will assume control at some point given the age gap. I recall you making that commitment when you took over from me?'

'And the timing was agreed to be entirely at my discretion.'

'Indeed. And I'd like to understand your thoughts as to the timing.'

'Why? It's really none of your business,' said Dayton, querulously enough for nearby diners to turn their heads.

'Shh, keep your voice down. It's entirely my business. You are my sons. This is the company I have given most of my life to building since your grandfather died and will continue to support in any way I can. How dare you tell me otherwise.'

'But I'm chief executive now. I decide what happens and when, including any handover. And I can tell you it won't happen until Ed's got enough experience.'

'What else does he need to learn?'

This was why Dayton hated confrontation. Adrenaline released by mounting anxiety was already making his hands shake and they were now jammed between his crossed thighs to stop the others from noticing. Worse, it was slowing his pace of thought and leading him into rhetorical dead-ends. To state Eddie was lacking specific experience was sure to cause further debate, to admit he had the necessary knowledge and skills would remove an obstacle Dayton was desperate to keep in place. When trapped the default manoeuvre was to answer one question with another, preferably loaded in his favour.

'Well, what do you think, Ed? Are you ready to take on my full remit and all the tedious responsibilities that brings? The endless balance sheets, the regulatory reviews, the statutory reporting?'

Eddie took his time, delighted the issue had been raised but knowing his next words would send him almost irrevocably down one of two paths. Did he want the job? Yes, partly to satisfy his ego but mostly because, after seven years of close observation, he could surely do it better than his brother - differently, but undoubtedly better. Maybe their father had come to the same conclusion. In any event, the timing all boiled down to his willingness to commit. Should he continue to defer or, finally, was he ready to grow up?

'Yeah, I am,' he said simply.

Dayton's mouth opened but emitted no words.

'Excellent,' said Richard. 'That was my judgement too.'

'But it's not... not true,' whined Dayton, finding his tongue at last.

He wanted to take control of the situation, to be as commanding as his father would be in his shoes. Alas, the anger required to fuel his courage was safely barricaded away with all his other emotions, only becoming accessible later to fuel nothing but self-recrimination. At this point even logical argument was prevented by a confusion of thoughts making him almost sick with vertigo.

'You're just not ready. Not yet.'

'Yes, I think I am,' replied Eddie, more confident now the choice was made. 'I've been meaning to talk to you about it for a while.'

'But–'

'Why don't you sit down over the next day or two,' said Richard. 'No need for me to be involved but I'd like to know the plan before I leave. To be clear, Julian, I think we'd all prefer an orderly transition than anything rushed. Unless of course you're careless enough to lose the case with McGlynn's.'

Unsure as to the seriousness of this last remark, Dayton stayed silent, brow furrowed. The relative comfort of his well-ordered world had been plunged into ambiguity and he needed time alone to determine the options retaining the most advantage. Delay was the likely strategy. Depending on the outcome of the trial he would delay the conversation with Eddie, then the agreement of a timetable and then the expected end of the process. Anything could change in the meantime and lead to a reprieve, anything to avoid the stigma of a forced departure.

'That's settled then,' continued Richard. 'Now, what's on your agenda for the day?'

'I'm heading down to court again,' said Eddie. 'Proceedings were suspended overnight but I reckon Wynter will have to testify today. Keen to see how she does.'

'I'm at a loose end until your mother arrives. Mind if I join you?'

'Sure.'

'Julian? How about it?'

Broken from his reverie, Dayton looked up and saw the Nilssons heading in their direction. With no inclination to feign politeness, he rose, crumpled his napkin and threw it onto the table.

'No, at least one of us has work to do. I'll be in the office. *My* office.'

Threading his way towards the door, he was forced to wait for Annika and then Fredrik to squeeze between chairs in their path.

'Good morning,' said Nilsson, courteously enough.

'He's over there,' came the reply with a jerk of the thumb. 'Enjoy your breakfast.'

16

The temperature at street level, already a degree higher than at the same hour the previous day, caused McGlynn to regret her choice in walking to court. She had managed to pry herself away from the laptop and into bed after midnight only for the alarm to wake her in time for Jacob Wiesenberg's arrival at six. They fell at once into discussing her preparatory work, how she wanted to articulate her understanding of the case and the defence's probable tactics. Wiesenberg then switched sides to role-play Dayton's lawyer, peppering her with difficult questions until they felt her testimony would pass close inspection. Jaded by two hours of mental gymnastics she had decided against his offer of a lift, the lungfuls of fresh air working wonders for her sense of wellbeing. The route took her up in the direction of Merchants Square but, rather than veering left along Jubilee Street, she was still climbing the steep gradient of Hamelin Road and could feel damp patches developing. A hot and sweaty arrival, she reflected, might not make the most auspicious of first impressions.

At least she had made productive use of her journey by chasing Detective Campbell again, now out of pure concern for Rohan's welfare rather than any expectation he might miraculously be available today, sending personal messages to Charlie and Jack and clearing down most of her inbox. About to return the phone to her bag, she was startled when it rang in her hand.

'Hello?'

'Ms McGlynn? It's Kenise Campbell. Are you free to talk?'

'Yes, of course. Sorry for the background noise, I'm walking through town.'

'That's no problem. I'm outside your warehouse waiting for Mr Brookes or Mr Valente to arrive.'

'Didn't you make it over there last night?'

'Uh-hmm. And I didn't appreciate being stonewalled after your promises on Monday.'

'I'm sure my staff are being as helpful as possible, within the constraints of their own priorities.'

'Mmm.' A tone of resignation. 'Perhaps I shouldn't have expected anything else. But how about showing each other some good faith today?'

McGlynn's interest, already piqued by the call, soared. Sure the detective had new information and was confirming a trade in return for cooperation, she needed to solve the dilemma playing on her mind since the previous afternoon. On one hand, she could easily defer Campbell's offer before agreeing this evening to the Mayor's request for public support. Following a call with Commissioner Petrucci, City PD would presumably be redirected elsewhere leaving her safe to clean house in private. On the other, she could trust that Campbell's information would help in the search for Rohan, follow her instincts in opposing Santoro's independence crusade, live with the police intrusion and potentially face criminal charges. Either way, there would be no going back. What should she do?

Do your duty, she had heard in the corridors of City Hall and again McGlynn asked herself where her duty lay - to her own principles, to her company and its staff, to the populations of the City, the surrounding region, the country or even the migrants who might be using her ships. Now that the problem required an immediate solution, the only acceptable answer was obvious.

'Yes, I think some good faith is exactly what's required,' she replied, staying true to herself.

'Very well, so... We have no reason to believe Rohan Mehta or Wenling Kim have left the country and there's no record of them making electronic payments since the weekend. I have a phone number for Ms Kim but she doesn't appear to be on the payroll of any City-based organisation. She's listed as living with Mr Mehta but her passport is registered in Singapore and I have that address if you want it. We also have a log of Mr Mehta's car from a camera on the Six Hills road. It crossed city limits at four-fifteen Sunday afternoon and I can give you the make, model and licence plate.'

'Yes please, to all.'

Campbell recited the details and waited as they were repeated back.

'Anything else?' asked McGlynn, disappointed at the lack of anything more useful. 'Any chance of a photo from the camera? Or triangulating their phones?'

'I take it you don't understand the boundaries within which I operate, Ms McGlynn?'

'Not really, no.'

'Then you should know that I've already overstepped my authority by quite a way. Further inquiries will require a missing person's investigation.'

'Alright, thanks.'

'Mr Brookes has just arrived so perhaps you'd call him before I waste any more of my time here.'

'Will do. I'll probably come down later too.'

'See you then.'

McGlynn stood at the roadside, thinking fast. Time was scarce as ever with only ten minutes until she was expected and another half a mile to walk. Mind made up, she pushed on while typing out a short message to Brookes. Once the delivery notification appeared she found Hallam's number, hit the dial button and increased her pace in spite of the temperature.

'Wynter?' came the gruff voice.

'Morning. Sorry, haven't got long. Just to let you know I've given Andrew and Hugo instructions to cooperate with City PD.'

'Sounds risky. What changed your mind?'

'Long story. I'll fill you in some other time.'

'OK. Did you see my feedback on their report?'

'No?'

'Only sent it five minutes ago. I've added notes and suggestions which I'll pick up with them directly if you like.'

'Sure, I'm heading over later so will read it on the way. No need for you to catch a flight.'

'OK. But I'd still like to come across tomorrow. Anything else I can take off your plate beforehand?'

'Mmm, maybe. Have you heard I'm struggling to find Rohan this week?' she asked, betting the older woman's access to the company gossip was as strong as ever.

'Yes, lots of rumours around. Is it causing you problems?'

'Several. I'm about to take his place testifying against Dayton's for one. But I am worried and I've just been given a few details which could help track him or his partner down. If I give you those, can you try and make headway before I resurface after lunch?'

'Fire away.'

McGlynn repeated Campbell's information from memory, confident of its accuracy.

'I think Wenling's number is the starting point, then her overseas address. And keep trying Rohan directly. I've spoken with his father and can call him again if we're stuck. Let's check in again first thing, your time.'

'Right you are. And good luck this morning. Give those bastards merry hell.'

'Ha! Will do.'

With all her other problems stowed, McGlynn's attention turned to the next few hours. Coming up on her left were the ugly, squat civil court buildings - much younger but already more dated than their elegant criminal counterparts near City Hall. Although no stranger to the inside of a courtroom, company issues from the trivial to the serious having had to be settled through due process, this would be her first time as a key witness. With or without Rohan, the need to prove Dayton was in the wrong threatened to consume her and she knew her testimony, which could even be delivered in front of him, would have a significant bearing on the verdict. She had promised herself three victories this week. Success today was the first and should lead to the second - the Nilssons confirming McGlynn-Lansing as their preferred bidder - leaving only Saturday's triathlon to complete the set. Swamped by the desire to win, she felt exhilarated by a heady blend of anticipation and apprehension.

Wiesenberg was waiting in the drab reception and a look of naked relief crossed his face as she stepped inside.

'Cutting it fine, Director?'

'Plenty of time,' she said breezily, knowing there were only minutes to spare.

He thrust a visitor's badge into her hand and led the way down a long, featureless corridor into what could have been easily mistaken for a classroom. On the far side, in front of windows offering nothing more inspiring than a view of the car park, were four unoccupied chairs behind utilitarian rectangular tables. More lay across the intervening area, those to left and right facing each other with a third in the centre, then twenty or so chairs set out theatre-style with their backs to where she stood, all but one of which were empty. Whiteboards covered with handwritten text and diagrams in blue ink took up much of the wall space and only the expensive-looking, free-standing microphones suggested this was anything other than a place of learning.

Maybe that's exactly what it was, and at least there's air-conditioning, thought McGlynn gratefully, following Wiesenberg over to the table on the right. The two men already sitting opposite wore matching ties and had broken off their hushed conversation to stare with a mixture of interest and hostility. Recognising neither, she assumed they were Dayton's legal representation and allowed herself to breathe a little easier given the man himself was not present. After a brief introduction to Wiesenberg's deputy, a studious looking woman in her early thirties, McGlynn made her way to the front row of the public seating, vaguely recognising its sole occupant; an expensively-dressed, exceptionally attractive South Asian woman. She returned the small, unsmiling nod before movement at the doorway drew their attention.

'All rise,' intoned a clerk in tweed jacket and skirt, standing aside and allowing others to pass before following them across the room.

McGlynn remained on her feet while appraising the judges who would hear her testimony. All were middle-aged white men wearing a common apparel of dark suits, open-necked shirts and glasses. The sole dissimilarity appeared to be that the one in the centre was nearly bald whereas the first and the third were grey-haired. Another example of why we need to champion more girls into technology careers, she thought, wondering how difficult it would have been to find non-male, stale and pale magistrates with the requisite experience.

Once settled behind triangular nameplates too small to be read from any distance, the clerk invited the room to be seated and fiddled with a remote control until vivid green bands illuminated around the microphones. Justice Stepney then introduced himself and his peers as Justices Walther and de Haan and resumed proceedings. Wiesenberg confirmed Rohan Mehta would not be attending and called McGlynn instead, had her sworn in at the central table and ran confidently through the topics rehearsed earlier that morning. They worked well together - him asking a progressive series of questions in his calm, precise manner and her answering fluently until certain they had evidenced the agreed point. She sensed very little activity from Dayton's counsel to her left which seemed a positive sign.

'And can you summarise to what level the semantic analysis involved in performing this function for the Dayton

Global Industries application delivers substantially the same results as the previously available McGlynn-Lansing application?' asked Wiesenberg.

'Yes,' replied McGlynn, continuing to address the judges directly with her answers. 'The Dayton application returned a ninety-eight percent matched result to ours in the independent comparison and benchmarking exercise. The algorithms involved in–'

Noticing the panel's attention had switched to the doorway, she broke off and half-turned, barely concealing her disdain when Richard and then Eddie Dayton strode in. They scanned the room to get their bearings, smiling wolfishly as their eyes met hers, and selected front row chairs by their lawyers. Eddie looked stylishly pugnacious as always but it had been years since McGlynn last set eyes on Richard. The supercilious plutocrat who fought an underhanded campaign to ruin her father's reputation seemed to have changed very little and her relief at Dayton's absence swiftly dissipated. Never mind, she thought, raising her chin and facing forwards again, if they had come with the aim of putting her off they would be sorely disappointed.

'And the algorithms involved in semantically determining these outcomes should therefore be considered identical once quantum error correction has been applied,' she finished calmly.

McGlynn's deposition continued, her awareness of Richard and Eddie dwindling into the background, until Wiesenberg appeared satisfied.

'Mrs McGlynn,' he said with finality. 'In your position as Director, and with all the information made available to this court, do you have any doubt that Dayton Global Industries gained a competitive advantage by illegally infringing your intellectual property?'

'I am left in no doubt whatsoever that this is the case.'

'Thank you. Justices, I have no further questions at this time.'

'Thank you, Mr Wiesenberg,' said Stepney. 'Do you have any objection to cross-examination of this witness on the basis of it causing significant distress or diminishing the quality of evidence?'

'No objection.'

'Mr Franklin, Mr Lister, does defence counsel have any questions for Mrs McGlynn?'

'Yes Justice, we do,' said the older of the two, rising.

A tall and austere man who had become much more interested in objecting to her testimony since Richard and Eddie's arrival, the lawyer's academic demeanour was well-suited to the room.

'Mrs McGlynn, I'm Anthony Franklin from Blanchet, Franklin and Lennon. Could you please explain to the court how these algorithms, exact copies of which you claim have been made by my client, could possibly produce different results based on identical inputs?'

'Certainly. It's partly due to progressive machine learning in natural language sentiment analysis, and partly to quantum decoherence which is why we apply the error correction I mentioned earlier. This combination will generally mean a small percentage of outputs differ each time a benchmarking scenario is run. However, for the ways in which we're applying the technology to consumer use cases, the variances are negligible.'

'These variances might be negligible to your customers, who perhaps have lower expectations than the members of this hearing, but they're not acceptable in your attempts to prove that my client's technology is identical to yours, are they?'

'Yes, they are. With error correction applied, the variance drops almost to zero meaning it's exceptionally unlikely the data is being processed through anything other than an exact copy of our code.'

'Exceptionally unlikely, but not impossible?'

'I don't think it's reasonable to suggest their technology is in any way different to ours based on the evidence we've provided.'

'But not impossible?' repeated Franklin in a bored tone, looking down the length of his hooked nose.

'Not impossible, but it's beyond reasonab–'

'Thank you. So, it's actually possible that my client's technology, which was authored to perform similar functions for the same target audience and will necessarily have a level of similarity in its design, is different to yours?'

'Theoretically, but–'

'But didn't you say earlier that the two sets of algorithms must be considered identical? Based on the benchmarking conducted by ACG Research Services and paid for, let us not forget, by McGlynn-Lansing?'

'Yes, and I absolutely believe they are identical. And I'd like it acknowledged again that ACG Services is fully independent - we only paid for their work as it seemed highly unlikely for your client to do so.'

'Noted. But if we can return to the algorithms in question, is it your opinion they're identical, rather than established fact?'

'It is my opinion, supported by all the evidence we've provid–'

'That's fine, thank you. I only wanted to confirm my understanding that your previous answer was opinion rather than fact. I'd prefer to ask about something else if I may. Could you please explain how your error correction technology works? I'm specifically interested in the assumptions you've made in the…' Franklin made a great show of returning to his table and leafing through an expensive-looking journal. '…in the application of Shizoku's theorem.'

'We're nearly able to do away with error correction altogether. Once we reduce decoherence to zero, it becomes even more obviou–'

'I'd be very grateful if you could restrict yourself to answering the question I put to you? About how your technology works? Could you try and manage that for me please?'

'Would you understand the answer if I did, Mr Franklin?' she asked pointedly, seeing the direction being taken. The man's patronising tone and tendency to interrupt were beginning to grate.

'Let's find out shall we. Please could you answer my question?'

'As I'm sure you're aware, I'm not the best person to explain the quantum theory behind that specific technology. But it's irrelevant to–'

'Ah, I see,' said Franklin with satisfaction. 'Would I have more success if I were to ask Mr Mehta, your, um… forgive me… your chief technology officer?'

'Objection,' said Wiesenberg. 'My client can't be expected to speculate on how well Mr Mehta may answer a question in his absence.'

'I'll rephrase. Mrs McGlynn, in your view, is Mr Mehta an expert in quantum computing?'

'He is, which is why I employ him. Rohan has several doctorates in the field, one of which was on error correction.'

'And, by definition therefore, you are not an expert?'

'I am Rohan's direct manager and make it my business to learn as much as I can about his work.'

'Thank you. If I may, I'd like to summarise our discussion and then ask a follow up question,' said Franklin, turning to the panel. 'Based on Mrs McGlynn's answers, we have discovered it is indeed possible for the technology developed by my client to *not* be the same as that developed by McGlynn-Lansing, in direct contradiction to her earlier testimony and the case as previously laid out by Mr Wiesenberg. Further, we understand it is Mrs McGlynn's *opinion* that my client infringed the patents held by her company but also, by her own admission, that she is not an expert in the field. It appears we still lack an expert opinion conforming to your personal view then, doesn't it Mrs McGlynn?'

McGlynn waited as long as possible, not daring to risk a glance at Wiesenberg, before answering.

'Much of our evidence was developed by Rohan. If he were available to testify, then his expert opinion would support mine.'

'But there's no written testimony from Mr Mehta, I believe? Which means, to paraphrase Mr Wiesenberg, you're speculating?' Franklin pulled a mock grimace. 'Where is Mr Mehta? Wasn't he scheduled to testify today? If his opinion is so crucial, then why isn't he here?'

'I'm not sure.'

'Which of my questions is that in response to?'

'If you can restrict yourself to individual questions, Mr Franklin, I'll do my best to provide individual answers.'

'Ha, an excellent point, you clearly missed your vocation, Mrs McGlynn. I'll withdraw those and perhaps come back to Mr Mehta shortly. In the meantime, could you please tell me whose decision it was to bring this case?'

'Mine, why?'

'This was your sole decision, rather than collaboratively with your investors or management team or legal counsel?'

'I sought their advice of course.'

'But you made the ultimate decision to proceed?'

'Yes, I'm Director of the company and accountable for its actions.'

'Accountable for its actions and its performance?'

'Obviously,' replied McGlynn, trying to deduce Franklin's intent.

'And how would you describe your relationship with Dayton Global Industries?'

'Personally or from a company standpoint?'

'Both.'

She mulled a range of adjectives, selecting one of the milder options.

'Competitive.'

'As competitive as with others in the same markets as you? Or more so?'

'Very competitive. More so.'

'And why is that?

'Objection,' noted Wiesenberg. 'My client accepts her company operates in competition with the defendant. Aside from that, I can't see the relevance of these questions.'

'Mr Franklin?'

'Certainly, Justice. I'd like to ascertain whether the long and, as I understand it, fractious relationship between Mrs McGlynn's company and my client is a sole or contributory reason as to why this case was brought.'

'I'll allow it, with due caution.'

'Thank you. Mrs McGlynn, why would you consider yourselves to be at a higher level of competition in this particular instance?'

For the first time since their arrival, McGlynn looked to Richard and Eddie, thinking about how much truth would be appropriate in her reply. Why has there been such intense rivalry for so long? Because they use immoral and illegal methods to gain any and every unfair advantage. Because they have tried to slow our progress and put us out of business since we first dared to set up in opposition. Because they spread disinformation to my staff, customers, suppliers, investors and peers. Because their company has been owned and operated by an unbroken line of malicious individuals since the day it was founded. Because it's currently run by one such individual who doesn't dare insult me to my face but who lies behind my back and for whom I have no respect. Because to him it isn't business, it's personal. Because I object to this and to him and to them and therefore because I will not stop until I have taught them the meaning of humility. That's why.

'Because they're slightly larger than us and would consider themselves number one,' she said, coolly holding Richard's gaze.

'They would only consider themselves number one? That's an incontestable fact isn't it?'

'Larger doesn't equate to better,' she said, returning to Franklin. 'We're growing much more quickly and will overtake them in several markets this year. I suspect they've resorted to copying our software because they're unable to compete solely on the merits of their own ability.'

'I'll remind you that's yet to be proven. But your point here is you would consider McGlynn-Lansing to be a better company than my client's?'

'I would.'

'And does this opinion stretch to all of McGlynn-Lansing's various subsidiaries? Specifically, do you believe your computing division to be better than the equivalent at Dayton Global Industries?'

'I do.'

'Then why is that business operating at such a large loss?'

'Excuse me?'

'If your company is so much better, and if your capabilities outstrip those of my client by such a distance, then why do you lose so much money in your computing operations?'

'What you're referring to isn't publicly available information, Mr Franklin. Why do you believe we make a loss?' she replied, unnerved by the implied specificity.

'Do you make a loss here, Mrs McGlynn?'

'It's a relatively new market and most of the players are investing heavily to capture market share. So yes, costs are currently higher than revenues.'

'By how much?'

'That's confidential.'

'It might be confidential outside these walls but I think it's important for the figure to be known to this courtroom. Please could you answer the question?'

McGlynn mooted the benefits of holding her ground. Even if Franklin did not already know the sum involved, she was not naive enough to believe the information would stay privileged from the Daytons if the gallery was removed and she revealed it to their legal team. However, Eddie and Richard were not the only members of the public present.

'I'm prepared to answer solely on the basis that the information remains confidential to these proceedings.'

'That's acceptable to the counsel for the defence. Justices?'

'Understood and agreed. All members of the court, including those seated in the public gallery, are directed to treat this information confidentially,' said Stepney. 'Please respond, Mrs McGlynn.'

'For the last twelve months, our quantum computing division made an operating loss of thirty-eight million,' she said, citing the latest figure from the board report.

'Thirty-eight million!' exclaimed Franklin. 'Isn't that an extraordinary amount for a company claiming to be the best in the industry?'

'No, not when you consider the potential mark–'

'How do your staff and your investors feel about the size of the losses you're making?'

'Objection,' said Wiesenberg again, exasperation in his voice. 'My client is unable to–'

'I'll withdraw it. Mrs McGlynn, was your decision to launch this case a direct result of such an eye-watering loss?'

'I fail to see how I can answer that without inferring this was a factor in my decision. It wasn't, it's irrelevant.'

'Is it? I'd have thought the reparations you're seeking would be very useful, even a necessity some might say, in propping up such an unprofitable endeavour?'

'We made a conscious decision to incur early losses in anticipation of future reward and our other businesses provide ample cash generation in the meantime. It has nothing to do with our rationale in holding Dayton's to account for–'

'Sorry, but why the use of these plural pronouns? I thought you mentioned only a few moments ago that *you* are solely responsible for the performance of your company and that *you* personally made the decision to litigate against my client?'

'Correct, I am and I did. But the point is–'

'The point I put to you, Mrs McGlynn, is that you and you alone must take responsibility for a fundamentally flawed decision, influenced entirely by long-standing jealousy at my client's success and the substandard performance of your computing operations. That, in–'

'Nonsense–'

'–bringing such a fallacious case, you conveniently divert attention away from your own failings of leadership–'

'My staff and investors are fully supp–'

'–and stand to gain significant financial reward without which your business is unsustainable. Those are the real reasons we're all here today, aren't they Mrs McGlynn?'

'No, that's not true at all,' retorted McGlynn, who had caught the murmured "hear, hear" from Richard's direction and was dangerously close to losing her temper. 'We're here today because of your client's blatant disregard for fair competition and, indeed, the relevant law.'

'Then, to return to my earlier question, why isn't Mr Mehta appearing as a witness?'

'He's unavailable.'

'I see. And why is that, given his testimony would presumably have been supportive to your case?'

'How should I know, Mr Franklin? You'd need to ask him.'

'Could it be that he doesn't want to appear because he realises there's no case to answer here? Because–'

'Objection!'

'–he has no wish to perjure himself under oath? Because he's actually rather embarrassed at what is–'

'This is ridicul–' snarled McGlynn.

'Objection! Objection!' the normally mild-mannered Wiesenberg nearly bellowed.

'–nothing other than an opportunistic, egotistical attempt to tarnish my client's good reputation? Is that why–'

'Mr Franklin. Mr Franklin!' shouted Stepney, overriding all three. 'Can I remind you this is a civil case in a civil court and that the word should be considered an operative term for these proceedings. Enough! Please withdraw or restate your last three questions.'

Franklin made a passable attempt at satisfied contrition and waited until the atmosphere subsided.

'I should like to withdraw them, Justice, my apologies. Notwithstanding our right to additional cross-examination should the witness provide further testimony, we have no other questions,' he concluded.

'Very well. Mr Wiesenberg, do you have anything further for Mrs McGlynn?'

Holding her tongue, still furious at Franklin's arrogance and her own reaction to it, McGlynn caught Wiesenberg's eye. She had an intense desire for him to say that yes, he did have more questions and then to work together in demonstrating just how egregious each of the defence's accusations were. The old man seemed to understand what she wanted but was clearly weighing up whether to offer Franklin another opportunity for interrogation.

'No, Justice, we have no further questions,' he said at last. 'And no more witnesses to call.'

'Mrs McGlynn, that concludes your testimony, thank you. Mr Franklin, does the defence wish to call anyone else?'

'No, Justice.'

'Then I suggest we break for lunch and return at one o'clock for summing up. This session is adjourned.'

Ignoring the Daytons and their legal team, McGlynn met Wiesenberg halfway between their respective tables.

'Let's get some fresh air, Jacob.'

Making for the door, she noticed the South Asian woman still watching attentively from the public gallery. Malik, she realised, Sunita Malik from the Post and God only knows what she must have made of the session. Deciding it was better to find out now rather than read about it later she pushed her frustration aside and diverted her course.

'Miss Malik, isn't it? I don't think we've met.'

'Hello,' said Malik, taking the proffered hand. 'It's nice to meet you, Mrs McGlynn.'

'Wynter. I've had more than enough of being called Mrs McGlynn this morning.'

'Thanks. Sunita.'

'What brings you here, Sunita? I'm surprised the Post is interested in our rather dull disagreement?'

'It didn't look particularly dull from my perspective. My editor suggested I come along to listen first hand.'

'Bill Rutter?'

'Do you know him?'

'We've spoken a few times. My father knows him better than me.'

'Ah. Well I'm working on an adjacent piece and he figured your case might be useful context.'

McGlynn's heart skipped a beat. Was she the target of Malik's next character assassination and, if so, why? What had she done to offend the Post? Or could Santoro, wanting to force her hand further, have found a way to tip them off about City PD's investigations?

'Interesting,' she said. 'Well, I can't say the last few hours were particularly enlightening, at least not from where I had the misfortune to be sitting, but maybe you came to a different conclusion?'

'To be honest,' said Malik, lowering her voice, 'I thought you gave as good as you got. That lawyer, Franklin, he's a bit of a prick isn't he.'

'Ha! I couldn't possibly comment. My own advocate… Jacob, come and meet Sunita Malik from the Post… would caution me against it in the strongest terms, I'm sure.'

Having been waiting politely on the fringes, Wiesenberg greeted the journalist as McGlynn decided on the best way to probe further.

'I won't be long, Jacob, see you outside,' she said, wanting Malik alone again. 'Have you heard anything which made your trip worthwhile, Sunita?'

'A few things. The size of the loss in your computing division for one. But of course I'm now gagged from talking about it even if I wanted to.'

'It's only temporary. We'll be profitable once the supply chain's optimised.'

'Once you've acquired Malmotec, you mean?'

'Ah, I suppose I shouldn't be surprised. It's certainly one of our aims.'

'I presume you know Dayton's are bidding? You do seem to take great pleasure in knocking lumps out of each other. Why is that Mrs McGly– Wynter?'

'It's complicated.'

'So I hear.' Malik looked across the room. 'I recognise Eddie Dayton but is that his father?'

'Uh-huh. They're the spitting image, aren't they. I'd offer to introduce you to the Baron of Inverlochy but I can't say we're on particularly good terms.'

'Sorry? The Baron of…'

'Inverlochy. It's a mediaeval hamlet on the west coast of Scotland. Richard took the title when he was appointed to the Lords.'

'A baron of a Scottish hamlet… *mashallah*. That was around the time you became Director of McGlynn-Lansing wasn't it?'

'You really are well-informed about my affairs. Should I expect to see my name in print anytime soon?'

'Perhaps.'

'Then why don't you come to my office? I'd be happy to show you what we do.'

'I'd like that,' said Malik. 'When might be convenient?'

'Any chance you'll be at the Portland tonight?'

'At the ball? Yes, I'll be there.'

'Then let's compare diaries later. I'll see you later, Sunita, it was lovely to meet you.'

Based on initial impressions, she liked Malik much more in person than by reputation and was mildly surprised to find herself so keen to meet again. Passing through the building's cheerless reception, she reminded herself to be careful - life was complicated enough at the moment.

Wiesenberg was sheltering under the broad branches of a sycamore to one side of the approach road.

'Christ but it's hot,' she said, hurrying to join him. 'Thoughts?'

'I think you did well enough, but I have to say the panel remains difficult to read.'

'Mmm, I agree. Stepney seemed reasonable but the other two might as well have not been there for all the eye-contact they gave me. Has Franklin been so condescending all along?'

'No, but he rather enjoyed showing off in front of his client, didn't he?'

'Loved it. I was hoping you'd go again after the cross-examination. Some of his comments were outrageous.'

'Happy for the truth?' enquired Wiesenberg, looking up at her directly. 'In my view he didn't land a knockout blow but was marginally ahead on points by the end. If I may say, you were starting to look rather agitated.'

'Ha! You're more than welcome to say. How dare he question my integrity.'

'It's his job I'm afraid.'

'Yeah. Sorry I took the bait.'

'He knew which buttons to press. Particularly in front of the, um, unexpected visitors.'

'Don't think I've seen old Richard Dayton more than once or twice since he moved to London. Can't stand the man, even now.'

'For what he did to David?'

'Mostly. Although my father didn't help himself much at the time either.'

'How is he?'

'To be honest, I don't really know. I get occasional updates via my mother... I spoke with her about him only yesterday in fact... but we're still not on good terms.'

'He's a proud man, Wynter, always has been. Give him time.'

'It's been seven years. I'm hopeful, but not as much as I used to be. Anyway,' she said briskly. 'Back to today's problems. Do you need me for summing up?'

'No, I'll stick to the objective evidence as much as possible. Let Franklin take the provocative approach if he wishes but I don't think it plays as well in such a technical case. Either way it's going to be a close call.'

'Don't worry, Jacob, the sun always shines on the righteous, especially on a day like this. Will we get a verdict this afternoon?'

'Tomorrow's my guess.'

'OK,' she said, checking the time, 'I'm going back to the office and then the port. Call me once you're through?'

'Of course.'

Grateful as always for his counsel, she watched the old man's measured pace as he walked away, wondering if Matthieu had organised lunch with her mother yet. Would David put away his pride and want to come?

No, she thought, not a chance.

17

McGlynn called a car for the return journey to ML One and even then was late in meeting Brookes. Stepping into the private garage led to a profound sense of déjà vu, although this time she was dressed for running in a sleeveless blue tri-suit and white athletic shoes, her hair spilling in a makeshift ponytail through the back of a navy baseball cap. As before, Brookes was already waiting beyond the security grid.

'Hey Andrew, sorry I'm late. Had the pleasure of spending the morning in court and needed to make some calls before I could change.'

'No problem, saw your message. How're you feeling today? Any tiredness or niggles I should know about?'

'Nope, all good.'

'Warmed up?'

'Not yet.'

'Then let's do some stretching. Quads, hams and hips, ten reps and fifteen seconds each side please.'

McGlynn leant her shoulder against the cool concrete wall and grabbed the toes of her left foot, bringing it up behind her.

'Talk to me about your morning,' she said. 'How are things at the warehouse?'

'Hectic. Where do you want to start?'

'Cameras?'

'All seem to be working properly. I watched some recordings from the reconnected ones - nothing unusual.'

'Did you watch with Turner?'

'Yeah. He's like my shadow again. Particularly as City PD have been making their presence felt.'

'Good. What have Campbell and her team been up to?' she asked, switching legs.

'There are four of them and she's in a better mood than yesterday but only just. Hugo and I had half an hour with her and a Sergeant Garnett. Asked mostly the same questions that I did on Monday afternoon but at least we were able to give better answers. Garnett's going through the warehouse whilst she seems more interested in the offices.'

'Have they been aboard the *Santa Rosa* yet?'

'Don't think so. We're making sure each container is signed for by a named operator so only about a quarter of the cargo has been offloaded so far.'

'OK. Keep up the checks until we're at least two-thirds of the way through and then we'll review. Did Campbell say how long she expected to be on site?'

'No. But it's not a formal investigation, so they're limited in where they can go and what they can ask for right?'

'Right. There's no warrant. Yet.'

But there might be very soon, thought McGlynn. Either because news of our cooperation with City PD reaches Santoro's ears and he works out the implications or because I have to give him the good news in person this evening.

'Presumably you've kept the info about what you found in the compound to yourself?' she asked.

'Yeah. Haven't been asked the direct question so, you know, never volunteer.'

'Keep it that way. I don't think it'll matter so much by tomorrow though.'

262

'Roger that. Feeling stretched out enough?'

'Four more,' she replied and finished off a set of lunges. 'Where are we going?'

'How long do you have?'

'About fifty minutes.'

'OK. Then out towards Conley and back to Merchants Square along the last couple of miles of Saturday's course. They're moving some of the barricades this year so I don't want you getting caught out.'

'Sounds good.'

They set off, jogging through the garage to the exit ramp they had ridden up two days previously. McGlynn slipped on a pair of wraparound shades and braced herself as they surfaced from the partial darkness. Again forcing her lungs to inhale, they crossed Cornelian Lane and headed up the hill a couple of blocks before turning northeast along Fairview. The semi-pedestrianised street was quiet enough to pick up the pace and they kept close to the buildings on their right, taking advantage of the shadows where they could, hearing the keening of the gulls and occasionally glimpsing the ocean down the side streets. She stayed on Brookes' shoulder, allowing him to set the tempo and not expecting any feedback about her technique. Running was her favourite discipline, effortless compared to the other two, and McGlynn was up on her toes, relaxed limbs moving fluently and efficiently in line with the forward motion. She had spent hours poring over the splits from previous City triathlons and knew Dayton was faster in the swim and on the bike. He would probably be well ahead as she exited the second transition but his run times in particular were declining and she could catch him this year if she was able to keep his head start to no more than three or four minutes.

'What else have you found since yesterday?' she asked, breathing easily.

'I've had to fix a hole in the perimeter fence but it looked rusted through rather than cut. That section's covered by two working cameras so low risk I'd say. Also, one of the admin team quit unexpectedly. Zoe Mears, know her?'

'Don't think so.'

'She's only been on staff two months and I hear she was well liked. I was in Hugo's office when she came in. Burst into tears and said she wasn't prepared to work there anymore. Hugo shushed her and took her off for a chat before she could say much else. Other than that, I'm still working through the process documentation and making notes about where we could tighten up.'

'Any luck in finding someone to run local security?'

'Hopeful. Talking at six to an old army buddy. She just finished a job in Dubai and is looking for contract work. Ex-MP. Knows her stuff around logistics operations in particular.'

'She sounds ideal. And I'm sure Jonah would be delighted to have a woman managing the team.'

'Got the impression he's a bit of a throwback. Gina would break his legs if he tried anything.'

'No harm in that. Well some, for him I guess.'

They ran in silence a while, McGlynn revelling in the heat, the exercise and the freshening air as they increased their distance from the city centre. At the end of Wheaton Boulevard, where Brookes forked left to take them along the edge of Palisades Park, she kept her eyes on the opening stretch of the Six Hills road for as long as possible, scanning for cars matching the details from Campbell. There had been no time to call Hallam between leaving court and coming out, and it was the middle of the night in Australia in any case, but she had sent a message asking after progress.

'Have you spoken to Jane Hallam at all?' she said.

'Not yet.'

'I asked her to look over Hugo's report and it came back this morning with her recommendations, mostly things only she would spot from knowing the dockyard operations inside out. I'm coming back with you to the warehouse so I'll tackle it with Hugo in person.'

'No problem.'

Brookes slowed to check her form.

'How are your energy levels?' he asked, evidently satisfied with what he saw. 'Want to up the pace a bit?'

'You've no idea. Taking it easy this week is killing me.'

'Come on then, but it's not a race, OK?'

From the western tip of the park, they pressed on along the Rangeway and then zig-zagged down through the narrow, tree-lined streets of Thornwood. The whitewashed five-storey townhouses kept most of the sun at bay, the cooler air a welcome relief until they dropped onto the much busier Crown Road, having to dodge the two lanes of fast-flowing traffic each side of the huge stone fountain. Reaching the other pavement in safety, they slowed again and Brookes began to point out where the latter stages were expected to differ.

'OK, the big change this year is that athletes are being sent around the edge of the Necropolis rather than through the middle. The marshals have shortened the course near Tattershall Place to make up for it.'

'Makes sense. They'll be able to pack more spectators into the park.'

'Yeah. And there'll be more drinks tables too so definitely worth hydrating given how hot it's going to be. I'll get you the last split somewhere around here. If you're still behind, see how you feel and decide how early you want to kick for the line.'

They looped around the cemetery's northern perimeter to join the end of Jubilee Street. The wide boulevard driving straight as an arrow for over a mile and a half into Merchants Square was easily her favourite part of the course. Not only would the end of nearly three hours of intense physical exertion be almost in sight but the combined noise and spectacle of the crowds made it a gladiatorial parade, sure to give her a fresh burst of energy for the final push. The onlookers here would be at their densest; often packed five or six deep behind the temporary barriers already installed on each side. Today though, the road was its usual midweek hubbub of cars and buses and she had to run shoulder to shoulder with Brookes along the pavement, merely imagining how she might feel come Saturday. Where would Dayton be by this point? Already finished? So far ahead he was unable to be caught? Or already overtaken such that the only thing between her and the week's third victory were fewer than ten minutes of easy running and blissful, liberating euphoria?

By the time the traffic had been forced left to the south of the square, Brookes was slackening off even more, no doubt mindful of McGlynn's reserves, and they entered the plaza at a jog.

'The marshals were still forty metres short so you're going to end up bearing right here and following the barriers around to the front of City Hall. The elite athletes have a separate filter lane but that'll be closed off by the time you get here so just keep left. Drink plenty afterwards and I'll find you near the obelisk again.'

She looked over at the monument. A cylinder of black granite erected to commemorate the seventy-nine people lost in the bombings, it dominated the western side of the square.

'No problem. Jack and the girls are coming down so I'll make sure we're somewhere nearby.'

'Good stuff,' he said, checking his wrist. 'OK, I reckon there's long enough to get you back on time without having to break our necks. Let's go.'

They retraced their route before veering off Jubilee Street towards the bay. All at once, and almost directly ahead among the few skyscrapers puncturing the blue and silver waterline, McGlynn saw the uppermost floors of ML One. She ran alongside Brookes down the incline, trying to concentrate on the road but finding her eyes inexorably drawn back to her building's roofline, drawing in its strength and purpose, bolstering the effects of the endorphins flowing in her bloodstream. The morning's frustrations receded to nothing, even the lingering annoyance at Franklin's presumption and Eddie and Richard's presence, and she felt fully reinvigorated, her boldness and optimism wholly restored. How could there possibly have been any doubt that the case would be won, the deal finalised with Malmotec and Julian Dayton bested for a third time come Saturday morning? What a privilege it was to be granted this exceptional existence.

'What else do you have planned for me, Andrew, tomorrow and Friday?'

'Absolutely nothing. If you've still got your lunchtimes blocked, then make sure you spend them eating properly, plenty of carbs. You can't afford to skip meals.'

McGlynn nodded unconvincingly.

'Is that clear, Director?'

'Crystal,' she laughed, trying to mimic his tone from the previous day's conversation but unable to sufficiently deepen her voice. 'But on Monday, I'm the boss again. *Clear*?'

'Ma'am, yes ma'am!'

'Ha! Come on, let's speed up a bit. It's less than a mile back and I bet you thirty sit-ups we can time the crossings between Marigold and the office so they're all on green.'

'You think? Alright you're on, but it's on you if you fall.'

'Not a chance!'

Lengthening her stride, she turned right and then left onto the much quieter Avenue San Domingo which led directly to the northern end of Cornelian Lane. McGlynn had run this route dozens of times and knew the pattern of the four intersections well. Once the lights at Marigold Street turned green, it was possible to catch each of the others at exactly the right time to avoid having to stop, although the length of the gap between the third and fourth made it nearly a sprint.

The first were on red as they arrived but the moment they changed and the crossing traffic started to slow she was away, exulting in the freedom to run at the pace she wanted and leaving a surprised Brookes to lag behind. Ninety seconds later, she hit the second junction perfectly and checked swiftly to each side before flying straight across the black and white stripes. Down again, towards Fairview where she was early and had to take more of a chance that none of the cars would jump the signals. Now onto the final stretch between Fairview and Cornelian, she raced onwards, throwing caution to the wind, exhilarated by the effort, determined to win the wager.

Around halfway, McGlynn looked up to see a minivan parked at the kerbside, an adjacent man standing in profile and another seated beyond next to Delilah's, in the shade of the restaurant's red awning. Subconsciously, she started to shift her position on the pavement, aiming to fly squarely through the gap without having to slow. Even so, the situation struck her as odd. Not only was the van stationary on a road where signs indicated no stopping but it was unusual for the small restaurant to be open at lunchtime. As the distance rapidly diminished she identified the reason. Both men were built like weightlifters and dressed identically in black – boots, jeans, t-shirts, shades – and slanting across the neck of the standing man she could make out a coiled wire. Private security, she thought, intrigued to know which minor celebrity or local bigwig had persuaded the famously indifferent Delilah to cook this early.

She glanced over her shoulder and saw Brookes also easing towards the kerb a couple of seconds behind, arms and legs driving smoothly, grinning with pride at the effort required to keep up with his well-coached protégé. Satisfied the intervening distance would allow them through the space in turn provided the bodyguards stayed exactly where they were, she turned back. Both now looked in her direction but were otherwise immobile and she committed to the risk, too late to shout a warning in any case.

Twenty yards to go, fifteen... and suddenly the two men moved with practised fluidity.

The first gave a small hand signal, flexed his shoulders and turned fully towards the oncoming runners. The second, a giant of a man, propelled himself upright with a thrust of his powerful arms and took a half-step around the table, stooping to avoid contact with the canopy above. A collision became unavoidable if he moved any further outwards and McGlynn began to desperately fight her momentum and lessen any impact. Somewhere in her peripheral vision she registered the van's sliding door yawned open by the kerb, the interior ominously dark.

Five yards... still going much too fast.

She passed the first bodyguard who, one foot up on the pavement, ignored her completely. To her increasing horror she watched the second man lunge diagonally into her path, swinging his right arm up to the horizontal where, a split second later, a brawny forearm hit her like an iron bar across the chest.

The upper half of her body came to a short-lived standstill but the forward motion of her abdomen and legs continued unchecked, lifting her feet off the pavement, snapping her head and shoulders back and down, and launching her into a reverse somersault. For the briefest of moments a winded, disbelieving McGlynn was completely upended in mid-air and glimpsed a dizzying picture of Brookes further up the street. Then the movement continued and she hit the pavement like an elite swimmer diving into a pool. Hands, elbows, head, breasts, pelvis, knees colliding with the concrete - flaying skin, tearing the tri-suit and driving the remaining air from her lungs. She came to a crumpled stop fifteen feet beyond her attacker, badly disoriented by the landing and a jumble of confused thoughts.

What the...? What the fuck just happened? This can't be, *impossible*, no... How could this *enculé*...? Not here, not in my city. What does he want, what do they... want from me? How dare he hit me? *Sale fils de pute*. Why can't I breathe? Broad fucking daylight... Why me? *Why*?

From where she had come to rest, sunglasses gone, one cheek on the ground and one eye obscured by the peak of the dislodged baseball cap, her view back towards the restaurant was rotated by ninety degrees. A long way away she could see Brookes well short of the van, rooted to the spot, mouth agape. Closer, the other man remained where she had passed him, facing Brookes with fists balled and legs braced but apparently making no attempt to interfere. Closer still, blurred pairs of black boots and jeans, impossibly tall from her lowly perspective, made leisurely progress in her direction.

He was coming for her again.

Run, screamed the signals from her amygdala, run, run...

But her battered, breathless body refused to comply and she lay like a rag doll for the moment it took him to cover the intervening distance. She tried to shout at Brookes, to demand that he move and do something, anything to help but no sound came other than a rasping, reflexive inhalation. Then a hand reached down into the edge of her vision, encircling her bicep as though it was nothing more than a broom handle, and McGlynn found herself being jerked unceremoniously off the floor. A second hand came into view, covered in the calluses of thousands of hours in the gym and smelling faintly of expensive cologne, knocking the loose baseball cap from the back of her head and taking hold of her neck. Effortlessly, the man drew her upright, her rising eyes inches away from the intricate stitching of his jeans, the protrusion of a belt buckle under his t-shirt, the edge of a tattoo above, the lizard-like skin at the base of a thick, brown neck. Deltoids and pectorals and biceps bulging like footballs, the huge man lifted her higher until only the tips of her white shoes remained in contact with the pavement, scraping frantically from side to side as she strove to bear any weight. She seized his wrist, slippery with sweat which might have been hers, and hauled upwards to relieve the pressure on her throat. Over the slope of his trapezius she could see Brookes finally come out of his stupor and into action, hurling himself at the man's accomplice, the pair crashing backwards into the minivan.

The van door, my God, the van door is open, oh my God, they mean to take me, *mon dieu, mon dieu,* not again, not again…

Long-suppressed fear gripped her and it took all McGlynn's remaining willpower to dominate the impulse to panic. To panic would be to lose. She must stay in control and find a way to turn the tables, find a way to escape before these men could force her into the van and whatever wretchedness lay beyond. However, much to her bewilderment, her attacker continued to raise his arm until she was clear of the concrete and then suddenly thrust her backwards, away from the road. He crossed the width of the pavement in two easy strides, a struggling McGlynn suspended from one hand, and slammed her into the front

272

wall of an abandoned bar, pinning her to the graffiti-covered stonework with her feet several inches off the ground.

Partially dazed, her fingers slackened as she stared at the grinning caricature of a bodybuilder. Only a sunbed would account for the deep tan and a long relationship with performance enhancing drugs for the pockmarks on his clean-shaven chin. Thin fair hair, buzzed close to the scalp to disguise male pattern baldness, exposed a vein squirming along the side of his right temple above a damaged ear. There was nothing in the black lenses of strangely asymmetric glasses except her own reflection - a desperate, contorted face perched atop a pyramid of narrowing muscle.

McGlynn clawed her way back to full consciousness and renewed her purchase. The excruciating grip around her throat seemed designed purely to hold her in position, the pressure upwards rather than outwards, leaving just enough of an airway to breathe. She was amazed he allowed her to carry so much of her weight and guessed frantically at his intentions. Did he mean to wait until the strength in her arms gave out before dragging her to the van and forcing her inside? Or was he waiting for help, for his partner to overcome Brookes so the two of them could more easily do the same?

Either way, these men had retained possession of the initiative for long enough. She contracted her abdomen, brought up her knees and lashed out with the ball of her right foot, unsighted but aiming for the man's groin. The blow missed, the inside of her shin bouncing harmlessly off his thigh, the momentum pulling her hips away from the wall. As she regrouped for a second attempt he broadened his grin and moved to stand side-on, presenting a much more difficult target. She tried again, twisting violently at the waist and driving her toe towards his genitals with a passable roundhouse kick. This time much softer flesh gave way and he grunted in pain. Encouraged, she bucked for a third time but, before she could launch her foot once more, he curled his free hand into a fist and punched her lazily in the stomach, using only enough force to subdue rather than injure.

McGlynn subsided limply back against the stone, the fight in her gone, realising she was hopelessly outmuscled. Her solar plexus was in spasm and her legs refused to cooperate. The agony from her jaw and the soft tissue at the top of her neck was virtually unbearable and even if her arms had been as long as his, long enough for her nails to reach his eyes, it would mean releasing the only support keeping her from strangulation. No longer able to contain the terror of certain defeat, she fought instead for another breath, the air whistling through her constricted windpipe. When might she get another bid for freedom? What did these people want with her? Was it money they wanted? Was this really about fucking *money*?

She tried to refocus on the man's face but could only see soft edges. The grin had returned, that much was discernible, and his head was now slightly inclined in a parody of interest but her vision was blurring, distorted by the pain or the lack of oxygen or both. One second passed, then another, McGlynn increasingly confused as to why he was waiting any longer before taking her to the van - surely he could see she had no resistance left to offer? Then she felt the pressure on her neck gradually pivot away from the vertical towards the horizontal, closing the remaining airway completely.

Her terror exploded into unconditional panic.

This was no abduction, this was an execution.

The giant man held her effortlessly, choking the life from her body with careful precision while McGlynn flailed and gouged as far as she could reach. He caught one wrist between the thumb and first two fingers of his free hand and then fished for the other as her legs and feet beat impotently at his shins.

The last of her strength ebbed away. Tongue protruding from her mouth, face blackening and irregular dark spots bordered in fiery red growing and joining in her sight, McGlynn still aware enough to know the end was near. The pain was gone, the panic replaced by the great emptiness of resignation.

Dying in the prime of my life on a beautiful day in a safe city. How stupid. How could it have come to this. What did I do to deserve such a death. Where were you Andrew, where were you when I needed you? Goddamn you Brookes, I needed you. But this wasn't your fault, not your doing, I know, I understand.

Who will look after my company with me gone? It'll be alright. The company is strong, I have cherished it and built it and leave it solid enough to survive without me. Thom will be alright and my sister and Auntie Jane and Jacob and others will help. Perhaps even *Papa*.

Adieu Sylvie, Michael. *Adieu Maman, adieu.*

Goodbye my beautiful family. I'm so sorry Jack to leave you like this. Goodbye my darling girls. Are you in danger? Are you next? I pray to a god in whom I do not believe. I pray you show them mercy, I beg of you, keep them safe, protect them as I would if I were here. Too young to lose their mother at all, let alone in such a manner. What damage will that do and how well will you cope? Be brave my darlings as I have tried to teach you, to show you through my example. You are my light, my passion and my reason and my only wish is that I could have done more. I should have done more, I'm sorry, I'm so very sorry. Please, please forgive me. Wherever I find myself next I will wait for you. I will stay until you are ready to join me and then I will adore and look after you forever. Know always that I love you, I will always love you, I love you always love you always you always love love love…

18

Hundreds of girls, dressed in the purple and grey of the Escola Maria Imaculada, meandered towards the tall iron gates or loitered under the fig and trumpet trees. Heady with excitement for the weekend, she ran.

The long-planned safari would be one of those rare occasions when the whole family was together, even father, all five of them hiking in the mountains where she was dying to see ocelots, monkeys and maybe even a wolf. She loved wolves and had been studying their habitat in geography lessons, memorising interesting facts which were sure to impress her brother and sister, especially the former who thought he knew everything. It's taken forever but the trip is finally here, she rejoiced. The thrill of a helicopter ride and then campfires, toasted marshmallows, stories from their guides and sleeping bags under a galaxy of stars.

Turning right beyond the school entrance, she hurried eastwards along the Rua Atalanta, impatiently scanning the waiting drivers for Rodrigo. Doors slammed and the occasional horn blared as limousines and SUVs pulled carelessly away from the kerb, the Friday traffic as chaotic as usual.

'Miss Wynter?' asked one as she passed.

'*Sim*,' she replied cautiously.

'Senhor Rodrigo is ill. I am to take you home today.'

She looked up at him, politely trying to keep the suspicion from her face while heeding her mother's endless warnings to never trust anyone she did not know. The uniform was similar to Rodrigo's, and the car behind was definitely his - she knew the licence plate by heart - but she was sure of having not met this man before.

'*Momento Senhor, por favor*,' she said in her piping voice.

Taking her phone from the inside pocket of her blazer, she tapped the sequence of keys required to call her mother and stole another furtive glance at the driver while waiting to be connected. He was older than Rodrigo and much fatter but wore a kindly expression on his face.

'We should leave little *senhorita*. You have an exciting holiday planned, yes? The mountains and the animals?'

Still no answer from the other end of the line.

'My name is Miguel,' added the man, seeing the girl's doubt. He opened the rear door of the car and raised a hand in invitation. 'Come, let us go, eh? Your brother and sister will be waiting.'

The ringing in her ear finally diverted to voicemail. She dared not call her father, who would be working and displeased at unnecessary interruption, and her older siblings were sure to still be finishing their lessons at the *Internacional* a mile away. Persuaded by the familiar car and the driver's knowledge of her family and their weekend plans, she clambered wordlessly up onto the back seat, clutching her phone and schoolbag in the gloom as the door closed. The man disappeared from the tinted window and she rapidly typed a message, her thumbs moving expertly across the tiny keys, hitting send and turning off the screen before the front door opened and he sank heavily into the driver's seat. He did not smell as nice as Rodrigo, she noticed, wrinkling her nose behind a hand.

They set off, queuing slowly through the intersection with Avenida Primavera then filtering into better traffic, northwards beneath the looping power cables in the direction of Vila Santa Clara. Miguel drove in silence and without hurry and she began to relax, reassured he was following the normal route. Maybe she would hear the howler monkeys again or feed the same adorable troop of capuchins which had visited camp last year. Shortly after passing the magnificent façade of the Catedral Paraiso, a chime from the phone intruded on her daydreams and her limbs went rigid on reading her mother's reply - *Chérie, make sure your phone's location tracking is turned on. Get out as soon as the car stops. Find a policeman if you can. Run.*

Up ahead the way was blocked by the lights prior to where Rodrigo would normally fork right and join the down ramp, accelerating hard onto the fast-flowing Avenida Central. Realising this might be the last time the car came to a standstill for a while, she double checked her phone settings and looked up to find the man who called himself Miguel watching carefully in the rear-view mirror. Gently, keeping her head very still despite the hammering of her heart, she moved the bag from her legs and slid her hands as close to the seatbelt buckle and door handle as she dared, aiming to be out and away before he had chance to react. The car drew to a halt in line and she jammed the belt release, simultaneously yanking the silver lever and shoulder-barging the door with as much force as she could only to rebound painfully off the leather and plastic trim. Wildly, she tugged over and over at the unresisting metal swivelling uselessly in her grip, unaware child-locks even existed let alone that they might have been engaged since the morning run.

'*Senhorita*, give me your phone,' said Miguel, half-turned in his seat and holding out a powerful, hirsute hand.

She shook her head, shrinking into the corner of the car, eyes searching everywhere for another means of escape.

'Give me your phone or I will tell my friends to hurt your brother and sister.'

Tears welling, she passed the device across as the lights turned to green and the traffic moved off. Miguel ignored the slipway and continued straight ahead. On reaching a cruise he moved into the outside lane, opened his window and threw the phone at the front of an oncoming truck where it blew apart, pieces scattering like confetti as she watched through the rear window.

'Where are you taking me?' she asked in a fearful whisper.

'Stay quiet.'

They drove for another hour, up into the hills where he pulled into a lay-by, bound her wrists and placed a roughly-sewn cotton sack over her head. Sometime after that the car stopped again and she was led into an old barn containing nothing but a mattress, a bucket and an iron hoop set into the concrete to which her ankle was chained.

She would remain at the farm for nearly a fortnight, meaning her eleventh birthday would come and go uncelebrated.

19

P ain. Pain was good. Any sensation was worthwhile given it signified awareness. *Cogito ergo sum.* I am, I still am.

More pain, especially in her neck and chest and the distant sound of shouting, all of which were gradually intensifying. Where was she? Prostrate on an unyielding surface, she could smell dust and ozone and warm concrete - was she still at the farm in the hills? She tried to move her legs to see if she could feel the metal bracelet or hear the clanking chain but they refused to obey. Was Miguel nearby, or one of the others who brought her food and emptied the bucket? Silent men with hard faces. She disliked the one with the small moustache the most, the way he looked at her as though he was always hungry. When would Rodrigo come and collect her? Poor Rodrigo, he couldn't come, could he? Because he was dead. The mutilated and bloated body dragged from the mud at the mouth of the river three weeks after Miguel took her away. But how could she know that if she was still at the farm, especially when she was fully grown before *Papa* had let that information slip?

The discomfort was building to a level where it was no longer welcome and she consciously wanted it to stop. Huge swells of nausea rose and receded, covering and revealing the scorching in her throat, the throbbing in her chest and lesser but sharper pains from her forehead, hands, knees and hip. A siren began to wail. Then scuffling nearby and a man's raised voice, distressed, not Miguel or any of the others.

'Director… Wynter, can you hear me? Oh Jesus fucking Christ, she's dead, she's de–'

Pressure on the side of her neck, away from the main agony but unwanted all the same.

'Wynter, it's Andrew, can you hear me? Wake up, please wake up, please…'

She grudgingly tried to open her eyes and succeeded in catching a snapshot of Brookes above, half his face covered in blood, before lapsing back into semi-consciousness. She was in the City, not the farm, that's right. She'd been out running with Brookes and feeling free and alive and indomitable when they had been attacked by men dressed in black, two men who might have wanted to abduct her…

McGlynn's eyes flew open, frantic to know whether the threat remained, and she pushed her aching body away from the ground only to immediately collapse again, her strength and balance not yet ready to comply.

'Easy Wynter, take it slow,' said Brookes, huge relief in his voice but lisping and sounding very shaken. 'They're gone. Don't worry, they're gone.'

The siren was much closer now and had been joined by a second, their rising and falling pitches slightly out of sync. She opened her eyes once more and this time they stayed open without effort, giving a sideways view of the pavement and the road and the plot of scrubland opposite. Beyond a baseball cap lying a foot or two away, occasional cars slowed before accelerating away again. Groggily, she pushed at the ground until her arms were nearly straight and then, with some help from Brookes, sank back into a slumped position against the stone wall. He looked a mess. Most of the blood dripping from his chin flowed from a deep cut above the left eyebrow but the whole area was already heavily swollen and there was another, less productive bleed coming from a tear in his upper lip.

'Are you OK?' she attempted to say but managed only a wheeze, accompanied by a searing sensation at the top of her throat.

She dared not try to swallow although her tongue felt huge in her arid mouth. Disjointed echoes of the assault and her childhood abduction kept flooding her thoughts but again and again the overriding image of her own desperation reflected in cold, black, asymmetric lenses surfaced unbidden and unwanted in her mind. She could not understand why the men had left her behind, or indeed allowed her to live at all.

Lights ablaze and siren blaring, a City PD car rounded the corner and came racing up the hill to stop with a scratch of rubber on grit. Two uniformed patrol officers climbed out, one coming to crouch next to McGlynn while her male counterpart attended to Brookes at her shoulder. Paramedics appeared in similar fashion, conducting an initial assessment then helping them both into the ambulance where McGlynn was offered small sips of water, given a cold gel-pack for her throat and had her fingernails swabbed at the policewoman's insistence.

She communicated in silence, gently nodding or shaking her head at their questions with Brookes providing more detail when required. Others in City PD uniforms arrived, closing and sectioning the road with tape and cones, until more than a dozen could be seen coming and going through the ambulance's rear doors.

A harassed-looking officer carrying stripes of authority came by, introduced himself as Sergeant Young and asked permission to begin an interview which the crew refused, saying they were satisfied with triage but ready to depart for St Stephen's. At this, McGlynn grasped the lead paramedic's arm and shook her head firmly despite the pain it cost.

'There,' she whispered, pointing in the direction of ML One, clearly visible to the south.

'What's over there?' asked the medic, a woman with flecked grey hair and an unassuming manner, surveying the skyline. 'Is that where you work? Not a good idea, love. You and your friend need to go to hospital, make sure nothing's fractured. And he needs stitches. You should be going home after that, not back to work.'

McGlynn knew by some miracle no bones had been broken and craved the security and familiarity of her own apartment. Looking directly at the paramedic, she pointed first at herself and then again at ML One.

'Alright, alright, I can't force you,' she said reluctantly. 'Let me finish patching you up. If you can stand by yourself without feeling faint, we'll drop you off. Andrew, you're still coming with us for a scan of that cheek.'

'OK then,' said Young. 'Sir, I'll follow you to St Stephen's and take a statement, then I'll come back to talk with you, miss. What's your surname and where can I find you?'

'Her surname's McGlynn,' answered Brookes.

'McGlynn?' said the officer, eyes widening. 'Were you pointing at the McGlynn-Lansing building just now?'

She nodded and the sergeant's features rearranged themselves into a frown. An unprovoked street assault in this part of the City was bad enough but the involvement of a semi-public figure meant extra scrutiny and paperwork - not what he wanted with the end of his shift in sight.

'Apologies for not recognising you, Miss McGlynn. But we'll be there within a couple of hours so please don't leave without contacting us, OK?'

The crew finished their ministrations and packed away for the short journey. With the ambulance nearing ML One, Brookes gave directions to the underground garage where he and both medics watched closely as McGlynn climbed determinedly to her feet, careful not to overbalance and give them any reason to demand she go to hospital. Stiffness was creeping into her hip and knees but she stayed erect.

'Sure you'll be OK on your own?' asked Brookes.

She pointed upwards and mouthed "Thom" at him.

'Alright, but be careful. Please. I'll be back once I'm finished.'

'Here honey,' said the older paramedic, handing over a wad of packaged gauze and tape. 'I bet the first thing you're planning on is getting cleaned up. Just make sure you cover your open wounds immediately. And if your breathing gets worse or you start feeling sick or dizzy, you need to phone an ambulance straight away.'

Baseball cap and spare dressings in hand, McGlynn climbed gingerly to the floor, tapped in the code for the shutter, made sure it was coming down again and limped to the elevator door without looking back. Once inside she leant against the cool metal wall and allowed the exhaustion to show. She felt hollow, devoid of adrenaline and all emotions except a pathetic gratitude at the prospect of a hot shower and some privacy. Even so, sly dread skulked nearby, constantly hunting. It whispered the men in black had somehow found their way into her apartment to lie in wait. Absurd as this was, she hesitated when the steel doors slid apart, having to force herself across the threshold into the quiet and empty space.

Reassured of being alone, she undressed and dropped everything except her shoes into the kitchen bin then hobbled to the bathroom and stood in the shower, enduring nearly scalding water as it sluiced from her head and shoulders, soaking the fresh white dressings and stinging the open flesh beneath. Gradually, the soreness lessened and the heat alleviated the tightness in her muscles. She drooped down the tiled wall, arms wrapped around her legs, and stared blindly at the rivulets running and twitching across the screen.

Time lost all meaning until the tape holding one of the pads let go and it slid sideways to hang by an edge from her knee. Roused from lassitude by needle-like jets of water on raw nerve endings, she gritted her teeth, peeled off the other dressings and coerced her body upright. She used nearly a full bottle of soap to wash twice from head to toe then stepped from the stall and dabbed herself dry, trying not to look at the red blemishes on the cotton. Only after carefully brushing her hair and applying new gauze to the abrasions on both hands, elbows, hip and knees did she dare look in the mirror, afraid of what might be seen there. Her cap had saved the heavily swollen skin between the right eyebrow and hairline from being broken, and seeing the rest of her bruised and bandaged body was bearable, but she recoiled at the timidity in her eyes. A stranger stood opposite, not the woman she knew.

More worried by this than any of the physical wounds, she dressed, sent brief messages to her nephew and the company providing her domestic security, then ground up two high-strength co-codamol tablets and stirred the powder into a glass of water. Taking small sips, she reclined clumsily on the sofa until hearing a knock at her apartment door. She made sure to use the peephole before tripping the release.

'Hey–' began Dalkeith. 'Jesus, what the hell happened to you?'

McGlynn simply beckoned him inside. Sitting side by side on the couch, she picked up her laptop and typed an answer, having concluded the pain in her throat outweighed that in her hands.

Running with Andrew. Jumped by two men. Unprovoked.

He turned and stared, his initial surprise swamped as generations of clan blood loyalty surfaced.

'Where?' he growled, looking murderous.

Outside Delilah's.

'Are you OK? Why aren't you talking?'

Knowing he would detect her wheeze, but afraid of putting what happened into words, she had to compel her fingers back to the keys.

One of them held me against a wall. Big guy. By my neck. Hurts. McGlynn flinched as he looked involuntarily at her throat. *Not bruised externally yet. Something to look forward to.*

'Was he just holding you there? Or... worse?'

Hard enough for me to pass out. Not long – think less than a minute.

'This is bloody awful. Is Andrew alright?'

Yes. Looks same as me. Gone to St Stephen's for a scan.

'Shouldn't you be in hospital too?'

No. Sure nothing broken. Just grazes, bruises. Lots. Going home soon.

'Absolutely. Best place for you. Ach, I'm so sorry,' added Dalkeith more softly, sympathy tempering his anger.

Disliking her dry-eyed brittleness, he considered hugging her but decided against it. Although they were kin, he and his aunt had never had or wanted a particularly tactile relationship and he was unsure what injuries lay beneath the familiar shirt and trousers. Or how appreciative she might be of being touched again so soon, particularly by a man of his size. There were a thousand more questions he would have liked to ask but knew that others, more competent and needful than he was, would soon be making her go through the same.

'What can I do to help?' he said instead.

A few things. Can you cover for me tonight at the ball? Here as well. I need time out.

'Of course. Christ, of course, no problem.'

I'll send a note to the team to say I'm sick. A pause, during which she noticeably began to shiver. *I can't face telling them. Not yet.*

'Alright. But you've never been too ill to work before. They'll be worried about you. I'm worried about you.'

I'll be OK. You're in full control. Take decisions as you see fit but message me if you want help. The only urgent thing is Malmotec but you'll need sign off from the board to spend anything like four hundred. If the court ruling goes our way that is. Talk to Elliott first, not the others.

'Right you are.'

I said Matthieu could use the chopper tomorrow. See what the news is and make a call on whether he needs more time off. And get someone in to review security, particularly for the senior team.

'Shit… sorry. Do you think we might be at risk too? I'll talk to Andrew Brookes, if he's OK to work.'

Not Andrew, someone else.

'You sure?'

Yes. Last, did you find anyone who's spoken to Rohan since the weekend?

'No. I asked around but no one's heard from him since Friday.'

I talked to Auntie Jane this morning. About him and problems at the docks. Go to her on those and anything else if I'm not available.

'Will do. What do–' Dalkeith stopped as his phone rang. 'It's Natalie, want me to answer?'

McGlynn nodded.

'Hi Natalie, what's up? Why…? OK… Hold on.' He pressed the mute button. 'She wants to know if I've seen you. City PD's in reception, Sergeant Jayden Young.'

Are you free to sit in? We can use my office.

'Sure you're up to this?'

Another tiny nod.

'Natalie? Yeah, I'm with her now. Can you collect him please? We'll be in the Director's office by the time you get back.'

They made their way through, Dalkeith guarding the door and McGlynn, still shivering and now feeling sick, choosing to sit again. Hoping the nausea was a result of the co-codamol entering her bloodstream and therefore might presage some welcome pain relief, she concentrated on her laboured breathing - inhaling and exhaling to the count of six through her swollen windpipe. In due course Natalie appeared with

Young in tow, unexpectedly followed through the doorway by Detective Campbell.

'Ms McGlynn… Wynter. I hope it was OK for me to come? Sergeant Young knew I was at your premises today and had the presence of mind to call. This isn't really my remit but it's possible there's a connection, and I… I wanted to come and make sure you're alright,' she added, seemingly embarrassed.

McGlynn smiled but said nothing.

'Would you like anything else, Director?' asked Natalie, hovering nearby and plainly unnerved as much by McGlynn's appearance as by the police presence for the second time in nearly as many days.

Both Campbell and Young declined but McGlynn held up her empty glass.

'Then just some water please, Natalie,' said Dalkeith, swivelling the desktop monitor to face the two officers. 'If it's OK with you both, Wynter would prefer to type rather than talk.'

'We understand completely, Miss McGlynn,' replied Young. 'And I spoke with Andrew Brookes at length so we can keep this reasonably short.'

Thanks.

'If you need a break, just say. But perhaps you could start by telling us what happened from your perspective?'

Over the next half hour, McGlynn relived the events on Avenue San Domingo in as much detail as she could recall. The easy body language between the two officers suggested they had worked together before with Young, who asked most of the questions, seeming to value Campbell's occasional interjections. Both took copious notes as Dalkeith sat adjacent like a hulking, overprotective brother, responding to her answers with expressions varying from troubled concern to outright fury. Twice he asked if she would like to stop but, wanting the interview over and with the co-codamol noticeably alleviating her discomfort, she pressed on.

'I think that's nearly everything,' said Young, scanning back through his notes. 'We'll cross-check what you've told us and then prepare a written statement for you to read and sign. I have one more question but do you have any for us first?'

Yes. What else did Andrew have to say?

'His account matches yours, pretty much exactly. You both have excellent observational skills.'

What about when I was unconscious?

'Ah, I see. He said he was still fighting the first man when he saw the other one let go of you. That guy then joined his partner and they both continued to assault Mr Brookes. They shoved him away from the minivan then he felt them kicking and stamping on him several more times. By the time he'd got back up, they were in the van and pulling away from the kerb, north towards Fairview. He was smart enough to take a look at the licence plate and then went to check on you. He's mighty relieved you came round as soon as you did. We've run the plates but, no surprise, they're fakes.'

What about Delilah's? She's normally closed at lunchtimes.

'Good catch. There was no one inside but we found signs of forced entry and the security system had been disconnected. Mrs Ntuli wants you to know how sorry she is.'

Not Delilah's fault. How did City PD get there so quickly?

'Someone saw what was happening from a passing car and called us. She's over seventy and said she didn't feel able to stop. Fair enough I think.'

More than. Forensics?

'Still on scene. The samples we took will be back soon but I'd have expected them to be wearing gloves if they already had records.'

That's all I have.

'OK then. I know it's difficult but we have to ask - can you think of anyone who would have sufficient motivation to attack you in this way, Miss McGlynn? Either you directly or because they want to hurt or intimidate someone close to you?'

McGlynn had been constantly asking herself the same.

Not really. I have rivals. In business. Perhaps even one or two enemies. But I'm positive none would do this.

'What about outside of your business interests? Anyone who might want to gain some other sort of influence over you?' asked Campbell.

McGlynn thought immediately of Nathan Santoro but quickly dismissed the idea as absurd.

No. Do you really think there's a connection to you being at the warehouse?

'Possible, but very unlikely. I only met Mr Brookes and Mr Valente late yesterday, no one else knew City PD was on site until this morning. From what I've been told, I'd say this attack looks too professional and premeditated to have been organised inside a couple of hours.'

Young seemed in agreement with this but Campbell, who had been paying close attention to McGlynn, leant forward.

'However if I may say so, Wynter, I think you might actually have someone, or something, in mind?'

McGlynn hesitated, fingers poised over the keyboard, before her shoulders slumped a little more and she began to type. She knew what impact the words would have on her nephew but would have to volunteer the information sooner or later.

Thought this might have been an abduction attempt. At the time.

She stopped again, hands shaking, breath whistling.

'We'd appreciate any ideas at this point,' coaxed Young. 'No matter how unlikely.'

I've been abducted before.

Having been half-expecting her to make a connection to Julian Dayton in some way, Dalkeith was staggered. By the time he was old enough to have been told about McGlynn's kidnapping, the incident had long been consigned to family history - if not forgotten then at least deliberately avoided.

'What...? When?' was all he could say.

I was ten. South America. My father was negotiating the purchase of mineral rights but a local cartel wanted to keep control of the land. They took me as a bargaining chip to begin with. Then asked for a ransom anyway. Held me for two weeks.

'I'm very sorry to hear that,' said Campbell gently. 'It must have made today even more frightening. Does your father still have interests or influences going back that far?'

Don't think so. He's retired. Seven years. But it ended badly for the kidnappers before. The cartel swore revenge and we left the country. Probably too long ago to have any connection but thought you ought to know.'

'Ok, thanks Miss McGlynn, and for your time,' said Young. 'There are specialist counsellors available if you'd like to speak to someone and please be assured we're working flat out to identify and bring these men into custody. If we need to contact you again, where will we find you?'

Laurel Valley. Natalie has the address.

'Right. Do you need a ride? Or an escort? We'd be happy to send a patrol car with you.'

Thanks but I've made other arrangements.

Everyone stood, Young shaking hands with Dalkeith, McGlynn rounding the edge of her desk to stand with Campbell.

'I'm going back to the port,' said the detective. 'Would you like me to say anything to Mr Valente?'

McGlynn gave a small shake of the head, wanting her privacy although she knew the rumours would soon spread. They probably already were.

'OK, and again, I'm so sorry. I'll stay in touch with the investigation and make sure you get updated on our progress at the warehouse too. I hope you feel better soon.'

And with that, she gently embraced McGlynn.

'Thank you Kenise.'

The words were almost too quiet to be heard but McGlynn was pleased the pain in her throat had subsided enough to make the attempt. Despite Campbell's professionalism, which would no doubt result in the exposure of her company to the permissible extent of the law if the investigation identified culpability, she instinctively supported the level of trust they were building. As Dalkeith escorted the two officers out, she glimpsed Brookes slumped in a chair. Preparing herself, she beckoned him inside.

'Hello Andrew. How're you doing? Anything broken?' asked the returning Dalkeith.

'Not so bad,' lisped Brookes. There was a white dressing above his eyebrow, stitching in his upper lip and the whole left side of his face looked horribly swollen. 'Just a hairline fracture. Those morons had me at their mercy, so pretty lucky all told.'

'I take it you came to see Wynter?'

'Yeah. I wanted to make sure you were alright, Director.'

'Shall I leave you to it?' Dalkeith asked.

McGlynn shook her head and indicated the chairs recently vacated by Young and Campbell. Returning to her side of the desk, she tapped at the keys.

What's broken?

'Zygomatic. Here.' Brookes pointed to the top of his cheek and she noticed the grazing along his knuckles. 'Doc says it should heal itself but, if not, it'll need surgery.'

Everything else OK?

'Much like you I guess. Apart from your... your neck. Any idea who they were? Or why they were there?'

No. Not even sure if I was the target. Or you.

'Definitely you,' he replied without hesitation. 'Sorry. But once you'd gone past the first guy, he just stepped between us while the big man knocked you over. Made no attempt to engage me.'

What happened then?

'I saw you get picked up and pushed to the wall. So I tried to help and that was when the other guy got involved. He was good, they both were, reckon they were ex-military too. I didn't make it past the restaurant.'

Why did my guy let me go?

'Don't know.' Brookes closed his eyes. 'He must have come up behind me afterwards because next thing I know, he grabbed me and literally threw me across the pavement, as if I weighed nothing. Thought I was going through the window. I tried to get up but it was all over so fast…'

Any theory about motivation?

'Nope. I was kinda hoping you might give me a clue.'

No idea.

'Shit. So I guess we don't know whether they might come back.'

Each of them was lost in their thoughts until McGlynn broke the silence.

'Appreciate you trying to help, Andrew,' she whispered. 'Sorry you've been mixed up in this. Whatever this is.'

'That's OK, Director.'

'But I'm removing you from your role with us.'

'What? What the hell's that supposed to mean?'

'I need… we all might need more personal protection for a while. And I need someone I can rely on.'

'But you can trust me, surely? Particularly after today?'

'I thought so, and I value your experience, but you hesitated today.' McGlynn winced, the plosives and glottal stops hurting. 'That's not a risk I can afford to take.'

'Hesita–… bullshit. I followed you into a highly unpredictable situation and did my best to help.'

'I know you tried. But your best wasn't good enough.'

'Not good enough? Why the hell do you think I hesitated? You couldn't see what was going on from the moment it kicked off. You've no idea what happened, do you?'

Brookes had become noticeably agitated and Dalkeith slid towards the front edge of his chair.

'I saw plent–'

'How could you have seen anything? You were upside down and then against a wall! Look at my fucking face... I risked my life trying to–'

'You froze Andrew!' rasped McGlynn, aware good judgement was being subjugated by her anger but not strong enough to resist or care at present. 'You just froze! I saw you stop. On the pavement before you even got to the first guy. I saw you standing there, doing nothing, mouth open like an idiot! You fucking froze!'

They glared at each other, Brookes halfway out of his seat and McGlynn in visible pain from the unreasonable demands on her larynx.

'This is bullshit,' he said, coming to some decision and standing up. 'Total bullshit. I wouldn't want to work for you any more anyway, you ungrateful bit–.'

'That's enough,' said Dalkeith, also on his feet and considerably taller and broader than the other man. 'More than enough. Time to leave. I'll be in touch to arrange severance.'

Brookes looked up at him, down at McGlynn and left without another word, allowing the door to bang against the wall. Dalkeith closed it and returned to kneel by her chair.

'Are you OK?'

She twitched her head from side to side, appalled at her loss of control.

I need to go home.

'Yeah,' said Dalkeith, watching the words appear. 'I think that's best. Want me to drive you?'

Tiredly, McGlynn picked up her phone and checked her latest messages. The first, from Jack, confirmed the twins were staying at school overnight and asked whether everything was alright. The second was from her security company saying they had personnel available and had dispatched armed bodyguards to ML One. Holding the phone so Dalkeith could see, she tapped out a reply and asked for them to meet her in the basement.

Looks like I'll be OK. You're needed here.

Returning to her apartment, McGlynn gathered the few items she wanted in an overnight case. With a last look around the familiar space in which she now felt like an interloper, not the same person who had once spent time here, she pressed the elevator button and rode down to the garage.

There was no sign of the bodyguards beyond the grille so she limped over to the two vehicles parked against the wall. For an hour's drive home on a fine day like today, she would normally have pulled the dust sheet from the old German convertible, dropped the roof and fired up the lovingly-maintained, air-cooled, flat-six engine. The car was beautiful but tail-heavy and its capricious nature required respect upon reaching quieter, faster country roads. Clipping corners and snicking through the manual changes, the exhaust echoing from the trees, she could lose herself completely in the visceral engineering and the artistry of driving.

However, today was no longer a normal day. Wanting anonymity and security, she stopped at the rear of the convertible's much younger cousin - a massive, dark grey

SUV - and heard the squeak of tyres announcing a car bearing nudge bars, decals and a light-rack.

'Wynter McGlynn?' asked the man behind the wheel, pulling up alongside the shutter. He looked somewhere in his thirties, tough and capable. 'We're from Triple S Security. Would you like to see ID?'

The chances of these men not being with the company from which she had just commissioned new protection were beyond remote and she shook her head.

'I'm Officer Schnitzer, this is my colleague, Officer Long. We'll be with you until at least midnight. Our first job is to escort you home, right? OK, any specific reason to believe you'll be targeted en route? No? Good. If something unexpected happens though, please stay in your vehicle with the doors locked and keep moving if possible, we'll take care of it. OK? Officer Long has sent you a message with our numbers so call anytime if you're concerned or want to stop. Once we arrive we'll join up with the rest of the team until relieved. If you want to go out again, you'll just need to let us know.'

Very much doubting that would be the case, McGlynn pulled the SUV's door closed with a reassuring thud and tapped on the central display screen. The two-and-a-half tonne machine obediently reversed away from the wall and nosed out into the main garage. Climbing the exit ramp with Schnitzer close behind, she slipped on a pair of rum-coloured sunglasses, reclined the backrest away from the rotating wheel and loosened the seatbelt pressing against her injured chest and hip, uncomfortably aware the painkillers were wearing off.

Rush hour had begun in earnest outside the tinted windows. Foreshore Road teemed with life and they made laboured progress within a constantly contracting and expanding queue of vehicles. Despite the presence of the team in her mirrors, McGlynn saw menace whenever the car slowed - cyclists pulling up alongside, dark-coloured minivans nearby, occasionally an approaching man in black shirt or jeans. She drew away from the glass several times, thumb hovering over the phone's call button, but they quickly proved to be false alarms and the car moved on eastwards without incident, all the way to Sloane Corner and the Garvarmore Road, leaving the outskirts of the City behind.

The small convoy increased its pace through the rolling hills of Greenford County. Each time they crested another incline, the distant mountains grew imperceptibly taller and a little more of McGlynn's tension ebbed away. Sinking back against the headrest, her concentration turned to what she was going to say to Jack. She had avoided sending a response to his earlier message asking if everything was alright because, well, what does one say when life deals a blow as unexpected and traumatic as this? So sorry, but I nearly died today? In fact I was nearly murdered and oh, by the way, you and the children might be in danger too? Hopefully he was yet to detect the additional personnel already stationed by the house, and she was relying on the well-funded security of the twins' school until she could discuss it further with him and with them, but their lives would inevitably have to change until they were sure the threat had been mitigated. With no obvious source though, how long might that take?

Past isolated farmhouses marooned within fields of young wheat, through the small market town of Garvarmore and back into flat arable land, the bucolic scenery sliding unnoticed past her window while she gazed vacantly at the roof lining. Was it somehow her fault? Had she done something to bring this upon herself and her family? Mounting guilt, already outweighing the sum of all the cares with which she had awoken that morning, threatened to tip the precarious balance of her reason.

McGlynn's foreboding peaked as the dashboard indicator blinked for the single-track road winding lazily upwards to a dead-end in the forest. Inclining the backrest to its normal position, she automatically sought her reflection in the rear-view mirror but had cause to regret the gesture at once. The red swelling to the side of her forehead, the beginnings of discolouration in the shadows beneath her jawline and the burst capillaries in her eyes all combined to give a wild, macabre appearance. Dismayed by the sight but adamant she would at least be in full control of her rationality before presenting the same to Jack, she mentally dusted herself off. Maybe these superficial injuries could be attributed to a fall until he had been persuaded into a comfortable environment, the kitchen or lounge would be best, where she would recount the day's events and guide the conversation towards the measures needed next. For his sake she must stay as composed as possible.

A few minutes later they rounded a curve and came upon uniformed guards standing beside an identical Triple S car. Both men raised their hands in silent acknowledgement and then bent to exchange words with Schnitzer and Long who were coming to a halt behind, leaving McGlynn's SUV to travel alone as it slowed and swung sharply between automatic five-bar gates. The driveway bore immediately left, obliquely up the gradient between occasional plinths carrying modernist sculpture, past the paddock in which the twins' ponies incuriously raised their heads and towards the stable block at the side of the main house. Tapping another button on the centre console, the vehicle passed the garage and crunched over the gravel frontage to pull up next to the house. McGlynn remained immobile for a moment, collecting her thoughts and taking as deep a breath as her ribs would allow, then stepped out into the sunshine and retrieved her bag, accompanied all the while by a furious barking from within.

Their front door was rarely locked and she pushed it open to be greeted by three large mongrels of indeterminate breeding. She petted their furry heads at random until they settled and began to whine, perhaps sensing not all was as it should be.

'Hello? Wyn, is that you? Down in a second.'

A resonant voice, his, somewhere on the floor above.

Home. That unique smell, that distinctive palette of light playing over such intimately familiar objects, implying the comfort and safety and dependability for which she had been desperate all afternoon. Home, *dieu merci*. Her determination to remain impassive and objective for Jack's benefit began to crack.

The dogs milled around her knees, sniffing cautiously, until he appeared on the landing and trod down the stairs, making them creak under his weight.

'Hey you, what's up? Thought you were at the ball toni– ah no, what happened? What happened, Wyn, what's wrong?'

Overcome by his compassion, with the enormity of the day's events washing over and through her, McGlynn stood stock still as her resolve crumbled. And then, for the first time in their long relationship, she took a pace into Jack's outstretched arms and wept uncontrollably against his chest.

20

Dayton heard the unmistakable sound well before entering the foyer - hundreds of elevated voices, each trying to be heard over the rest - and girded his loins while crossing the Portland's lobby. Of all the unfavourable elements comprising his role, forced joviality at large gatherings was probably the worst. Fake laughter, punishing handshakes, conversation which was both strained and dull. Knowing he was on show and that his participation was expected made it all the harder to bear. At least the lobby was virtually empty given he had left his arrival as late as possible. With his father meeting the Nilssons in the bar upstairs, and Eddie no doubt wooing Suzanne Connaughton for all he was worth somewhere, his absence from the champagne reception was unlikely to have been noticed. However, dinner would be announced in ten minutes and he had not quite dared be so late as to miss the prearranged conclave with them beforehand.

Huge easels carrying table listings flanked each of the four open doorways and he stopped beside one, pretending to study the board but in reality an excuse to delay his entry into the pit by a further few seconds.

'Mr Dayton?'

He looked round to find a fair-haired man of about thirty, similarly attired in black tie, standing next to a rather plain woman of the same age wearing an overly-revealing pink cocktail dress.

'Yes?'

The first uncomfortable pause of the evening.

'Um, it's Sam. Sam Del Valle? I work for your brother, Eddie?'

'Ah, sure. Good to see you Sam. And this must be…?'

'This is my wife, Andrea.'

'Nice to meet you, Mrs Del Valle. You look lovely this evening,' he lied, thinking she looked like a mid-range prostitute. They exchanged sickly smiles until Dayton could bear it no longer. 'Afraid I need to catch Ed before they call us through for dinner. See you later. Probably.'

The lights in the foyer were dimmed and Dayton had to be careful as he edged through knots of baying strangers lest he spill anyone's wine. Although nearly all the men conformed in black tuxedos, he noted a rebellious few wearing muted colours and even one or two in white, perhaps in solidarity with the serving staff. The women though, as befitting one of the most glamorous functions in the City's calendar, had been much more adventurous. A vast spectrum of gowns from the sober to the brazen wrapped all manner of figures and offset sparkling necklaces, bracelets and earrings likely making their one and only annual appearance. He retrieved a glass from the tray of a roaming waiter and completed a full circuit, nodding to a few whilst ignoring others, then gave up and headed to the side of the room with the intention of phoning his brother. Close to the wall, a hand tapped his shoulder.

'Evening,' said Richard, standing alongside Eddie. They were dressed identically and looked eerily like a before and after picture.

'Evening. I've been looking for you for ages.'

'Mmm. I've only just managed to leave Fredrik and Annika with your mother. We had a drink then came down and spent the best part of fifteen minutes trying to work our way over to the mayor. No chance though, he's absolutely surrounded. We'll have to try again later.'

'Right. How'd it go with them?'

'Generally well, although there's still some detail missing. I could do with filling those gaps before the end of the evening so I took the liberty of giving Sandy a list. You're copied so can you chase him up before nine.'

'Yes, OK. I'll take a look.' Dayton switched his attention to Eddie. 'All good? Met one of yours on the way in, Sam something or other.'

'Del Valle? Solid chap.'

'That's him, and his wife, Anthea. They on your table?'

'Andrea. Think so. Plus the Havillands and Scott Tobyn from Inspiron.'

'Great, he's about to sign isn't he? Fourteen million over three years?' said Dayton, knowing full well this was the case but taking any opportunity to reinforce his father's meddling was neither wanted nor needed.

'Tomorrow. I promised to get him properly pissed first.'

'As long as he can hold a pen. Looks like I've picked up Don and Imelda Finch as a result of Fredrik joining us. Also that chap from Gentronic and the Fitzwilliams.'

'Can you apologise to Don for bumping him across tables and tell him I'll see him later,' Richard said. 'He'll understand.'

'Who's your plus one?' goaded Eddie.

'Todd Secker,' replied Dayton, ignoring the taunt. 'In return for the introduction to Blacktree.'

'Fair. Looks like they could be good for us.'

'Indeed. Listen, I don't suppose either of you looked through the auction listings? Haven't had time myself.'

'Not me,' said Eddie as Richard shook his head. 'But I bet it's the usual fare - cheap plonk and spa days.'

'Let me know if there's anything you're interested in. If not, I'll do the same as last year and pick something we can give away as yet another bloody staff incentive if we don't want it.' Dayton fiddled with his cuffs, irked by the thought of spending money unnecessarily. 'How did it go earlier, did you both get down to the trial?'

'Franklin did a reasonable job, I thought,' said Richard. 'We stayed for the summing up too - rather dry. Have to admit I didn't understand most of it but at least the judges seemed attentive.'

'Agreed,' added Eddie, restlessly scanning the crowd. 'They've adjourned to consider their findings so we'll probably hear either way tomorrow. You should have been there this morning though, Jules, very entertaining. Franklin nearly got her to lose her temper.'

'In that case, I'll come down tomorrow for sure. It'll be even better to watch her face when we win.'

'From the little I've seen, it's hard to call either way,' said Richard.

Over the speakers came a disembodied voice, enthusiastic and unctuous as a gameshow host, inviting them to be seated for dinner.

'We'll win,' repeated Dayton with a confidence he did not feel.

Having spent at least some of the afternoon fretting over how Mr Sharma might behave, Sunita Malik was feeling much relieved. The diminutive urology surgeon who took her hand on meeting at their table was evidently no womaniser and looked more akin to a newly informed lottery winner. And why not. Malik expected to need the full arsenal of her charms in securing the conversations she wanted during the course of the evening and had prepared accordingly. The classic symmetry of her face, touched here and there with a trace of make-up, was fully exposed by the thick, lustrous hair piled high on the crown of her head. Save for a modest solitaire ring she needed no other jewellery, carried only the faintest perfume and wore an off-white halter neck dress accentuating the dark gold of her neck and shoulders to perfection. Thinking that Indrani, queen of the devas, had somehow fallen from the cosmos, Sharma gawked upwards and blinked several times in rapid succession.

'M… Miss Malik,' he stammered. 'It is indeed my pleasure to be meeting with you. So unexpectedly, that is. I am… my… my name is Sanjeev… Sanjeev Sharma.'

'The pleasure is mine Mr Sharma. I appreciate you letting me accompany you this evening. I'm only sorry that it was made possible due to the illness of your wife.'

Delicately, she extracted her hand from the moist grip and accepted his help in taking a chair.

'May I ask how she's feeling?'

'Fine, fine. Well, truth be told she's come down with quite a nasty virus. And unfortunately, it's caused an acute case of the dees and vees. Ah, um, that's diarrho–'

'Yes, I understand, how awful. I hope she feels better soon. Tell me, have you been married long?'

The poor man seemed unable to maintain eye contact so Malik, occasionally breaking off to greet others joining their table, fed him a steady stream of open questions and let him prattle on. His shyness gave her the freedom to survey the still-circulating guests and appreciate the opulence of their surroundings while reflecting entirely on other things.

Built to cater for money which had been old even then, the Portland remained lavishly appointed and the Grand Ballroom, befitting its moniker, was no exception. High above her head hung twenty-five crystal chandeliers on chains anchored in elaborate roses, illuminating a ceiling painted in the style of the Old Masters and full height Corinthian columns in lightly veined marble. Acres of ruched velvet and wide plasterwork cornices covered in gold leaf lent the room a timeless opulence. Other than the lectern, amplifiers and shiny drum kit set up on a low stage, Malik could have imagined herself as a debutante attending a high society dinner dance more than two centuries ago.

She had arrived at the hotel unfashionably early, stationing herself near the entrance to make sure she was able to watch people coming through the doors. Of her thirteen targets, she had identified at least six before the crowd became too dense and she moved off, circulating close to the groups in which they were standing. One of the men would invariably catch her eye and provide an opportunity to join their discourse, often to the displeasure of wives or girlfriends. Never mind, having established contact and made interesting but chaste conversation she now had the perfect excuse for bumping into them again later, hopefully after several glasses of champagne and liqueurs.

Three in whom she was most interested were female. There had been a fourth but given she and her husband had been in close dialogue with Vincent Evesham and his wife in the foyer, and all had turned to glare at Malik as she drifted past, any approach was unlikely to be fruitful. Without vanity she knew these women presented a different challenge. Her beauty, normally such an asset in meeting both hetero and homosexual men, could be threatening to her own gender and a variety of other devices would be needed to bring them into her confidence.

'Yes, you see I studied at Stanford… although that was a long time ago, maybe so long ago that you were a little girl… and then I undertook postdoctoral research and a fellowship at UCSF, which allowed me to…' Sharma spoke as though suffering from a slight nasal obstruction. She hoped it was a perennial condition rather than anything to do with Mrs Sharma's illness, especially as he shuffled a little closer at every opportunity. '…and then, when I was twenty-six, I moved to Montréal to take a job at McGill's. I was the youngest attending physician and…'

Leaning further back in her chair, Malik inspected the nearby tables. Only a few empty place settings remained and they were being rapidly filled ahead of an advancing army of waiters carrying shield-sized trays of appetisers above their heads. As expected there was no one she recognised. The seating plan at the foyer door, in which she had determined an informal hierarchy predicated on distance from the mayor, showed McGlynn-Lansing's group next to Santoro's beside the stage. She was looking forward to seeing Wynter again and wondered how open she might be on the subject of her relationship with Julian Dayton. His tables were immediately beyond hers and she had been particularly pleased to note he was hosting Imelda Finch. Malik had scoured the woman's extensive social media accounts the previous evening, gleaning she and her husband were avid patrons of the Mayor's Ball and, more importantly, old friends of Richard and Vanessa. If they could be inveigled into sharing stories, the Finches were likely to have known Julian since he was a boy and could be a very rich source of information indeed.

The waiting staff finally reached them, breaking Sharma from his monologue, and she stole another glance at her phone to refresh her memory of the blurred headshot Rutter had sent across. Bill said he had seen the man discussing some sort of deal with Richard Dayton, in The Guardsman of all places, and speculated the two of them might continue their negotiations at the ball. In such an event, Malik was under instructions to try and determine both his identity and the subject of their dialogue, reporting back immediately once successful.

Understandably, neither Thom nor Sylvie Dalkeith was concentrating fully on their hosting duties and the mood at the McGlynn-Lansing tables remained subdued halfway through the meal.

Sylvie had promptly seen through her sister's message about a mystery illness for the fabrication it was. Confronting her son to demand the truth, she had called McGlynn several times without success and was now feeling every bit as impotent and desperate for news as they all were during those final weeks in South America. Four years McGlynn's elder, it had taken a long time after their return to the City until she had quelled either her own conscience or the urge to act as her constant guardian and yet, somehow, here they were again. Peter held her hand beneath the tablecloth, sitting patiently at her side as he generally did at these events, and she gripped it tightly while paying as much attention to the conversation as she could manage.

Dalkeith, constantly reminded of McGlynn's absence by the empty place next to him, felt adrift. He had helped cover his aunt's breaks away from the office before but under very different circumstances. In addition to worrying about her wellbeing and his mother's reaction, the burden of sole leadership was already proving unexpectedly heavy. Directly opposite, Matthieu Gautier looked particularly downcast. Dalkeith surmised he and Natalie would have shared what they had seen and heard earlier and probably come to conclusions not far from the truth. Which was the lesser of evils, he wondered, to go against McGlynn's wishes for a second time in as many hours, tell Matthieu precisely what had happened and swear him to secrecy? Or leave him and Natalie open to speculation and the risk of spreading inaccurate gossip? He mulled the dilemma, picking at the remains of his salmon and trying to ignore the braying laughter nearby.

'And then,' boomed Simon Fitzwilliam, barely able to contain his mirth. 'And then... hold on, give me a second, one second... and then the silly sod knocked a whole glass of red into her lap!'

'That's right!' shouted Jonny Havilland in reply. Not content with sharing the highlights of last year's ball with those at Dayton's table, Fitzwilliam had commandeered the attention of Eddie's too. 'I remember! She was fucki–... she was livid, absolutely livid. Took her ring off there and then. Threw it at him and stalked off without another word. Poor Freddie!'

Havilland, Fitzwilliam, Eddie and their partners all roared whilst Del Valle and the various customers, being outside this circle, smiled tactfully. Lubricated by three glasses of wine even the normally taciturn Dayton found himself sniggering at the memory. Only Don and Imelda Finch remained impassive, concentrating on their meals and no doubt rueing the circumstances which had resulted in their reallocation to such juvenile company.

'Yeah, Freddie's not around tonight is he?' asked Eddie, tears in his eyes but having recovered most of his composure. With a hand resting lightly on his arm, the daringly-attired Suzanne was also in high spirits and full of promise. He lived for nights like these. 'We'll have to see if we can find him after dinner and remind him what an arse he is.'

'He's away on holiday, Eddie darling, in Biarritz,' gushed Boudicca Fitzwilliam. A florid, moon-faced woman who knew that her husband's friend disliked her but had no idea why, she sought to curry favour whenever possible.

'Wise,' decreed Eddie, disgusted by her sycophancy.

'Well, he's not the only one who hasn't shown his face, is he,' said Dayton, both to fill the lull and remain engaged in the conversation. He nodded in Dalkeith's direction. 'I see that Wynter bloody McGlynn hasn't bothered to grace us with her presence either. No wonder they all look so miserable.'

Several heads turned to stare at the vacant chair.

'Actually, I didn't believe it at the time but there was a rumour going round this afternoon,' volunteered Havilland. 'I heard she was out running and got beaten up by a couple of thugs. Over on San Domingo. Quite nasty by all accounts.'

Seizing upon a perfect opportunity to restore the jocular mood, Dayton laughed.

'Ha! Couldn't have happened to a nicer person!'

A brutal silence fell, reactions ranging from embarrassment amongst those who worked for him to outright shock from the others. One by one he scanned their faces, seeking validation but finding only the enormity of his mistake. Even his father had looked over in surprise at the sudden hush and wore an accusatory scowl.

'Um… not true is it? I mean… oh God…'

With infinite care, Imelda Finch rearranged the cutlery on her empty plate then eyed him with hostility.

'What a cruel thing to say, Julian, whether it's true or not,' she said, sagging jowls shaking. 'Despicable, even for you. What were you thinking?'

Totally unable to justify himself or deflect the blame elsewhere, Dayton rose abruptly, caught the underside of the table and set the crockery and glassware rattling.

'Um… sorry, sorry. Please excuse me a moment.'

He made his way unsteadily towards the foyer doors.

'What the fuck,' he muttered in anguish. 'What the absolute… what were you thinking? You utter, utter cunt. Why would you say that? Out loud. Why… why? The absolute fuck… Oh God, oh God, oh God…'

There were restrooms in the lobby which offered privacy and, if the sudden cramps in his stomach were to worsen, suitable facilities.

Watching him go, Richard leaned towards his younger son and beckoned him close.

'What's happened?' he asked quietly.

'Julian,' said Eddie, as if this was explanation enough.

'What about him?'

'Jonny said he heard something about Wynter McGlynn being assaulted this afternoon. Jules made a joke of it.'

'Is it true?'

'What, that he made a joke?'

'No, about Wynter.'

'No idea. Said it happened while she was out jogging. Any mention of it at your table?'

'None, although I saw she was missing. And that boy Dalkeith certainly looks as though he's carrying the weight of the world on his shoulders, doesn't he? Interesting. How badly did Julian's comments go down?'

Disliking his brother's character but never having been one for telling tales, Eddie hesitated.

'Not great. Everyone heard and Imelda called him out over it.'

'Oh for pity's sake.' Richard despaired of his elder child's seemingly incurable ability to cause problems. 'Where's he run away to?'

'Not sure.'

'In that case, give him five minutes and then go and find him. Tell him to get back here immediately, apologise if he has to and get on with his sodding job for the rest of the evening. I'll talk to him after dinner and see whose feathers we need to smooth. If you can't find him, I'll make my excuses here and swap tables.'

Waiting for some acknowledgement, Richard followed his son's line of sight and saw a dark-skinned woman gliding by in a white halter neck dress. He failed to recognise her from the courtroom earlier, his eyes not being what they once were, but could just about make out she was half-smiling and seemed to be examining the guests at their tables.

'Edward,' he hissed. 'Edward, concentrate!'

'Sorry. No problem.'

'If Wynter's not here, then it gives you a perfect opening to strike up conversation with young Gautier, doesn't it? Looks like him over there.'

Eddie grunted, a sour taste in his mouth.

'Ladies and gentlemen, please take your seats and give a warm, warm City welcome to Mayor Nathan Santoro!'

The gameshow voice reverberated around the room as the house lights dimmed. Dessert had been cleared and the phalanx of waiters roamed with silver coffee pots in hand, squeezing past diners already standing in loose social groups. Dayton, having come back to resentful glares after a short and rancorous debate with his brother, turned in his chair beside Todd Secker and offered a silent prayer of gratitude that their stilted dialogue could come to an end. At least the introverted Secker had been open to conversation which was more than could be said for anyone else.

Bright music and dutiful clapping accompanied the mayor as he bounced up the few steps to the stage, stopping at the lectern to pull a cordless microphone from its holder.

'Thank you! Thank you,' he cried, using his free hand to dampen the already dying applause. 'And welcome to each and every one of you! Let me start by saying how much I appreciate your continuing support for this fantastic event and the wonderful, amazing organisations we work with! As you know, we're raising much needed funds this year for a new treatment centre at Woodlands Hospital and of course they're here tonight… where are you, where… ah, there you are… welcome, welcome! Let's give them a big round of applause!

'Now, before we get to the auction - remember to dig into those deep pockets my friends, all for children facing life-changing illness, such a great cause - I'd like to say a few words about how proud I am to represent the citizens of this city and express my gratitude for those without whom this evening just wouldn't be possible!'

Delivering what was effectively a campaign speech without once mentioning the forthcoming election, Santoro danced back and forth across the dais like an overweight celebrity preacher, exhorting his congregation to believe. With hard work and optimism there were no insurmountable obstacles, no limits to their combined potential. An even brighter, even more affluent future was there for the taking if only the progressive communities of the City, and especially those in this room, maintained the courage of their conviction. He came to a crescendo with sweeping words of appreciation, making it sound as though he had personally organised an event which typified the City's egalitarian, entrepreneurial spirit and then, with a glance towards the empty chair next to Dalkeith, reluctantly withdrew waving both hands high in the air.

Had Dayton been listening, the connotations of the mayor's saccharine rhetoric would have been obvious but his mind was resolutely preoccupied - a tireless critic with the sharpest of pens, bent on self-examination.

Drums rolled and an auctioneer, sparkling like tinsel in a tight cherry-red gown, took her place behind the lectern. The bidding etiquette was already well understood by the regular patrons comprising the majority of the room. Other than the year's charitable cause, each table or group of tables was expected to offer a number of credible bids whilst entering as few lots as possible, thus ensuring the session did not become overly protracted. The available prizes followed proven themes – from cases of wine, through interior design consultations and overnight stays at country hotels, to corporate boxes at the racing and adventure holidays abroad - and it was considered poor form if the less-valuable items were snapped up by the bigger companies or wealthier individuals.

'Lot number one, ladies and gentlemen,' she declared over the hum of conversation. 'A behind the scenes tour of Fentimans Theatre for up to eight people, including VIP seats for the show and afterparty drinks with the cast. A night out that you and your family or friends will always remember. Who'll start me at a thousand?'

Bidding was brisk. The first twenty-odd items sold in three quarters of an hour with much backslapping and cheering for the winners alongside commiseration or good-natured accusations of tightfistedness for the losers. Malik noted Vincent Evesham picking up a dozen lessons with the professional at Montclair Golf Club and maliciously wondered if he expected to have more time on his hands. At her elbow, Sharma showed no intention of participating but bobbed up and down with excitement as the gavel hit the block on inflated sums. With the auction nearing completion, she was reasonably sure nobody from Dayton Global Industries or McGlynn-Lansing had yet raised their numbered cards and began to stir at the thought of a bidding war erupting.

Eddie was thinking precisely the same but for very different reasons. He still remembered the year when his father and David McGlynn, their tables being too far away to see each other properly, had inadvertently entered competitive bids. Neither had been prepared to back down and the price for a relatively modest item, dinner for four in the kitchens of a Michelin-starred chef as he recalled, escalated to a level where every counteroffer drew a gasp from the audience. Recognising there could be unpleasant scenes should the process continue, the then mayor stepped in once David had surpassed the forty thousand mark to declare both men as victorious, stating each was to be offered the same prize if they agreed to split the sum at twenty thousand apiece and, to much accompanying laughter, enjoy their evenings on different dates. Ever since, the first of them or their successors to put in a bid was by unspoken custom allowed to win unimpeded by the other. Provided one side took the initiative before the final item went up for sale such a strategy worked well. However, with only the current lot and two more remaining, and perhaps Thom Dalkeith intending to deputise for the more experienced McGlynn, Eddie was beginning to fear history might repeat itself.

'At seventeen thousand, two hundred... anybody else? Last call... Sold! Thank you, table thirty-four. Moving on to our penultimate listing, an unforgettable, all-inclusive diving holiday in the Maldives sponsored by our friends at Reynard Travel. Who'll offer me fifteen thousand for this spectacular week away? Fifteen thous– thank you at the back there. I have fifteen. Any advance on fifteen? Now sixteen, thank you madam.'

Eddie studied Dayton's profile, willing him to participate, but the furrowed brow and the thousand-yard stare indicated he was elsewhere, doubtless stewing on the earlier faux pas. Allowing problems of his own making to take precedence over those of the company was entirely typical of his brother. He turned towards Richard who at once caught his eye and gave a tilt of the head towards the lectern.

'Any advance on eighteen thousand, ladies and gentlemen? Now at the second time of asking…'

Eddie raised his hand.

'New bidder at nineteen thousand, thank you! Now twenty at the back. Twenty-one at the front.'

Neither knowing nor caring whom he might be competing against, Eddie continued to nod each time the bid returned, deciding to withdraw if and when the price reached twenty-eight thousand. That should be high enough to publicly demonstrate the company's charitable commitment and with luck be low enough to avoid an unwanted prize.

'I have twenty-five from the gentleman here,' said the auctioneer, smiling directly at him.

She looked up again to survey the room and he felt Suzanne place a warm hand on his upper thigh.

'Are we all done at twenty-five thousand? Going once…'

Risking a glance at Dalkeith, Eddie was satisfied to see him in close conversation with his mother and paying no attention.

'Going twice... Twenty-six! I have twenty-six. Also at the front.'

Something in the tone of her voice, some trace of confusion, made him turn sharply back again only to lock eyes with his brother. Dayton had one hand in the air and a malevolent expression on his face.

'Sir, the bid is against you. Any advance on twenty-six?'

Instead of surprise, Eddie's principal feeling was one of sadness. Not for the lack of kinship, which had been beyond repair for a long time, rather for the man's need to make such a gesture. Eddie loved nothing more than competition when it involved a true test of his mettle, a chance to prove himself against a worthy opponent, but here was further evidence Dayton no longer offered any kind of challenge. On the basis there was nothing to be achieved in engaging, he shook his head and turned away.

'At the front then, at twenty-six thousand...?' A rap of the gavel. 'Table number eight, thank you. And now to the final lot of the evening, your last opportunity to win...'

The final prize went for a much higher figure than anticipated due to a combination of previously frustrated bidders and those yet to participate finding their nerve, the formalities concluding with the gratifying announcement they had surpassed the quarter of a million milestone. Unannounced but of equal significance was McGlynn-Lansing failing to enter a bid for the first time in living memory. When combined with the Director's absence, speculation amongst the milling crowd was rife as to why. Were McGlynn's in financial trouble? With the verdict in the court case imminent, had Wynter backed away from a confrontation with the Daytons? Did that mean she expected to lose? Or win? Was it true she had badly broken a leg while out training for the triathlon? Why else would she have decided not to take what was obviously her empty chair next to Thom Dalkeith? Who were the Nordic-looking couple on old Richard Dayton's table and did they have anything to do with it? Fuelled by alcohol and an insatiable desire to know more than one's neighbour, rumours began to leap like wildfire between mingling groups.

On stage, half a dozen musicians dressed in Latin costume were moving towards their instruments or plugging them into amplifiers, signalling to Malik the most important part of her evening was about to get underway. She had managed to speak with a few people on her list between courses, none of whom had yet been persuaded to reveal anything untoward about Julian Dayton - he was hard-working and determined, often difficult to get along with and always difficult to know - but loud music, low lighting and high spirits ought to provide the perfect cover for soliciting gossip. The interplay between the Daytons during the auction had fascinated her. Sure that Eddie's hesitation before declining to bid against his brother had stemmed from pity rather than deference, she came to the instant realisation that the arrogance she had assumed in Julian's demeanour was in fact insecurity. She now wanted to test this theory with as many of her remaining quarry as she could find but, alas, Sharma had resumed his monologue.

'...and therefore you see, I had no choice but to attempt a difficult and quite revolutionary procedure–'

'I'm so sorry to interrupt Sanjeev, but I've promised to meet a few people before I head home. Please excuse me and do pass on my best wishes to your wife.'

'But I was just about to ask you if...' he began dolefully.

'Yes?' Malik stood, towering above him on her stilettos, impossibly beautiful. 'What is it that you would like to ask me?'

'N-nothing, nothing. Well, if you're sure that you have to go.'

'I'm afraid I must. Thank you again for a lovely evening.'

Giving him no time to pluck up further courage, she made a swift escape passing close to Eddie and his cronies who remained drinking at the tables along the front. One arm around the half-naked woman at his side and his head thrown back in laughter, the claustrophobic atmosphere she had perceived before was entirely gone, but then so were his brother and father. There had been no sign all evening of the man in the blurred image from Rutter and she was reasonably confident he had not been amongst the Daytons' guests.

In the foyer, a sizeable vodka luge in the shape of an ice dragon was proving popular with the overspill from the ballroom. Spotting Imelda Finch's floral dress making for the doors beyond, Malik had to skirt the disorderly queue at its base as she hurried to catch up. Imelda looked like she was alone, probably visiting the restrooms, which might offer the opportunity to strike up conversation. This proved to be the case and she joined the old woman in the queue behind two animated, expletive-prone teenagers where, inevitably, Imelda began to tut and suck her teeth.

'I don't know,' she grumbled to nobody in particular. 'I can't understand a word they're saying.'

'Well that's alright then, isn't it, grandma. No need to sound so fucking offended,' replied the taller of the two to the hilarity of her friend.

'Where are your manners girls,' cut in Malik sharply. 'I don't want to listen to your bad language either. Or see fifteen-year-olds being so disrespectful to their elders.'

'We're eighteen.'

'Well you look fifteen to me. Now hold your tongue.'

The girl tried to stare her down but was no match for the mien of imperious womanhood perfected by Malik long ago. After conferring with her accomplice, they skulked away to find facilities with less opprobrium.

'Thank you Miss... er,' said Imelda, peering upwards. 'Goodness, what a pretty girl you are.'

'I'm Sunita. And you're very welcome, it was nothing.'

'It was certainly something to me. There's hardly any courtesy on display these days, especially for the older generation. Don't ever get old, Sunita,' she said, wagging a finger. 'That's my advice, it's not what it's made out to be. These children are so often spoiled and simply don't seem to have any boundaries. What are their parents thinking? If they haven't learnt their airs and graces then they shouldn't be allowed to come out and enjoy social occasions like these, should they?'

'Absolutely not. Do you have children Mrs... um?'

'Ha! Here am I, lecturing you on good etiquette and I haven't even introduced myself. My name is Imelda, Imelda Finch. And yes, my husband and I have two daughters, five granddaughters and three great-granddaughters. It seems the production of boys doesn't run in our family but we feel very lucky all the same.'

'I have a sister as well, no brothers, and I'm sure my parents felt the same way.'

'Do you have any children of your own yet?' Imelda asked, keenly inspecting Malik's waistline as they shuffled forwards. 'Forgive me, my dear, of course you don't. But is that something you and your fiancé hope for one day?'

'Maybe. But I don't think it's something I should enter into lightly. And don't be fooled by the ring, Mrs Finch, it's purely for show. I find it helps reduce the volume of unwanted attention a single woman tends to receive.'

'Very sensible. And call me Imelda, it helps me feel less old. I might not look it anymore but I used to be quite the catch too. When I was your age, I was swimming and playing tennis every day, sometimes twice a day. I had long black hair and a tan and a figure just like yours. Not as tall and perhaps not as pretty but fit and healthy enough to catch the eye of more than a few young men, I might tell you. And now, well, what a disappointment. No bust, no buttocks and better hair on a coconut. Still, I suppose that's the price we women pay for the privilege of growing old. And getting on a bit is certainly better than the alternative, isn't it?'

'It is indeed,' agreed Malik, maintaining her own counsel on the topic.

The line moved at a reasonable pace and she held the door ajar for Imelda to enter the restroom first, although the term seemed something of a misnomer given the noise levels inside.

'Forgive me for asking, Imelda, but your dress is very distinctive. Weren't you sitting at one of the tables next to the stage?'

'Yes, that's right. Don and I came with Vanessa and Richard Dayton. Do you happen to know them?'

'Not personally, no. But I did meet with their son, Julian, on Monday.'

'Really? What a coincidence. What line of work are you in?'

'I'm a writer,' said Malik easily. 'And I'm actually working on a piece about Dayton's.'

'How interesting! It's a good company isn't it? Richard did such a fine job before being called to London. As did his father before him.'

'Yes. But I've been asked to focus on the business as it is today and Julian in particular. Do you know him well?'

'Since he was a baby of course. Such a bright child. So unfortunate.'

'Unfortunate? In what way?'

Imelda studied Malik more closely.

'A writer you say? Have you been retained by Julian or one of the family?'

'No. I work independently.'

'Then by whom, if you don't mind me asking?'

'For this piece, the City Post.'

'The Post? Are you a journalist? I shouldn't like to talk to a journalist without Richard's permission.'

A cubicle door opened and she began to move away.

'Listen my dear, it was so nice to–'

'I appreciate your position, Imelda, I really do. But to be open with you, I'm struggling to find somebody, anybody who'll give me a balanced opinion of Julian. Everyone I talk to seems to think he's… well… quite unpleasant.'

'I'm sorry, Sunita,' she said after the slightest of pauses. 'But it wouldn't be appropriate for me to comment. I'm sure you understand. It was nice to meet you. Goodbye.'

Malik had no need to use the stalls and except for the hesitation before Imelda's reply would have headed back to the foyer to find another person on her dwindling list. Instead, she crossed to the handbasins and pretended to inspect her appearance in the mirror. Many others stood alongside her doing the same - some alone, most swapping makeup and scandal with friends. Imelda stepped out after a few minutes. Finding Malik still present, she slowly joined her at the adjacent sink.

'You didn't leave,' she said, shrewd eyes watching in the mirror.

'No. I thought there might be something else you would have liked to say.'

'Beautiful and clever, eh? Lucky girl. Alright, let's go outside, it's much too busy in here.'

Once in the lobby and ambling back towards the ballroom, Imelda spoke again.

'I might be prepared to talk with you about Julian. Under certain conditions. You have to understand that Don and I go back a long, long way with the Daytons. Must be nearly sixty years. And I won't jeopardise our friendship.'

'Of course. There would be no need for me to attribute anything if you prefer.'

'If we were to speak, I would want to be completely off the record. No recordings, no note taking, no quoting me and no using specific details or anything of the kind in this article or any other. It would be purely to give you some context rather than bringing skeletons out of closets for your or anyone else's gratification. Every family is entitled to their privacy but, as you say, it's perhaps important for you to have a more balanced view of Julian.'

'OK.'

'If I may say, that wasn't particularly convincing. You might think I look like a gentle soul, maybe even a touch beyond my prime, but I can assure you otherwise. And if I propose to share something with you in confidence, I expect it to remain that way. Now, do you agree, explicitly?'

'Yes, I agree.'

'Well then,' she said at length. 'I'll tell you what, Don will be out in the morning so why don't we arrange to meet around eleven, at Milburn's. Have you been before?'

'I'll find it.'

'It's on Butcher's Row, at the back of the square. They know me there so just ask if you need to. Well, goodbye again for now, Sunita. I hope you enjoy the rest of your evening but I'd caution you to be careful about asking too many questions. Everyone in that room knows everyone else, one way or another, and we don't take kindly to criticism from anyone. Least of all outsiders.'

21

Laurel House had been in the family for three generations. Her grandfather Kenneth McGlynn had fallen in love with the foothills of Cairn Fell and purchased a spread of more than a hundred acres, demolishing the old shepherd's cottage to make way for a home fit to match his aspirations. This was the house to which she had returned from South America. Determined to put down roots and establish some routine, some domestic familiarity and security after their previously nomadic existence, Cécile had been indefatigable - establishing the children in nearby schools and new friendships, overseeing the renovation and extension of a building which had stood empty for more than a decade and organising ever-larger social occasions to bring noise and colour and joy to the house and its occupants. She had even persuaded David to spend more time at home in the years before he became Director, realising he would necessarily commit his energy elsewhere on taking up Kenny's mantle.

McGlynn had grown to love the house and what it represented, even after Michael and then Sylvie departed for university and it lost some of the carefully cultivated atmosphere. At eighteen, when she took up her own place at college, Cécile also decided to move on and relocated closer to the City and her husband. The house fell largely silent for another decade, used only for big family Christmases or summer breaks, but never lost its pull and when she returned from her sabbatical, pregnant and with Jack in tow, she had asked for permission to take it as her own.

The place was too big for them, of course, even once Catriona and Adeline had been born. Most of the land, which included several outbuildings in various states of disrepair and was better suited to subsistence farming than their contemporary lifestyle, had been left alone for nature to reclaim - only the garages, workshop, paddocks and gardens were maintained to a high standard. Facing south-west, clad in time-darkened hardwood and modelled after a nineteenth century landowner's ranch, the main residence cut into and sprawled across the sloping hillside. Within the lower level were a grand entrance hall and reception rooms converted into a playroom, home office, studio and a boot room where the dogs slept. Upstairs comprised the study, kitchen, a huge dining room, two interconnected lounges with picture windows on both sides and access to the rear terraces and lawns. Eight bedrooms branched off a central corridor along the top floor, each with its own bathroom and spectacular views of either the mountains behind or Greenford County in front. On a clear day with a powerful enough pair of binoculars, it was possible to watch ships criss-crossing the horizon from the balcony outside the master suite.

Facing the cornflower sky and the tips of the Douglas firs on the opposite side of the valley, McGlynn lay awake after a short night of broken sleep, repeatedly sliding unconsciousness only to be roused again by some disturbance, real or imagined. She could tell it was still early from the angle of the sunlight and wished it was possible to remain in the security of the oversized bed for longer, but the need to relieve her bladder and take more co-codamol could no longer be ignored.

Easing herself upright she hobbled to the bathroom and closed the door quietly to avoid waking Jack. Everything hurt and fought for her attention as she moved, even urinating made her bruised abdominals groan in protest. Taking two tablets from their shelf in the cabinet, she crushed them under the bottom of a glass, scooped the gritty powder into her hand and swilled it down with water from the faucet. The storage tanks were fed from a stream further up the hill and, notwithstanding her swollen tongue and the waves of pain in her neck as she swallowed, the cold liquid tasted fresh and sweet. Only then did she slide Jack's old t-shirt over her head and tease away the gauze pads to stand naked in front of the mirror.

New scabs were forming over the grazes, becoming much more conspicuous as the blood dried. Those which were pink and still wept stung the worst. Near her temple, the contusion appeared to have receded slightly but was beginning to purple and remained as tender as the smaller lump on the back of her head. Perhaps most noticeably, the skin across her upper neck was now blotched with a variety of shades, the darkest of which matched the circles beneath her eyes. Nevertheless, despite all the physical evidence to the contrary and even acknowledging a lingering vulnerability, she felt remotely better on seeing her reflection - those steady grey eyes seemed to have regained some resolve.

Clinging to whatever reassurance she could, McGlynn showered and had nearly finished applying new dressings when she heard a soft knock.

'Everything alright?' asked Jack.

Unable to reply loudly enough, she shrugged on a robe and opened the door.

'Hey,' she whispered. 'Yeah.'

'Are you coming back to bed?'

'I need to be up.'

'Want any help?'

'Just coffee, please. And I ought to eat. Haven't touched anything since yesterday morning.'

'I'll see what I can find.'

He disappeared. Spurred on by the thought of caffeine and food, she joined him in the kitchen fewer than ten minutes later wearing another loose t-shirt and shorts. The house had air conditioning but they rarely used it, preferring open windows and the smell of the countryside. On the breakfast bar was a steaming mug of black coffee and a bowl of what looked like narrow strips of honeydew.

'The melon's straight from the fridge. Thought it would be soothing for your throat. And I figured scrambled eggs might go down OK too?'

'Sure,' she said, satisfying the dogs' immediate need for affection. Molly and Blue relented after a full minute and returned to lie on the tiles by the back door, tongues lolling, eyebrows twitching. Roscoe waited until she perched on a stool then settled by her ankles.

'Want any painkillers?'

'Had some upstairs.'

'OK. Let me know if I can do or get you anything to help. Anything.'

Grateful as always for his thoughtfulness, she forked slivers of the fruit into her mouth and waited for her coffee to cool while watching him move around the workspace.

Jackson Connelly was still a couple of years shy of his fortieth birthday, a blonde, bearded bear of a man standing six-five in his bare feet and with the heft to match. As with many big men who led simple lives and had nothing to prove, he carried a sensitive heart and could not help but glance surreptitiously in her direction as he busied himself with the eggs. She recognised the underlying worry in his expression, first seeing it when she told him about their pregnancy three days before flying home from Bali. Having decided to keep the unexpected gift of a baby, she had placed no expectation on him - they barely knew each other after all - but her news had drawn a profound reaction. Much to the fiercely independent McGlynn's secret amusement, his first instinct had been one of protection, a need to keep her and their unborn child out of harm's way. They talked long into the humid night and ultimately agreed for him to return with her to an unfamiliar life and the chance to build a family. That had been more than a dozen years ago, she thought, the notion never failing to surprise. How short those years have seemed, racing past much more swiftly than the weeks and months in between.

'Here you go. I've left them runnier than usual. Eat as much as you want and I'll finish the rest.'

'They smell amazing, thanks *Chéri*.'

'We missed a message from Queenswood. The headmaster's asked for a call at eleven. Feeling up to it?'

'Whatever they need. Any idea what we should say to the girls?'

'I don't want to worry them,' he said. 'Not if we can help it.'

'Me either. I can't decide if it's better to bring them home or leave them there. Let's see what the school recommends? They might have worked with similar threats before.'

'The Triple S guys just checked in as well. They've walked the perimeter every thirty minutes and say there's been nothing out of the ordinary. They want to come up to the house in a bit though, if you're well enough, to cover off more stuff with the both of us.'

McGlynn nodded in reply, took a scoop from the heaped plate and managed to swallow it at the second attempt.

'Is it bad?'

She nodded again and sipped the coffee.

'Felt better,' she breathed. 'Assholes.'

'I know how much you hate being looked after but please, please tell me you're not expecting to keep working?'

'No. Thom's in charge at the office. I said I'd keep an eye out but he knows to go to Sylvie or Auntie Jane if he needs help. He'll be fine for a few days.'

'What about the triathlon?'

'No chance. After all the goddamn training I put in too.'

'Good. You need time to recover. And proper rest, you hear me?

'Uh-hmm.'

Jack leant on the other side of the breakfast bar and looked at her, blue eyes unassuming beneath the craggy brow.

'Want to talk any more about yesterday?' he asked gently. 'Always happy to listen if it helps.'

With every mouthful marginally easier than the last she continued to blunt her appetite, delaying an answer to this question. Finally settling in his arms last night, there had been only enough strength left to relay the barest of details and reliving those, on top of the earlier police interview, was more than enough. What she really wanted was to never discuss yesterday's events again, or perhaps to wait until her vocal cords recovered and then scream alone into a cashier's box, wreathe it in heavy chain and sail far across the ocean before dropping it overboard.

Avoiding his eyes, she reached for her phone and Jack, after a moment's pause, returned to the washing up.

She scrolled absently through the list of new messages. Most only had her on copy although a couple were direct from Dalkeith. He asked where he could find this or that but emphasised there was no urgency and was at great pains to say he and Sylvie had everything in hand. Their hospitality at the Mayor's Ball had gone smoothly, their guests sorry but understanding, and he planned to head over to court today with Wiesenberg. Assuming the judges returned a favourable verdict, the Nilssons had accepted a follow up meeting on Monday which he hoped was a positive indication. She was not to worry.

As her inbox refreshed, three more message headers appeared, gliding into the top of the stack in bold font. Two were replies to previous threads of no particular interest but the third was new, had a title of *Security Review - Wednesday* and contained a link to a video sharing service. Wondering whether it might offer useful insight about Campbell's progress at the docks, she tapped the screen. While loading, she noticed the video had been added by an anonymous user and, by the time it started to play, revealing nothing but a silent black rectangle, her overwrought brain was questioning why her team would share anything via a public website.

Further rational thought, however, became impossible as a moving image faded into view.

The video was of her.

There was no audio, the colour quality was poor and the viewpoint meandered and jerked, but none of this mattered in the slightest. McGlynn's entire being was transfixed by an image she had last seen reflected in cold black lenses. The pyramid of a powerful arm rising from the base of the screen, white-knuckled hands clamped to its wrist and a squirming, tortured face at its summit. Unable to speak, to make any movement at all, she watched the recording run on in excruciating detail, the massive hand covering the length of her throat flexing slightly and both of hers flying towards the camera, clawing and beating uselessly like birds trapped in a net but failing to obscure the gradually darkening face, the bulging and reddening eyes, the tongue extending grotesquely between bared teeth.

'Something wrong?' asked Jack, half-turned with his hands in the sink. Birdsong and the sound of a distant agricultural engine filtered through the open windows. Roscoe sat up, head cocked. 'Wyn?'

Riveted to the screen, air whistling through her windpipe, a single tear slid down McGlynn's cheek, then another to chase the first and splash on the wood. Indifferently, the video played on to show the moments of her dying, of losing her life in pain and terror and sorrow, of praying for the safety of her family whilst cursing the men responsible for its destruction. Horror-stricken at both the spectacle and the sadism of those who wanted it filmed, she was made to endure the moment her swollen face became unresponsive before the picture faded and five words in large white lettering appeared - *STAY AWAY FROM CITY PORT.*

Fists jammed against her eyelids as if to crush unbidden images, McGlynn broke into great, heaving sobs. After what seemed an eternity, Jack's arms went around her and she spun to bury her face in his neck, wretchedly grateful for the soft beard against her forehead and the sounds of murmured sympathy.

They shared his strength that way for a long time and, by degrees, the dread receded and her weeping lessened.

'Sorry,' she croaked at last, partially muffled but in control again. 'I'm so sorry.'

'You've nothing to be sorry for, honey, nothing,' he said, his own lashes wet and an immense fury lurking behind the concern. 'This wasn't your fault.'

'But I feel so guilty that I've somehow put you all in harm's way. The police didn't think it was to do with them visiting the docks but I–'

McGlynn suddenly remembered Matthieu's account of an unknown man trying to establish her whereabouts earlier in the week, leaping backwards again to her feeling of being watched while inspecting the warehouse with Turner on Monday. If someone had been stalking her down those gloomy aisles, or heard her asking Hugo Valente for the site security reports, there could have been two full days to plan and carry out an ambush. Who else, other than organised criminal gangs like those dealing in the misery of human trafficking, had the wherewithal to conduct a daylight assault on the city's streets and then the gall to issue such a blatant threat?

'What is it?' asked Jack.

'Just that this has to be linked with their investigation, that's all. Hopefully it means you and the girls shouldn't be in as much danger.'

'But what about you? Can you stay away from the port like these people want? Call City PD off?'

'Wouldn't be the right thing to do and it's too late anyway – I gave up the only chip I had to bargain with. Don't worry, I'll be alright.'

'That's not good enough. What about that security guy, Andrew, what's he doing to help?'

'I screwed up with him, Jack, lost my temper. There were personal protection terms in his contract because of South America, but he hesitated right after I got hit. Said I'd have to replace him and it went badly from there.'

'He'd understand, it was a hell of a day for both of you.'

'Mmm.'

'Are you going to let the police know?'

'Guess so.' Still trembling, she picked up the phone, wrote a short forewarning to Campbell and sent the offending message onwards. Shuffling into a more upright position on his lap, she sniffed and dried her cheeks with the palms of her hands. 'Goddammit, I need to go wash my face again.'

'Tea?'

'More coffee please, I could use the caffeine today.'

'OK baby. Remember I love you, and anytime you want to talk, I'm here.'

'You've always known the right thing to say haven't you, Mr Connelly? I love you too. Back in five.'

She headed upstairs, thinking how lucky she was to have him in her life. Through their shared adoration for the twins and with proximity and time, there was no doubt he had become her closest friend even though they had little in common other than the girls. A sometime sculptor, from a poor but creative household, Jack had no interest in the world of business in which she was steeped. He crammed himself into a suit and supported her at public functions in the City when required but generally stayed away if possible, much preferring the tranquility of home. To her recollection he had never seen the inside of a gym, taking his exercise in the guise of manual labour or hillwalking, plenty of both being on offer in the vicinity. When the girls wanted to stay at school for a few nights, and if she was over in town or away on business, she knew he liked nothing better than to fill a rucksack and head directly upwards from the back of the house with the dogs by his side. They would disappear for days at a time to return dirty and tired but always happy.

Rarely did they make love anymore, hence Charlie, but he was a good man, honest and true, and she loved him. Thank God for the French blood flowing in her veins which allowed her to understand the difference between sex and love, that adultery and infidelity were not necessarily synonymous. McGlynn had thought it wise to remain ignorant of Jack's own views on the subject but, if similar, wished him nothing other than equal fulfilment.

A slim, dazzling triangle of sunlight had encroached upon the far end of the bedroom floor by the time she re-entered, the quilt of tall firs on the ridge opposite now a subtly different shade of green. Avoiding her reflection, she ran the faucet, cupped her hands and carried icy water to her face. The cold helped ease the prickling but the memories of the previous day's events and the loathsome video remained untouched. There had been no space for anger in the hours since regaining consciousness on Avenue San Domingo but McGlynn felt a swelling rage now the source of danger was clearer. If the time spent chained to a dusty concrete floor in the hills of South America had taught her anything, it was that fairness could not be taken for granted, of the need to fight each and every day for what was morally right, and she wanted, no, she demanded justice to be served upon those culpable. Justice or vengeance, either would do and she had the savage desire and extensive resources to pursue them both.

Her phone rang, Campbell's number flashing up.

'Hey Kenise,' she croaked. 'That was quick.'

'What was at the link? It's been taken down.'

'Ah. It was, um, a close up of me being attacked yesterday. And a warning to stay away from the docks.'

Campbell hissed through her teeth.

'Are you OK?' she asked. 'Are you safe? There's no chance this happened at random now is there, what extra precautions are you taking?'

'We're alarming the house overnight plus four security personnel around the clock, all armed. We're speaking to the girls' school this morning but expect them to stay until the weekend.'

'Good, that sounds good. I can probably arrange for City PD help if you like?'

'No thanks. I'll have it covered privately,' said McGlynn, wanting no favours from Commissioner Petrucci.

'OK. Now, how in hell did they get a close up of you?'

'Remember me saying they both wore sunglasses? And that the glasses on the guy who came after me looked strange? Well he had a camera built into one side, his right I think. Recorded the whole thing from a distance of three feet.'

'Ah no, that must have been, uh…'

'It was.'

'Do you need any support? There's no point in toughing it out by yourself.'

'Not as long as they're caught.'

'We're working on it. Forensics might have figured out some more if we'd had the video. Never mind, we'll try and trace the user but that'll take time. Same for the message itself.'

'I think you need to be careful too, Kenise. Something's going on around the warehouse and whoever's behind this isn't worried about serious intimidation. Or worse.'

'Agreed. I'll talk to Garnett and the team - we're all here again today. Do you want me to speak to Mr Valente too?'

'Would you mind?'

'No, that's fine and I won't mention what we've just discussed. How about Mr Brookes? Haven't seen him since yesterday.'

'I don't think he'll be back. Thom Dalkeith is arranging a replacement and I'll get him to make introductions. But can you please chat with him about what other precautions we should be taking?'

'No problem.'

'How's your investigation going?'

'Steady. I think we'll be here until early next week.'

'And anything else on Rohan?'

'As I said, I've done all I can there. I hope he turns up but you should log a missing persons case if not.'

'Ok,' said McGlynn, hearing the buzzer for the front gate sound in the hallway. 'Have to go, sorry, speak soon.'

She looked in the mirror and picked up a hairbrush, wondering what the Triple S team might recommend for situations like these. Would they insist on cameras around the house? Self-defence training? Personal alarms? Even a live-in guard or two? As far as she was concerned, privacy away from McGlynn-Lansing was sacrosanct, or at least had been before being stolen by the men in black.

On reaching the landing, amid the clatter of pans from the kitchen, she heard a knock at the front door and continued straight on down the next flight of stairs to let the team in. Were Officers Schnitzer and Long already back on shift? Instinctively, she liked Schnitzer based on their brief interaction yesterday. He had the calm, professional demeanour which would suit an inevitably close working relationship. Nearing the foot of the staircase though, she saw the handle turn and the heavy door begin to swing through its arc. Coming directly into the house without asking was not acceptable and boundaries would need to be set and respected if this was ever going to work.

However, the person crossing the threshold was neither employed by Triple S nor someone who looked as though they would meekly accept her instructions. Of a height with McGlynn, with modishly chopped grey hair, blue jeans and unpretentious poise, the newcomer stopped dead on seeing her and sucked in a sharp breath.

'*Alors Chérie, Qu'est qui s'est passé?*' demanded Cécile, stepping into a half-embrace whilst inspecting her all at once. 'What have they done to you? Let me see. What animals! Just look at you.'

'*Maman*…but… how?'

'Sylvie of course. Your sister has always known when to ask for help, not like you, *hein*? Thinking you should carry all your troubles on your own. *Pfft.* She calls me first thing this morning. Are you alright? Is anything broken?'

'No, just cuts and bruis–'

'Are you certain? Have you been to the hospital? What did they say?'

'Come up and have some coffee. Jack's making a fresh pot and–'

'Ah, just one moment,' said her mother before McGlynn could close the door. 'There is someone else who came to make sure you are alright.'

She heard footsteps outside and a figure materialised, coming to a halt on finding her, seemingly unsure whether to venture any closer. Thinner shoulders, deeper lines, hair so fine she could see the sun reflecting from his scalp, the man appeared far more careworn than when she had seen him last, a world away from the dominant figure of her childhood. Perhaps most troubling of all, he bore an air of acquiescence so acute it hung over him like a pall.

Lingering just out of reach, they eyed each other cautiously until David broke the silence.

'My darling,' he began.

22

A stone channel eight inches wide and two deep ran down the centre of the cobbled street. Each of the sixty-four sections of limestone block used in its construction weighed a third of a tonne and had been laboriously carved using pick, hammer and chisel. Smaller contributory runnels joined the main artery at an angle from the front of each premises, giving the effect of feathers fletched to the shaft of an arrow where its head was buried in a target of ductile iron; a circular grate two feet in diameter leading directly to the City's sewer tunnels. In times gone by, the central channel would run almost constantly with the gore of animals slaughtered in back rooms and hung in front windows for townsfolk to peruse. These days, the runnels were fed by drainpipes pinned to shabby-chic façades and carried nothing more grisly than rainwater and the occasional stray napkin.

Although unfamiliar with her exact destination, Malik knew Butcher's Row reasonably well and had swapped stilettos for sandals in anticipation of the uneven surface. She strolled upwards from the rear of City Hall, scanning left and right in case anyone interesting happened to be sitting outside the bistros and cafés, and eventually found *Milburn's Coffee House* engraved on a pedestal menu towards the street's upper end. Like most of its neighbours, the enclosed frontage was crammed with slender furniture to maximise occupancy and the original plate glass shop window had been retained. However, the upper storeys were painted in beige and blue and festooned with a riot of trailing Begonias to give the impression of a Greek taverna. Maybe it was the colourful exterior, perhaps the quality of the coffee but, either way, something was working because the place was packed.

She weaved her way between tables trying to find Imelda Finch, a task made all the more difficult by a clientele sporting oversized sunglasses and sharing similar characteristics - older, white, female, monied. After five minutes, she gave up and approached the team of baristas squeezed behind the counter. To a man they were young and good looking, suggesting a further reason for the café's core demography.

'Excuse me, I'm looking for Mrs Imelda Finch. Do you know if she's here?'

'Miss Malik? Mrs Finch is upstairs on the terrace. May I show you the way?'

'If you could just point me in the right direction.'

'Through here, up two flights and the terrace is on your left. Would you like something to drink?'

'An iced tea please.'

Passing through a door marked for staff use only, Malik climbed the stairs. She emerged onto a rear-facing terrace no bigger than the bedroom of her apartment but affording a spectacular outlook across the eastern downtown area. Imelda sat sipping tea beneath the parasol of the sole table causing Malik to wonder how she had secured such an enviable spot.

'Good morning Imelda and wow, what a view.'

'Yes, isn't it?' replied the old woman cheerfully, rising to her feet. In fashionable light trousers, sleeveless shirt and a chunky necklace, she looked much less grandmotherly. 'Have you been asked what you'd like to drink?'

'I have. Your staff are very polite. Do they know all their customers by name?'

'Unlikely, although they seem like good boys. But they know me because I've owned this building and the one next door for some time, considerably longer than they've been alive actually. I saw the potential for the Row back when it was all but derelict and decided to invest early.'

'Smart move I'd imagine.'

'Yes, I believe we've done quite well. Thank you Henry,' she added as Malik's tea was delivered. 'Could you close the door for us please? There's a dear.'

'Do you manage the properties yourself?'

'Well I can't be crawling around on all fours these days but I still look after the tenants and do the books. Stops me losing my marbles plus the ice cream gives the great-grandchildren an incentive to visit. Have you been before?'

'Not to Milburn's, I'm sorry to say, but I like one of the restaurants lower down. Siam Thani, do you know it?'

'Indeed I do,' said Imelda with a chuckle. 'But do you know who owns that property? In fact the first four on that side of the Row?'

'No?'

'Your good friends Vincent and Donna Evesham… Exactly. I suspect you might think twice about dining there again, eh?'

'Mmm. I take it you've been doing some research of your own.'

'I didn't recognise you at the time but of course it clicked when I went online and found your surname. The famous Sunita Malik, scourge of City society. I have to say that I rather admire your nerve in showing up to the ball at all.'

'All part of the job. I'm not in it to win any popularity contests.'

'Then what are you in it for, if I may ask?'

'It's interesting work.'

'Yes but so is zoology. And lions and pandas are much less likely to take you to court. Why this in particular?'

'I have my reasons.'

'My dear Sunita, I'm afraid that just won't do,' replied Imelda more firmly, refilling her cup from a china pot. 'May I ask you to remember we're having this meeting because you would like to learn about Julian Dayton. Given your reputation, I should imagine you're on the hunt for ways to smear him in one of your forthcoming columns. So even though I've made it clear you may only use our conversation for background research, some context if you will, what guarantee do I have that you'll honour my wishes? You've given me your word and that's admirable. However, in return for a private discussion, I'd like to know something about you which you would normally choose to keep to yourself. It doesn't have to be how you came to journalism but, and please forgive me for being frank, it will need to be a secret of sorts. In that way, we both have something to lose should it ever come to it. Do you see?'

Malik saw only too clearly and spent a moment weighing her options.

'It's a long story.'

'Oh good,' said Imelda, settling herself with cup and saucer in hand. 'Those are the best sort.'

'Right.' Malik stopped again, surveying the rooftops, entirely unused to playing the interviewee. 'Um, to begin with it's probably worth saying I had no great ambition to be a journalist. My parents expected my sister and me to become doctors, like my grandfather. He was a cardiologist in Srinagar. The Kashmir Valley's such a beautiful place. Have you been?'

'Never had the opportunity, not yet at least.'

'The icy waters of the Jhelum, the perpetual scent of saffron, surrounded by the eternal mountains, the roof of the world… you must if you can. Anyway, Grandpa was quite famous in those parts and wanted his children to follow in his footsteps, but my father's interests were in business, not the wonders of the human body, so they reached a compromise and he came to the City to study pharmacy instead.'

'So why did he want you to be a doctor?'

'Status. After marrying Mum, he'd scraped together enough money to lease a small unit at the bottom of Epstone Street, then grown it fast enough to finance a new one every year until he had fifteen across town. By then he'd diversified into general retail too. Basic foods, toys, anything he could trade at a profit. He was so busy he hardly ever came home but it didn't matter because it meant he could pay for his children to go through medical school. Even though he'd graduated top three in his class and had a thriving business, he never really lost the underlying insecurity that running a company was a little bit, I don't know… plebeian compared to the prestige of a doctor.'

'I see, then why did you end up doing something different?'

'My father committed suicide when I was seventeen.'

Suddenly it was Imelda's turn to feel uncomfortable.

'Oh my, Sunita, I'm sorry to hear it.'

'We were too. There was no note, no explanation, but once we started going through his paperwork we found unpaid bills, letters from debt collection agencies, repossession orders, you name it - he'd been declared bankrupt. Mum asked the family for help and discovered how much he'd already borrowed. Uncles, cousins, even Grandpa had sent tens of thousands expecting to be paid back with interest. When they heard what happened, they cut us off completely. The only good thing from around that time was a competitor offering to take over the business as a going concern. No money in it for us but at least they settled the debt and we didn't have to go to court. Our staff were kept on and the shops were rebranded to Howlett's Pharmacies.'

'Howlett's? I remember those, Don used to go there for his statins. Didn't they end up going into liquidation too?'

'Sort of, I'll come back to them in a minute.' Malik took a sip of her drink. 'But I bet you're still wondering what all this has to do with why I'm a journalist.'

'I'm sure you're coming to that.'

'I am. But it's important you understand why I felt the way I did, why I still feel the way I do. So, despite Howlett's takeover, we'd lost the house, the cars, the jewellery and pretty much everything else just as I needed to think about applying for college. I already had one job and offered to take a second or go full time to help pay the bills but Mum was having none of it. She took on more hours and persuaded me to continue with my studies. With Dad gone though, I opted for law instead. The idea of being a lawyer, fighting for people's rights and holding them accountable for their wrongs, well, it was naive but it appealed. And I thought a lawyer would have as much status as a doctor which could be a way back into the family. My grades had slipped but I worked and worked and made it by the skin of my teeth onto a course at New College.

'By then we were living in this tiny welfare place. It was awful and besides, we didn't want to live off the state, we wanted to pay our own way and rid ourselves of the shame we carried, the shame of taking handouts, the shame of Dad's decisions and actions. So for three years we worked, studied or slept for every hour Allah sent and prayed for his divine mercy.

'By the start of my final year at college, we'd managed to scrape together enough to move out near Granton. It was basic but we had our own bedrooms and even a garden, such luxury. In the first few days, a van turned up with all of Dad's old stuff – Mum had put anything left into cheap storage when we'd first moved. Going through his personal effects again, even the smell of his clothes, it's so hard to describe but it brought him back to us in some way, you know? We spent our Sundays unpacking those boxes, donating to charity, choosing mementos and so on. A dozen were filled with paperwork which should probably have gone to Howlett's, but everything was out of date and besides, I wanted to try and figure out why he'd gone bust, where he'd gone wrong. Wasn't hard in the end, particularly as I'd been studying contract law that semester.

'Fourteen of his property leases were with a company called Mobius Developments. They all included terms for an annual rent review and, after years of modest rises, I saw that Mobius had suddenly doubled their rates during the last twelve months of Dad's life. But rent was already running at thirty percent of costs and it was no wonder he'd gone bankrupt.'

'Why would they have done that? Retail's a low-margin business - they must have known your father would struggle to pay?'

'That's what I wanted to know too, so I started looking into their ownership. The only common thread seemed to be the boss of the holding entity. I switched my attention to him and noticed he'd been involved in lots of dissolved companies. And then I found a record of him acquiring the assets of a small, privately owned pharmacy chain which had gone bust a couple of years before Dad died. Right here in the City.'

'Ah,' said Imelda, her voice flat. 'Howlett's.'

'You got it. For whatever reason, the guy who ultimately owned Mobius had decided to go into retail pharmacy, bought what was left of Howlett's and then seen an easy opportunity to pick up another fourteen stores without spending a penny. He'd doubled Dad's rent, forced him out of business, then had Howlett's ride into our lives like knights in shining armour.'

'But he couldn't have known your father was planning to take his own life?'

'No, probably not. But my guess is he'd have made an offer for the remaining assets once the banks foreclosed. Just a matter of timing.'

'That's dreadful Sunita, truly dreadful. What did you do?'

'What could I do? I'm twenty years old and I know enough to understand that what this guy did was permitted by the contracts Dad signed. Immoral for sure but I couldn't prove it was illegal, at least not without hiring lawyers and investigating a bunch of shell companies for which I had absolutely no money. I tried City PD but from the ten minutes they gave me it looked like a tonne of work, was ancient history and involved a high-profile name from out of town. I'd just about made up my mind to visit the Capital and confront the guy in person when I had a better idea. If I couldn't drag him into a court of law, then I'd drag him through the court of public opinion instead.'

'And how did you manage that?'

'That's how I became a journalist, of sorts. I secretly deferred my last year and went hell for leather in pulling together enough of a story to get the media interested. Got to know some of his associates, not too close but enough to pick up information outside the public domain, and met some of the people he'd screwed over. His speciality was asset stripping. Acquiring problem businesses, preferably those he could push further into distress, and dismantling or offshoring them. Most of it was perfectly legal but I heard about shadier things too. Bribes to officials, boasting about how little tax he paid, some insurance and bankruptcy fraud. After six months of hard graft, I started pitching to the press.'

'Was anyone interested?'

'Nearly. I had no idea how the media worked back then and didn't want to give away too much too soon. Nor was I ready to have my name linked to some of the frankly unsubstantiated claims I was making. So I put half the research on a private website and sent anonymous messages to a few of the papers and networks, three of whom were interested enough to see the rest, especially if I knew where the money went. Unfortunately I didn't but there was no way I was giving up, so I picked the journalist I trusted the most and said here, go check it out and I'll have the money trail by the time you're done. You see, I'd heard who did my guy's accounts, the real ones. Hadn't dared talk to him but I knew he lived here, in the City. Name of Leo Vergari.'

'Impossible,' Imelda almost snorted. 'Leo Vergari was convicted of abetting multiple counts of tax fraud and went to prison years ago. It was a huge scandal at the time because he took several people down with him. People even Don and I knew in passing.'

'The only person I cared about was Gideon Wade.'

'Gideon Wade? Really? He was the man in the Capital who owned Mobius and Howlett's?'

'Uh-huh. Not directly but he was at the top of the pile.'

'But he was exposed well before Vergari if I remember correctly? And the paper that broke the Wade story was The C–'

'The Courier,' said Malik with satisfaction. 'Shaun Strickland at The Courier to be precise. Made him famous actually, but I got what I wanted and didn't mind. He'd filled in some of the gaps in my research by the time I gave him the financial details, then published the story and Vergari found himself caught in the backlash. Gideon got sixteen years, Leo got eight and neither ever knew it was me.'

'Wade killed himself recently didn't he?'

'Mmm. Not sure I'd have told you this if he was still alive.'

'Astonishing. I never knew they were connected. But how did you get Vergari to give you the information you needed?'

'I was desperate. And of age.'

'Ah.'

'After Wade had been jailed, and in the absence of any better ideas, I finished college. Graduated with first-class honours but by then I'd realised that people like him and Vergari, they weren't going to fall foul of the law unless someone uncovered what they did behind their public personas, their expensive lawyers and accountants. And those were the people I wanted to see humbled, Imelda. The rich, privileged, untouchable men who use the system to push obstacles, people like my father, out of the way.'

'Only men? Are you a… I'm not sure of the word. The equivalent of a misogynist?'

'Misandrist. It's used so rarely isn't it? Because nearly all the public conversation is about men who hate women.' Malik's expression was blank but Imelda heard the undercurrents in her voice. 'No, not a misandrist. It just happens that the abuse of power, the vast majority of it all the way back through history, is committed by men. Dictators, warmongers, dishonest politicians, corrupt business leaders, religious zealots, terrorists, rapists, paedophiles, bullies in all walks of life. For every woman's name you can remember, I'll give you ten men, twenty, fifty. Maybe it's a testosterone imbalance, maybe it's the perpetuation of the stereotype, but it keeps happening.'

'And you're going to stop it, all by yourself?'

'I'm doing my bit. Do what you love and never work a day, right? And I'd loved bringing Wade down, not just the result but the process as well. The research and the critical thinking to deliver justice for someone who couldn't fight back. Shaun made sure the Courier gave me a fee for handing them all the credit. Not millions but enough to provide a cushion for Mum and Meerah and for me to buy my own place, so I was no longer poor and had some choice in what I wanted to do. I saw an advert in the City Post offering internships and applied. Do you know Bill Rutter?'

'Yes, I know of him at least.'

'Poor man. None of the other applicants stood a chance and neither did he. He has no idea about what I've just told you by the way. He's been good to me. Taught me how to do the job properly and gave me enough of a free hand to pursue the stories that I chose.'

'Like Vincent Evesham?'

'And Julian Dayton.'

'Would you class them in the same category as Wade, or Vergari?'

'Almost certainly not, although I suppose it depends on what you're prepared to tell me. There are only so many Wades or Vergaris in the City. But it doesn't make Vincent or Julian any less guilty of abusing their power, does it? And, when they do, they should be held to account.' Malik smiled for the first time. 'So, is my secret valuable enough, Imelda? Do you have sufficient collateral and, if so, may I ask you a few questions now?'

'More than. Thank you for sharing such a difficult part of your life and yes, I'll talk with you a while about Julian, although the same rules still apply. But first, I'm afraid an old woman needs to visit the bathroom and order another drink. Can I bring something for you?'

'Another iced tea, please.'

'Shall we enjoy something a little stronger? It is lunchtime or thereabouts and they have a rather nice pink prosecco here.'

'Sounds lovely but perhaps the iced tea as well?'

A glass of wine might loosen Imelda's tongue but Malik wanted her own memory as sharp as possible. Imelda disappeared inside, leaving her alone in the company of the humming streets and the crying gulls. Distant buildings danced in the air as she dwelt on those faraway times, how angry she had been, how frightened. How did crime journalists like Strickland ever sleep at night? Wade was the first and most dangerous of those whose malpractice she had exposed, even more so than she had suspected at the time. Once they started to dig, the police uncovered links to prostitution and the drug trade alongside a litany of racketeering. Sixteen years was not enough justice for what that man did to her father and many others, even though it turned out to be more than enough for him. Would she have had the courage to do what was needed at the time had she known? Or do the same now? Maybe. She had sworn to never again debase herself as with Leo Vergari, a perfect example of the exploitation she now fought to prevent, and these days was older, wiser and had something to lose. For the foreseeable future, Sunita Malik was content to keep her eyes and ears open, finding no shortage of people in this hot and sinful city who, whilst not as felonious as Gideon Wade, nevertheless abused their position to hurt those with the misfortune to be weaker.

And almost always they happened to be men.

23

H ere we are,' said Imelda, holding the door for an overburdened and perspiring youth. 'Leave the ice bucket in the shade, Jasper, there's a dear. Sunita, you're getting no protection from the parasol, would you like Jasper to move it?'

'No thanks, I'm something of a heliophile.'

Having cast sly glances in Malik's direction, Jasper seemed disappointed. Imelda shooed him away, poured two flutes of prosecco and resettled her weight in the creaking wicker chair.

'Now tell me, how was the rest of your evening? I seem to remember you still going strong.'

'Were you there when the ice dragon was knocked over?'

'Goodness, no.'

'A couple of people were getting a bit physical and fell into it. There was quite a bang then a rush for the bar.'

'There's a reason we don't stay to the bitter end these days, even if my knees were up to it. Was Julian still there?'

'I think he left after the auction.'

'Sounds about right. How much time have you spent with him?'

'Only the interview in person, but I've done a fair bit of asking around for opinions.'

'And how do you intend to describe him in your column?'

'Unapproachable is probably the best way of saying it,' said Malik, brow creased. 'He projects this aura of not wanting to be engaged in conversation, which I thought was arrogance although now I'm not so certain. He doesn't like to be challenged, even fairly, and can be rude in response but I'm not sure if that's down to a lack of manners or simply an overreaction to confrontation. He seems to consider his position a chore which is almost unique in my experience - most of his peers love the status and work incredibly hard to stay there. If he doesn't, then it suggests nepotism and perhaps a lack of intrinsic motivation. From what I'm told, he's intellectually clever but not clever with people. Those who know him well tend to steer clear if they can and I think he prefers keeping them at arm's length anyway. But those who have to work with him variously describe him as manipulative, grumpy, cold, socially inept, prone to sulk–'

'Ha! You missed out crass,' interrupted Imelda, chuckling by this point. 'And egocentric, and misogynistic, and overprivileged.'

'Why's that funny? Isn't he?'

'Probably. But the more interesting questions are to what degree, and why, and what else. You can find nearly any trait in any person if you look long enough or hard enough. Or under the stress of certain conditions or through a suitably jaundiced lens. What do you make of his family relationships?'

'I'd say there's not much love lost. Eddie and Richard turned up to the trial against McGlynn-Lansing yesterday but Julian was nowhere to be seen which is strange given it's his reputation on the line. And anyone could see there was animosity during the auction.'

'What about his mother, Vanessa?'

'I don't know. She was there last night but I didn't see them together.'

'To understand Julian, you have to know something of the dynamic between him and his parents,' said Imelda. 'Just as Edward is the epitome of his father, so Julian is very similar to his mother. She's a viscount's daughter and a very clever lady but in a different way to Richard. A generous and gentle soul, always thinking of others. Julian took after her and was sensitive as a younger child, perhaps overly so.'

'It's strange to think of him as a child.'

'Richard was away a lot with work, as was Don, and I often used to take my two out with Vanessa and Julian for the day. He always seemed such a happy and loving little boy. Fi is a year older and Beth's a year younger and they used to play well together, the best of friends.'

'What changed?'

'I suspect being packed off to boarding school at six didn't help. Rovingham was one of the best in the country, elite or elitist depending on which way you'd prefer to look at it, but he was terribly homesick. Vanessa was against the idea but Richard wanted a son graven in his own image, you know, a macho, rugby-playing, alpha-male type. He thought time away in the company of other boys might toughen him up.'

'So his dislike for his father goes back that far?'

'Children love their parents unconditionally at that age, or want to love them at least. Julian was like any other boy and idolised Richard. But being sent away from home is confusing for a child, especially one so young and especially unwillingly. They can't rationalise what's happening. I remember him coming home for the holidays and being quite introverted. Didn't get on with my two anymore and spent his time reading or playing by himself. It was painful to see such a change. Then, when Edward came along a few years later, it was obvious how alike he and Richard were. The closer they became, the more time Julian spent with Vanessa, not that either minded as they remain exceptionally close even now. It's funny how even small families can split along certain lines, certain axes, and that probably cast the die in terms of Julian's relationship with Richard as well as creating a certain jealousy regarding his brother. Don took a job in Oman for a few years but when we came back occasionally, it was clear that Julian was turning into a polite but very serious young man who had lost the ability to connect with others his own age.'

'So that's what you'd put Julian's character flaw–... traits down to? A silver-spooned but unhappy, perhaps emotionally starved childhood on his father's side? And maybe some sort of Oedipal complex on his mother's?'

'I think that's stretching what I've said much too far but I don't see why he'd be any different to the rest of us. Our early experiences shape us as adults, wouldn't you say? Although Julian hasn't had the most fortunate of adulthoods either. Have you spoken to him or anyone else about his marriage?'

'I didn't know he was married?'

'He's not anymore,' said Imelda, leaning forward to pull the dripping bottle from the bucket. 'Would you like a top-up?'

'No thanks, I'm still half-full. When was this?'

'Must be at least twenty years ago. Vanessa was starting to want grandchildren and hoping one of the boys would settle down. But Edward was still quite young, in his early twenties and behaving like a teenager in any case, and Julian hadn't really shown any interest in a long-term relationship.'

'Had he had girlfriends? I wondered if he might not be, um…'

'Gay? Why, because you don't think he likes women? No, or at least I'm fairly sure he wasn't at the time. He was very eligible you know, a good-looking boy with manners and obvious prospects and I remember being introduced to a girlfriend or two. Tall, dark-haired and pretty was the type - although I don't think any of them lasted more than a few months. But then out of the blue we were invited to his wedding.'

'What was she like?'

'His wife? Oh my, do you know, I've quite forgotten her name. We didn't really get to meet her properly other than to exchange the usual pleasantries. She seemed kind-hearted and clearly doted on Julian but was different from the others. Mousey, very shy. Vanessa didn't think she was right for him, I imagine mothers rarely do, particularly mothers of sons, but she was trying to be happy because he was. However, Richard was at pains to make it known she was not at all suitable to be marrying into the Daytons. No doubt worried about the shallowing of his bloodline.'

'Were they getting married because she was pregnant?'

'Not that I'm aware. I think they were in love, same as almost everyone else who takes the plunge. They did have a child reasonably soon though, a boy named Adam. Easy enough to remember that one, being his firstborn, but now, well, what on earth was… Sarah, yes, that was her name, I'm sure of it. Sarah Dayton.'

'Julian has a twenty-year-old son? Nobody's mentioned him at all, not once.'

'Adam was never terribly well. He sickened as a baby and the doctors diagnosed a brain tumour. Very rare, very serious. The poor boy underwent a lot of surgery and spent months in hospital as a toddler but never recovered. All the family were devastated, even Richard.'

'He... died? I... losing a child must be... I can't imagine.'

'No, it's unimaginable isn't it, every parent's literal nightmare. Such an innocent as well. Poor, poor boy.'

'Awful. Is that what caused the breakdown of his marriage?'

'I assume so. One didn't like to enquire too closely at the time but we didn't receive any more news of Julian or his wife for a while. Not until Vanessa rang one night in floods of tears. I remember it very well because Don and I were on holiday in Santorini, having dinner and watching the sun slide into the caldera. I picked up the call expecting to say I'd ring her back but she was in such a state I had to leave him sitting there with the entrées.'

'What had happened?'

'Well, I'm sorry for mentioning this, Sunita, given your own circumstances. But I'm afraid Sarah had taken her own life.'

'He lost his son... *and* his wife?' said Malik, stunned.

'Vanessa managed to tell me that he'd turned up at home almost catatonic. Wouldn't or couldn't talk about anything other than Sarah. They'd been living apart by then I think, but even so, losing Adam had broken both their hearts and, well, she just didn't have the strength to go on, poor thing. From what I understand now it's more common than you might think. Premature mortality rates for women increase noticeably after the death of a child, much more than for men although Vanessa was terrified in case Julian was considering the same...'

Apparently lost in thought, Malik had already turned away.

Imelda watched the haughty profile for a while then, careful not to disturb her preoccupation, refilled her glass and leant back, sipping the floral wine and allowing her gaze to flow over the City's rooftops. Life is so fragile, she mused, only truly understanding the idiom having witnessed so much, having lived so long and being unavoidably closer to an expected ending than an unexpected beginning. Every day threatened to consume her with worry for her daughters and theirs and theirs. What kind of a world had she brought them into without their permission? Did every mother feel the guilt of bestowing life and an uncertain future upon their children? Was her generation leaving behind a better planet than they inherited, one which would be kinder or at least more tolerable for the next? Such imponderables could drive one mad if left unguarded.

'And he's been on his own ever since?'

The journalist was back, although Imelda thought she detected a very slight softening of the tone.

'I don't know. Although I haven't seen or heard of him being romantically linked with anyone, male or female, since Sarah died. Understandable wouldn't you say?'

'I heard a rumour,' said Malik, deciding to leave no stone unturned. 'That he'd once made a pass at Wynter McGlynn. Is there any truth in it?'

'Ha! Well, well. Where on earth did you hear that?'

'Sorry, but I really can't say. Is it true?'

'I wouldn't call it a pass,' replied Imelda, the prosecco making her feel pleasantly light-headed. 'But if you're referring to the incident at the Levines' party then yes, I was there.'

'What, really? Who are they?'

'Bob and Chase Levine. She used to run Canterbury's? Before your time I expect. She passed away a few years ago although I believe Bob's still grimly hanging on despite the dementia. They had a big place up on the Rangeway and threw enormous socials for the sheer hell of it. There was always a fantastic atmosphere and half the City used to turn up whether they were invited or not. But Chase never cared, she'd just hand over a glass of champagne and introduce herself. Always fascinated by people was Chase, fabulous woman.'

'When was this? The incident with Julian and Wynter?'

'Oh, a long time ago. We were back from Oman but well before Julian got married. Edward was still at Oxford but must have been home for the holidays because he was there too. That was another hot summer, every bit as much as this one's shaping up to be, although I have a feeling this was later on in the season.'

'And Julian was there with Wynter?'

'Not in that sense, no, but Wynter had come with her parents. She might have been home for the holidays too. She's slightly younger than Edward I believe, can't have been more than eighteen or nineteen. Probably an opportunity for her to catch up with friends who'd all gone off to college.'

'And?' prodded Malik again.

'And sorry to disappoint but there's really not much to tell. It was a typical Bob and Chase party. At least a couple of hundred people milling around, generally in their forties and fifties but also some grown-up children. There was a buffet and a band but most of the attention was on drinking and catching up with old friends. We were in a group on the lawn with Richard and Vanessa, and the Claytons I think. It must have been mid-evening because the tree lights had been switched on, long sets of fairy lights with enough of a glow for people to stay outside until the early hours. Brought a magical feel to the place, like an enchanted forest, albeit one populated by the rich and noisy. From what I remember, Edward had come to join us and said something to Richard at which point they both turned towards the end of the garden, towards the border with the park and away from the crowd. So being as nosey as anyone, I looked as well and saw Wynter and Julian sitting next to each other on the wall, deep in conversation.'

'Was that unusual?'

'Very. Do you know much about the rivalry between the Daytons and the McGlynns?'

'I'm learning.'

'Richard detests David McGlynn, always has. Not just dislike, but active hatred and I'm sure the feeling's mutual. Never made much sense to Don or me. David and Cécile always seemed pleasant enough. But then, other than our friendship with Richard and Vanessa, we've no axe to grind. There was an unwritten rule that your loyalties lay on one side or the other, never in the middle, and that went for their children as well as their friends.'

'Any idea what the two of them were talking about?'

'No, none. But as we watched, the conversation stopped and then, apropos of nothing, Julian leaned in to kiss her.'

'He did what?' asked Malik. The man was full of unsavoury surprises.

'There was no mistaking his intent. He'd meant to kiss her on the lips but she backed off in the nick of time.'

'And she was still in her teens, which would have made him what, around thirty? How well did his advances go down?'

'I suspect he was younger than that but I agree it's a bit distasteful. However, such age gaps weren't all that uncommon and if she had been willing then it would have been up to her wouldn't it? To answer your question though, the attempt didn't go down at all well. From what I remember, Wynter recovered the quickest and put her hand on Julian's arm. Edward started to laugh, loudly enough for Julian to hear. He saw we'd all been watching and went from embarrassment to anger almost instantaneously. Stormed off without a word. I probably didn't see him again until his wedding.'

'Any idea why he'd tried to kiss her?'

'No. And I knew better than to bring it up given how Richard was. Incandescent is putting it mildly. Maybe Julian talked to Vanessa about it afterwards, maybe not, but it would have been disloyal to even ask.'

'Uh-hmm. Doesn't really fit in with my picture of him but it was a long time ago as you say. I was half-thinking of asking Wynter for her opinions but sounds like I should save my breath. She's unlikely to be available anyway.'

'Is it true then? About her being attacked?'

'Yes. I'd heard the rumours and had it confirmed this morning. Two men ambushed her and her fitness trainer. Put the trainer in hospital and choked her unconscious.'

'Good God, how appalling. What is this city coming to when the streets aren't safe in the middle of the day.'

'Mmm. And it goes without saying the two offenders were male, of course.'

Malik drained the last of her tea, studiously ignoring the remaining prosecco and itching to lay hands on her notebook.

'Well, thank you for meeting me today, Imelda, I appreciate it. Is there anything else you'd like to tell me about Julian?'

'Nothing springs to mind. But I hope you feel as though you have a slightly more rounded view of him. Yes, he can be difficult at times but maybe there are reasons as to why that is.'

'Those don't excuse his behaviour.'

'No, they don't. But they might account for some of it and I think that's an important distinction when you're deciding what to write.'

'I'll bear it in mind. Oh, one more thing,' said Malik, finding a picture on her phone and sliding it across the table. 'I don't suppose you recognise this man do you? The other with his back to camera is Richard Dayton.'

'The face is familiar,' said Imelda, squinting. 'I want to say he's an old university friend of Richard's but I couldn't swear to it. I might not have seen him in fifty years or more. People change, you understand.'

'No problem. If it does come back to you I'd appreciate a call - reach me at the Post anytime,' replied Malik, taking to her feet. 'Please, don't get up.'

'Well, goodbye. And I hope you don't mind me saying I shouldn't like to find my name in any of your future columns either.'

'I'm sure that's very unlikely.'

Imelda watched her go, envious of the woman's limber elegance and hoping the zeal which burned so brightly within it had been tempered, even if only a little. She owed that much to her friendship with Julian's mother. Once upon a time, she too might have had similarly unassailable courage in her own conviction but knew better these days. *Let she who is without sin…*

Beadily eyeing the half-finished bottle of wine, which it would be shameful to waste, Imelda's thoughts turned towards what to order for lunch.

24

Curled up on the sofa with the dogs, McGlynn was increasingly aware the fatigue she had resisted all day was gaining the upper hand.

Although appreciating their good intentions, the unexpected arrival of her parents had brought with it an additional burden at a time when she already felt stretched thin, like an over-washed and threadbare blanket incapable of fulfilling its function. Her father had proven particularly enervating. No doubt wanting to give the two of them some privacy and keen to obtain a second opinion on her daughter's condition, Cécile had disappeared to find Jack. However, this left McGlynn alone on the doorstep to console an old man descending into tears, pained more by the incoherent apology tumbling from his lips than by the clumsiness of his touch against her bruises. Once she had persuaded him upstairs, David's remorse knew no bounds. He laid the blame for their years of acrimony squarely on his own shoulders, confessing at length what she already knew about his pride. Yesterday's news brought back such terrible memories of South America, he said, renewing his guilt and making him realise the need for reconciliation before it was too late. After all, he was no longer young and anything could happen, to either of them. Did she understand? Could she forgive?

McGlynn was unsure what feelings she might have anticipated at this longed-for resolution but whatever they were - joy, regret, vindication, anger, love - proved elusive.

Perhaps already drained of emotion, all she felt was weariness as David sought and found absolution at the expense of her depleted stamina. Cécile and Jack eventually returned to save them from further discomfiture, then the prearranged call with the twins' school provided enough justification to suggest her parents might visit again early the following week.

She thought the staff at Queenswood had been excellent, coming with open minds and a list of recommendations to which she and Jack listened carefully. Ultimately, they agreed to fund a temporary strengthening of the school's physical security measures and increase the frequency of status reports, keeping Catriona and Adeline on-site until the nature of any ongoing risk to the family could be determined. They would need a few extra things for their extended stay so, with one of the Triple S teams in support, Jack had left an hour ago promising he would explain the need for vigilance to the girls without going into detail.

Without him as a distraction, her thoughts returned again and again to the overhanging threat. Detective Campbell had rung back to say City PD were withdrawing to await further orders, leaving McGlynn more anxious than ever. Recognising it would be foolish to visit the warehouse herself, and with Hallam so far removed, she realised there was only one good solution, and with it the chance to right a wrong.

The first call went to voicemail, the second answered only moments before.

'What do you want?' came Brookes' hostile voice.

'To apologise,' said McGlynn, knowing the significance of her first words. 'I made a bad decision, Andrew, I shouldn't have said what I did.'

'Is that it?'

'Yes,' she said, stopping and forcing herself to wait.

'Alright,' he said at length. 'I guess we were neither of us ourselves.'

'Thank you. How're you feeling?'

'Not great to be honest. It's been a long time since I last had that kind of treatment. You?'

'Same. At least I know who's behind it now, or what.'

McGlynn apprised him of the morning's events.

'Shit,' he said when she was done. 'Without the police there, you're wide open. I wouldn't trust anyone at the warehouse to deal with what might be coming next.'

'Me either. I'd understand if not... but I was hoping you'd still give me the details for your army friend.'

'For a moment, I thought you were going to ask me back.'

'What would you have said if I did?'

'Mmm, I'd have had to think pretty hard about it. Let me give Gina a call, see if she's still interested.'

'I appreciate it, Andrew, thanks. Please pass on my number, I'm free to talk anytime.'

Brookes rang off leaving McGlynn to wrack her brain for other options, none of which appealed. Cursing her stubbornness in delaying Hallam's travel from Brisbane, she resolved to call once time zones allowed and set about contacting her close network for recommendations in the event Gina, or Brookes, declined. Rectangles of sunlight crept towards her feet as she worked, Roscoe, Molly and Blue dozing peacefully at her side, until the intercom for the front gate set them growling.

'This is Officer Wiley from Triple S.' A female voice, competent but with undertones of exasperation. 'Sorry to disturb but there's someone down here asking for you. I've told her you're not receiving visitors but she won't take no for an answer. Has a passport in the name of Jane Hallam.'

'She never takes no for an answer,' sighed McGlynn, wondering how Auntie Jane had come halfway around the world unannounced but brightened by the thought. 'OK, but no one else please.'

'Yes ma'am. I'll bring her up.'

With the dogs ranging excitedly ahead, she made her way downstairs to watch the Triple S car crest the driveway and stop immediately outside. Both doors opened simultaneously, Hallam struggling with her seatbelt as Wiley rounded the rear of the vehicle.

'With you in a second,' called Hallam. 'Damn thing, won't undo.'

'Thanks for giving her a ride,' said McGlynn quietly to the guard.

'Pleasure. Will Ms Hallam be staying for long?'

'Not sure. We'll let you know. Hi Jane,' she added to the tiny, scowling woman now standing before her. 'Guess I don't need to ask why you're here.'

'No you bloody well don't,' said Hallam fiercely, staring upwards and searching for signs of injury, physical or otherwise. 'Thom tried to convince me you were poorly but I'd heard the rumours and was having none of it.'

'Come on up, you must be ready for a drink.'

In the kitchen, McGlynn poured two large glasses of homemade lemonade over plenty of ice and carried them through to the lounge. Hallam was perched on the sofa with one hand buried in the thick fur of Roscoe's neck and the other in Molly's. Blue sat by her knees looking on jealously.

'Thank you, my love. And sorry to just turn up but I had to make sure you were still in one piece. I've been worrying about you all the way over.'

'Honestly, I'll be fine. But glad you came.'

'Pah, I should have been here already.' Hallam took a grateful sip of her drink. 'I don't want to rake it all back up but did I hear right? You were mugged?'

'Sort of. Andrew Brookes too. He's OK apart from a broken cheek. We weren't sure on the motive but there's been a related threat, telling us to stay away from the warehouse.'

'Oh, that's not good.'

'No. Have you been to see Hugo yet?'

'I came straight from the airport and was heading there next. Can't quite believe he'd know nothing about any smuggling, or people trafficking, if it's going on under his nose. How are Jack and the children?'

'He's as pissed as you'd expect. We're keeping the twins at school and not giving them too many details.'

'Sensible, poor darlings. Give them my love when you see them. Other than taking Hugo by the scruff of the neck and liaising with City PD, what else do you need me to do? Does Thom want any help? I hear he's in charge.'

'He is. Ask him by all means but try not to crowd him, running the business is a useful lesson. The priority has to be a new head of security at the warehouse. Andrew knows someone but it'd be great if you can find other options. And I'd also like to catch up on how the Australian business plan's going. I read the RBA's economic forecast over the weekend and it's not as rosy as last month. Could you arrange a couple of hours with Matthieu and Thom next week, possibly Damian.'

'You shouldn't be rushing back,' said Hallam mildly.

'I want to keep working if I can.'

'No surprise. How did you get on in court yesterday morning?'

'The testimony went OK but I haven't heard much more. Thom's there with Jacob waiting for the verdict. I don't suppose you had any luck reaching Rohan in the last twenty-four hours did you? Or Wenling? I'm still worried about them.'

'Ah, a little. I made a dozen or so calls before I left Brisbane but no joy. As it happened though, the first flight out wasn't direct and I had a long layover, in Singapore. So I went through immigration at Changi and took a cab to that address you gave me.'

'You did what?'

'What else did I have to do for six hours when you're all asleep? It was less than a thirty-minute ride - Nassim Hill, near the Botanical Gardens and very nice it is too. Big, flashy houses, a bit like Cornhill Road but newer and even more ostentatious. Eventually managed to find the right place, rang the buzzer and asked for a Ms Kim, then spent at least ten minutes arguing with a maid before she'd even let me through the gates, bloody woman.'

'Sounds like a bit of a trend for you recently.'

'Don't you start, young lady. Officer Wiley might have a pretty face and think she's super smart but she was just being obstructive.'

'That's her job, Jane. Remember?'

'Hmph. Well anyway, I manage to bluff my way up the drive where I'm accosted by an older woman who I assume is Wenling's mother. Dressed like a newsreader, clearly in charge and clearly ruder than the maid - able to tell me off for interrupting her day in much more colourful English. I ask if I may speak to her daughter and she says no, I may not, then demands to know who I am and which of her daughters I want to speak to anyway. I say it's Wenling and she tells me she's overseas so I'm entirely wasting my time and hers by standing on her porch. Then I explain who I work for and that Rohan Mehta works for the same company and she obviously has no idea who he is.'

'Odd,' said McGlynn. 'I got exactly that reaction from his father when I asked him about Wenling. Felt as though I'd put my foot in it somehow.'

'Same here. And Mrs Kim is now even more suspicious so I change tack and ask if Wenling's over here, in the City, to which I'm told in no uncertain terms that it's none of my business and if I don't leave immediately, she'll call her husband to come and deal with me. Apparently, he's at work ten minutes away.'

'Bet that scared you.'

'Ha! Took all my famous self-restraint to avoid tearing a strip off the old bat. But I wanted to find out where he was so I'm ashamed to say I kept goading her until she let it slip. While she's telling me off - she's having a full-blown tantrum in Mandarin by this point but I still recognised some of the names I was being called - I look the place up and she's right, his office is in the Mapletree business district. So I apologise not very sincerely, beat a hasty retreat and go off to find Mr Kim and see if he'll tell me where Wenling is, or at least when they last spoke.'

'Amazing. Did you reach him?'

'I found the address alright. His block was the biggest in one of those parks where all the buildings look like spaceships. I put on my most serious VIP face, wander in and ask for him at reception, then look like a bloody fool when they tell me they have fourteen Mr Kims and want to know which one my appointment is with.'

'Ah, tricky. Mrs Kim hadn't let his name slip?'

'No, and I was well and truly stuck. I pretended to take a call and hung around, half-hoping she'd tipped him off, but no luck. One of the receptionists eventually came and asked me to leave or he'd have to call security, very politely I might add.'

'Not to worry. Appreciate you trying. What was the name of the company?'

'Um, Refrenix Corporation I think. Hold on, I'll still have it in my phone.'

'Refrenix?'

'Yes,' Hallam confirmed, looking up from the screen. 'That's it. Why? Do you know them?'

'No, at least I'm fairly sure we don't work with them. But the name sounds familiar. What do they do?'

'All sorts. I had a look at their website and it's mostly specialised manufacturing and distribution for cold storage companies. You know - industrial fridges, freezers, insulated shipping containers and so on. But they also have a professional services arm dabbling in transport, telecoms, healthcare, construction, you name it.'

'Mmm. Refrenix… Never mind, it'll come to me. Would you try Rohan and Wenling for me again today and tomorrow? I might too but there's no harm in both of us calling.'

'Don't you have any idea at all where they could be?'

'I have it on good authority they haven't left the country and my gut tells me they're not far. But if they don't want to be found, then there's not much chance of us figuring it out without access to the phone network or vehicle tracking or whatever else City PD can use. I'll get Thom to log a missing persons case tomorrow.'

'Right,' said Hallam, setting her glass down and appearing keen to be engaged in something productive. 'Is there anything else? If not, I'll be on my way unless you'd like me to stay until Jack gets back?'

'No, just let me know how you get on with Hugo.'

'I'll call later but not too late so don't wait up. You need plenty of sleep, do you hear me, Miss McGlynn? Now, give me a hug and I'll be careful not to squeeze too hard.'

As the two women embraced, McGlynn grateful for her friend's company and not looking forward to being alone in the house, whatever she might have said only moments ago, her phone picked up its shrill ringing. Glancing down, her stomach tightened and she showed Wiesenberg's name to Hallam before accepting the call.

'Hello? Jacob? No, that's fine, go on… uh-huh… Is Thom there? OK… Anything else we should be doing? OK…yes, once you're back at the office and we can make a plan from there. Call me whenever, I'm not going anywhere... Yep, thanks for letting me know. Bye.'

'What news?' asked Hallam.

'The panel just returned a unanimous verdict.'

'And?'

'Not proven. Jacob says we should expect a counterclaim for defamation to land sometime next week.'

McGlynn sucked in an uneven breath, staring at a point on the wall above Hallam's head as she processed the immense damage that would result.

'Fuck. We lost Jane. I lost. Julian Dayton has won it all.'

25

W ell done, my boy! Very well done indeed!'
A delighted Richard clapped a hand on Dayton's
shoulder. Unaccustomed to praise from anyone, let alone his
father, he found himself at a complete loss as to the
appropriate reaction.

Including Eddie, the three of them stood together in the
front row of a public gallery where the expectation of a
verdict had drawn something of a crowd. The room was
abuzz with conversation and Dayton could see the Nilssons,
Malik and Dalkeith interspersed between a dozen or so others
whom he suspected were mostly from the media.

'Yeah, well done Jules,' said Eddie. 'Good result.'

'Thank you. Thanks very much, both of you,' he replied,
vastly relieved and trying to maintain the bearing of a
wronged party.

Truth be told, the panel's findings had been far from
emphatic. Whilst the plaintiff's argument was not without
merit, noted Stepney, he and Justices de Haan and Walther
concluded it had not been proven to the required standard and
only on that basis were they dismissing the litigation. The
defence would do well to provide greater transparency in
explaining their development processes when required,
especially given the similarities which existed between the
two organisations' products.

Never mind, the outcome was good enough and Franklin
already had his instructions to file the libel suit on Monday.
Having outmanoeuvred and mortally wounded that bitch

McGlynn, he would take great satisfaction in personally delivering the *coup de grâce*.

On the other side of the room the wizened old lawyer in the yarmulke had finished his phone call and was talking closely with Dalkeith. Dayton watched them, enjoying their troubled expressions and wondering if this oversized boy might be his next adversary. Be that as it may, the idea of seeing off McGlynn's successor was undeniably appealing. On the assumption he was able to prolong his own tenure, of course, a problem he intended to address first thing in the morning now the case had been won.

'Are you happy, Mr Dayton?'

He turned to find Malik looking at him with more curiosity than might be expected.

'Ah, hello Sunita and yes, yes I am. Pleased but not satisfied, shall we say. Absolutely the right result.'

'Not proven? Hardly an exoneration, wouldn't you agree?'

'No, I wouldn't. We've been found innocent of McGlynn-Lansing's mendacious and unwarranted allegations through due process and I'm delighted to have cleared our good name.'

'Will you be seeking damages in return?'

'Ha! No comment.'

'No doubt time will tell. That's Fredrik Nilsson over there isn't it, in the white shirt?' asked Malik with a tilt of the head. 'Will you be confirming the acquisition of Malmotec anytime soon?'

'I believe it is Mr Nilsson. But no comment on any transactions you might have dreamed up. And you'd be well advised not to go asking him the same questions.'

'No comment again? Are you prepared to comment on anything today? How about a word or two regarding the assault on Wynter McGlynn, your adversary in this lawsuit?'

'I was sorry to hear of Mrs McGlynn's unfortunate accid–'

'Accident? Is that how you'd describe an unprovoked assault on a woman out running?'

'No, no, if you let me finish, I was going to say that I was sorry to hear such unfortunate news and how we all wish her a speedy recovery.'

'I'm sure you all do.'

'Genuinely. By the way, I don't think I've seen a draft of your article yet, have I. Any progress in actually writing it? Or perhaps I should give Bill a call and ask him?'

'It's coming together, thank you. But feel free to talk to Bill.'

'I shall. Sorry Sunita,' said Dayton, seeing the Nilssons heading their way. 'I'm afraid you're going to have to excuse us. Perhaps you might go and ask Mr Dalkeith how soon McGlynn's will issue an apology.'

Malik saw the cause of his invitation to leave and a mischievous smile played over her lips.

'Ah. Good luck in closing your deal.'

She moved off before Fredrik and Annika joined the group, shaking hands with each of them in turn, even Dayton.

'Many congratulations,' said Fredrik. 'You must be very pleased.'

'Yes, I am,' he said before his father had a chance to reply. 'Particularly as you were able to hear us vindicated in public. I take it you're now comfortable to firm up our appointment for Monday? We should be in a position to complete contracts by then, no?'

'I'm a little surprised to be discussing this with you already, in a courtroom no less. But yes, I think this would still be convenient.'

'Good,' said Richard. 'And I'm also delighted you were able to come along this afternoon. I hope you've both recovered after last night's entertainment?'

'I admit we had slight headaches this morning but have to say it was most enjoyable. Thank you again for such kind hospitality.'

'Think nothing of it. In fact, as we're done for the day here, how about going for a drink to celebrate? There's a champagne bar at the Dune Plaza hotel. It's only a ten-minute walk and they have a first-class restaurant. Assuming they're both still open that is, haven't been to the Dune in a while. Edward?'

'They are,' confirmed Eddie. 'And the Dune's on the way back to the Portland.'

'Then why not?' said Nilsson. 'Perhaps we could also talk some shop, as you say over here, and find a middle ground on the last few points?'

'An excellent suggestion. I'll ask Vanessa to meet us there. Edward, are you free to join?'

'Sure,' said Eddie, thankful that dinner this evening would not affect his plans for tomorrow. Sophia Moretti was due on the six o'clock flight from Milan, a table at Vecchio Castello was reserved at seven and he expected they would be in bed by nine.

'Very good. Julian?'

Dayton had been weighing up how to answer the inevitable invitation. With the relief of the verdict developing into cheerfulness, he actually wanted nothing more than to raise a glass to victory and McGlynn's ruination. The tension built up for so long in the pursuit of these goals cried out for a release, an opportunity to drop his guard, revel in the plaudits and perhaps, for the first time since he was a boy, even acknowledge his father's approval. Yet still enslaved by the lessons of his childhood, the thought of socialising with people who would merely tolerate his presence while making conversation around him filled him with dread. He remained afraid to risk the misery of exclusion.

'Come on, my boy, you deserve it,' cajoled Richard, ignoring the Nilssons' interest in the hesitation.

'I, er, I can't unfortunately,' he replied at last. 'I've other plans. Another time though, maybe Monday assuming we're signed by then, eh Fredrik?'

'Maybe so.'

'You sure, Jules?' Eddie asked.

'Quite sure.' He pretended to check his watch. 'In fact, I need to be off but I hope you all have a nice evening. Tell Tony Franklin I'll call him tomorrow.'

Dayton took great satisfaction in declining questions on his way to the door. The time to answer these and make a statement regarding his own countersuit would be once thoroughly prepared and supported by his legal team. He also mooted the idea of maximising McGlynn's discomfort by convening a formal press conference, even though it would expose him to the level of scrutiny he would normally shun, and made a mental note to investigate the notion in the morning.

Stationary traffic stood nose to tail in both directions along Hamelin Road and he opted to walk home in the waning sunshine rather than wait for his car. The more distance he put between himself and the courtroom, sauntering down the incline beneath broad-leaved trees, the more his feelings of relief dissipated until, by the time he crossed Jubilee Street, they had all but vanished. Relief inferred the pre-existence of doubt. Recognising that doubt inferred a lack of the performance required to be certain of winning, his subconscious had busily rewritten recent events. Without question, his conduct in architecting that woman's downfall was exemplary and the outcome had therefore been guaranteed. Using nothing other than his own shrewd diligence, had he not undertaken the painstaking research required? Had he not discovered the pieces of the puzzle and devised a plan for success? Admittedly, he needed help in its implementation but for what else was the responsibility of leadership than to direct available resources in the appropriate manner? Relief was therefore gone, replaced by immodesty and a feeling he barely recognised - elation.

The City thrummed on all sides. Thousands of people flowed seemingly at random along the roads and pavements. He felt subsumed by all of human existence but for the first time in many years enjoyed this proximity to the masses. Their ambitions must lie before them, hence their haste, whereas his were surely being realised, hence his leisure. A probable changing of the guard at McGlynn-Lansing would deliver a longer period of respite, of not working harder than he would wish. Having already selected a suitable reward as motivation for today's result, Dayton was cheered by the prospect of an increase in his free time. His prize was scheduled to arrive next week, which gave him enough notice to postpone should it have been required, but meandering through the winding paths of Valiance Park he pulled his phone from an inside pocket and typed a message to see if delivery might be possible tomorrow evening. Why should he wait, especially as there was no longer any chance of McGlynn competing in Saturday's triathlon?

After a swim in the basement pool, lazily sculling the water past his flanks and ignoring fellow residents, he rode the elevator up to his apartment to shower, shrug on an old shirt and jeans and open a bottle of good champagne while cooking dinner. On a whim he ate the steak and pasta on the balcony where he could savour the unusual sweetness of the air. By the time his plate was empty the park below lay obscured by dusk and the city's heartbeat had slowed to a lower frequency. Listening to the ebbing soundscape, in the seclusion of the gathering darkness, most of the wine gone, his euphoria abated and his mind slackened.

Coming home may have been a mistake, he admitted, thinking of the group at the Dune who by now were surely raising toasts and swapping anecdotes. He had grown used to living alone, the isolation no longer as oppressive as it once had been, but still missed the company of others on occasion. The absence brought back the sting of long evenings and unending weekends, particularly those after Sarah had gathered her few belongings and moved out.

He had met his future wife at work, where else. The company in those days occupied an entire block further inland, a concrete monstrosity with labyrinthine corridors and offices built for a different generation. His own, a dingy space almost permanently in the shade of the building opposite, but on the same floor as Richard and symbolic of his upwards trajectory, required the climbing of several flights of stairs from street level where, on one of the tiny landings, he had come across a flustered paralegal collecting scattered papers. Neither seeming to recognise him nor notice his displeasure at being asked to help, she had suggested coffee afterwards, then dinner the following week and before long Dayton found himself settled in a serious relationship.

Pinpointing exactly how that came to pass was troublesome. Sarah was admirably prosaic, attractive in a homely sort of way and there was no doubting he liked her company, her endearing servility, but at no time did they observe the usual milestones of a developing romance. A memory of their first kiss escaped him, for example, as did their first lovemaking and he struggled to recall any conversation where they discussed living together, getting married or the possibility of a family. Yet those things must have happened because within a year or so of their meeting, he drove up to the wooded cabin overlooking the shores of Lake Pleasant and informed his parents that he intended to ask for her hand. Richard had ignored Vanessa's plea for restraint and launched into a forceful explanation of why someone like Sarah was not an appropriate match for any progeny of his. She came from a poor background, the lone, probably illegitimate child of a single-parent social worker for heaven's sake, and did not have the requisite education, extraversion or political connections to make a good society wife. At best she was hopelessly naive, at worst a gold-digger. Prenuptial agreements were regularly being voided by the latest batch of liberal magistrates and Julian was foolish to even be contemplating the idea of lending her their surname. If he were to go through with this misconception, then he would have no other option than to question his son's judgement and reconsider his position as heir to the company throne.

Dayton proposed later that day. Primarily, he wanted to prove he was a man capable of correctly making his own decisions, to himself as much as anyone, but there was a hint of pure rebellion too. He had never dared to go explicitly against his father's wishes before yet having the security of another's affection left him light-headed with possibility. Sarah had become his anchor now, and if she was not the partner with whom he could forge a lifetime of happiness then nobody was. He felt certain of being in love.

Although permeated by Richard's disapproval and his own resentment, the wedding passed without incident. Sarah then moved to another firm, concluding that to stay at her new husband's company might jeopardise their marital harmony, and promptly earned a promotion and a chance to study for the bar. Dayton ploughed on with the daily grind but took the opportunity at each of her steps up the ladder to thumb his nose a little higher in the direction of the office at the end of the hallway. Richard, by then focused on the whirlwind expansion underway at McGlynn-Lansing, paid scant attention.

The newlyweds were also soon seeing much less of each other. Evenings lasted an hour at best, weekends were lost to his business travel or her studies and, perhaps most troubling of all, Sarah appeared to be thriving under a newfound sense of purpose, no longer setting aside the time to dote on him. Dayton began to worry they were drifting apart. Too frightened to volunteer his concern and be the cause of an argument, or God forbid any tears, he tacitly resented her success instead. As she rose he sank lower into peevishness, all the while searching for a way of restoring what he considered the correct order of priority. Before long he landed on the perfect solution. With a new baby, Sarah would have to give up her job and become reliant on his support, at least temporarily, maybe longer with some persuasion, spending her time at home where he could choose to see her as and when he wished. During an expensive birthday dinner he therefore announced his desire they should try for a child and was both surprised and hurt when she declined. She was already happy, she said, enjoying her vocation and young enough for there to be plenty of time, so why start a family so early? Pretending to agree, he hid his indignation but some months later, after a failure in their usual method of birth control, she fell pregnant.

Swigging the last of the champagne, Dayton brooded over how swiftly their marriage had soured.

It became clear from the outset that she rightly suspected him of somehow engineering this state of affairs. As her belly grew so did her hostility. Coming home each day to find her progressively bloated and irritable, he felt overwhelmed by her provocation and played his part in the petty spats which neared but never reached the point of a direct accusation. She withdrew from him emotionally, then physically and sexually and his frustration grew to enormous proportions. However, a week overdue and after a difficult delivery, Adam's arrival finally provided a moment of joy and some substitute for intimacy.

The Renaissance masters could not have described a more cherubic child. With soft curves and owlish aquamarine eyes,

Adam was a beautiful, healthy, gurgling delight and duly supplied his first triumph by uniting his parents under a veneer of civility. They adored him without judgement or question and took shelter in the warmth of his presence. Dayton's eagerness to spend time at home returned and even his wife seemed content and at peace. After too short a time though, the boy took to complaining almost constantly and would only settle for a nap when held. The ensuing sleep deprivation took its toll, particularly on Sarah who refused a nanny and bore the brunt of his care, and they began to argue bitterly over the best way of soothing the pitiful cries. Soon, Adam could not be appeased at all and they visited the doctor in the hope of a diagnosis, something on which they could act, but were sent home again with an explanation this behaviour was normal in infancy and several hints they had been wasting her time. New, more serious symptoms began to surface and they sought a second opinion then a third until, when Adam was nearly a year old, a paediatric specialist at St Stephen's ordered a cranial scan and the unthinkable discovery of a medulloblastoma brought them to a standstill. Given the way the tumour impaired motor skills and affected balance, Adam never learned how to stand unaided or take his first steps. The diagnosis drove his short future onto a path of invasive and aggressive treatment and his frantic parents first to hope, then despair.

A year later and a week after the funeral, Sarah left for her mother's house saying she needed space to grieve. Dayton, as he had been taught, would have grieved alone anyway. They tried to stay in touch but as their bond dwindled so did the frequency of their meetings and messages and he became increasingly concerned for her wellbeing. She had begun to mention her desire to join Adam, to make sure he was safe and loved and cared for wherever he might be. Providing psychological support to others was beyond Dayton's ability but no matter how much he asked, then cajoled, then begged, she refused to seek help elsewhere. At a loss, he betrayed her confidence by talking with her mother and was then excluded from further contact until news of the suicide arrived with a policewoman at his door.

Dayton held up the empty glass, refracting light from the faraway windows and agonising over what sort of man he might have become had his family survived.

Bound together by the responsibility of parenthood, surely he and Sarah would have made more of an effort? Found ways to revive their connection and tried for a younger brother or sister for Adam to play with, perhaps more than one? By now they could have built shared memories to gladden them in the good times and fortify them through the bad. With children who loved him unconditionally in the way only children can, he may have discovered the courage to truly love someone in return, thereby laying the cornerstone for happiness, becoming less insecure, more empathetic, able to build lasting relationships. He would have been a more tolerant man and grown closer to his brother and his father in all the same ways he envied their own ties.

Instead however, he saw no option except to guard against further loss through self-enforced separation from others, making himself invulnerable through the discipline of having nothing or no one to lose. No man was an island but for the last two decades Dayton had assiduously cut a trench across the last spit of earth connecting him with the continent.

Looking up at the brightest stars, he knew another drink was a poor decision but wanted one regardless. Going to bed now would only mean lying awake and giving his psyche the freedom to punish him without distraction. He pushed his way upright, clumsily stacked the crockery and carried the pile through to the kitchen sink. With a generous measure of whisky decanted into a cut glass tumbler, he foolishly decided to take the bottle as well and weaved his way onwards to the lounge.

By its window lay a piano, a black concert grand nearly nine feet long carving a void against the balcony beyond. At his mother's insistence Dayton had taken lessons at Rovingham but had always avoided the repetitive boredom of practice. Nevertheless, he remembered enough basic theory to play the instrument and would compose simple melodies or every so often memorise a piece of music, bar by laborious bar. Sitting heavily, thrusting a coaster between the tumbler and the unblemished lacquer, he rested his fingers on the keys. Anything towards the more complex end of his repertoire was beyond him and he fell into a composition of his own; a revolving progression requiring no more conscious thought than breathing. Safely hidden from the world, varying the volume or tempo and adding occasional grace notes to each side of the root triads, he closed his eyes and sank further into melancholy.

Sarah had hated it when he played. She wanted to know why he chose such plaintive melodies, why he insisted on using an acoustic instrument rather than a machine with a headphone socket. Please could he stop. Stop waking the baby, stop making her feel so depressed, stop endlessly repeating the same pieces.

But Sarah wasn't here to tell him what to do anymore.

Four chords then - G# major, C minor, F# major, B*b* minor - over and over and over for as long and as loudly as he likes.

McGlynn could play too, so he believed, apparently quite well. Sitting here sometimes, he liked to imagine how her music might sound; classical or modern, improvised or rehearsed, allegro or legato, intimate or remote. However, the McGlynn he pictured and heard was not the hated rival, not the woman who cast judgement from afar or the despised nemesis only recently overcome, but the summertime girl of his twenty-ninth year.

G# major, C minor, F# major, B*b* minor.

Prior to that summer he had been away on a long secondment, restoring their Sydney operations to profitability before coming home to a favourable reception. Even Richard had been impressed enough to volunteer one or two veiled compliments in passing. Uplifted by a new sense of self-confidence, the tanned and unattached Dayton found invitations arriving out of the blue from an expanding list of admirers and threw himself back into the City's roster of social occasions.

At one of the first, a beach party arranged by an old college friend of Eddie's, which would have been turned down had his presence not been specifically requested by the classmate's elder sister, he had been sprawled out by the campfire when his concentration was lured away by laughter nearby. Two women with long brown legs, white lace kaftans and hair still wet from the sea approached, crossing the sand with such effortless grace that he caught his breath. Taking care not to alert the babbling elder sister by his side, he watched them enter the light thrown from the fire and was startled to realise the taller girl was Wynter McGlynn. She had changed almost beyond recognition in the two or three years since their last encounter. The demure and watchful adolescent was gone, replaced by a woman who carried herself with calm authority and spoke with her friend in confident, humorous tones. Choosing a space by the bleached tree trunk opposite she glanced around the circle and he saw the flicker of recognition. Far from looking away, she raised her brows and inclined her head in greeting instead. Here was the daughter of his father's arch-rival, not only breaking the unwritten code to deny each other's existence but doing so in a manner which appeared polite, almost friendly. On all counts, Dayton had been amazed.

They bumped into each other several times during the following weeks. Wariness steadily gave way to familiarity, guarded words of hello to longer strands of conversation. By mid-summer, echoes of her voice and laughter would catch him unawares, thoughts of how she walked or smiled or simply tucked her hair behind an ear invaded his waking hours. He began to look for her at every turn, daydreaming almost constantly about where she could be and what she might be doing. Most surprisingly, she gave the impression of liking him in return and, unable to deny it any longer, Dayton came to believe he was falling in love. The notion warmed and appalled him in equal measure but he drowned out any disquiet by adopting a narrative of the star-crossed lovers, destined to unite their warring houses. Together, they would be a power-couple the likes of which the City had never seen. A formidable partnership, uniquely capable of

393

brokering a lasting peace between their fathers, maybe even a consolidation of their competing businesses.

G# major, C minor, F# major, B*b* minor.

Eyes closed, hunched over the keys. The whisky makes the darkness slowly spin but the autonomous fingers still move with fluidity and precision in their endless accompaniment.

Major, minor, major, minor.

He thought of how, at one of Bob and Chase Levine's weekly soirées, he managed to inveigle her away from the crowd to the end of the garden where the shadows were deepest. Sitting half-turned in the glow of the tree lights, knees touching, him almost feverish with desire at the lines of her face, the curve of her neck, the subtle perfume. Wynter McGlynn was a grown and beautiful woman, the discovery still an astonishment, and he had let himself be drawn into the kind grey eyes, only half-listening, bewildered by the keenness of his love. He had felt truly and totally happy, right up until the moment she mentioned her imminent departure. After three months of summer holiday, a return to university beckoned and she would be leaving early the following week. He tried to keep the disappointment from his face, not yet ready to admit his feelings but realising permission to visit would require exactly that, while hunting desperately for another solution. Mistaking his silence, she had been quick to reassure him how much she enjoyed their conversations and how different he was from her own father's description, his never-ending tirade against the whole Dayton family. Surprisingly, she liked him much more than expected. Maybe they could meet again when she returned for Christmas or, failing that, Easter?

He remembered the panic, how the castles he had built in the sky rumbled in protest. Here was the first woman he had loved in a long time, perhaps the first ever in truth. How could he have been so short-sighted as to think they had the luxury of time?

Summoning his limited bravery, emboldened by the wine as much as the sense of fate, he had waited for her to draw breath then leant forward, intent on showing he would wait for as long as necessary. The kiss failed to land but his eyes had flown open in time to witness the change in hers. Confusion at first, then a trace of revulsion, then pity.

Oh God, oh God...

Worse than misreading her sentiment, worse even than her rejection, he saw that Wynter pitied him. And somewhere in that fog of humiliation, in the distance far off to his left, he had heard laughter sounding suspiciously like his brother's.

G# major, C minor, F# major, B*b* minor.

An emphasis on the minor chords now, breathing more raggedly. Eyes screwed shut and fingertips brushing the edge of discordant notes.

What else could he have done? In the following days and weeks, under the weight of his own mortification, Richard's temper and Eddie's ridicule, he chose the only path left open to him - betrayal. He fabricated a story, telling them how the better part of his summer had been spent befriending McGlynn in a strategy designed to extract information about her father's company, that the plan was starting to work and she had shown signs of trusting him. What they had misinterpreted as a kiss was actually him leaning forward to catch secrets from a girl plied with alcohol and drawn expertly into his confidence. The more elaborate the plot became, the more he found his internal rendering of the story changed. McGlynn began to pivot inexorably from hero to villain. She was the culprit here, entrapping him with typically feminine subterfuge. How could she have led him on? How dare she decline his advances? Outraged by her deceit, Dayton threw himself afresh into the denigration of McGlynn-Lansing, telling anyone who would listen about the disgraceful behaviour of the whole family and their youngest daughter in particular.

During a chance encounter later that year, he had felt shamed by her frigid expression and hence the die was cast. He buried the memories of his love and the false alibi endured as his reality. McGlynn was transformed from lover into implacable enemy. In his fractured mind however, the summertime girl from his twenty-ninth year and the hated figurehead of McGlynn-Lansing separated by degrees into distinct characters. From time to time he was able to think of the former without prejudice, especially under the influence of alcohol, but her image always resurrected the emotion of that time like an undead corpse, eager to demean him with confused memories of impropriety and regret.

G# major, C minor, F# major… then the long fingers lose their way and the melody falters into dissonance, draining slowly away beneath the sustain pedal.

Despite feeling suffocated by sentimentality, Dayton knew there was no catharsis to be had in reflecting upon his own misfortune - after all, his psyche was incapable of self-pity no matter how much liquor he might drink - and therefore he resolved to suffer release by proxy instead. Topping up the glass, he staggered to the couch and fumbled with a remote control. A large, wall-mounted screen sprang into life and he flicked through the channels, hoping to find a live broadcast with which to satisfy his needs but comforted by having access to suitable content on demand if not.

Dayton liked to think of himself as a connoisseur when it came to emotional pornography. He had invested significant time in researching the genre. Film was his preferred fictional medium and he had a penchant for high-achieving anti-heroes, self-sacrificial bravery or the death of a loved one. However, no matter how high the standard of acting, such manufactured scripts paled by comparison with their factual equivalents.

Sporting triumphs were towards the top of his real-life list, especially so if they represented a world-class athlete or team reaching the ambition of a lifetime. During the competition he would contemplate their unseen labour in the pursuit of such a singular goal; the self-deprivation, the endless hours of practice, the years of commitment required to reach the global elite. Then there was the winning of the contest itself; how they stretched the limits of their ability, took outlandish risks, dominated the fear of defeat, denied themselves the luxury of exhaustion. At the moment of realising they had won, at the enormity of their achievement, often the sheer disbelief at victory, Dayton would think of how dissimilar he was and find he was able to cry with them, for their success.

Beyond sporting metaphor, there was pathetic empathy to be had in documentaries about the work of emergency room nurses or videos of soldiers returning to families after long tours of duty. Nearing the end of the channel listing though, he struck gold. A television awards show renowned for its celebration of everyday heroism was midway through its primetime slot. Letting the controller fall from his fingers, he exhaled and lay back in expectation.

Two immaculately attired network anchors guided proceedings, introducing six-minute segments of charity fundraisers, pioneers of civil rights, first responders, altruistic inventors and community stalwarts from across the nation. The show's producers pulled at his heartstrings with poignant backstories and tributes from friends and relatives. Even the cutaway shots of celebrities and politicians, damp-eyed but for once in the audience and not centre stage, developed his rapport with such selfless people. At some point during the story of a twelve-year old girl, paraplegic and coping with a painful skin disorder yet even so the primary carer for her heavily disabled mother, a tear dribbled slowly down his cheek. As she wheeled herself onstage to a standing ovation, a half-choked whimper broke from his lips.

Sipping at the whisky, Dayton lay in the dark and tried to keep his blurred vision focused on the screen. Every teardrop, every sob, chipped a tiny sliver of self-loathing from his ego and discarded it forever. Each was a morsel of relief.

Achieving any higher emotional state was as yet impossible but he would continue to practise. Maybe one day he might even be able to cry for himself. In the meantime, watching those who faced adversity with stoicism, humility and good humour, he would compare them to his own image and find solace by way of their example.

26

McGlynn was alert at dawn and out of bed shortly thereafter. Other than waking around midnight, confused and sweating, she had slept deeply. In defiance of recent events, her mind and body had succumbed to their exhaustion and dragged her into unconsciousness the moment her head hit the pillow.

Jack dozed on, the house quiet and peaceful, but still she made sure the blue and white of the Triple S cars could be seen at the gates before venturing downstairs. The night seemed to have contributed a small but perceptible improvement to her injuries. The assorted bruises and scrapes were more vividly discoloured but the headache was virtually gone, the stiffness in her hands and joints was easing and swallowing was much less painful. Her heart felt heavier though, the consequences of losing the case to Dayton on top of the last two days adding a sickening burden. Nevertheless, trusting this represented an overall gain, she decided to forgo more co-codamol and see whether coffee would suffice instead.

Cradling a freshly brewed mug at the breakfast bar, the dogs settling their breakfasts by her feet, she thought about another unavoidable day's work. A plan for the forthcoming litigation was the priority - she knew Dayton well enough to believe his paperwork was probably undergoing final review – and there was the small matter of keeping the board informed. McGlynn was not prepared to leave either of these duties to Dalkeith, even with help from Hallam, Sylvie and others. She felt obliged to clear up her own mess and the younger man lacked the capability for such risk-laden assignments, especially given he was managing both their workloads already. After these, she would talk to Hallam for the latest on Hugo Valente, a replacement for Brookes and City PD's investigations, she and Jack ought to meet with Triple S again, there was the continuing search for Rohan and she needed to call Fredrik Nilsson regarding the no doubt faltering bid for Malmotec.

Thinking progress could be made before Jack came down and caught her working, she switched on her phone. The missed notifications included several calls from Hallam and a message to ring her urgently. At once tapping the green button, McGlynn braced herself.

'Hello, my love. Feeling any better?'

'A bit. What's the matter? Sorry for the phone being off but I wanted to try and get a decent night's sleep.'

'Quite right. But I have news.'

'Tell me it's not bad news, Jane. Please. I really can't face any more right now.'

'It's not all bad. There's been progress at the warehouse.'

'Well thank fu–... thank God for that.' McGlynn eased her dry mouth with coffee. 'So what's up?'

'When I got here last night I met that detective friend of yours - I like her by the way, she's smart as she is tough, isn't she - and we ended up talking about what the police have found so far, mostly what Hugo already covered in his report.'

'Any direct evidence of stowaways?'

'No mention of food or clothing if that's what you mean, and I didn't get the sense she was holding out on me. But when I sat down with him afterwards he looked so ill I thought he was going to throw up, even though he still claimed nothing was wrong.'

'Much what I got from him on Monday.'

'Mmm. But with respect I've known him much longer than you. I interviewed him for his first position when you were still at school and had what I'd consider a trusting relationship ever since. So I pushed him on it. Hard. Told him you'd been attacked and subsequently threatened and that, if he had other information, it wasn't fair of him to hold out on us. Laid it on pretty thick.'

'And?'

'And he broke down. Literally cried in front of me. Turns out he's being blackmailed too.'

'He's what?' exclaimed McGlynn.

'I know. He found a letter on his desk last summer telling him to ignore any suspicious activity and make sure his team did the same. If they didn't, there'd be consequences. Whoever it was knew his home address and had photos of Erica and the kids. Apparently there was nothing to notice at first but then things started happening which he knew were connected.'

'*Merde*,' said McGlynn, half in sympathy for Valente but growing angry too. 'Didn't he think about talking to us? Or the police?'

'Of course. He's not the type to scare easily but the detail frightened him, and then there was another warning. He noticed one of the cameras wasn't recording properly and gave instructions for it to be fixed. Next morning, Erica found one of their Alsatians with a screwdriver in its chest. He stopped looking so closely after that and I'm not surprised.'

'How in hell did I miss this? I knew he was acting strangely but put it down to me criticising his work.'

'The assault was probably the tipping point. He'd already been spooked by your visit and having Andrew and Detective Campbell poking around but knew he had to come clean after that. Just a question of when and to whom.'

The phone buzzed in McGlynn's ear. She glanced at the message notification but the number was unfamiliar and could therefore wait.

'Right,' she continued. 'We need Campbell in the loop first thing. She's going to wa–'

'Already ahead of you. When I couldn't reach you, I rang her instead and she came back last night. Also called Andrew and he came in as well.'

'Did he?'

'Said he wants to help catch whoever jumped you both. Sounds like his friend Gina's on the way over too.'

'Ah, that's fantastic news,' said McGlynn, feeling some of the burden start to shift. 'What else did Hugo have to say?'

'Well he'd kept the original letter. And he also handed over a log he's been secretly keeping. Dates, times and locations of unusual events.'

'Did you get to read it?'

'No, Campbell wanted it. But he thinks there were only a couple of occasions when our infrastructure's been used for actual people smuggling. Unfortunately, he also said at least two containers not registered on their manifest have been through the compound in the last six months. Took an almighty risk on the first one. Paused the cameras, sent the overnight team off to a false alarm and took a set of bolt cutters to the seals.'

'What did he find? People? Drugs?'

'Guns. Sixteen cases of assault rifles hidden between crates of soft toys.'

McGlynn was unable to speak for a moment. No wonder these people were prepared to go to such lengths.

'I can't believe I'm hearing this, Jane. We've always had the best security money can buy.'

'I know. But the police say there's not much you can do once the gangs get you involved.'

'Gangs? Whose cargo was the container in?'

'It was a mixed manifest, on the *MCV Golyat* out of Ambarli.'

'Turkey? Eastern Europeans?'

'Campbell thinks so,' said Hallam. 'Apparently there's no Turkish mafia presence in the City but there are a couple of Balkan groups trying to establish themselves, and that means bringing in people and weapons.'

'I don't know whether to feel better or worse. Hugo must have been out of his mind with worry.'

'He thinks a few of the staff have started to cotton on as well. One of the team quit this week, said she knew something was going on and felt frightened, Zoe–'

'Mears, I heard. Look this needs to be sorted, immediately. Did Campbell say what we should do next?'

'She went off to talk with her boss. She thinks not being onsite actually reduces the risk. But I don't like it.'

'Me either. We're sitting ducks.'

'Well I'm here and Andrew's set up camp. He has that look about him so I didn't dare try to send him home. We're ringing round the private security world to see what we can rustle up so don't even think about coming down yourself, do you hear?'

'Uh-huh, I'll see. Although there's a heap that needs doing here today.'

'Good, leave it to us. Listen, hope you don't mind me mentioning it, but I think we should talk to our freight partners, let them know we want a temporary strengthening of protocols in Turkey, Bulgaria, Romania and possibly Greece.'

'Yeah, good idea, can you give them the heads up. Who do we have in Istanbul? They're not new are they?'

'Kaya Shipping and no, we've used them for years. It's hard to find good distributors there, or anywhere for that matter. I know the Daytons have the same problem.'

A half-formed memory, lingering since the previous day, thrust itself to the forefront of McGlynn's mind.

'*Oh mon dieu*,' she whispered. '*C'est pas possible.*'

'What's the matter?' Alarm in Hallam's voice. 'Is everything alright?'

'Oh sweet Jesus… Yes, yes, but I've got to go, there's something I need to check. Everything's fine I promise. Keep me posted on Campbell and I'll call you back as soon as I can.'

Startling the dogs, McGlynn scraped the stool back and made for the lounge, opening the new phone message along the way - *Heard about Wednesday. Wishing you a speedy recovery, Sunita M.*

'Morning,' said Jack, looking sleepy on the stairs. 'Hey, Wyn? How're you doing?'

'I'm good,' she called over her shoulder. 'Need a few. Coffee's in the pot. Fresh.'

He would have to wait and so would a reply to Malik. Dropping to the sofa, she pulled open her laptop and began to search for evidence to corroborate the half-memory. Fewer than five minutes later, she found it.

'Sonofabitch,' she said softly, staring at the short text. 'Absolute son of a bitch.'

Her fingers returned to the keyboard, typing and scrolling with even greater urgency. Jack came in carrying a steaming mug but, seeing her expression, set it down without being noticed. Finally sitting back in frustration, she drew her lower lip into her mouth and massaged it with the tip of her tongue.

At length she located Dalkeith's number and hit the dial button, grimacing at a mouthful of cold tea.

'Morning Wynter.'

'Morning. How're you?' she asked, thinking he sounded downcast.

'Ach, I'm fine. But I'm so sorry about the result yesterday, I really am. More importantly, how are you?'

'Feeling a bit better actually. And don't worry about the verdict, it's my fault, not yours.'

'We all agreed to go after them and I was no help in finding Rohan, was I? You know, that old bastard Richard Dayton came straight over afterwards, saying how unfortunate the whole situation was and wanting to shake my hand. I told him he could sod off.'

'Ha! I'd like to have seen that. How did he take it?'

'Not well.'

'Good for you Thom, standing up to him. Did Julian put in an appearance?'

'He was there but left almost immediately. Sorry to say I saw Fredrik and Annika leaving with Richard and Eddie though, looking very friendly.'

'No surprise. They're going to decline Monday's meeting aren't they?'

'I'd say so. Want me to give him a call?'

'I was thinking of doing the same but let's leave it this morning and see what happens. Have you and Jacob booked time to prep for the counterclaim?'

'Aye. I know you shouldn't be working but do you want to join?'

'I'll leave you to it, there's something I need to do which might help. Though don't mention anything to Jacob just yet,' she said, trying to keep the hope from her voice. 'Anything from Elliott or the other investors?'

'Nope.'

'If and when they get in touch, refer them to me please. And what about Matthieu? Did he get away to see his parents?'

'He went but the chopper came back without him. His mother hasn't got more than a week or two.'

'Oh no, poor Matthieu and poor Eloise. Tell him to take as long as he needs. We'll cover his work and I'll send Granny Cécile a note in case she hasn't heard. Anything else I need to know?'

'Only that one of the reporters asked for your number yesterday. Sunita someone from the Post. Promised me it was for a personal message.'

'Mmm, she's my next call as it happens. But please don't make a habit of giving out my number, especially to journalists.'

'Yeah, sorry. This one was, um, persuasive.'

'Good looking too.'

'Aye. That too.'

'Stay in touch Thom.'

McGlynn rang off and collected her thoughts before dialling Malik.

'Hi Sunita, it's Wynter McGlynn.'

'Oh, hi. There was no need to call me back. It's just I heard what happened, how outrageous it was, and wanted to let you know I was thinking of you. Are you OK?'

'It's been a rough a couple of days but I'm on the mend.'

'Any idea who did this? They need to be caught.'

'Off the record?'

'Honestly, I wasn't looking for an interview.'

'Then yes, the police are following up on a few leads as we speak,' said McGlynn. 'But I wanted to ask about something else if I can. You said on Wednesday that you're working on an article relating to the case, rather than the case itself. Specifically on the topic of Dayton's?'

'Am I off the record too?'

'Totally.'

'Then yes, it's about Dayton.'

'Ah, thought it might be. What's your opinion of him so far?'

'Mixed. But if you're looking for more than that, you'll need to wait and read it in the Post, same as everyone else.'

'I heard you were at court again yesterday. Did you agree with the verdict?'

'Nope. Julian thinks it's a full vindication but I don't - his product seems too similar for coincidence. I'm sorry you didn't win but, with all due respect, where are you going with this?'

'I need a favour.'

She let the word hang, knowing Malik would interpret it correctly.

'I'm listening.'

'To be clear, this is still off the record. But hypothetically, what if I were to tell you Julian found a way to prevent one of the key witnesses testifying?'

'Rohan Mehta? Your technology guy who didn't show up? Then I'd be very interested, if true.'

'I can't prove anything yet. I need help from someone with your skills.'

'If I found anything would there be conditions on how I can use it?'

'Nothing absolute,' said McGlynn, wondering how far Malik could be trusted. 'I may offer some advice but you don't have to take it. Fair?'

A pause.

'Fair.'

'OK, check your messages. I've sent you an old press release about one of Dayton's distributors.'

'Right... What am I supposed to be looking for in here?'

'I need to find a personal link between Julian and that company, likely nothing to do with their business relationship. I've already spent an hour on it and will keep looking for the rest of the day, longer if I have to. But I'm hoping you have access to resources that I don't.'

'It's not much to go on.'

'No, sorry. I'd imagine the relationship goes back further than the article, but that's only speculation.'

'Then why this company in particular?'

'Can't say, but I don't think it'd help.'

'That's the interesting bit though, isn't it,' replied Malik, nobody's fool. 'Even if I find what you want, it'll be no good unless I know how it relates to Rohan. What's the connection?'

'Look, I'm not prepared to be the cause of rumours about my staff if this turns out to be no more than wishful thinking. But if you help prove the whole chain beyond doubt then I'll lay out the missing pieces. Deal?'

'Mmm... alright, I can make a start. If it needs longer than today though, I'll want to know why I'm not wasting my time.'

'Perfect. Call me if you find something. Anytime.'

'Understood. Keep your phone nearby.'

The line went dead and McGlynn's attention returned at once to the laptop.

27

My office Becca,' growled Dayton in passing, his pitch a full octave lower than usual. Staying up late and mixing his drinks had produced exactly the outcome he feared. There had surely been worse hangovers but none in recent memory. 'And find me a coffee on the way.'

Choosing to ignore whatever it was she muttered under her breath, he strode onwards. Today was no day to pick a one-sided fight with his PA, not when he expected much stiffer opposition from Eddie in a contest carrying far greater importance. As was typical in the run up to a confrontation, he felt underprepared and anxious but knew spending even a little time on the former would ease the latter.

Stripping off his damp jacket, he sank gratefully into the cold leather chair and waited for the thudding between his temples to subside. Seeing ML One along the shoreline helped, although the corner office was almost certainly empty. Was it his imagination or did the building look a little more drab this morning, more jaded, as if the pristine sheen had been dulled by its owner's miscalculation? He had thought about sending flowers or a note of commiseration in advance of Franklin's papers but such a move might be considered poor form given current circumstances, especially if she determined to make the gesture public in some way. No, waiting for the next round of litigation to complete showed the quality of his judgement and besides, the barb would find a softer mark following a second defeat.

McGlynn's absence from the triathlon tomorrow was a real shame, a missed opportunity to gloat in person. Whilst he might still participate for the cardiovascular benefit alone, the arrival of his self-awarded prize had been confirmed and likely meant a third late night in a row. Dayton felt himself stir at the prospect.

Feeling moderately better, he swung the chair back around as Giordani entered, coffee in hand.

'Here you go, sorry about the wait,' she said, stifling the temptation to mention his appearance.

'Shut the door and have a seat Becca, there's a few things. First, have you seen my brother or father yet this morning?'

'No, but Eddie should be in soon. Don't think I was expecting Richard?'

'Probably not. Can you give him a call. I want some time with him here, ideally this afternoon. Shouldn't need more than thirty minutes but book an hour, OK? And no later than four, I need to leave by five.'

'Sure. And if he's not available?'

'Then try for Sunday or early Monday. I don't think he's flying back to London until after we've met Fredrik Nilsson. You can go for tomorrow as a last resort but tell him I won't be able to confirm until mid-morning.'

'Got it.'

'Next, it's my brother's birthday on the sixteenth. Can you pick up a gift before he flies out? It'll save you from messing around with couriers or whatever.'

'Um, OK. Any ideas?'

'Not really, but I'm sure you'll find something. Not too expensive though. Call me for a second opinion if you have to.'

'Yep, I'll try.'

'Last, I want a copy of the job spec we used for your recruitment. HR will have one if you can't lay your hands on it.'

'OK. Please can I ask why?'

'Because I need to hire your replacement,' said Dayton, reciting the carelessly rehearsed speech. 'I'm moving you across to Simon Fitzwilliam. You'll get to work with somebody else at a reasonably senior level and exposure to a new part of the business. If you keep your performance ratings up well, who knows, I'd say there's a fair chance of promotion next year. Perhaps an increase at pay review.'

He saw the change in Giordani's expression and ran on hastily.

'And, um, I'd also like to say thank you for all your efforts over the last year. Or two.'

'Right. Just for the sake of argument though, what if I didn't want to work for Simon?'

'Well it's not really up to you. But why wouldn't you? He's OK isn't he?'

'He's no worse than you, if that's what you mean.'

'Eh? No, that's not–'

'Did it even cross your mind to think about what I might want?'

'Of–'

'Did it?'

'I decided this was the best–'

'You decided. Don't I get a say? Aren't I capable of making my own decisions?'

'Yes, but list–'

'Uh-uh, no Julian. You listen to me for once,' she said, flushed and with her fists bunched on her knees. 'For two sodding years I've worked my arse off for you. Yeah, I get paid OK and yeah I get to sit at a nice desk and eat my lunch overlooking the sea but this job is boring. Don't you get it? Mind-numbingly, totally fuc–... boring. I've a full diploma in business and finance for Chrissake, with distinction at that, and you've got me making coffee and doing your expenses. Giving me orders day and night - fetch this, do that - but never helping with my career. I've got ambitions, I want to do more, be more, but you've no idea because you've never listened and you've never asked. And working for Simon's just gonna be more of the same, isn't it? And it's a step downwards.'

'It's not–'

'Yeah it is. You don't get to decide that either, I know how it works. At least Simon's got manners. He'd say please and thank you and he'd ask me on a date if he wanted to gawp at my legs, my boobs. Not like you. You think I don't notice but I do Julian, I really do. I see you and so does every other woman under the age of thirty around here. We all talk about it behind your back. It's not just a disgrace, it's harassment.'

'Now hang on a minute. You can't–'

Giordani stood and punctuated her words with a jabbing finger.

'Be quiet, OK? I don't want to hear what I can and can't do anymore, not from you. If I was to work for anyone else in this company it'd be Eddie. He's twice the man you are, three times. You're just... pathetic. But I don't want to work for him or for Simon because it'd mean I still have to come within twenty feet of you. So you know what Julian, I quit.

Yeah, you heard me right, you'll get your two weeks' notice and then I'm gone. If you want anything done between now and then, you'd better send it in writing because I don't want to speak to you in person and there's no way I'm coming back in here alone. Not with you. And if you don't want me buying something stupid for Eddie's birthday, then you'd better get off your arse and do your own shopping. Understand?'

'You're… you're going to leave, just like that, after all I've done for you? Where do you think you're going to go? I know you need the money. More to the point, what do you expect me to do?'

'I'm not afraid of hard graft, unlike you. I'll go to the agencies and get temp work, bar work, anything until I find something else. But I already applied for six other jobs this week so I reckon it won't take me long. Proper jobs too. And if it's not obvious already, I don't really give a shit how you'll manage.'

'Well… you won't get a reference, not one you'd want.'

'Like I care. But if I hear you're badmouthing me to other companies, or anyone at all for that matter, then I'm calling the compliance helpline. Get it? I'll put in a formal complaint about your behaviour. And then I'll be calling Sunita Malik at the Post to tell her exactly what goes on here. She's not afraid of you, she's not afraid of anyone and you'll get shamed in front of the whole fucking city, no more than you deserve either. So just pay me what I'm owed. That's how this place works isn't it - keep your mouth shut, I'll do the same and we'll all pretend everything's OK. Well it's not OK and I'm done with it, Julian. I'm fucking done with you.'

Giordani stalked out, tears of anger on her cheeks, chin in the air, and slammed the door.

414

'Fuck's sake,' he breathed, rubbing his pounding forehead. 'Fucking stupid little slut.'

In all his time working at the company no one had ever spoken to him in such a manner. Who did she think she was? Nothing but a secretary, a menial worker half his age, lucky to have had the benefit of his experience whilst enjoying a sinecure funded by his largesse. Good riddance. Taking a slug of coffee to mask the bitter taste of the truth his thoughts turned to damage limitation. He picked up the desk phone and stabbed at a speed-dial.

'Chloe? It's me. I've just had Becca in my office and she's been bloody disrespectful... How should I know? Time of the month, anything. All I did was tell her we were moving her into Simon's line... No, I don't care about the process, I care about her mouthing off to anyone who'll listen. I want her on severance leave and out of... OK, I'll pay the two weeks but only if she goes quietly... One of the others will do in the meantime... Yes, yes, thanks.'

Staying very still, he waited for a commotion to ensue beyond the frosted glass wall. After ten minutes his heart rate slowed and the nausea receded to its earlier level. The mug by his elbow was empty but, not daring to venture into the kitchen, he set about reviewing his meeting notes for Eddie with a parched mouth instead.

At eleven he rose and stood by the window, wanting to be on his feet when his brother arrived. At a quarter past he sat again, cursing the man's disregard for punctuality. At least the hangover was settling - one of the sales team had come to ask a question and was promptly dispatched for more coffee - only the underlying tiredness persisted.

Eddie arrived towards the bottom of the hour, blowing in without bothering to knock.

'Morning. Sorry I'm a bit late.'

'Right,' said Dayton, staying where he was, the solidity of the desk between them a reassurance. 'I've pushed back my twelve o'clock but could still do with getting a move on. Grab a chair.'

'What's happened to Becca?'

'Why?'

'She wasn't at her desk and Jess is outside looking upset. Told me she's gone?'

'Turned out she didn't want to work for Simon so we agreed terms for her departure. How was last night?'

'Ah, that's a shame, she's a bright one. Always thought she might be interested in bigger things. I can give her a call if it helps?'

'No chance I'm afraid. How was the Dune? Still one of the best?'

'Food was good but the service isn't what it used to be, not for the price. Fredrik was on form. Bought a bottle of schnapps after dinner and went through most of it himself. He's a funny guy once there's a drink inside him.'

'He can be as funny as he wants provided he signs on Monday. Looking likely?'

'Yeah. It'll happen.'

'Excellent.'

'Just so you know, Richard's agreed to keep Anders on for at least two years. One of Fredrik's redlines. Or Annika's more likely.'

'What? I'm not comfortable with a clause like that. Why wasn't I consulted?'

'You weren't there. It'll be difficult to withdraw, plus I happen to think it's the right thing to do, but talk to Dad if you want.'

'Mmm, I'm seeing him later,' said Dayton, jotting a note given he would personally have to arrange the meeting. 'And how are the houseguests? We should really ask them to leave unless there's anything else we want.'

'Can't think of anything. I'll drop in this afternoon on the way to the airport. Do you still think it's best to have him resign? What about a role here?'

'Once you've burned someone like that, they're not to be trusted. And we're going to have a better option soon anyway. Give him my regards though, and my thanks.'

'I wouldn't expect those to be reciprocated.'

'No, but there we are. Presumably you're out that way collecting Miss Moretti?'

'Uh-huh. We might come and spectate in the morning, depends what time we're up. Fitz was trying to organise a boat trip but the forecast's dicey so I think we'll stay in town.'

'Doubt I'm going to bother racing but will let you know. It'll be good to get rid of this sodding heat though, can't even walk home without needing a shower…'

The conversation ground to a halt. With the small talk over, Dayton found broaching the main topic even more difficult than anticipated.

'When's your flight back?' he asked instead.

'Wednesday.'

'Perfect.'

'Perfect…? What's on your mind, Jules?'

'Mmm, so. Before you bugger off, I thought we should continue our discussion, on… ah… making a plan for you to take over.'

'Really? Yeah, that'd be great. I got the impression you wanted to avoid the subject.'

'I was just surprised, that's all. Didn't think you were keen on all the drudgery I have to deal with. What's changed?'

'Nothing specific. Just a growing realisation that this is what I want, what I'm ready for.'

'Uh-huh, let's come to that,' said Dayton, adjusting the position of his notepad fractionally. 'First though, what are your thoughts in terms of how to effect a transition?'

'Look, no offence but why don't we save ourselves the time and start with whatever plan you've already cooked up?'

'No, no, come on, I'm genuinely interested.'

'Alright,' sighed Eddie. 'I'll admit there are some elements of the job I still need more experience in, is that what you wanted to hear? Mostly the detailed finance reporting, tax liabilities, analyst relations and so on. I'm not against a p–'

'Yes and I suspect you could do with brushing up your knowledge around the fiduciary duties, plus the management and capitalisation of our product development centres, working with the banks, auditors, regulatory frameworks and a few other odds and sods. All very dull but essential I'm afraid.'

'Is that a list you're reading from?'

'It's only my perspective but I thought we should combine our views and come up with a development plan.'

'Depends how long your list is.'

'Not long,' came the easy reply. 'I'll send it over. Come back to me once you've had a chance to reflect and then we can arrange for you to start shadowing me where needed. I think it's important for the team that we maintain stability, that a handover is gradual and smooth rather than short and sharp, yes? Now, how do you feel about your international experience?'

'Pretty good actually. You know I've travelled a lot and spent a decent amount of time in Asia-Pacif–'

'I wouldn't say a few months is long enough to properly understand an overseas territory. My international postings were all eighteen months or more. Richard thought it essential - and I happen to concur by the way - for me to fully understand global trade before I took the top job. You'll need to get to grips with more than just the local sales pipelines.'

'I don't agree. We've invested in decent territory leaders since your time. They're–'

'Yes, but they'll be reporting to you. Which means you need to know at least as much as they do.'

'What's the point in hiring at this level of experience if I have to tell them what to do? These are smart, capable people.'

'If you're not able to keep them on their toes, they'll take advantage of you, that's why,' said Dayton, prodding at the surface of the desk for emphasis. 'There's no shortcut here, Ed, you're going to have to spend six months minimum in each of our main regions. I know you're particularly keen on developing Asia so, with proper oversight, I'd be prepared to give you full control of our business there, all aspects, to help address the gaps in your experience. How does that sound?'

'Honestly? Sounds like crap. I don't want to run Asia-Pac tied to a leash. And I don't want to wait forever before sitting in that chair either. So do me a favour and get to the point - how long?'

'There's no getting away from the fact I had more than twenty-five years of executive experience before taking over. You've only really had what, six? Seven? I wouldn't be doing my job properly if I appointed someone without the requisite training. And trust me, you wouldn't enjoy it if you're not ready.'

Eddie's eyes narrowed further.

'How long?'

'Before we answer that, why don't we work on this list and see what it suggests?'

'Because I want to know where your expectations lie.'

'Well, what do you think is reasonable given our discussion so far?'

'If you're prepared to help as much as you claim, then I can't see me needing more than a year, eighteen months max.'

'Ha! No, no, no, I think that's quite an understatement. Rather proves my point. Legally transferring all the directorships will take more than a year alone. Then we'll have to find and train a replacement for your current role before starting a transition. All of this alongside business-as-usual projects like the Malmotec integration, the various offshoring initiatives, new product launches et cetera, et cetera. You know, we might even be able to tip McGlynn's into distress. I don't think she'll have the cash to pay what I'm seeking in damages and there'll be a fire sale of their assets, some of which I'd certainly be interested in. We're lucky there's no need to rush here, you simply wouldn't have the capacity to get all this done by yourself.'

'How long Jules?'

Dayton leant back and interlocked his fingers.

'All in all, I don't think it's unreasonable to suggest you'd need, say, five or six years to–'

'Five years…?' exploded Eddie.

'Minimum. Remember that'd still only get you to about half the tenure I had before–'

'So what? We're different. You can't seriously expect me to roll over and just accept working for you for another five years?'

'Why not? It's a sensible timeframe given how much you need to learn and how much there is to do. If everything went incredibly smoothly we might shave off six months, maybe a year. Subject to certain conditions.'

'Jesus. Which are?'

'I hadn't really considered it. But Richard's not getting any younger and five years puts him well past eighty. If he was thinking of retirement, I could perhaps step up towards the end of the transition. Executive Chairman of course.'

'So whilst I did all the work, you'd hang around in the background and call the shots? Is that the idea? You can piss off.'

'I thought you wanted a proper discussion?' chided Dayton, now enjoying himself enormously. 'If you're not ready to be civil, I suggest we adjourn to a future date.'

Eddie fumed at the condescension but managed to bite his tongue. A lack of preparedness, mistakenly assuming his brother would avoid this negotiation until forced, was nobody's fault but his own.

'It's too long,' he said flatly. 'We're stuck in a rut with you in charge. The comp–'

'No, not true, not true at all. We've grown substantially since–'

'Look at the charts. It's obvious most of that was driven by the tailwind you inherited from Richard. Since then we've plateaued which effectively means we're going backwards in this market. The company needs to be modernised and that's going to require an appetite for risk and a bucketload of change. Who's going to do it? You? I don't think so. You're happy enough running dirty little schemes behind closed doors but you don't like taking risks in public because they expose your own lack of confidence. Nor do you like change, it's hard work and you don't have the stomach for it, never have. That's why the company needs you out of the way, as do I, as does Richard, else we're stuck in limbo while all our competitors, not least McGlynn-bloody-Lansing, stroll past us and off into the distance.'

'I can't believe you'd even think that, let alone say it,' Dayton retorted. 'After the time and effort I've put in, over half my life dedicated to the company. What gives you the right to criticise my achievements or my work ethic, eh? Where were you for the fifteen years after you left Oxford? When Dad needed help, when I needed help, before we finally backed you into a corner and a real job? Too busy drinking, whoring after women and stumbling around a muddy pitch, that's where. You worked here in name only and frankly still do much of the time. You've–'

'Careful.'

'– always been more interested in getting drunk or getting laid than getting on with the job. Out with the boys on

Monday, Suzanne on Wednesday, Sophia tonight, doing God knows what else or who else in between. You don't have the temperament for my job, or the level of detail. The only reason you want to take over is because you can't bear the thought of me being senior to you anymore. That's it, isn't it? A simple case of jealousy. You think you're better than me and don't like the fact that I'm in charge.'

'You're not in charge, Jules, stop fucking kidding yourself. I've been ready to follow good leadership all my life, in sport, in business, wherever, but the problem is you're not it. A leader doesn't maintain their authority because of what it says on a piece of paper, they have to earn a mandate every day through the quality of their actions, how they care for the people they presume to lead. But your lack of action reeks of laziness and you don't give a toss about the people who work for us, to you they're just disposable assets on a spreadsheet. The trouble is they all know it. If it wasn't for me and a few others who clear up after you there'd be a mass exodus–'

'That's bullsh–'

'– and the whole company would come crashing down around your ears. Richard knows it too, why else do you think he brought the subject up? In charge? You're delusional. Take my advice and get out of the way. Get out before you're thrown out.'

'You can't threaten me,' sneered Dayton, voice and body quivering at much the same frequency. 'You or the old man. The company articles are quite clear and you need both his consent and mine to get them revised. You might be the favourite but I can't be removed against my will and I'm not going anywhere until you learn some respect, do you hear me? Five years could easily turn into ten, and ten into fifteen. Yeah, that's right, I'm staying in this office for as long as I want and… and if you don't like it, then you can be the one to fuck off and leave.'

Eddie laughed, partly to antagonise but mostly at the absurdity of the situation. Ignoring the petulance Dayton was right and could not be forced to vacate his position without consent. Their father should have foreseen the scenario and made provisions ahead of leaving for London but, given Eddie's own lack of commitment at the time, probably lacked any viable alternative. At least one thing had been resolved through today's argument - there was no possibility of an amicable handover.

'Yeah, it'd be much easier for you if I walked, wouldn't it?' said Eddie, calm again, dangerously so. 'Probably for me too, truth be told. But I'm not going to stand aside and watch you grind the hard work of our forebears into the ground, Julian, not anymore. I know what it says in the articles but if you're not willing to leave of your own volition, then I'll find a way to get them changed and have you pushed out instead. Consider this fair warning. You're not fit to run this company, I don't think you ever were, and you can't cling on forever.'

28

How's it going?'

'I'm alright,' said McGlynn between spoonfuls of soup. Having worked at the laptop until the battery gave out early-afternoon, she had come to find the charger whereupon Jack forcibly suggested she replenish her own energy too. 'I know you don't like it, but I need to do this, sorry.'

'So long as you're not making yourself worse.'

'Sitting on the couch isn't exactly tiring. And it's helping take my mind off... you know.'

'I know you. But please don't overdo it, promise?'

'Promise. What time are you collecting the girls?'

'Pick-up is at six so I'll be gone by four-thirty.'

'We'll spend the weekend together even if I don't find what I'm looking for today, OK? That's a promise too. I can't wait to see them, I've missed them so much,' she continued, thinking about how much detail would be appropriate when their inevitable questions came.

'If you're up to it, how about we take the dogs up the hill in the morning? I'll make a picnic.'

'Sounds good. We could, er...' McGlynn broke off, distracted by Malik's number. 'Sorry Chéri, have to take this. Hello?'

'Free to talk?'

'Absolutely.'

'Do you have a screen to hand? Bigger than your phone? Need to send you a picture.'

'Wait a sec. OK, got it. It's a... a rugby team?'

'The Oxford University Blues first fifteen to be exact. Now, front row, third from the left.'

'Good-looking Asian guy?'

'Uh-huh. That's the scrum-half apparently, name of Kah-Wing Tang. You wanted me to find another link between Julian and Refrenix Corporation? Well, Tang's father Li-Wei is the founder and majority shareholder. Owns over sixty percent of the stock. Kah-Wing's now all grown-up and runs the place day to day.'

'So what's the link to Julian?'

'Take another look. See anyone else you recognise?'

McGlynn scrutinised the faces. Twenty-five or so young men and coaches arranged in two tiers before an old-fashioned sports pavilion. Mostly Caucasian, they stared back with puffed-out chests and swaggering grins. Reaching the end her eyes widened.

'Shit!' she yelped. 'That's Eddie, isn't it? A young Eddie Dayton with a beard, back row, last but one?'

'Yeah. What are the chances.'

McGlynn stared at the laptop. There it was - the last connection in an unbroken line from Julian Dayton to Rohan Mehta through five degrees of personal separation. The image proved nothing as yet but she knew the chances of this being a coincidence verged on zero.

'How in hell did you find this? I spent all morning at it.'

'Wasn't too bad. You probably know that Refrenix is registered in Shanghai? I've a friend there and he got hold of their corporate breakdown for me, a full list of directors, shareholdings and subsidiaries. When I couldn't connect anyone with Julian directly, I built out short bios on both sides, starting from the top. Richard, Julian and Eddie for the

Daytons. Li-Wei, Kah-Wing and his younger sister Shihan for the Tangs. I saw Kah-Wing and Eddie had both been up at Oxford around the same time but couldn't link them until I went back through social media. Turns out Kah-Wing used to go by Fender. And that's who you're looking at in the photo, Fender Tang.'

'Oh you're a goddamn genius, Sunita. I'm so grateful.'

'Enough to say what links him to Rohan Mehta?'

'Ah, not yet, sorry. Will you give me the weekend?'

'Do I have a choice? I'd really like to know by Monday though. My article's nearly ready. With or without your theory, Julian's not going to like it.'

'Leave it with me. And thanks again.'

'Good news?' asked Jack innocently, encouraged by the first unalloyed smile he had seen for days.

'You bet. Fill you in soon as I've made some calls.'

Laptop in one hand, phone in the other, she made for the office on the lower level to decide how best to use Malik's information. Knowing there was a chain of communication was one thing, proving its use another. Several next points of contact presented themselves - Dayton himself, Eddie, Richard, Fender Tang, Wenling's father, even Jacob Wiesenberg or Kenise Campbell - but each came with a unique perspective and held motivations which would lead down different paths. Not all could be trusted to deliver the outcome she needed and choosing the right place from which to start was crucial.

McGlynn stood before the view across the valley, sifting through the pros and cons until, finally satisfied with her rationale, she placed a call and waited for an answer.

'Dayton.'

'Eddie, it's Wynter.'

Silence.

'It's Wynter McGlynn.'

'Just a moment.'

Sounds of muffled footsteps and a door latch closing made their way down the line. She wondered what he was thinking.

'Twice in one week, Wynter? People will talk. I'd ask how you are but, um, I heard. For what it's worth I was sorry about what happened.'

'Thanks. I'm doing OK, nothing broken but plenty of cuts and bruises. They'll heal.'

'Good, good. There's no place for that here, or anywhere for that matter, none.' He tailed off. 'Should I assume this isn't a social call?'

'I know about Fender Tang.'

Silence.

'And I know you used him to stop Rohan Mehta testifying.'

Silence.

'Eddie, are you listening?'

'You don't know anything.'

'Try me. This is a courtesy call and a one-time offer. My next call is to City PD.'

Silence. She held her breath but could hear his, slow and steady.

'What's the offer?'

'I want to trade.'

'Mmm. I'll listen, then we'll see. In person though. Thirty minutes, the Establishment.'

'I'm at home. I can be there in sixty.'

'See you then.'

Ignoring her protesting knees, McGlynn took the stairs two at a time up to the bedroom where Jack found her hurriedly changing into shirt and trousers.

'You going somewhere?'

'I need to go into the City for an hour. Sorry but it's urgent.'

'Then I'm coming with you,' he said immediately, pulling off his t-shirt. 'There's enough time before I leave for Queenswood. No arguments.'

Ten minutes later they were in the front of the grey SUV and halfway back to the Garvarmore road, Officers Schnitzer and Long close behind. Jack drove manually, always disliking the lack of control when autopilot was engaged and doubly so today when a sudden manoeuvre might be required. Away from the familiarity of the house, McGlynn's excitement was tempered by returning anxiety. She resisted the urge to check over her shoulder by laying out her theory for him in detail.

'So you don't know exactly how this Tang guy got to Rohan yet?' said Jack. 'Other than it was probably through his girlfriend's father?'

'Nope. But there's no chance Eddie'd want to meet if there was nothing to hide. I'm going to have to bluff my way through and see what he lets slip.'

'I can't believe he or Julian did what you say. I know the bad blood goes back a long way but, even so. You're certain there's no connection to what happened on Wednesday?'

'Julian's a vindictive and devious man but he's no gangster. Not unless he's being blackmailed too I suppose. It'd be quite a leap from coercing someone not to testify at a civil trial to being involved in gun running and people trafficking. Talking of which do you mind if I give Auntie Jane a quick call?'

'Sure.'

The muscles in the front of her neck had begun to hurt again. Sneaking a peek of the blue and white car in the passenger mirror, she relaxed against the headrest as the call connected, eyes on the City's towers shimmering in the haze ahead.

'Hi Jane. Sorry it's taken ages to come back to you.'

'That's alright. But what happened earlier? Sounded like you'd had an almighty fright.'

McGlynn brought Hallam up to speed. The news prompted a similar response to Jack's albeit liberally peppered with expletives.

'And you're going to see young Eddie Dayton right now?'

'Yep. Don't fret though, I've Jack and two security guards as chaperones.'

'I want to know who's chaperoning Eddie. Wait till I get my hands on him or his brother.'

'Totally, they'll have stooped to a new low if it's true. How are things your side?'

'Busy. I've had to put Hugo on extended leave. Poor man was in no state to work when he came in so I gave him a couple of numbers for private security, sent him home and suggested he gets away with his family for a while. I let Detective Campbell know and she told me City PD are arranging for a round-the-clock surveillance team. Should arrive tomorrow.'

'Christ. What are we doing in the meantime?'

'Andrew's right here, want to speak with him? Hold on.'

'Morning Director,' said Brookes.

'Appreciate you coming in, Andrew. How are we fixed until the police come back?'

'The cameras are being continually monitored and Gina should be here in an hour so we'll up the number of site patrols. I could really use a few extra bodies though, there just aren't enough people I trust.'

'I've had offers of help and can probably get you a dozen guards before nightfall – see what you think and keep however many you want.'

'That'd be great, thanks. I also told Jonah Turner the new security protocols are permanent. He's moaning about it but at least the cargo checks are still being done properly.'

'OK. The *Santa Maria* put to sea last night, didn't she? When's the next shipment due?'

'Late Sunday. The *Katsonis* out of Athens. Jane and I spoke to the freight partners and they've all been helpful. Too late for the *Katsonis* but the next one from Eastern Europe is the *Murtrans Bulk*. She won't berth until the end of the week and will have undergone extra inspection at loading.'

'OK. Need anything else?'

'No. If someone tries to get in without the police here watching though, they'll be sorry,' he said with grim determination. 'One second, I'll pass you back to Jane.'

'So, don't worry,' continued Hallam. 'We're fine.'

'Mmm. I'll talk to Campbell and push for the surveillance team,' said McGlynn. 'Have you spoken with Thom?'

'I have. Sorry to be the bearer of bad news but he said Christopher Boland has been in touch. Wants to know whether you're well enough for an emergency meeting on Monday. Thom wasn't sure whether to ask.'

'Just Christopher or the full board?'

'Thom got the impression he was proposing the whole shebang.'

McGlynn had known the demand would arrive sooner or later. That it came from Boland rather than Elliott Hounslow was indicative of the likely agenda.

'I'll contact him later depending on how I fare with Eddie,' she said. 'Something else to look forward to, eh? Sorry but I have to go, we're coming into town. Wish me luck.'

'The very best, my dear, always.'

Relieved to be approaching from the east rather than the north and Avenue San Domingo, McGlynn's head rolled towards the side window. In her heightened state of awareness, strangers scattered along the Esplanade or riding in adjacent cars seemed to stare at the big SUV more than usual but she paid them little regard. The game was on and most of her focus was elsewhere, refining strategy, double-checking assumptions and rehearsing arguments. Eddie had the reputation of being a strong negotiator yet she felt galvanised by the prospect of engaging him in a battle of wits, undaunted by the stakes involved.

With both cars parked under ML One they crossed the basement and emerged into the concrete oven of Willis Lane. McGlynn took Jack's arm and pushed the pace, almost as keen to be off the streets as she was to begin. The Friday evening rush was still an hour away and spotting her opponent in one of the Establishment's wall booths proved easy enough. She squeezed Jack's hand and approached alone, leaving him, Schnitzer and Long to find a table out of earshot.

'Hello Eddie.'

'Afternoon. There's mineral water on the way unless you'd like something else.'

'That'll do fine, thanks.'

Neither made an attempt to extend a hand as McGlynn took a seat opposite. Unsmiling, Eddie lingered on the half-hidden bruise under her hair and the discolouration around her neck. She appraised him in return, the expensive haircut, suit and watch, thinking he somehow looked older and wiser than when she saw him in court. The philanderer's chutzpah had been replaced by something akin to gravitas yet the substitution had done nothing to diminish his handsomeness.

'Who's the big guy with your security detail?'

'That's Jack.'

'Is it now?' he replied, looking across with new interest. 'Don't think I've come across him before. What is he, six-three, six-four?'

'A little more than that. And very protective.'

'Mmm. And how are the children? You've twin girls I think?'

'They're fine. Still none yourself?'

'Far as I'm aware.'

A bow-tied waiter arrived. Avoiding eye contact he poured hissing liquid over ice and quickly withdrew, wanting no part of an encounter requiring the nearby presence of two armed guards and a glowering man mountain.

'Right. Let's get into this shall we?' said McGlynn, leaning forwards. 'How did Fender Tang persuade Rohan and Wenling to disappear?'

'Who are they?'

'Mmm. You want to waste our time? You know Rohan Mehta was due to give evidence when you were at court on Wednesday. Wenling's his girlfriend and her father works for your friend Fender Tang at Refrenix Corporation in Singapore.'

'Haven't spoken to Fender in years.'

'Really. You're not aware of your distributor agreement with Refrenix, or that Fender is the senior executive there. Or that his father is the founder and majority shareholder.'

'Julian deals with distribution.'

'I know you've spent time abroad recently. Wouldn't take much to find out where, or whether your social life has involved Mr Tang. Are you seriously telling me Wenling's father working for him is coincidence?'

'Uh-huh.'

'I don't believe it. I'd bet a month's wages you've been in Singapore and that Fender's doing a favour for an old friend. He has some sort of leverage over Wenling and she was told to warn Rohan off.'

'No. Perhaps your chap Rohan had an accident? Unfortunate, but it happens.'

'We filed a missing persons case yesterday and the police have trawled the traffic accidents and hospitals,' bluffed McGlynn. 'Nothing. And I'm told they haven't left the country either. What's Rohan going to say when he comes back up for air? You can't keep him hidden forever.'

'Maybe he didn't want to testify. You heard what Franklin said, maybe he's embarrassed at your misplaced accusations. He wasn't under subpoena, was he? As I understand it there's no obligation to be a witness in a civil case.'

'True. But I know he wanted to. He's as pissed as me about you stealing our code. Couldn't wait to testify then disappears two days before he takes the stand. Coincidence again?'

'Must be.'

She looked at him, weighing his resolve.

'This was a one-time offer Eddie. If you choose to be unhelpful, I'm calling City PD the moment I leave this bar. My bet is that you and Julian dreamt this up between you so no one else around here knows. But the police will be interested in the chain connecting you and Rohan, that's for damn sure, especially given the sums involved in my litigation and the countersuit you'll inevitably issue. They don't much believe in coincidence either which means they'll start asking questions and the two of you plus your father will be fielding difficult calls from staff, family and friends very soon. I doubt Richard's involved, he wouldn't want to get his hands this dirty, but will he have to disclose to the Upper House that his not-so-honourable sons are the subjects of a criminal investigation? And after the police I'll call the Post because I'm goddamn sure they'll be interested. I hear they're doing an article on you and this is great material, especially if they can break a story before you get a summons - obstruction of justice is a criminal offence, civil case or not.'

'Empty threats. If you had any actual proof you'd have gone to the police already.'

'I considered it but a drawn-out investigation isn't in my interests either. There's plenty else I should be spending my time on.'

'You know what, Wynter? I feel bad at you coming all the way into town for no reason. So I'll indulge you. You wanted to trade? Go on then, tell me what your opening offer was going to be if you could have proved any of this.'

He took a slug of water and spread his big hands on the tabletop, still much too relaxed for McGlynn's liking. If Fender Tang had a lasting hold over Rohan then Eddie might be able to stonewall indefinitely. Was now the time to show her cards or should she try and crank the jeopardy even higher? Instinct told her to play an open hand.

'I want the countersuit dropped immediately. Then a public apology within a fortnight for stealing my code, a hundred and twenty million in reparation and a written resolution to remove the software features you've copied within three months. And I want Wenling and Rohan left alone, including a promise that Tang stops threatening her or her father. I'd also ask for a personal commitment to free and fair competition, for you to stop these underhand, illegal business practices permanently, but I suspect I'd be wasting my time.'

'I've never had a problem with fair competition.'

'So this was all Julian's idea?'

'No comment, obviously. But why didn't you approach him with this nonsense? You must have realised those conditions, which are wholly unjustifiable by the way, would need his approval. Why call me?'

'I've known you both a long time. If you were going to fight dirty you'd be man enough to tell me to my face and even then there's still a line you wouldn't cross. You and I appreciate the value in competition, we know the only way to show you're better than your opponent is to win while obeying the laws of the game. But Julian's different. For whatever reason, he takes it all so personally that he'll stop at nothing to try and bury McGlynn-Lansing and me along with it, so long as he thinks he can get away without a scratch. I don't think he ever learned the satisfaction to be had in playing fair such that a victory actually meant something.'

'If what you're alleging were true then I'd be as complicit as my brother, no?'

'Everyone has lapses of judgement, particularly when dealing with family. It's whether you can accept those for what they are and make amends which matters. This is about character, and I have less faith in his which is why I called you first. You know how joyless and spiteful he is and therefore you must realise he's a liability. To you, to Richard and to the long-term success of your business.'

'Ahh, I see, you mean to flatter me into fratricide so I can take his place? Which'd then give me the authority to agree to your demands?'

'Are you different from your brother? Or have you sunk to the same level?'

'We're different, I can assure you.' He paused. 'Want to know by how much?'

'If it eases your conscience.'

'You've a youngster working for you. French. Matthieu something or other.'

'Matthieu Gautier?' she replied, thrown by the non-sequitur.

'Yeah that's him. Would you like to know just how fucked up Julian really is? He wants to enlist Gautier as a mole. Asked me to tell him our latest radiotherapy machines have unrealistic rates in treating gastric cancer.'

'I'd like to say I'm surprised,' said McGlynn, feeling sickened. 'Should I take it you've been unsuccessful?'

'Couldn't do it. Saw him at the ball and the lad looked glum enough already. Thought you ought to know in case Julian tries directly.'

'Thank you, genuinely, the Gautiers are good people. Eloise is probably closer to the end than your brother might think but yes, you've illustrated my point perfectly. Sorry to say it but the man's a disgrace to the family name, an absolute… *bâtard*.'

'Quite.'

'Then you must realise he needs to go?'

'Nothing lasts forever. But he's still my brother.'

Intuiting the magnitude of the debate underway behind Eddie's impassive face, McGlynn stayed quiet. If he were to reject her proposal then, having already decided it would be pointless to reason directly with Dayton, there would be no choice but to talk with Detective Campbell. However, that option ran a poor second to dealing with these problems swiftly and discreetly at source. Moving only her eyes she risked a glance in Jack's direction and found him looking directly back. Perhaps he could read the body language and knew this to be a critical moment because he nodded in encouragement.

'Maybe I could intercede for you,' said Eddie eventually. 'With Julian. If you were prepared to compromise.'

'I think I'm being more than fair under the circumstances,' said McGlynn, recognising the opening gambit. 'But what did you have in mind?'

'If other terms were acceptable I could probably persuade him to drop the countersuit. Removing the features you've contested within three months is impossible though.'

'How long would you need?'

438

'A year. Even then you have to accept they make sense for the market so we'd end up redeveloping them anyway.'

'A year's too long but let's come back to that. What else?'

'How did you arrive at a hundred and twenty million? Isn't that twice the initial amount you tried to sue us for?'

'I want the original sixty and the same again to fund new software development, to restore the competitive advantage we held beforehand.'

'That's unreasonable. Pending the verdict, we'd made a provision for sixty and that sum's still available within thirty days. We could perhaps top it up to seventy-five at most, payable in a hundred and eighty.'

'What about the apology?'

'Not going to happen if we settle out of court. And we'd want the usual contractual protections to prevent you talking to the public and specifically to City PD, the Post or any other media outlet.'

McGlynn took a moment. The extra sixty million was actually intended for her Malmotec war chest. Forcing Dayton to contribute held undeniable karma and the additional funding would mitigate her board's objection to an increased price. However, agreeing to confidentiality meant reneging on her promise to Malik about the link between Tang and Rohan. That would have to be made good in some other way, she decided, the priority here was protecting her company.

'I can agree to those if you'll agree to the hundred and twenty million. Sixty up front, the remainder in six months. I still want the features dropped in three and a commitment to no redevelopment for three years. The offer's also conditional on me hearing from Fredrik Nilsson by midday tomorrow that you've withdrawn your bid and are recommending he completes with us.'

'What the f–... Why on earth would we give Malmotec to you?'

'Because without a public apology and with gag clauses in place I'm giving up leverage to win it from you directly. And not buying them leaves you with plenty of money to pay my hundred and twenty million, doesn't it?'

'Jesus... Seventy-five up front only. Nine months for the software remediation and no redevelopment for two years. We'll withdraw from Malmotec but you're dreaming if you think we'd recommend him to you.'

'Seventy-five up front and another forty-five into escrow within thirty days. If you complete the software work to an agreed specification within six months, I'll accept twenty-five as final payment and you get twenty back, else it's all forfeit. Agreed on two years and on Fredrik but I still want a copy of your letter withdrawing from the process by noon tomorrow.'

'Sixty up front, thirty into escrow with half of that refundable. All other terms remain as is.'

'Sixty up front, fifty in escrow, half refundable.'

'Sixty and forty, no more. But a personal commitment to free and fair competition from this point on.'

'From you or from Julian?'

'You know I can't make a commitment like that on his behalf.'

'And you know I can't finalise a deal with someone who doesn't have the authority to agree it. So what's it going to be Eddie? Can you get this done? Can you find a way to make this your commitment?'

She waited for him once more, watching intently, feeling for signs of a decision either way. Having judged the silence had continued long enough, she deliberately interrupted his thoughts and noisily leant back as if ready to rise.

'Wait...'

McGlynn breathed again.

'Wait... I, um, I'd need some time. But if you're happy with those terms in principle, I'll talk to Richard, then Julian.'

'How long?'

'Probably tonight, first thing tomorrow latest.'

'OK. I'll accept on two further conditions - a favour and a show of good faith.'

'Shit, you're killing me here, Wynter. What else do you want? What's the favour?'

'After you've spoken to your father, I want to be the one to tell Julian.'

'Alright,' he said after a moment's thought. 'It'd save me the job and it's no more than you deserve. And the show of good faith?'

'So far, other than a frank exchange of views, I have nothing more tangible than I walked in with.'

'So?'

'So you could leave and forget this conversation ever happened. I want some collateral, for you to put some skin in the game before we part company.'

'And how do you propose I do that?'

'Tell me where Rohan and Wenling are.'

Eddie almost blanched.

'Tell me Eddie. You need to talk to Richard before you can commit? Well I want to talk to Rohan.'

Watching and waiting a final time, McGlynn willed him over the line of no return.

This was why she loved to compete. This was the moment in which the first of three defeats could be reborn as a victory and perhaps signal, if not the end of the war, at least the beginning of the final onslaught. This was Darwinism made real within the dominion of mankind.

After a full minute, Eddie exhaled loudly and looked at the table.

'They're up at the cabin,' he muttered. 'Lake Pleasant.'

29

T he short stack of iron plates rose and fell, rose and fell. Pressing the handles away from his chest and supporting their return, Dayton was in excellent humour. The earlier meeting with his father had gone well. True, he had probably overplayed Eddie's willingness to accept a minimum five-year transition but the long list of his personal development activities had been agreed without debate. And with Richard on board his disrespectful, impatient little brother would find it very difficult indeed to get his own way.

So fuck you Eddie, fuck you very much.

He finished the set and gently returned the weight to its starting position. Today's workout had been light, sufficient to engorge the arms and chest without taxing his strength and causing only a slight sheen of perspiration in the gym's conditioned air. Nevertheless he gulped the last of the water bottle and dabbed at his forehead with a towel while climbing the stairs to the penthouse - the easy, rhythmical movement loosening the tendons in his lower body.

The housemaid had cleared away last night's detritus and the kitchen was tidy again. Retrieving his favourite ingredients - banana and spinach for fibre and energy, peach and pineapple for vitamins, Greek yoghurt for protein, calcium and probiotics, lime and ginger for taste and digestion - Dayton tossed them into a blender and flicked the switch. The oven clock told him there was just over an hour to go.

To kill time as his bladder filled and his core temperature normalised, he meandered into the nearest of the three spare bedrooms, being careful not to spill any green liquid as he sipped directly from the jug. Although not as spacious as his own, the room still swallowed the super-king bed, large fabric sofa and matching twin armchairs with ease. In common with the wider apartment, the decor had been professionally styled and tasteful off-white predominated, from the open voile curtains to the decorative array of cushions on the patterned duvet. Early evening light streamed through the windows to give the whole space a warm and inviting glow. As always on these special occasions he searched for the cameras; one in the fake fire sensor directly above the bed, one in the modernist lampstand to one side and the last behind the top corner of a mirrored wardrobe. They ran off wires buried in the walls and fed a hard drive in his dressing room. Satisfied the tiny lenses and microphones were undetectable unless one knew where to look he turned back to the view. From this aspect the ocean could be seen above and between the office blocks opposite. Much squatter and older than his own, these were reliably deserted by this time on a Friday and he loitered by the glass, in no rush to finish the drink.

With pressure growing in his lower abdomen he crossed to his own bedroom, closed the blinds and stripped his gym gear into the laundry basket. Taking a tissue he laid on the bed and watched pornography until erect enough to masturbate, then ejaculated neatly onto the absorbent white paper. The process took no more than three minutes and involved little pleasure other than the moment of climax. Once the light-headedness subsided he moved to the bathroom, dropped the limp tissue into the toilet bowl and sat, waiting for his urethral sphincter to relax.

After a hot shower, using liberal amounts of a tangerine and bergamot wash to scrub from head to toe, he took a fresh blade from the cabinet and shaved with great care before massaging a linseed moisturiser into the marble-smooth skin. Clean and refreshed, he returned to the bedroom, switched on a single light above the full-length mirror in the corner and stopped a pace short of the glass.

Not many men his age could lay claim to such an attractive physique, he thought. Regular exercise and a healthy diet were only half the reason. For the rest, the slim frame and fine bone structure so vulnerable to injury but so aesthetically pleasing, he should no doubt be thankful to his mother's aristocratic genes. The only disappointment was the loss of skin tone but, with the spotlight directly overhead, this was rendered all but invisible leaving him free to enjoy the image without distraction.

When fewer than fifteen minutes remained, he reluctantly donned a pair of trunks, well-worn jeans and a tailored but informal white shirt, leaving the cuffs rolled partially up his forearms. Leaning against the piano, aware of his trembling, Dayton's heart missed a beat when the elevator chimed. He waited long enough for it to seem as though he had not been waiting at all, then padded softly to the door.

Photographs never fully conveyed how someone might appear in real life. Even video failed to capture the uniqueness of another human in such close proximity; the subtle energy, the minute vibrations, the hair shifting in natural light. However at the sight and sound and smell of the woman returning his smile across the threshold, he felt a mixture of relief and desire flow through him. He had chosen well.

'You must be Madeleine. Please, come in.'

'Hey there. Nice to meet you, Mr Dayton.'

She wandered into the apartment, unsure where to go. Of medium height with honey-coloured hair curling halfway down her back, her movement was as lithe as he hoped. At his request she was dressed casually - jeans and a t-shirt with no obvious make-up – and a mid-sized messenger bag in brown leather hung from her shoulder.

'It's Julian,' he said kindly. 'Not Mr Dayton or Jules, never Jules. Have a seat wherever you wish. Would you like something to drink? There's nothing open so please, whatever you'd prefer. Wine, champagne, something stronger, or softer…'

'White wine? The drier the better, thanks.' Depositing the bag by her feet Madeleine perched on the edge of the sofa, knees together and still a little wide-eyed. 'I like your apartment. You been here long?'

'Mmm. Much longer than I care to remember. Belonged to a Russian chap who wasn't staying in the City often enough and wanted the cash for a villa outside Rome. I probably paid more than it was worth but it's so unique. Right place, right time, you know how it goes.'

'Not yet, I'm still renting. Maybe one day.'

'I'm sure of it.'

Dayton passed her a glass on which condensation was already forming, took a chair nearby and crossed an ankle over a knee. Gently moving air and the hum of the City reached into the apartment through the balcony doors.

'Health and happiness,' he said.

'Absolutely.'

They drank, his sip significantly smaller than hers.

'Now, if it wouldn't make you uncomfortable, perhaps we could start by you telling me something about yourself?'

'Mrs Carmichael said she'd given you my details and portfolio, eh?'

'She did, yes. But I can imagine how you might feel, coming up to a stranger's apartment by yourself, and I'd very much like you to feel at home here. So how about you do the talking for a while?'

'OK, for sure. Well, um, I'm thirty-one years old. Originally from a small town near Vancouver but over here since college. I've a Masters in visual arts from UBC and work at the Timpson Gallery, that's on Denstone Street, not far from the library. And I, uh, well I guess that's about it.'

'Very interesting,' said Dayton, knowing all this already. He smiled encouragingly. 'Who or what inspired you to study the arts?'

'That'd be my grandfather. He was a teacher, a physics teacher, but painted as a hobby. Oils mostly. I used to go up to the attic in his house when I was a kid and he'd let me sit and watch as long as I was quiet. The way he'd mix the palette and throw the... Ah sorry, but I'm rambling, eh?'

'Not at all. You were saying? About throwing something?'

'Yeah, well he'd almost throw the paint at the canvas, like magic, you know? And these beautiful pictures would emerge from nothing. My parents wanted me to enlist, they're both ex-navy, but it was Gramps who gave me the confidence to follow my passion.'

'Good for him, and for you. Do you still paint?'

'Some. I'm still learning though. Art's a lifetime of study.'

'And how about your siblings? I believe you've three older brothers, what do they do?'

'Would it be OK if we didn't talk about my family too much? It feels kinda, uh, weird.'

'Of course. Then what else do you enjoy doing in your spare time?'

'I love to kitesurf whenever I can. Run every day. How about you?'

'Same, I try and stay healthy. My work keeps me very busy but I train for the triathlon most years.'

'Yeah? Are you there tomorrow then?'

'Maybe. It'll depend on, um, how tired I am. Do you normally come and watch?'

'Uh-huh. I've thought about entering but I'm not quick enough on the bike yet. No point racing if you're not aiming to win.'

'Couldn't agree more. I'm glad they split the field though, don't think I'm up to competing against men your age these days.'

'Which category are you in, if you don't mind saying?'

'I could make you guess,' he grinned, standing to refill her glass. Madeleine's initial nervousness was almost gone, the boldness he had liked in her showreel beginning to appear. 'Just for fun?'

'Over-sixties?' she replied immediately, eyes bright. 'Sixty-fives?'

'Ha! Over-seventies actually, so decrepit I use a frame for the last mile. You know what though, if I were a betting man, I'd say Mrs Carmichael already told you.'

'To be fair, you look alright for it.'

'Mmm. Not the finest compliment but I'll take it. What else did she say?'

'Honestly?'

'Please. Honesty is a prerequisite between us.'

'She said you were OK. That I wasn't the first and probably wouldn't be the last but she'd had no complaints from the others.'

'Ah. How about the contract she gave you? Did you have any concerns before you signed?'

'Nope. Everything seemed easy enough.'

'And what made you accept? Was it the money? Truthfully please,' he added, noticing the slight hesitation.

'The money's a large part of it, not gonna lie. It's more a month than I make in a year.'

'What else then?'

'I guess you know how I met her?'

'Through her agency. What gave you an interest in the film industry?'

'The money. And because I'm single and thought what the hell.' She took another sip and looked at him directly. 'And because I like sex.'

'And you prefer older men?'

'Mostly. My last boyfriend wasn't far off your age. Daddy issues.'

'Fair enough. But why take my contract rather than your first role?'

'Suppose I haven't totally made up my mind about going for it. And agencies pay by the film whereas your money's guaranteed, right?'

'For as long as we see each other, yes.' Dayton could see the uncertainty. 'But I'm very sure you'll have a few questions so please, fire away.'

'Really? OK. So is there anything I ought to know about, uh, unusual tastes?'

'I don't think so. No one's complained so far, as you've already heard, and there's nothing I expect you to do that you don't want to. Same goes for me. But I want you to know I'll get most of my pleasure from pleasing you. Not in a submissive way, that's absolutely not my thing, but by ensuring you have a good time, the best time possible. Make sense?'

'Not a whole amount to me. But I understand, I think.'

'I mean it, Madeleine. If you're only pretending it's a massive turn-off. So be brave and tell me what you want, when you want it. No faking.'

'Deal. Next question. Will you be getting anyone else involved?'

'No. I want you all to myself and the agreement is based on exclusivity. If you wish to see someone else, that's fine, but you'll need to terminate beforehand.'

'Yeah, I saw that. And you truly don't mind if I want out?'

'It's not a question of whether I mind or not, I agree to respect your choice. Likewise for me in return. You've also noted the confidentiality clauses I presume? They're the most important in the whole agreement. You don't talk about me or this apartment to your friends, family, anyone. Nothing on social media and it goes without saying that you don't talk to the press. Ever. Do you understand? The only people in the world who know are the two of us and Mrs Carmichael and she's no fool - I pay her too well. This is a fair contract and

I'll abide by it provided you do the same. And if you're ever stupid enough to try blackmail, well, let's just say that I'm a resourceful man.'

'Right, good to know. So we'll only be meeting here then, eh?'

'Mostly. Sometimes I might ask if you'd like to join me when I'm away on business but it's not expected. I pay all expenses although we'd almost certainly travel separately.'

'Because you don't want to be seen with me?'

'Yes. But that's not because of you.'

Dayton watched her toy with the empty glass.

'Why do you do this?' asked Madeleine. 'I looked you up and have some idea of what you're worth, financially I mean. Surely there's plenty of women who'd want to get close to you?'

'To be honest,' he said, marvelling at how often the phrase preceded an untruth, 'I like the transparency in this arrangement. Experience tells me that traditional relationships, romances if you will, are so often full of deceit. Don't you think?'

'Uh-hmm.'

'Anything else?'

'Do you play?' she asked, nodding at the piano.

'Badly.'

'I'd like you to play for me. Sometime.'

'Maybe I will.' He searched the lovely face, trying to discover anything hidden there. 'Now, if there are no other questions would you like to see our room?'

'Why not.'

Rising, he indicated the correct door and followed her through. The buildings opposite and to the east were ablaze with the last hour of daylight, stark against the indigo sea beyond. They stood in silence for a while, her shoulder brushing his arm, and Dayton's head swam.

Unable to bear the tension any longer he moved to the sofa opposite the foot of the bed. She looked at him inquiringly.

'Please would you undress.'

Madeleine backed away from the window, kicked off the deck shoes and with composed, unhurried movements removed her jeans and t-shirt, tossing them over the nearby armchair. She slipped a finger into the sides of her panties, slid them down toned legs and stood again, proudly naked. His erection, at this point more from exertion of control than sexual arousal, felt constricted but he resisted the urge for rearrangement. Instead, he waited a while, wanting her to know his next words were authentic.

'You're exceptionally beautiful, Madeleine.'

'Thank you.'

'Please would you lie on the bed, against the cushions.'

'You like to watch, eh?' she asked, taking her place as instructed.

'Only the first time. I much prefer to be involved.'

'So what happens next?'

'I'd like you to reach orgasm. In your own time and however you wish.'

'Mmm.'

She began. At the moment her eyes closed he silently eased his discomfort and settled more comfortably against the backrest, only half-interested. This was a necessary step in the overall composition but still within the opening bars of the prelude.

In the years following Sarah's suicide Dayton had put significant thought into what he wanted from any future relationship. Whilst considering himself far too young to give up altogether, his heart bore too many scars for the risks of conventional romance and so, through the application of intellect, he set about designing a methodology to satisfy both his libido and his very specific emotional needs. The principal issue was how to mitigate his now morbid and intertwined fears of commitment and rejection. Having been repeatedly abandoned by those to whom he had entrusted his love - most notably Richard, Eddie, McGlynn, Adam and finally Sarah - and vividly remembering how destructive those experiences had been, he had no desire to ever again be reliant on another's goodwill. The avoidance of humiliation, either linked to rejection but also due to the presence of a third party, especially a well-known third party, ran close behind.

The solution was a process in which information could be discreetly shared before any decision was made. Upon his instruction Mrs Carmichael, who had been only too easy to find and retain as broker, monitored the agency's applicants for women meeting his criteria. After initial enquiries their profiles and photos would be forwarded to him for review. Dayton was fastidious in their screening, finding as much pleasure in the choosing as in the ultimate choice, but one or two would eventually be approved and approached with a detailed proposal. If that was acceptable Mrs Carmichael asked for further information on their background, formative experiences, education, financial situation, current and prior relationships, sexual preferences and the presence of any offspring. A video accompanied the subsequent briefing documents and allowed him to make a final decision on whether to proceed. If so, the preferred candidate was given a copy of the contract plus an offer for access to legal advice should it be wanted. Once the highly punitive confidentiality clauses were in force, then and only then would he give permission for his own profile and photos to be made available in return. This was the point of highest risk, where rejection based on him as a person rather than the process or the principle might take place. Within reason this was also the step at which the candidate could take as much time as they wished to reflect. He would wait anxiously, hoping against hope and forcing himself not to push for a positive response. Assuming the reply was favourable, and the progressive management of expectations thus far generally meant that it was, Mrs Carmichael would reiterate the terms of the contract, share his identity and arrange a meeting.

By the time of that first encounter the bulk of Dayton's fears would have been assuaged. The privacy of using an intermediary had ensured no embarrassment and the chances of being rebuffed by a woman who gave informed consent to visit him at home were, he felt, minimal. As the perception of risk lessened so did his characteristic awkwardness. He became free to be himself and much to his surprise found good manners, humour and sometimes even charisma were all attainable in that liberation. There had now been five of these meetings in total. Five in sixteen years, each bringing new lessons and helping him refine his approach. Alcohol was useful in relieving initial anxiety provided it was served in moderation, as was offering the opportunity for questions to establish rapport. On two occasions his guests had proactively raised the topic of fornication and on the others he had found it expedient to do the same while still clothed. Taking time together was key but not hurrying her decision to attend in the first place was paramount. Such a mistake, where the lack of chemistry had been palpable and meant his self-consciousness quickly returned, had led to the only failure at this stage of the process to date.

'Madeleine?'

'Hmmm?'

'There's no rush, OK?'

'Call me Maddy… friends call me Maddy.'

'Slow down a little, Maddy, take it easy.'

'Mmmm, OK. Now hush, I'm trying to concentrate.'

Presuppositions of commitment were also as well-managed as they could be. The contract provided for termination in unambiguous, dispassionate terms. No long-term allegiance had been pledged and therefore no shame, no sense of humiliation, should be involved in the event of a withdrawal by either party. At least that was the theory, but where it went from here with Madeleine was anybody's guess.

Dayton had been completely truthful when he admitted his pleasure came from hers and would dedicate himself accordingly. This did not mean the adoption of a servile attitude or blunt demonstrations of virility, it meant diligence in his courtship. He would buy flowers and cook for her, play the piano when they were together, send teasing messages when they were apart, find ways of making her laugh, flatter her knowledge by asking for help with the visual arts, introduce her to literature and music whilst being receptive to her tastes, listen in the dead of night to her hopes and fears and whisper his affections as she slept. All of these things in the pursuit of twin goals; that he might fall in love and, although less likely, that she might do the same. Discounting the chances of them having entered a lifelong relationship only one of two further outcomes was then possible, the question being who would want to end the affair first. From the outset his intellect understood there would be an ending, a removal of affection, a rejection, but the dimension of time lent the inevitable a delicious uncertainty.

He knew the trauma of such endings well. Yet by constantly reminding himself the end would one day arrive he protected enough of his ego to ensure survival. Bound by the principles of Darwinism, he had adapted to suit his environment.

The first of these relationships spluttered to a close after six months, both of them knowing it was over before she took the initiative. Still somewhat confused as to what truly satisfied him, he had grown fond of her by that point but probably no more. The second failed at their initial meeting but the third progressed much further. Whilst he had been crushed when she broke it off, the accompanying self-abasement was surprisingly welcomed as a long-absent friend. Like the prisoner who dreaded interrogation but felt relief when torture arrived, he had discovered pain could be feared and yet still desirable. In that context the fourth engagement, and the last until today, had yielded the most successful results thus far.

The moment Lucia appeared at his door one late spring day Dayton had realised how far he would fall. Like Madeleine, she was slender with the same implied strength but taller, younger, her features perhaps a little more angular, hair a shade darker, eyes grey-brown rather than bright blue.

Those eyes had looked at him with innate curiosity, with wit, wisdom and warmth. They and she had reminded him of a young McGlynn.

Within a month, a fortnight even, he was hopelessly smitten. Masking his desperation he redoubled his efforts to win her heart and by Christmas believed he had met with victory. From thereon he faced an exquisite dilemma. Should he wait until her love waned and watch, increasingly frantic, as she began the inexorable process of retreat? Or was it better to take the initiative and strike first? That they could possibly maintain their love until death did them part never crossed his mind, he was simply comforted to know the inevitable grief would be almost unbearable. In the end Dayton rationalised he ought to have the advantage of looking back as the instigator. Such an act of masochism would sharpen his torment and hence bring greater long-term pleasure. This being the case, Lucia duly received a letter from his lawyers terminating their agreement and offering to pay for her relocation to the Capital which, after some ugly pleading on her part, was accepted. On deeper reflection during the two bleak years which followed, he realised the actual reason he had struck first was cowardice - he simply lacked the courage to have waited for her any longer.

It was set against this backdrop that he observed Madeleine, already satisfied in their beginning whilst wondering what the relationship might bring and how it would end. As always his first goal was the emotional intimacy so often denied him in the past. He wanted to feel as close as possible to her, to someone, close enough for him to suffer when they parted and even better if those feelings were known to be mutual. Sex, although undeniably a pleasure, was purely another instrument in achieving that aim.

From both her expression and the irregular breathing he could tell she was nearly there.

'Maddy?'

'Shhh.'

'Maddy.'

'Fuck. What now?'

'Come here please.'

She stared at him in resentment then obediently shuffled from the end of the bed and stood between his knees. He placed his right hand lightly against the inside of her lower thigh. She shivered at the touch.

'Are you comfortable?' he asked, ensuring he spoke clearly enough to be picked up by the microphones. 'Being here with me?'

'Uh-huh.'

'Are you happy to continue with our agreement?'

'Yeah.'

'What are the rules?'

'Rules?'

'About pretending.'

'You get your pleasure from mine. I tell you what I want, when I want it. And no faking.'

He slid his hand gently up her thigh until the tip of his thumb rested between her labia.

'And what do you want now?'

'I want you.'

'You want to make love?'

'Uh-hmmm. Please.'

He stood, slipping his thumb inside and cupping her buttock, causing her to sigh. Madeleine looked up at him with half-lidded eyes. Feeling like an Acapulcan diver, hanging his toes over the cliffs at La Quebrada, fascinated by the turquoise water below, Dayton summoned his limited bravery and leapt.

30

There had been no relief overnight, the City remained locked and sweltering in the mass of air blown all the way from the equator. At dawn, those for whom Saturday meant no work thanked their various gods and stayed in the shade. The less fortunate moved sluggishly between air-conditioned vehicles and buildings, nervously eyeing the unbroken bank of cloud far off to the southwest.

At seven o'clock the organisers, insurers and race controller took the joint decision to go ahead. The triathlon was a major event and nearly nine thousand participants and sponsors were either already here or on their way. In the interests of safety and because numbers allowed, the committee further agreed to collapse the last three groups, releasing them as one to ensure everyone had ample time to complete the course before the storm made landfall. By nine forty-five the elite, club and younger athletes were already gone and only the older, slower groups remained - milling around the dry sand or sitting silently on the boardwalk in accordance with their pre-race ritual.

Satiated and at peace with the world, such rarities in his lifetime, Dayton wandered between them. Last night's lovemaking with Madeleine had been everything he hoped for and afterwards, with her resting in his arms sometime in the early hours, they had drifted into sleep together. Their genesis was perfect, she was still perfect and he was content.

Awoken early by a message from Eddie, saying he and Sophia intended to come down but only if Dayton was going to race, he had thought why not? A cold swim, a ride and a run even without the competition he had trained for would trigger a flood of endorphins and replenish his vigour. Madeleine wanted to spectate as well. She would cheer him along the last stretch of Crown Road before the Necropolis, safely away from where his brother usually stood, before they headed back to the brownstone for a lazy afternoon. The prospect filled him with much anticipation. By the time he realised an erection in a thin tri-suit amongst company would be far from ideal it was too late. Chastened, he forced his thoughts toward the profound wish that McGlynn could have been here, to be beaten for the third time in a week, face to humbled face.

A gaggle of spritely septuagenarians and their scattered belongings blocked his path. Dayton barely slowed as he barged through their midst, but looking up again on the other side stopped him in his tracks.

His wish had been granted.

Against all the pleas from Jack and advice from Triple S, McGlynn had made the decision late the previous evening, arguing she was physically capable and that such a heavily-policed event posed little threat. Listening on the periphery, Catriona and Adeline seemed even keener than usual to support their mother, more than likely eager to see friends and take advantage of the ice cream stalls. Even so they had proved much less amenable this morning, hauled protesting from their beds at what they considered an ungodly hour to be bundled into the car. Jack had driven them back to the City accompanied by no fewer than three escort vehicles, their journey mostly a quiet one.

Coming to a standstill on the Esplanade beside the heaving ranks of competitors, family and friends, he had broken his silence to wish her luck. McGlynn had smiled back, wondering how much of that precious resource might be needed. Her overall condition was better than yesterday but under any other circumstances there would have been no chance of her competing. In addition to the enduring weariness she was vaguely sickened by the thought of immersing her scabbed skin in saltwater. Nevertheless, she felt strong enough to at least start the course and warmed up while methodically working her way along the beach, hunting her prey. Schnitzer and Long dogged her steps in return.

She and Dayton caught sight of each other at the same instant. After the initial surprise he scuffed his way across the hot sand and she planted her feet, ready.

'Wynter!' he exclaimed, pulling up out of reach. 'Delighted to see you!'

'Morning Julian,' she replied, unable to keep herself from glancing at the obscene bulge across the top of his thigh.

'Um, you see I'd assumed you wouldn't be well enough to come after the, ah, incident.'

'You underestimate me as always.'

'Good for you, good for you. Are those security chaps yours? They don't look dressed for a swim.'

'It's the dangers on land which concern me. I have to say you're looking very well, very pleased with yourself?'

'All in all, it's been rather a successful week, hasn't it. Commiserations on losing the case but I did warn you at the time how foolish these accusations were.'

'You did.'

Failing to register that McGlynn was much too calm, too predatory, for a conquered foe, Dayton cast around for another subject.

'Um, haven't we been lucky with the weather? Assuming we get round before the clouds blow over that is. If you don't mind me saying, your injuries don't look too bad... quite minor in fact... which I'm sure is a relief for... um, everyone. But what I meant to ask is whether you'll be able to compete, to anywhere near your usual level I mean?'

'I think so.'

'Marvellous. Keep at it and you might beat me eventually, eh? But it won't be today I'm afraid, so sorry, not today.'

'Have you spoken to Eddie this morning?'

'No? But he's coming to watch. Probably be on the left as you join the Rangeway from the park, so be sure to give him a wave. Why do you ask?'

'What about Richard?'

'Not sure. Why?'

'They'll want to talk to you afterwards.'

'And how would you know?'

'Because I spoke with them last night. On my way home from Lake Pleasant.'

'Really?' Dayton's stomach performed a sickening backflip. 'Um, the lakeside's certainly a picturesque place to spend an evening. But I fail to see the relevance.'

'You should be more interested in the consequence. You're done Julian. I struck a deal with your brother and father. You'll be out of a job by Monday.'

'What? What on earth are you talking about?'

Somewhere in the middle distance a whistle sounded and nearby conversation wilted as people shuffled towards the flags.

'Let's get to the starting line. It's going to be busier than usual.'

'What are you talking about, Wynter? What deal?'

'You've the best part of three hours to figure it out, haven't you. If you're still none the wiser come find me at the finish and I'll fill in the blanks.' McGlynn moved off, leaving him rooted to the spot. 'Best of luck, Julian, I'll be sure to give you a wave on my way past.'

At the siren's blast the mob raced for the sea, as desperate for action as they were for the cold water. McGlynn ignored Andrew Brookes' advice and waited until the most zealous of them, including Dayton who could be seen sprinting off to her right, were away. She had no desire to compound her injuries and jogged across the sand, picking the line she wanted in the surf. Submerged up to her thighs, the salt stinging but not as much as feared, she gritted her teeth and dived headlong. Initially she concentrated on her regular stroke pattern - a breath every three, checking her direction and for nearby swimmers every nine - but with a rhythm established she relinquished control to her training and allowed her mind to drift towards the problem of what to do with Rohan.

After leaving Eddie at the Establishment she and Jack returned to ML One then parted ways. He took the SUV and made for Queenswood with the Triple S team. McGlynn, waiting for a back-up crew to arrive, had pulled the dust sheets from the old convertible and thumbed the ignition, allowing the engine to warm and listening to the guttural exhaust notes bouncing around the concrete box. The blast up to Lake Pleasant had taken an hour.

Finding the Daytons' cabin proved simple enough although she had thought the designation something of an understatement. Two storeys of oiled cedarwood with generous verandas and immaculate lawns almost encircled by the forest pines - a jetty, a flagpole and a breathtaking view of the lake beyond. As she pulled up a familiar face appeared at the front door. Rohan had been expecting Eddie. At finding McGlynn he appeared so shocked, so ashamed the door almost closed again but, with gentle words of reassurance that the two officers were in fact private security rather than City PD, he was eventually persuaded to let her inside. There, in a vaulted lounge overlooking the water and with a fidgeting Wenling to one side, he had stared at the floor and given monotone answers to her patient, unflinching questions.

Rohan said he received the unexpected call late the previous Friday. A man introducing himself as a Mr Kah-Wing Tang informed him Wenling's father was in a precarious situation. He had found himself in substantial debt through financing his wife's expensive tastes, paying two mortgages on a property in Nassim Hill and all the while indulging a beautiful but rapacious mistress on the side. Tang held the old Singaporean's fate in his hands. Not only could he fire him and thereby remove his main source of income, but he claimed there was also sufficient evidence of corporate malpractice to indict the man for misconduct meaning a forfeit of his stock options too. The shame within the island's insular business community would be unrecoverable and make it impossible for him to find alternative work. Did Rohan understand the problem and would he like to help?

While listening, Rohan had been able to substantiate enough of Tang's background online to be persuaded by his story. On that basis he said yes, of course he wanted to help and was told he and Wenling should pack enough for a week away, leave their phones and laptops in Willowborough and relocate to the lake by Sunday evening, remaining out of contact there until further notice. Nothing had been said about the trial but it was obvious the two were connected. Sure enough, Eddie Dayton paid a visit the following day to reinforce Tang's instructions. Most unfortunately, Wenling made the mistake of asking whether her father knew about Rohan and from there the younger Dayton quickly worked out that neither set of parents would approve of their relationship. A delighted Eddie departed having uncovered a second inducement with which to secure their compliance and Rohan had been left guilt-ridden all week, particularly when he heard the verdict had gone against them. Much as they wanted otherwise, he said he and Wenling believed there had been no other choice than to do as they were told.

He had begged for forgiveness in the face of McGlynn's apparent sympathy. Needing time and space to reflect she had deferred. Sympathy was one thing, absolution something else entirely.

She lifted her head from the water to check what distance remained to the beach. Rounding the second of the marker buoys, the field had tapered substantially with athletes sorting themselves into an elongated formation predicated on ability or effort or both. The first time her fingertips made contact with sand she was up and striding into shore; hands, elbows, hip and knees itching rather than stinging, numbed by the cold. Feeling able to continue, she ran easily up to the Esplanade then between the bike racks to find the right station, unceremoniously stripping and cramming the wetsuit, cap and goggles into her kit bag. Officer Long had positioned himself opposite and they exchanged looks before he returned to sweeping left and right in one-hundred-and-eighty degree arcs. With shoes and helmet donned she was back on her feet, unhooking the blue and white bike and running alongside it to the mount line.

Dayton was nowhere to be seen. She glanced at her watch - well over forty minutes. Not terrible but probably not good enough to catch him either.

Charging past the marina with the wall of bruised cloud rising ominously to his left, Dayton was head down, knees pumping and breathing hard. He had pushed himself in the swim, fighting through the bay's lazy ebb and flow, and was among the leaders of this final group riding the smooth tarmac of Foreshore Road.

'Shitshitshitsh–'

So mired was he in confusion and anger that he nearly missed the turn inland, swerving dangerously and escaping the barriers by inches.

'Concentrate you… stupid… fuck…' he rasped.

McGlynn must have realised the frustration giving him almost nothing to work on would provoke. His mind churned impotently, like a broken propeller, trying to establish who or what might have led her up to Lake Pleasant and what transpired while she was there. Surely Eddie had enough common sense and enough loyalty to have kept his mouth shut? He was just as culpable in their plot after all. Was Fender Tang somehow the initiator? Not probable yet still possible. Could it be that Rohan's conscience had been pricked, leading him to make contact with her directly? But why would that happen after the verdict had already been handed down? And why would she travel up to the lake rather than waiting for him and that Chinese girlfriend of his to come back to the City? Then there was her mention of having spoken with both Eddie and Richard. Had his father really been a participant in the alleged phone call? Did he now know the manner in which Dayton had delivered Thursday's victory? What would his reaction be?

Wynter fucking McGlynn. What did she actually know? Everything, something or not very much at all?

So many unanswerable questions.

Bare shoulders burning, thick beads of sweat evaporating from his cheeks, there was no respite from the sun out here. Baked air hitched in his lungs as the incline began to bite. On the Shillingham bypass he rose from the saddle to keep pace with a faster group but lost contact well below the summit, leaving himself without a pacemaker or other rider to draft. Cursing his own impatience, he leant the bike northeast and laboured solo along the ridge before dropping back down through Granton and Barlaston into the city centre again.

There, in its winding streets, he muscled his way past backmarkers from prior classifications, sped through the short shadows of the grand old station buildings on Blake Street then veered right down Ironbridge Way. Although trending downwards to the shoreline he began to glance over his shoulder on re-joining the Esplanade. Like McGlynn, he was well aware the first two disciplines suited him the better but was starting to worry at the growing hollowness in his hips and thighs. They burned with lactic acid and were unresponsive to his demands for greater urgency.

Spectators stood several deep along the coned channels filtering riders into the transition area. Most had been there for hours yet still clapped and yelled encouragement.

'Julian! Julian Dayton,' came a distinctive baritone. 'Over here, Julian!'

Trying to maintain his balance he peered through filmy lenses and spotted a man in the crowd, much taller than those close by. Dayton lifted a hand in greeting before realising who it was.

'When you get to the Crown Road, look at the fountain,' shouted Dalkeith. 'Look at the fountain, Julian, and you'll see she's already won!'

Fearful of triggering a crash, he freewheeled over the dismount line before hauling the brakes, letting the frame fall between his knees and spinning around to challenge the Scot.

But Dalkeith had already disappeared.

There was no chance of McGlynn having caught him yet, none, but that young pretender had sounded so bloody cocksure. What did Dalkeith know that he didn't? Had she somehow slipped past unseen in the swim? Rather than putting further distance between them on the ride, had all his effort simply represented a failure to catch up? Or did she plan to take some kind of shortcut, to cheat, to steal his victory by ignoble means?

More questions, more uncertainty, anxiety now ablaze in his stomach.

He abandoned the bike where it lay, not caring whether it meant disqualification as long as it meant beating her, dashed for his changing station and frantically crammed his feet into running shoes. After yanking off his helmet he ran for the exit.

Directly above his head, the midday sun vanished for the first time in more than a week, swallowed up by the storm's edge, and the world was suddenly a much darker place.

McGlynn banked through the final corner then bullied her protesting body towards the entry channels. They seemed equally busy so she defaulted to the furthest left and scanned the crowd for Dalkeith, finding him opposite the flags. A brief look at his wrist and he raised both hands - all five fingers up on the right, none on the left.

'Come on Wynter!' he roared as she went by. 'Five ten but he's all over the place. You can catch him!'

Five minutes and ten seconds. A far wider gap than she wanted.

Decelerating, she drained the drinks bottle, slipped out of her shoes, swung a leg over the saddle and jumped into a run at the line, wincing as her bare feet made contact with the concrete. Even with the sun obscured the heat was merciless, the dead air and sea-level humidity holding every drop of sweat prisoner against slick skin.

Five minutes ten. She racked the bike and tugged on new shoes while working on the split calculations. If he maintained the same pace as last year then catching him before the square would require a significant improvement on her personal best. And there was zero chance of that today.

In motion again, she jogged through the exit lane and tried to picture him ahead. He must have gone out exceptionally fast to establish such a big lead. How fatigued was he? Was his form good or poor? Dalkeith, no expert, suggested the latter. She might yet reel him in if he faded badly but it was impossible to know how hard to push - too much and she risked the same outcome, too little and it would all be academic in any case.

With no time to overthink a wrong answer McGlynn made her decision, committed to a tempo and pressed on up the incline towards Fairview, oblivious to the good citizens of the City cheering lustily from the pavements.

She had to catch him, had to.

He fought his way along Fairview and Wheaton Boulevard, confusion developing into paranoia. Logic told him she was somewhere behind, probably through the second transition and therefore gaining ground, but the irrational part of his mind whispered she was somewhere ahead, waiting to taunt him at Crown Road or Merchants Square or somewhere in between. Either way, every dragging breath, every painful stride cost him as much mentally as it did physically. Rather than overtaking others he was now the one being passed, his technique already deficient and rapidly worsening.

Along the edge of Palisades Park the crowds thickened again, drawn by the refreshment stalls and the street artists as much as the race, but Dayton paid them no attention. Nor did he notice the absence of seagulls overhead, the birds having sensed and sought shelter from the storm. He focused solely on keeping his head down and taking the next forty paces without stumbling, and the next, and the next.

Joining the Rangeway he risked lifting his eyes. Coming up was a huge mound of earth in the shape of an upturned pudding bowl, once the site of a wooden watchtower protecting the eastern city walls but these days covered in lush grass and a popular vantagepoint. This was where his brother should be if he was actually here at all. Dayton no longer had any confidence their earlier exchange of messages had been genuine. Maybe it was Eddie's way of surreptitiously confirming his plans such that he could tip off McGlynn, or maybe it was as simple as him being there to gloat in person.

The spot was busy as usual, almost everyone in shorts and t-shirts or vests, sunglasses pushed onto foreheads in the gathering gloom. Coming closer he recognised a couple towards the top. The man's powerful arms rested on parted knees and his companion's auburn hair tumbled over her shoulders. Turning their heads like owls as he passed, Eddie merely stared back and Sophia wore her typical expression of disdain. Dayton, although desperate to put an end to the awful speculation, dared not slow even for a moment and forced his attention back to the roadway.

The gradient in Thornwood's leafy streets offered temporary relief. Midway down Chesford Avenue, he gave up trying to interpret Eddie's deadpan expression and gave in to the contemplation of whether McGlynn would be waiting when he reached Crown Road. What would he do if so? In a race to the finish there was no doubting who would win yet he refused to entertain the idea of being heckled all the way with her jogging easily alongside. No, if that objectionable nephew of hers had in fact been telling the truth and she was already beyond the corner then he would stop and cry foul. That remained the only palatable option.

Two course marshals in high-visibility vests stood by the junction, indifferently waving athletes around the tight angle with wands bearing a sponsor's logo. Safely through he swung his head left and scrutinised the long row of people atop the fountain wall. So intent was he on looking for McGlynn that he missed Dalkeith completely at first but saw him at the second attempt, aided by the cheerful wave. At his side stood an Indian man and an Asian woman. Dayton stared at all three in disbelief before tripping over a traffic cone and going down hard.

Regaining his feet, he lumbered on, shaking his head from side to side and moaning like the injured animal he was.

The last of McGlynn's concentration was broken by distant thunder as she rounded the barrier onto Crown Road. She immediately sought out her nephew, ready to give up or persevere depending on what he indicated. Too far away to shout, he held up two fingers on his right hand.

Her quarry must be slowing, there was still a chance.

Further around the slight curve, the Statue of Angels towered above the elm trees of the Necropolis and Dayton was in real trouble. Sweat he could ill afford to lose poured from him, his feet were leaden and he limped noticeably, blood leaking from a knee. The moaning had stopped - filling his lungs was proving difficult enough.

He hugged the barriers and shortened what was left of the course inch by precious inch. From the noisy throng on the other side a woman with honey-coloured hair called his name but he gave no indication of having heard. Most of his conscious thought was given over to the maintenance of forward momentum and dealing with the pain it cost. The remnants were ensnared by the panic of failure, of the humiliation he would feel when his father and brother came to remove him from office. There was no bluff here, no other plausible explanation for the events of this hateful morning. Eddie and Richard had indeed made a deal with the bitch McGlynn leaving him no other choice, he would have to go. In trying to hang on they would protect the company by making him a scapegoat, meaning criminal charges and personal as well as professional damnation. Very soon he would no longer be The Honourable Julian Dayton, the respected businessman running one of the largest firms in the City. He would be a different Julian Dayton altogether, without influence, without consequence, without purpose.

A City PD car with revolving blue lights lay at the cemetery gates to force runners around the perimeter. Checking over his shoulder yet again, he ignored the water stop opposite and stayed with the barriers through the corner. Four more obtuse angles to negotiate, three to the left and one to the right, and he would be on Jubilee Street with an arrow-straight mile and a half to Merchants Square. Whatever remained of his pride depended on crossing the line there first.

Fat drops of water splashed all around only to evaporate again almost instantly. McGlynn could not have cared less. Upon reaching the Necropolis, her sole concern was that she had not run swiftly enough.

This was where Andrew Brookes should have been waiting with a final split and words of encouragement. However, following their earlier call, she knew he was otherwise engaged at Bay West police station.

Just before three that morning, he had said, his lisping voice still taut, Gina noticed a dark-coloured minivan slow to a stop on the compound's perimeter monitors. Seeing only the occasional glow of a cigarette, they became progressively interested by the lack of other movement and headed out to investigate, alerting Hallam and taking two of the new warehouse guards for company. Brookes and his partner had approached the vehicle head-on only to be confronted by the driver and a nine-millimetre pistol. Unfortunately for them, both the driver and his passenger then failed to notice the others creeping up behind. The ensuing fight had been exceptionally violent, concluded Brookes with much satisfaction, with the passenger, a giant of a man bearing deep scratches up most of his right arm, suffering near-fatal injuries.

In the comfort and security of her SUV, gliding past Garvarmore's deserted market stalls, feeling the tension leak from her limbs, McGlynn had thanked him profusely. Surely, whilst she and Jack would need the services of Triple S a little longer, a return to some semblance of normality was in sight.

Pushing his absence aside, she grabbed a paper cup from the hydration tables, gulped a mouthful and flung it away. Rising up on her toes, limbs moving fluently and efficiently in line with the forward motion, she threw caution to the wind and kicked for home.

Dayton reached the eastern end of Jubilee Street uncontested. In the distance he could see the colonnaded dome atop City Hall, proud white stone against slate grey cloud.

Fatigue and dehydration were making him light-headed and his heart beat much too loudly in his ears. He put his head down and refocused on counting the paces, unaware he was drifting off the line. After the first forty he looked over his shoulder and saw no one he recognised. Facing front once more he was alarmed to find the barriers coming towards him, spectators with open mouths and half-raised umbrellas beyond. He readjusted his direction, ran another forty then checked again, still no one.

Hope sprang anew.

Another forty paces, another backwards glance… and he watched, transfixed, as she came round the corner. The long limbs, the graceful motion, the ponytail bouncing around, unmistakably her.

Fear flashed through him and his body responded with a surge of adrenalin. Suddenly his feet were not as heavy, his blood not as starved of oxygen. He turned and fled through the rain, knees up, arms pumping, stride rate doubling in a maniacal effort to escape this final indignity.

Another forty paces, even faster, nearly sprinting, not daring to look over his shoulder, terrified of what might be there. Another forty, or maybe thirty, or fifty, no longer caring provided he was still out in front.

Then sudden agony, an unbearable clenching in his chest, immediate paralysis everywhere else.

He pitched forwards, limp as a rag doll, and the ground rose up to meet him.

The clouds were inverted waves, silently rolling far above the head of a drowning man. Unable to blink away their moisture he searched for the beauty in their blurred, bulbous patterns instead.

He understood what had happened but knew nothing except relief. There was no pain. More importantly there would be no fall from grace, no ignominy of defeat, no one to blame him for failure this time.

His had been a strange existence, not that it mattered anymore. A long tapestry stitched with disappointments. Gazing idly at the underbelly of the sky he realised what it meant to waste a life chasing things not worth the cost. Whatever came next would be a chance to start over, to do better and he was ready to try. If anything came next, that was.

A face interrupted the view.

Hers of course. She looked older, overburdened, yet irrefutably the summertime girl of his twenty-ninth year.

Warm drops crossed the space between them.

Too late for tears my love, much too late.

Nevertheless those steady grey eyes looked into his with their customary kindness and wisdom, determining the greatness of his need. He felt hands on his chest and shortly thereafter she leant down and placed her lips upon his own.

This was what he wanted, the intimacy he had always craved.

This was enough and he was happy.

31

They had decided to stay in the City, the lure of a bed nearby more appealing than the long drive home.

Following lengthy negotiations over breakfast, primarily between Catriona who wanted to see a Manet exhibition at the Rotunda and Adeline who robustly championed the idea of quad biking, the four of them agreed on a day aboard the *Libertas III*. McGlynn drove the boat into the deep, running under full sail before the wind, the others all competent on deck and shouting with glee at seal sightings and the rainbows thrown up by the bow. Several hours on the ocean with her family, concentrating on little more than tack and trim and tide, worked an extraordinary magic and left her restored.

After goodbyes at the marina's main gate, she walked briskly up towards the hospital, plain-clothed replacements for Schnitzer and Long, who were on a rest day, hurrying to keep pace at her side. The sun shone brightly again but the breeze blew from the north and the temperature had plummeted by more than a third.

St Stephen's stood at the top of Blenheim Road, sandwiched layers of brutalist black concrete and glass. Asking at reception for directions, she rode the elevator up to the twelfth floor and found her destination at the end of the corridor. The Triple S bodyguards stopped short at a row of plain metal chairs allowing her to pass through the open door alone.

Dayton lay in the white bed in the white room, apparently asleep. Wires connected him to a bank of equipment displaying vital statistics and the steady, hypnotic pulse of a cardiograph. Except for the phone on the bedside cabinet there was nothing by way of personal effects, no clothing, no books, no flowers, but the Dayton Global Industries building could be seen from the window and, further along the shoreline, ML One.

Sensing a presence he opened his eyes. They were red-rimmed and made him look old.

'Hey,' said McGlynn gently. 'Sorry if I woke you.'

'You didn't.'

'How are you feeling?'

A better answer escaped him. In the end, he settled for the truth.

'Ashamed.'

'Would you like me to leave?'

'No. There are things that need to be said, aren't there. Now's as good a time as any. Have a seat.' He waited until she scooted a chair to the foot of the bed, keeping a distance. 'Where's your security?'

'In the corridor.'

'Must be an intrusion. Will you need to keep them long?'

'We're making progress. Two men were arrested yesterday.'

'Already? Surprised City PD managed to pull their finger out. Good news for you I trust, and the mayor's re-election stats.'

'Mmm.' She looked around the sterile space. 'Have you had many other visitors?'

'You missed Richard by twenty minutes. He came to, um, negotiate the terms of my surrender.'

'Did you get what you wanted?'

'I got what I deserved I suppose, but I shan't exactly starve, don't worry. And you'll be pleased to hear that Ed's taking over from tomorrow as predicted. There'll be an announcement in the Post later this week, citing my resignation on recent poor health. What a fuc–... what a joke.'

'Has he been to see you?'

'He's not welcome.'

'He's your brother Julian. And family feuds are never worth the pain, take my word for it, the effects always outweigh the cause in the end. What would you have done in his situation?'

'Kept my sodding mouth shut for a start. Idiot.'

'Seems smart enough to me. I'm sure he had his reasons.'

'Mostly concerning his own ambition and lack of patience. That's one of the problems with being in charge isn't it? You have to rely on people who want to replace you.'

'Can be a good thing if you direct their energy in the right ways.'

'Well, he's not ready, he'll realise it soon enough.' A pause. 'How did you work out what we'd done?'

'With Rohan? Luck. I asked one of my team to make enquiries at his girlfriend's address in Singapore. Those led us by happy accident to Refrenix and from there to Fender Tang and then Eddie. But what did you intend to do with Rohan? Surely you wouldn't have been able to keep him invisible much longer?'

'You wouldn't have seen him again. Tang can crush the girlfriend's father anytime he wants. And neither her parents nor his approve of mixed-race relationships.'

'Part of the deal was for them to be left alone permanently. I expect that to be honoured.'

'It's up to Ed now but I can't see why he'd renege. Will you be taking Mehta back?'

'Haven't decided yet.'

'I'm sure you don't want advice from me but I'd suggest not. He'd only ever leave you wondering.'

'Mmm.'

Dayton decided not to press the point. On seeing her again, McGlynn seemed to have become a confusing amalgam of her younger and older selves. He no longer knew where the boundaries of their relationship lay.

'How are you doing anyway?' he said instead. 'Rude of me not to have asked already.'

'Good thanks. Jack and I took the kids out on the boat today.'

'Thought so, or something like it. You look disgustingly healthy. Certainly healthier than me. No ill effects from the race?'

'Only the usual. Although my knees aren't going to forgive me anytime soon. I reopened the cuts when I was… you know.'

'When you were working on me.'

'Yeah.'

'I went down on Jubilee Street, didn't I, beyond the Necropolis. You'd caught me up by then I think.'

'Uh-huh. You just keeled over and hit the floor. At first I thought you'd tripped but then you didn't get up, didn't move at all. By the time I got there it was obvious you were in a bad way.'

'There were clouds.'

'That's right, it had started to rain.'

'No, I meant I could see clouds above me. Must've been on my back looking up at them,' he said, piecing together fragments of memory. 'Then I saw you. And you kept me alive.'

'Only until the paramedics got there - can't have been more than a couple of minutes. You'd have done the same.'

'The fact you would even think so tells me how different we are. Did you try to cheat yesterday?'

'What? Of course not. It would have been a fair race to the finish if you hadn't been taken ill.'

'Which you'd have won, no question, I'd gone out much too fast. Total stupidity on my part even though you'd done a decent job of winding me up beforehand. But do you know why I had a heart attack?'

'Running at that pace in that temp–'

'The doctors think it's more likely a result of me taking human growth hormone for the last three years. Mmm, that's right. The chap who sold me the shots said there was an increased risk of cardiac arrest but, fool that I am, I ignored him. The odds were low, age was catching up with me and I couldn't stand the thought of losing, not to you.'

'Bloody hell, Julian,' said McGlynn, unnerved by his candour. 'I don't like losing either but not everything's worth fighting for that much.'

'I know. At least, I know now. Perspective's a wonderful thing. Lying there, waiting to… to die, I realised I'd spent my life doing things that wouldn't matter to me or anyone else.

Seemed even more unfair than death itself. All I felt was disappointment... and perhaps a little hope. Hope that I might wake up from all of this... this...'

'This dream?'

'This nightmare. It's ironic but the dreams I remember are generally a kinder place than my reality. Sometimes I like to believe they're a window to better lives I'm living elsewhere. But there's one thing I'll tell you for free, after coming that close I wouldn't go back to my old life again, even if I could.'

'You should do whatever makes you happy.'

'Ha! The problem is I've no idea what that is. I used to think it was the winning, beating the competition, beating you, but not so much anymore. And there's precious little else... Anyway, true happiness? Nothing but a myth.'

'I disagree. But I think it's something that needs to be worked at. Happiness is an unstable state of balance, like spinning plates. You have to keep shaking those poles and put up with the occasional breakage.'

'And how do you know which poles to shake?'

'Find the beautiful things.'

'Come again?'

'You really want to know? So listen up because I don't want to overshare twice. The older I get the more I learn to keep close to what I regard as beautiful. Could be anything - family, friends, places, music, sunsets, books - whatever brings you joy when you think about it, see it, feel it, or are simply aware of its existence. Beauty's different for everyone but spending time with whatever it looks like for you will help you be happy.'

'You believe happiness is the appreciation of beauty?'

'Yeah, I think that's about the sum of it.'

'So why work as much as you do? Why run a firm as big as ours and put yourself through that grind each and every day? There's no beauty in that, none.'

'There is to me. But there's your answer.'

Dayton reflected on this a while, whether he had anything beautiful to appreciate, or could have. Maybe so if he looked hard enough. McGlynn stayed quiet too. Watching the gulls loop and roll outside the window, she tried to comprehend why this man seemed to have changed so much as a result of facing mortality whereas she felt not so different from before.

'So,' said Dayton, breaking into her thoughts. 'It seems I owe you a sizable debt.'

'Not for yesterday. And as for the rest I suspect we've settled as much as we ever will.'

'Please? For the sake of my conscience? Not that I have any right to ask.'

'You won't tell me anything about the company and I wouldn't want to listen anyway, I promised Eddie fair competition. And without wishing to be callous I doubt there's anything else you have to offer.'

'How about something that would mean a lot to you but is no longer of any use to my brother? Would that squeeze within these ethical boundaries of yours?'

'Try me if it makes you feel better. But I can't unhear whatever you might later regret saying.'

'Mmm, noted. Hold on.'

With an effort he reached for the phone and prodded at its surface. McGlynn felt a vibration and pulled out her own.

'What's this?' she asked as a message downloaded. The sender's address had nothing to suggest it came from Dayton or his company yet was oddly familiar. No subject or text but an attached document which she opened with a tap of her thumb. 'What am I looking at?'

'It's a heads of terms. In which Dayton's agrees to procure consulting services for the next three years from Boland Technologies. Signed by Christopher Boland and me.'

'It's what...?'

She scanned the preliminary contract - the parties involved, definitions, the basis of their future agreement, fee schedule, confidentiality clauses, completed signature boxes - all present and correct. Boland had implied he was prepared to offer Danny Zhao's work to the highest bidder but to actually sign something with McGlynn-Lansing's biggest rival? With whom there was ongoing legal action in the same area? The conflict of interest was staggering. Scrolling back to the bottom she rechecked his signature date. Tuesday. The same day as the meeting in which he had criticised her management of both the company's computing division and their litigation. And to have convened an emergency board meeting tomorrow at which he presumably intended to lead the calls for her resignation, she was nearly lost for words.

'Asshole,' she grated. 'What an absolute, fucking asshole. Sorry, not you, him.'

'I probably don't deserve much better. Not at the time I signed it anyway.'

'Was this at your instigation or his?'

'Did you run the background checks personally when you appointed him?'

'Of course. He was a decent fit, his references checked out and he had more than enough to invest.'

'What about his education?'

'Eh? It was a very long time ago but I think he's got a doctorate, computer science or something, from one of the Ivy League universities. Why's that relevant?'

'It isn't. But if you'd gone even further back you might have seen he's an old boy of Templecombe School. What you probably wouldn't have realised is he was there at the same time as Richard.'

'Are you… are you kidding me? Christopher and your father are *friends*?'

'Acquaintances. The old boy network's always been important to us Brits, you know, at least to people like my father. I believe they met for dinner on Tuesday prior to him signing the document. You'd had a board meeting that day, right? Christopher knew we'd found a way to keep Rohan from testifying, he expected you to lose the case and was convinced he'd get a vote of no confidence through. Once you were forced to resign he planned to dismantle your computing division and push the business in our direction, suitably and expensively advised by Boland Technologies of course.'

'I can't believe it. He's had access to all of our reporting for years.'

'You have my word he never shared anything beyond the scope of the agreement, even though I asked him several times. But I hope this is useful?'

'You know it is.'

Running through the implications, excitement began to steal away her anger. The agreement was sufficient to accuse Boland of gross misconduct, a very specific charge and the subject of special conditions in his contract. As Director, she would be able to fire him without notice and had first refusal on buying back his McGlynn-Lansing stock at the original purchase price, a figure much lower than its present value. Making the man pay financially for his misdemeanours was hugely appealing. Or perhaps she should consider forcing a transfer of Zhao across to her own business? He would be a more than capable successor for Rohan if needed. Wait, even better, what about striking a bargain whereby Boland had no choice but to support changes to the company's share structure, returning a majority stake to its Director? After nearly a decade of taking decisions by committee, of grey men pronouncing their findings in sombre tones, this could be the key to restoring the autocracy in which she so passionately believed. The more she thought through the options so others began to emerge. The information was potentially priceless and all she needed to do was choose how it should be used. Whatever that decision, Christopher Boland was going to find tomorrow's meeting significantly less comfortable than he expected.

'Are you sure this doesn't compromise you?' she continued.

'It's fine. I never liked the man and the deal you made with Ed means the contract's pointless anyway. I'm assuming you're unlikely to be out of a job in the near future.'

'This address you sent it from, looks familiar.'

'It's one of my personal accounts… Ah, now you mention it, I wonder if I used it to send something a few years ago, a tip about who'd won the sealed bids for the land near Valiance Park?'

'That came from you?'

'Couldn't resist… I've been the cause of a lot of your problems over the years, haven't I.'

'It's always seemed so personal with you, Julian. Ever since that party where you tried to kiss me and I didn't want to.'

'That was… ah… a very long time ago,' said Dayton, appalled by the raising of such a private matter face to face. 'As far as I can recall I was… ah… really quite drunk.'

'Thanks. But why turn on me afterwards? Was it some sense of being spurned which made you behave that way for so long?'

'Err, no… not at all, it was just… I… I, um…'

Seeing the cardiograph at his side begin to spike more frequently, sensing the shutters coming down over his panic, McGlynn felt the same ache of sorrow for him as she had in the Levine's fairy-lit garden. There were many things of which to be frightened in this world but, *mon dieu*, surely love was not one of them.

'Never mind, I had no right to ask. Not here, not now.'

'Yes you did,' he said miserably. 'It's just that I'm not capable of an answer. Probably never will be in truth… I know what I am, Wynter, I know what an unpleasant human being I've been. Can hardly bear it most of the time. Every time I try to do better I always find a way of fucking things up again, like I can't help myself, it's in my nature. But, um… before you go, whether you believe me or not… I wanted you to know that I'm, uh… um…'

'If you like,' she said slowly, reading the truth in his eyes, 'I could come back in the next day or two. See how you're doing.'

'That's kind,' he replied, reading the pity in hers. 'You've always been kind, even when it wasn't deserved. But in this instance, I don't think it would be wise.'

'Are you sure?'

The old man in the white bed nodded.

'Forgive me,' he said.

32

ML One was silent, lying in wait for the following day and a return of the industry for which it existed.

Standing at her office window, arms folded, most of her weight held carelessly in balance over one currently bare foot, she studied the building's fraternal twin along the shoreline. The top floor lights in the south-eastern corner shone brightly against the evening sky. Perhaps the new occupant was moving in, unpacking a cardboard box or two before leaving them refilled at the door for someone else to collect. She wondered what kind of rival he would make. Probably no better or worse than his predecessor, only different. He would make her productive, be a reason to improve each and every day, his very presence giving her the gift of purpose.

Even so he would need to wait until tomorrow. More urgent and important matters required her attention first.

Turning away, she swivelled neatly into the tan leather chair, cleared all else from her mind and settled down to concentrate on the task at hand.

Printed in Great Britain
by Amazon

45212532R00280